S0-ARA-491

RAVE REVIEWS FOR JENNIFER ARCHER!

ONCE UPON A DREAM

"This is an excellent magical story with a marvelous hero and an admirable heroine. If you want a fun, exciting, humorous, fast-moving story, this is it."

—*Romantic Times*

"Wildly entertaining. Wonderfully unique. Jennifer Archer gives readers another one for the keeper shelf."

—Ronda Thompson, author of *Violets Are Blue*

"Guaranteed to keep a reader turning pages long past bedtime!"

—*Under the Covers Book Reviews*

BODY & SOUL

"*Body & Soul*, Jennifer Archer's first book . . . promises readers new and exciting things in the future from this gifted author."

—*Calico Trails*

"I think I'll add Ms. Archer to my 'Get Next Book' list. . . . I can't wait to see what she'll come up with next."

—*Romance Novel Central*

"*Body & Soul* is a fun, fast read that's going to please a lot of readers. It's easy to recommend this one!"

—*The Romance Reader*

A SHOCKING ATTRACTION

"I'm sorry I've been rude to you, Rosy. I'd like to start over."

The cigar sent grew stronger, making her think J.T. had stepped closer. The hair on her arms stood on end. Goose bumps scattered across her skin. "Why do you call me Rosy?" she whispered.

"It suits you. I like it."

"It's too—" *Familiar*, she started to say. *Intimate*. But then her tongue went numb because she felt a tiny shock, then his hand covering hers. His fingers were warm against her palm.

She blurted out the first thought that came to mind. "Are you still naked?"

"Are you hoping I say 'yes' or 'no'?"

"I'm hoping you at least had the decency to put your clothes on before you came over."

"Are you sure?"

She felt his breath on her face a moment before his mouth brushed hers. Because her eyes were wide open, she saw the tiny spark flash between them, felt the quick strike of it against her lips. Roselyn pulled back. "Oh!"

Other *Love Spell* books by Jennifer Archer:
ONCE UPON A DREAM
BODY & SOUL

SHOCKING BEHAVIOR

JENNIFER ARCHER

LOVE SPELL

NEW YORK CITY

For everyone who has ever been called an oddball.
Or felt like one.

A LEISURE BOOK®

August 2002

Published by

Dorchester Publishing Co., Inc.
276 Fifth Avenue
New York, NY 10001

If you purchased this book without a cover you should be aware that this book is stolen property. It was reported as "unsold and destroyed" to the publisher and neither the author nor the publisher has received any payment for this "stripped book."

Copyright © 2002 by Jennifer Archer

All rights reserved. No part of this book may be reproduced or transmitted in any form or by any electronic or mechanical means, including photocopying, recording or by any information storage and retrieval system, without the written permission of the publisher, except where permitted by law.

ISBN 0-505-52507-0

The name "Leisure Books" and the stylized "L" with design are trademarks of Dorchester Publishing Co., Inc.

Printed in the United States of America.

Visit us on the web at www.dorchesterpub.com.

ACKNOWLEDGMENTS

I am grateful to Charlotte Goebel and Kimberly Willis Holt not only for reading and critiquing the entire manuscript of this book, but for doing so right before Christmas when I know their schedules were hectic. They couldn't have given me a nicer gift! Thanks also to Jenny Bent, agent extraordinaire, for reminding me to celebrate. And to Jeff, for being my biggest fan.

SHOCKING BEHAVIOR

The Invisibility of the Lonely

The invisibility of the lonely
Is known and is felt by all;
For even the kings on their thrones
Have felt transparent and small.

When no one notices their laughter,
When no one acknowledges their tears,
When a blind eye is turned to their triumphs,
And a deaf ear is turned to their fears.

Do you feel like you're fading, dear brother?
Fading faster than sight and than sound?
Transparent as wind over water?
Short-lived like dew on the ground?

Do you feel like there is nobody watching
Or caring for whatever you do?
Does it seem that there's a wave of darkness
Swallowing all of the life that's in you?

The invisibility is closing in now,
Because the fools won't see who you are.
They have stolen the light that was in you
That once made you shine like a star.

I will join you in your translucence,
Take your hand and teach you to run
Out of the darkness of the lonely and
Back to your place in the sun.

For the invisibility of the lonely
Will always be felt by a few
But I will not stand by, my brother,
If the lonely that's fading is you.

—Beth Wallek

Chapter One

J.T. Drake stood in the shadow of an elm tree across the street from his father's rambling old house. He glanced at the glowing face of his watch. *Midnight.* Pop was up to something. J.T. had suspected as much even before Wanda Moody, owner of the tree under which he now stood, called his L.A. office last week. The widow Moody informed J.T. that, for three days straight, green smoke with a smell like burning rubber had drifted from the back windows of his childhood home.

Despite old Mrs. Moody's tendency to exaggerate, J.T. didn't dismiss her claim. The last time Pop's creative wires tangled, all the windows in the house next door exploded. The time before that, every dog in a three-mile radius howled for hours on end.

Remembering the news coverage on that one, J.T. covered his eyes with one hand and rubbed his temples. The so-called "humorous human interest" story had garnered national press, though Pop's name had miraculously been

1

withheld. The reporters had simply referred to him as "a real-life absentminded professor in the small college town of Pecan Grove, Texas."

J.T. returned his attention to the window and whistled quietly. Even in Pop's younger days, some of his projects had gone haywire. And that was way back when he only got drunk on weekends instead of draining a bottle on a daily basis. His father's blundering was spiraling out of control, the repercussions more serious each passing year. If J.T. didn't take command of the situation soon, he feared what news the next phone call might bring. So it had come down to this—waiting like a thief to sneak into the house in the middle of the night, just like he'd done plenty of times in his youth before he finally figured out that Pop didn't care when he came and went; the old man didn't even notice.

A lightning bolt ripped the night sky. A rumble of thunder followed. Wishing he were back in his hotel room with the air conditioner blowing full blast, J.T. lifted the tail of his T-shirt to wipe his sweaty forehead and drew a breath of air so humid it felt like he'd sucked warm water into his lungs. The heavy, sweet blend of honeysuckle and roses drifted to him, bringing with it memories of stormy summers long past, memories that coaxed a smile from him one second then tightened his throat the next.

With an ease born of years of practice, he closed his mind to yesterday, forced his thoughts back to the issue at hand. According to Mrs. Moody, Pop's lights went out each night at 9 P.M.

Not tonight.

A muted glow lit the front bedroom window, illuminating a scrawny, slumped-shouldered silhouette. The silhouette paced back and forth, back and forth, again and again.

J.T. shook his head and cursed. No doubt about it,

Pop had something in the works. He couldn't begin to guess what; he wouldn't try. Considering all the crazy gadgets Pop had come up with over the years, a living, breathing replica of Frankenstein's monster strapped to a table in the basement laboratory would be no surprise.

Whatever this latest project might be, Pop had not been willing to discuss it over dinner four hours ago when J.T. asked how he'd been spending his time. Pop also, as usual, refused to discuss leaving Pecan Grove to move to an apartment in L.A. to be closer to J.T., insisting he was doing just fine on his own. J.T. scratched his nose. No surprise there. Pop had never pretended to need or want him around. Why would he start now? The old man could be down to his last dollar and dying of starvation, but as long as he had his experiments and inventions, he'd be satisfied. They fulfilled him; J.T. had accepted that fact a long time ago.

He cursed again. He didn't like the thought of moving Pop to L.A. either, and had hoped to work out some sort of a compromise. Pop was still a reasonably young man with the possibility of a long life ahead of him. But if he insisted on digging in his heels and continuing his reckless habits, sooner or later J.T. would be forced to chop off his feet at the ankles.

He studied his father's restless shadow as it, again, passed by the bedroom window. Pop's movements seemed steady. Surely that was a good sign. And the old man had only downed one whiskey sour at dinner. A double, granted, but only one.

Swatting a mosquito away from his face, J.T. listened to the steady drone of cicadas and counted blinks of tiny yellow firefly lights. July in south Texas was a ruthless, tormenting bitch. Though he'd worn running shoes, shorts, and a lightweight T-shirt to stay cool, the shirt, now clammy with perspiration, clung to his chest and back like cellophane. The threatening rain only added to

3

the unbearable humidity, and when the first drops hit the sidewalk, J.T. half expected them to sizzle.

He muffled a sneeze. Mrs. Moody's flowerbeds still teased his allergies, just like they had before he'd left Pecan Grove at the age of eighteen. He couldn't afford to get sick. This unexpected trip was a bad enough blip in his schedule at the magazine where he worked. And on top of that, a book deadline stared him in the face. By the end of the month, his editor expected to see the story he'd been investigating and writing for the past two years.

J.T. stooped, plucked a blade of grass, stuck it between his teeth. And then there was Giselle. Leggy, cat-eyed Giselle whose French accent would make the contents of one of Pop's boring *Scientific Quarterly* magazine articles sound sexy. Finally, after weeks of trying to coordinate their schedules, he'd booked a date with the busy model. If not for Wanda Moody's call, J.T. would be coaxing a kiss from those expensive, pouting lips of Giselle's right now instead of standing in the muggy Texas heat spying on his father.

When Pop's bedroom light finally went out, J.T. waited another fifteen minutes. Then he stepped from the shelter of the tree into the light drizzle of rain, crossed the street and unlocked the front door with his key. He disarmed the burglar alarm before moving quietly through the dark foyer toward the back of the house and down the basement steps.

White light shimmered beneath the door to Pop's laboratory. J.T. heard a steady, high-pitched hum coming from the other side. He stooped, lifted one corner of the area rug, found the loose floorboard and wedged it free. The key was still there, hidden away where it had been for as long as he could remember.

Seconds later, when J.T. inserted the key into the lock and touched the doorknob, a faint but steady vibration tickled his fingertips. He turned the knob, pushed the squeaky door open, stepped through.

The cluttered laboratory from his childhood had been transformed. Only the old sofa against the wall remained. Shelving and cages lined the other walls. Inside the cages, white mice ran to nowhere on metal wheels. Machines beeped. Computers hummed. A tall metal box with a glass door dominated the center of the immaculate room. On the floor beside it, connected by a host of coils and tubes, sat a generator and another large machine J.T. could not identify.

"What the . . . ?" He left the key in the lock and closed the door behind him.

The box emitted a tremulous radiance, making it unnecessary for J.T. to turn on the overhead light. Careful to avoid the wires and other hardware stretched across the floor, he circled the machine. When he returned to the glass door, he reached for the handle. Upon contact, a tingling sensation raced up his arm and prickled the hair at the nape of his neck. He stepped onto the metal floor inside, catching a faint whiff of the burnt rubber scent Wanda Moody had described. With his back to the door, he studied the knobs and switches on the control panel across one wall of the box.

"Jerome!"

At the sound of Pop's voice, J.T. jumped, turned, and stumbled against the glass door, slamming it shut. To right himself, he reached back, bracing a hand on the control panel behind him.

A thunderclap rattled the house's rickety rafters.

The white light brightened, the humming grew louder, the floor beneath J.T.'s feet quivered. A flash of heat entered his toes, shot through him with the force of a lightning bolt, froze him in place. His shoulders lifted with the surge; his body stiffened. A sharp, metallic taste tainted his tongue, and his nostrils burned from the harsh stench of the green smoke filling the box.

On the other side of the glass door, Pop's face contorted . . . blurred . . . then slowly faded from view.

Roselyn Peabody bolted upright in bed and reached for the trilling phone on her nightstand. "Peabody residence."

"Thank goodness . . . Roselyn. . . ."

"Professor?" She blinked away the last remnant of a very strange dream about accepting the Nobel Prize wearing only her underwear. "Is something wrong?"

"It's the electromagnetic refractor."

"The refractor?"

"It worked."

Roselyn's breath caught. She scrambled to the edge of the bed and switched on the lamp, warning herself not to become prematurely excited. Professor Drake might be tipsy or simply confused. The poor, sweet man was prone to both conditions more and more often lately, though he still exhibited moments of sheer, lucid brilliance. But premature or not, Roselyn couldn't extinguish the flame of hope that flared inside of her. "Are you certain?"

"Quite so. His hand hit the switch and then he—"

"He?"

For a moment, the professor didn't respond. When he finally did, he sounded a thousand miles away. "My son. He's a published author, you know. And a journalist in Los Angeles. Jerome writes a magazine column for—"

"What happened to your son, Professor?" Roselyn interrupted, trying to steer his mind back on track. Lately, he often jumped from subject to subject, telling her things she'd known for years. "Tonight. What happened tonight?"

"Oh . . . yes . . . tonight." The tension returned to his

voice. "Jerome slipped into the lab. I heard a noise and came down. I saw it happen, Roselyn. He . . ." The professor's voice trembled, then drifted off.

Roselyn pressed a hand on the nightstand to steady herself. "Completely, Professor?" She stood. "The refractor worked completely?"

"Completely," he answered. "The adjustments we discussed yesterday . . . I made them after you left. Then Jerome's unexpected arrival distracted me, and I didn't have the chance to test the results. Obviously, they worked."

Clutching the cordless phone to her ear, she stumbled across the clothing-strewn floor to her closet. She threw open the door and tugged the first blouse on the rod off a hanger. "Is he conscious?"

"No, but he's breathing, thank heavens. And his heartbeat is strong. Too strong for my liking, as a matter of fact. Rather sporadic, too. Beating like a frightened bird's wings. Speaking of wings, did I tell you about the bluebird that visits my pecan tree out back each morning? Such a delightful—"

"Professor Drake?"

"Yes, dear girl?"

"Your son . . . you were telling me about Jerome."

"Jerome? Oh . . . yes." He coughed. "I'm afraid to try to reverse the process until he's regulated. I thought of calling for an ambulance. But his pulse rate seems to be slowing. Then there's the matter of . . ."

He didn't need to finish the sentence. She knew exactly what else worried him. How would they explain this to a paramedic? To a doctor? To anyone? They had never experimented with a live subject, only inanimate objects— books, a chair, an apple, a baseball bat. In the past, they had met with no success. But now . . .

Roselyn dropped the blouse on the bed. She juggled

the phone, tried to tug the T-shirt she'd slept in over her head, then gave up.

Jerome T. Drake. The professor's conspicuously absent son. Truth be told, if she hadn't seen the man's photo on the back jacket of one of the true-crime novels he penned, she might wonder if he was simply a product of the professor's imagination. Other than town gossip, Roselyn knew little about Professor Drake's only child. Still, she'd formed a strong opinion. The younger Drake was the polar opposite of his father. Self-centered. Immature. Irresponsible. Heartless. In fact, Jerome Drake's disturbing lack of involvement in his father's life had been the knot that cinched her decision to move to Pecan Grove two years ago.

Roselyn balanced the cordless phone between her ear and upraised shoulder as a long-ago conversation came to mind—a drunken confession from the professor when she'd returned to Pecan Grove for a visit after hearing rumors of his faltering mental health. She wondered if Professor Drake remembered what he'd told her about his regrets regarding his distant relationship with his son? Though he spoke of Jerome often and always with a father's blind pride, in the years she had known the professor, she had yet to meet his only child.

"Jerome's my son, Roselyn," the professor said, interrupting her thoughts, his voice steady again, more coherent and firm than she'd heard it in weeks. "If his vital signs don't become completely normal soon, I'll be forced to call someone. I won't risk his health . . . his life."

She tugged on a long wrinkled skirt that she'd tossed into a corner last week. "Of course you won't. *We* won't."

When her zipper was zipped, Roselyn hurried to the closet again. She quickly rummaged through the jumble of shoes on the floor inside until she found two that matched, then shoved her bare feet into them and tied the ties.

"Roselyn?"

"Yes, Professor?"

"What if we can't . . ."

"Don't even think it. Failure is not an option. Try to stay calm. I'll be over in ten minutes."

A voice, J.T. heard a voice close by. It guided him slowly through a dense, dark fog, a mist of sleep so thick he was lost in it. His head pounded, and the mere effort of trying to open his eyes only increased the beat.

Something snapped at his temple then swept across his brow and into his hair. Cool . . . dry . . . the soothing touch somehow familiar, a touch he had long yearned for in some buried part of his soul.

J.T. forced his heavy lids open and gazed up into Pop's long, gaunt face, those wild gray eyes that had always spooked him a little. To J.T., his father's restless gaze often seemed to see things no one else did.

That was not the case now.

J.T. lay flat on his back on the floor. His father sat beside him. And though Pop looked at him, he seemed not to see him at all; in fact, he seemed unaware that J.T. had awakened. Pop stared down at J.T.'s nose and, rather than sharp, the gray eyes behind the little round lenses of Pop's glasses looked bloodshot, worried and blurred by tears.

"I'm sorry," Pop murmured. "You'll be fine, Jerome. I'll make this right. I won't fail you this time. I promise." He closed his eyes. "I swear to you, Evie. I swear I'll make this right."

An old ache spread through J.T.'s chest when he heard his mother's name. He tried to speak, but the words wouldn't come. Before he could make another attempt, a small, thin, woman with dripping wet hair rushed into the room. She made J.T. think of a broken kaleido-scope—dazzling, but off-kilter, a blur of scattered colors. Her sudden presence seemed to increase the energy level another fifty percent in the already electrically charged room.

"How is he, Professor?" she asked.

Pop glanced up at her. "His pulse is close to normal now. Much more steady. See what you think."

She stared at Pop a moment before shifting her attention past J.T. to the floor just beyond him.

Panic streaked through him. Why wouldn't she look at his face? Why wouldn't Pop or this woman meet his gaze? Why couldn't he talk? And his body . . . it felt tingly, numb.

J.T. tried to move his legs. He couldn't.

Pop's hand returned to J.T.'s forehead, generating a tiny shock on contact. His cool, dry fingers slid slowly down J.T.'s cheek, then settled at the side of his neck. "Here," he said.

The woman dropped to her knees beside Pop, then, squinting, leaned over J.T. A raindrop fell from one choppy blonde strand of her hair and plopped onto his chest. She didn't appear to notice that he studied her, that he cried out to her with his eyes.

Her own eyes were huge, framed by the uneven layer of bangs plastered against her brow. As odd and mismatched as the rest of her, the left eye was green, the right one blue. Her skin had the smooth, pale texture of someone who spent little time outdoors, but a flush stained her cheeks a vivid shade of pink. J.T. drew a weak breath. She smelled like baby powder.

Lifting a hand, she placed her fingers beside Pop's on J.T.'s neck, eliciting another brisk shock. "Oh!"

"Yes," Pop murmured. "Incredible, isn't it?"

"Amazing." She pressed her fingers against his skin,

then skimmed down to his shoulder. "His shirt is wet."

"The rain must have caught him before he let himself in here."

"He was outside?"

"Yes. Jerome's not staying at the house. He has a hotel room in town."

Her hand moved up again. She shivered. "Eerie."

Incredible. Amazing. Eerie. J.T.'s leg muscles jumped. They talked about him as if he were one of Pop's experiments. He'd been shocked, which was bad enough, but that was the extent of his injury, wasn't it?

Summoning what little energy he could muster, J.T. drew another breath, then moaned long and deep.

Pop flinched.

The woman uttered a startled noise, something between a squeak and a gasp.

"He's coming to," Pop blurted, as if J.T. had not been looking up at him for the past five minutes.

"Get a wet washcloth, Professor. A drink of water. It might help him regain consciousness more quickly if we sponge his face, and his mouth will be dry from the shock."

J.T. heard the slap of his father's rubber flip-flop sandals against the floor as Pop hurried from the room. A wave of panic swept over him. He was afraid. As afraid as he'd ever been in his life. He didn't want Pop to leave him.

"Hold on, Jerome," the woman whispered, staring at his chest. "You're going to be fine." She turned and scanned the room. "I should put something under your head, make you more comfortable."

When she started to stand, J.T. suddenly regained his reflexes. He grabbed her wrist. "J.T. . . . ."

"What?"

"Not . . . Jerome." He drew a staggered breath. "J.T."

11

He followed her wide gaze down to where he held her wrist. Her arm was raised and, though he could feel her skin and the flutter of her pulse beneath his fingertips, J.T. couldn't see his own hand.

Chapter Two

Once, as a child, Roselyn had wondered what hid behind the electrical outlet cover on her bedroom wall. Using a screwdriver, she tried to pry the plastic cover off. The tool slipped. Though only four years old at the time, she never forgot the feel of the electricity as it surged through her body.

That childhood experience had been far more severe than this. In fact, she had almost died. But the two incidents felt similar enough that the sensation shimmying through her fingers and up her arm now brought back the memory.

Roselyn tried to pull her wrist to her side but couldn't.

"Don't leave," Jerome Drake said. "Please . . . don't leave me alone."

She fought the urge to break free, to turn and run from the room, away from his disembodied voice, the invisible force that held her . . . the freak of nature she'd created. She and the professor.

13

"It's okay, Jerome." She swallowed, reminding herself that Mr. Drake was the professor's son, a flesh and blood man, not a ghost; his flesh and blood had simply gone into hiding. "I won't leave you. I promise."

The reassurance didn't slacken his grip on her wrist. "Who—"

"My name's Roselyn. Roselyn Peabody. I'm your father's partner."

"What happened?" he asked, his voice as scratchy and thin as sandpaper. "I was in that . . ." He cleared his throat. "I don't remember . . . I . . ."

Step-by-step Roselyn mentally recalculated the changes she and the professor had discussed just that afternoon. And suddenly nothing, not even her anxiety, outweighed her sense of accomplishment. They had worked long and hard toward this moment. Finally, *finally*, all the long hours had paid off. True, the breakthrough had occurred in a manner she and Professor Drake did not anticipate, a way that presented an entire new set of problems, but it was a breakthrough, nonetheless. Any problem could be solved; it would only take time.

"How do you feel?" She slowly went to her knees beside him again. "Are you experiencing any pain? Any numb—"

"My hand! I can't see it! What happened to me?"

"Try to stay calm. You—"

"Stay calm?" His deep voice raised an octave. "I can't see my hands . . . my clothes." He gasped a curse. "My legs! Where are my legs?"

Roselyn felt his body shift. She glanced over her shoulder at the door. What was keeping the professor? She wasn't sure she could handle a hysterical normal man, much less one she couldn't see. A moment before, she'd thought she heard a bell chime, a pounding at the door. Surely no one would be visiting at this late hour of the night.

14

He squeezed her wrist until her fingers tingled. "Talk to me, damn it. Tell me what you've done to me."

Roselyn spared another quick glance at the door. "You said you remember stepping into the refractor?"

"You mean that wired-up outhouse over there?"

"Outhouse?"

"That's as good a name as any for it considering the damn thing shocked the crap out of me."

She lifted her chin. "It's an electromagnetic refractor. Your father's and my invention. We've been working on it for almost two years." She decided now was not the best time to inform him of their lack of success. "To put it simply," she continued, "when an object is placed inside of it, the refractor is capable of generating an intense magnetic field. The magnetic field causes a refraction . . . a bending of radar waves around the object. It's somewhat like . . . ." She considered how best to explain it. "I'm sure you've seen heated air wavering over the highway on a hot summer day."

"I'm lost in a mirage, is that what you're saying? I'm the freaking *object* of some deranged scientific experiment concocted by you and Pop?"

"Now, Jerome—"

"*J.T.*, I told you. My name's J.T."

"Mr. Drake . . ."

He released her wrist. She heard his movements, felt the air stir, caught a whiff of the burnt rubber scent surrounding him.

"To put it *simply,* I'm invisible."

Roselyn looked up. His words came from a higher place than before, a space far above her head. "Well, you—"

"If you can make this happen," he said, his breathing erratic, "you can reverse it, right?"

Thunder vibrated the house. She wasn't sure if the racket it made, the odor in the room, or his question

15

caused her sudden queasiness. Blinking at the empty space where she'd heard his voice, she slowly stood and clasped her hands in front of her.

"*Right?*" he asked again. "You've done this before, haven't you?"

"I . . . well . . . *yes*. Of course. But your body can't handle another shock so soon. It's better for you if we wait . . . give the effects a chance to wear off of their own accord. We shouldn't subject your system to the trauma of a second electrical transference unless it's absolutely necessary."

She stepped back. "You'll need rest . . . plenty of fluids. Your father and I will monitor your vital signs and perform a few painless procedures to help the process along." Roselyn nibbled her lower lip, then added, "Trust me on this."

"Trust you?" His laugh pricked her ears. "That ridiculous machine was your idea, wasn't it? You got Pop into this. Two years, you said. You've been working with him on this for two years? That's about the time Mrs. Moody's regularly scheduled phone calls started."

Stung by his accusation, she took another step backward toward the door. "Your father is a brilliant man. He was my teacher, my mentor. He's ahead of his time. We—"

Roselyn paused for a breath. An explanation of her motives was unnecessary. She wasn't the cause of Jerome Drake's current situation. His snooping had placed him in this unique predicament. "The professor has been like a father to me. I owe him more than I can ever repay. That ridiculous machine, as you call it, is as important to him as it is to me. Do you have any idea of the refractor's significance? Not only for the world but also for your father personally? The American Institute of Scientific—"

Drake's huff of disgust cut her short. "Quit kidding

yourself. No legitimate scientific foundation would take this fluke seriously. You're wasting your life just like Pop wasted his. Pursuing the impossible."

"Impossible, Mr. Drake?" Roselyn crossed her arms. She understood that the man lashed out at her through fear and uncertainty. Still, she couldn't excuse his attitude toward the professor. "If your father and I are nothing more than a couple of idealist dreamers, a couple of mad scientists, then explain to me how it is that at this very moment I'm staring straight through you."

For several seconds, Roselyn listened to the agitated pace of his breathing.

"Where's Pop?" he finally asked. "I want to talk to him. I want him to fix this. Pop!"

"Sshhh!" She followed the sound of his footsteps and the pungent scent of smoke he trailed. At the door she collided with something solid, something she couldn't see. "Oh!" On instinct, Roselyn lifted both hands to push away. Sparks skipped off her fingertips. She felt damp cotton fabric and, beneath it, a hard expanse of bone and muscle and firm, warm flesh. Two arms encircled her waist, trapping her.

Roselyn stared at her upraised hands, pressed in midair against a transparent, yet concrete, force. "I think some-one's upstairs with the professor," she said, stunned by the breathless sound of her voice and the flustered emo-tions that swept through her—apprehension and desire and the same voracious curiosity that had consumed her all of her life. Her fingers itched to explore what lay be-neath them. "I heard the doorbell ring."

"You're trembling. What are you afraid of? That someone will find out you tried to play God and turned me into a freak?"

The deep resonance of his voice scattered goose bumps up her spine.

"You'd better be glad this can be corrected, darlin'. If

I found out I had to live as a phantom the rest of my life, I'd make it my business to haunt you the rest of yours."

Roselyn's stomach clenched. Heaven help her, she had been so thrilled by this breakthrough in her research she had ignored all the possible outcomes. A man's life was at stake. For the first time in her professional life, Roselyn worried that her scientific abilities might have limits. What if this was the one problem she could never solve? What if she couldn't make Jerome Drake whole again?

J.T. released his father's partner and started for the stairs on shaky legs.

"*Jerome* . . . Mr. Drake . . . come back here. Please. You need to sit down. You've suffered a terrible shock."

J.T. forged ahead, ignoring her whispered pleas. He felt dizzy. His head ached. The odor of burnt rubber made him queasy. Maybe it wasn't such a great idea to have Pop shock him again so soon, after all. Maybe his best bet was to trust that Roselyn Peabody knew a thing or two about science. Maybe, as she had suggested, he should wait for this *condition* to wear off. The numbness and tingling in his legs had receded. Maybe the rest would, too. Other than the fact that she was crazy enough to team up with Pop, J.T. couldn't think of any reason not to believe her.

He drew slow deep breaths. So the old man was like a father to her. How sweet. Clenching his teeth, J.T. hastened his step.

He should've thought to ask how long it might take for the effects to subside or how the transformation would take place. Would he slowly begin to materialize body part by body part? Or would he flash into view all at once like an image on a movie screen? However the event was destined to happen, he'd be damned if he'd cower in a corner to wait.

Glancing back, J.T. saw that she followed him with determined strides. In her peculiar eyes, he detected the same rash light of eccentricity Pop possessed. A thirst for knowledge of the obscure, an obsession for solving the mysteries of the universe, a driving need to prove the impossible possible. *Pure madness.*

J.T. took the stairs two at a time. After all these years, Pop had finally achieved victory with one of his projects. And, just as J.T. had with Pop's failures, he now suffered the consequences of the old man's success. All the old jokes came rushing back. Taunts from his classmates about his dad, the absent-minded professor, getting high on home-brewed chemical concoctions down in the basement. There'd been others, too. Snickered jibes that J.T. must have been the result of another fouled-up experiment in the old man's laboratory because no woman would do the dirty deed with a half-mad holdover hippie like Hershel Drake.

At the top of the stairs, J.T. stepped aside so that Pop's partner would be spared another collision. Not that he'd minded having her body pressed against him, her hands on his chest. She was attractive in a strange sort of way.

He almost laughed aloud at that particular thought as she stumbled past him. The electromagnetic thingamajig must have erased his good taste along with his body. He'd never seen a worse haircut on a woman or known anyone with less fashion sense—not even Pop. She wore a wrinkled white T-shirt with red letters across the front. He couldn't make out the word they spelled because the shirt was inside out. Beneath it, she wore a long, wrinkled brown skirt and blue ankle-high snow boots. As a wave of weakness rushed over him, J.T. grabbed hold of the stair rail to steady himself. Roselyn Peabody was no Giselle, that was for damn sure.

Still . . . His thoughts skipped back to that moment she'd bumped into him. She might be skinny, but she filled out her wrinkled damp T-shirt in a way that, under normal circumstances, he would thoroughly appreciate. Especially since, beneath it, she seemed to wear nothing but skin.

J.T. leaned forward, braced his palms on his knees, and gulped in oxygen. If nothing else, being invisible gave a person a certain measure of power. He recalled the breathlessness of her words, her quivering hands, the stunned look on her face when she bumped into him. If this had happened to another sort of man, someone who thrived on control and manipulation and taking advantage of women, Rosy the mad scientist might be fighting for her life right now or, at the very least, her integrity.

He lifted his head.

Two steps past the head of the stairs where he stood, Roselyn paused and turned to look over her shoulder. She squinted, sniffed, crinkled her upturned nose. "Are you there?"

He held his breath. He wasn't sure why, Maybe because, reasonable or not, fair or not, he blamed Roselyn Peabody for this weird crisis and for encouraging Pop's obsessions. Maybe because a part of him, the boy in him that had never grown up, wondered just how much he could get away with while in this physical state. Then again, maybe he just needed to lighten his apprehension with some harmless fun.

She took another sniff of the air. "That's you, isn't it?" Crossing her arms, Miss Peabody frowned. "Mr. Drake . . . this isn't funny. You're making me a nervous wreck." She lifted a hand, reached out, lowered it. With a sigh, she resumed her trek toward the den.

Relieved to discover he could still smile, J.T. quietly followed. He heard two people talking as they neared the den. Pop and Wanda Moody. There was no mistaking the old woman's voice. It crackled with static, sounding as old and scratchy as the antique phonograph his mother used to play for his amusement when he was just a boy, or so his father once told him.

Pop and his neighbor sat at opposite ends of the threadbare green velvet couch, the only den couch J.T. could recall his father ever owning. A folded umbrella lay between them. Like Pop, Mrs. Moody wore pajamas and slippers. Unlike Pop's faded blue tie-dyed T-shirt, baggy drawstring sleep pants, and rubber flip-flops, her lounging attire consisted of a loose housedress and fuzzy slippers with pink bunny ears. J.T. guessed Wanda must be close to eighty by now, and in the five or so years since he last saw her, Pop's neighbor had tinted her white hair violet and dropped another ten or so pounds from her stick figure frame.

"That was one incredible bolt of lightning," Mrs. Moody said. "Never seen anything like it. Lit up your house like a Christmas tree when it hit."

"Well . . . I appreciate you coming by to check on me," Pop said, glancing up as Roselyn entered the room. "Ah, there you are." Pop's eyes narrowed on her, as if he were telepathically sending a question her way. After all that had happened tonight, J.T. didn't doubt that he could.

Roselyn glanced slowly left then right then back at Pop. She sniffed.

Pop sniffed, too, then ran a shaky hand through his thinning shoulder-length hair. "I'd like you to meet my neighbor, Mrs. Wanda Moody," he said. "Wanda, this is my friend, Doctor Roselyn Peabody. Roselyn was once my student. She hails from Nevada. Las Vegas, to be exact. I've never forgotten the day she first walked into my—"

"I know you." Behind the wide, square lenses of Mrs. Moody's crooked black glasses, her eyes narrowed on Roselyn. "You're that teacher who took over Hershel's job at the University."

Roselyn smiled. "That's right."

"Humph." Mrs. Moody's nose twitched. She crossed one bony bare leg over the other. The bunny slipper tapped the air. "There's that smell again."

J.T. crept slowly past the threesome. Fatigue tugged at him, making it difficult to place one foot in front of the other. If he didn't sit soon he knew he'd black out. He didn't want that to happen. Not now when things were about to get interesting. Just before he reached the empty recliner beside the couch, a board creaked beneath his weight. He paused.

Roselyn stopped talking mid-sentence. Her wide-eyed gaze darted toward him, across to Pop, back to Wanda Moody again. "So you live next door?" she blurted.

Wanda's top lip curled up. She poked a finger into her hair and scratched. "Across the street." Leaning back against the cushions, she pulled a cigarette pack and a lighter from the pocket of her housedress and turned to Pop. "You don't mind, do you, Hershel?"

Pop's head jerked and bobbed like an anchored boat on a choppy sea. "No, no, not at all."

"I didn't think so. Not with what I've been smelling over here. And all that green smoke . . ." The widow Moody tapped a blood-red fingernail against the pack then pulled out a single cigarette. She turned, her eyes squinting behind her angled glasses as her gaze settled on Roselyn Peabody's clinging wet T-shirt. "You spend a lot of time over here. That'd be your bicycle out front, wouldn't it?"

Roselyn glanced down at herself and flinched.

J.T. bit his lip. For all the good that shirt did her, she might as well be naked.

Crossing her arms to cover her upper body, Roselyn nodded. "Yes, it's my bike."

"I've been trying to figure out what you cart around in that handlebar basket. Something for whatever it is you two are doing down in the basement, I guess. Seeds, maybe? Fertilizer?" Wanda stuck the cigarette between her thin lips, flicked the lighter until a flame appeared then lifted her gaze to Pop and added, *"Viagra?"*

Splotchy pink patches appeared on Pop's cheeks. "Miss Peabody is . . . well, you see, she's having some problems with one of her students. She comes by for my advice."

J.T. settled into the easy chair, relieved to be off his feet and more than slightly amused by Mrs. Moody's insinuations. He glanced at Roselyn. She seemed unfazed by the old woman's implications.

With her arms still crossed, she started toward his chair. "I often draw on the professor's years of wisdom," she said. "His experience is invaluable."

Mrs. Moody's cheeks collapsed inward as she took a drag from her cigarette. She blew out a stream of smoke. "I don't doubt that a'tall. I bet Hershel's eager as a young pup to share his wisdom with you."

When J.T. realized Roselyn intended to sit in the chair he occupied he tried to rise but his muscles were still weak from the electrical shock and he couldn't push up in time. He bit his lip harder and watched with mixed feelings of apprehension and amused anticipation as Roselyn's small, round bottom slowly lowered onto his lap.

Chapter Three

Roselyn grasped the arms of the chair and tried to stand. Pressure against her stomach restrained her and, without any thought to Mrs. Moody's reaction, she kicked her feet and beat her fists against the confining force.

A shriek drew her attention to the couch. The cigarette fell from Mrs. Moody's mouth as the old woman recoiled against the armrest.

Looking down at herself, Roselyn saw that her arms and legs flailed in midair, her fists struck at nothing, her bottom hovered a few inches above the chair's surface with nothing supporting it . . . or so it appeared. It was most definitely supported. She felt hard evidence that, though invisible, Jerome Drake's body still functioned properly.

When she stopped struggling, he shifted beneath her. Roselyn slid off his lap onto one side where she sat squeezed between his thigh and the edge of the recliner. She grabbed the arm of the chair with one hand and something warm, firm, and slightly hairy with the other.

Roselyn jerked her hand up from what she suspected was Jerome's knee, then folded her arms across her middle.

"Did you see that, Hershel?" Mrs. Moody lifted the umbrella, pointing the sharp tip at Roselyn. "She floated."

Professor Drake snatched the burning cigarette butt off the couch cushion. "You don't really believe that, do you, Wanda?" He reached for a glass of amber liquid on the coffee table and drained the contents before dropping the butt into it. "The floor's slick," he said, his laugh nervous as he set the glass down again. "Doctor Peabody simply lost her footing. Fascinating how the mind can play tricks on us, isn't it? I recall an article in *Scientific Quarterly* about the—"

"Hershel Drake . . . if you try to make me look like a fool, I swan, I'll . . ." Keeping the umbrella aimed at Roselyn with one hand, Mrs. Moody adjusted her glasses with the other, her face contorting with outrage. "That girl floated. You know it as well as I do."

The professor cleared his throat, looked down at his folded hands, coughed.

Standing, Mrs. Moody held the umbrella out in front of her like a weapon and stepped away from the couch. Then she backed her way toward the door with small shuffling steps. "You may be younger than me, Hershel, but you're the one acting like an old fool now," she said, her gaze fixed on Roselyn. "Something's wrong with that girl . . . something evil. Look at her eyes."

Professor Drake stood, too. "Look here, she's—"

"I don't know what that girl's got you mixed up in." Mrs. Moody stopped at the door. "But mark my words Hershel, if you don't nip it in the bud right now you'll live to regret it." She reached behind her, opened the door, then escaped into the rainy night.

Deep laughter erupted beside Roselyn as she pushed to her feet. "You, Mr. Drake," she said, swinging around to face the empty chair, "have a warped sense of humor."

"Sorry about that," he said, though he didn't sound the least bit contrite. "I couldn't help myself. Wanda's a little old for you, isn't she, Pop?"

"Yes, well . . ." The professor's face turned scarlet. "Seems she has a thing for younger men. Try as I might I can't discourage her."

"Well, thanks to you, Jerome," Roselyn said, "that poor woman obviously thinks I'm a witch."

"Are you?"

Stunned by his question, Roselyn stepped back. Over the course of her twenty-eight years, she'd been called many things—a nerd, an egghead, a freak. She'd become reasonably comfortable with those labels, had learned to pretend wearing them didn't, from time to time, make her itch beneath the collar like she wore a stiff wool coat. But "witch"? That label was new and startling.

"For pity's sake, Jerome." Professor Drake frowned as he tucked a strand of hair behind his ear. "What sort of question is that?"

"A fair one under the circumstances, don't you think?" The chair cushion shifted. "And maybe I should be asking it of you, too, Pop. I mean, look at me. I'm not exactly myself because of the two of you and your hocus-pocus. For all I know, maybe she's a witch and you're a warlock." His laughter chilled the stuffy air.

Looking stunned, the professor shook his head. "I'm sorry, son, but you've been told time and again you're not allowed in my laboratory without permission. After what happened the last time . . . well . . ." He coughed, looked down at the floor. "I thought you learned then to stay away from—"

"Your experiments?" Jerome's words shot across the room like bullets, making Roselyn jump. "I'm not a kid anymore, Pop. I don't want any part of your precious experiments. I couldn't care less about them. And now I am one."

The professor flinched. His head tremor increased, something Roselyn had come to recognize in him as a sure sign of stress. She had never in her life wanted to physically harm anyone, not even the old classmates who'd tried to hurt her with their names and taunts and manipulations. But right now she wanted to strangle the professor's son, wanted to slap him silly, as her mother would say.

Instead, she moved to the couch and stood beside Professor Drake, placing her hand on his shoulder. "We're all exhausted and overwhelmed by this development. I think we should try to get some sleep and start fresh in the morning."

"Yes . . ." Professor Drake reached across his chest to pat her hand. "A wise idea, dear girl. You can sleep in your old bedroom, Jerome."

"And then what?" Jerome sounded congested. "You said there were procedures, *Doctor* Peabody. Painless ones. To help the process of reversal along."

Roselyn felt the professor tense. "Roselyn and I," he said, "We haven't—"

She gave his shoulder a gentle squeeze to quiet him. "I said you needed rest and plenty of fluids first. We'll monitor you during the night. Then in the morning—"

"Do you mean to tell me this won't wear off by then?" Jerome asked.

"It might." Roselyn swallowed. "It might not. Every case is different. We'll just have to wait and see."

"And if you can't? See, I mean. If you can't see me in the morning, then you'll shock me again and reverse the process?"

She glanced quickly at the professor and drew her lower lip between her teeth. "If you're stable, yes." Roselyn started to add, *we'll give it a try,* but decided against it.

"All my things are at the Ambassador Hotel in town," Jerome said tightly, then sneezed. "I won't get any sleep without my allergy medicine, thanks to whatever it is that's blooming around here." He sneezed again. "I really hate Pecan Grove."

Roselyn thought he had made that fact painfully clear. She bit her lip to keep from telling him so. "If one of you would loan me a car, I'll be happy to pick up your bags at the hotel. I don't advise that you drive tonight."

"So you think an unmanned moving vehicle might raise a few eyebrows around Pecan Grove?" The air stirred. The cushion on the recliner expanded. "Why do you need to borrow a car? Did you walk over?"

Before she could answer, he added, "That's right, I forgot. You travel by bicycle." A lightning flash lit up the window. "Rain or shine I guess."

She glared at the chair, bristling at the mocking tone of his voice.

"A bicycle with a handlebar basket to carry around mysterious ingredients for your spells." His words moved across the room. "I wonder what they could be? Eye of newt and toe of frog? Or maybe wool of bat and tongue of dog."

Roselyn shifted her gaze to the hallway, following the sound of his voice.

"Adder's fork and blind-worm's sting . . . lizard's leg and howlet's wing . . ."

"Jerome Terrence Drake!" The professor bolted to his feet, his gaze darting left then right. "I will not allow this childish insolence toward Doctor Peabody. Roselyn is a respected scientist, a fine young woman."

"Scale of dragon, tooth of wolf . . ."

Roselyn squared her shoulders, her cheeks burning. She didn't understand why Jerome Drake's goading bothered her so. Derision was certainly nothing new in her life. Perhaps it was the fact that she couldn't see him but could feel him watching her, perhaps because she had harbored issues with him even before they'd met. Or maybe his taunts stung more than others she'd endured because she didn't understand his caustic attitude toward her. More than mere anger over her part in tonight's crisis seemed to bubble beneath the surface of his animosity.

She heard a jingle, then another as something hit her feet. With a gasp, Roselyn fell back onto the couch with her legs sprawled apart. She clutched her throat with one hand.

"My keys." Jerome's voice was near, so near she knew if she reached out she'd touch him. "I'd tell you where they landed but I can't see them any better than you can. Seems they disappeared right along with the rest of me."

The burnt rubber odor had dissipated. Roselyn smelled *him* now—a blend of something like sandalwood, the tang of tobacco, purely masculine sweat. The scent was disturbing . . . so close . . . too close. She held her breath.

A patting noise sounded on the floor beside her feet, another jingle, a tired sigh. "Ah, here they are." His words floated up from between her spread legs.

Though Roselyn's skirt reached her ankles, she slammed her knees together and stared at the empty space in front of her, too mortified to spare a glance at the professor.

The older man cleared his throat. "Jerome . . ."

"Relax, Pop. I'll behave myself." He chuckled. "Reach out your hand, Darlin'."

"My name is—"

"Oh, yes. Excuse me. Doctor Peabody."

Roselyn hesitated a moment before lifting her arm out in front of her. The cold weight of metal hit her palm, though she didn't see anything there.

Jennifer Archer

"The Dodge Intrepid I rented is parked on the side of Mrs. Moody's house," Jerome said.

She started to draw back her arm.

"Wait. Here's my room card, too. 308. Park in back."

The card was cool and flat, plastic, she noted as her fingers closed around it and the keys. Her heart tripped in her chest at the weirdness of not being able to see what she held in her hand.

Jerome's voice came from above her again. "I'd go with you," he said, "but to tell you the truth, I'm pretty damn shaky right now. And Pop doesn't need to be going out. Not after polishing off that glass of whiskey."

Roselyn looked up at the professor. His pale face reddened and he suddenly looked every minute of his age and more.

"Go lie down, Jerome," he said quietly. "I put linens on your bed. When you said you were coming for a visit, it never occurred to me you'd stay at a hotel."

Jerome seemed unaware that his subtle cruelty had snuffed the last, faint spark of vibrancy from his father's eyes. Either that, or he didn't care. "Fine," he said. "I think I'll turn in now. Just leave my bags outside the bedroom door."

Sensing he'd moved away from the couch, Roselyn slipped the keys and plastic room card into her skirt pocket and stood. She glanced around, sniffed, smelled only the musty air of a room seldom used. "Goodnight, Mr. Drake."

"Goodnight, *Doctor* Peabody."

She peered deeper into the hallway from where she'd heard his distant reply. A hinge squeaked. A door opened, then closed.

Roselyn turned to the professor in time to see him shudder.

Exhaling her own wobbly breath, she linked an arm

30

through his, understanding all too well how it felt to need another human being's support.

J.T. turned on the light, then leaned against the door. He didn't like the way Roselyn Peabody had squeezed his father's shoulder to shut him up when Pop started to comment on the process of reversing the invisibility. He didn't like her vague answers about the procedure. He didn't like her . . . period. At least he didn't want to.

He scanned the room. Like the scarce few other times he had been in here since moving away from Pecan Grove, he felt as if he'd stepped into the past. Everything was the same as he'd left it. Usually that fact unnerved him, even annoyed him, but not tonight. He felt oddly comforted by the images of rock-and-roll legends and sports heroes and bathing-beauty blondes staring back at him from the faded posters still covering the walls. At least *this* was constant. Here was solid proof of his existence, echoes of the boy he'd been, bits and pieces of the interests that had helped to form the man he'd become.

His cross-country track medals still hung from their red, white, and blue ribbons on a cork board above the desk in one corner. J.T. walked over, ran a finger he couldn't see across one gold medallion, then moved to the fake mum beside it. He skimmed the black silk petals, the flowing black and gold streamers beneath the flower. Lifting one of those streamers, J.T. read the word *Wildcats* spelled in sparkling white glitter down the silky length. The ribbon to the left of it bore his name, the one on the right, the name *Libby*.

J.T. traced the letters. *Libby Bakersfield.* Senior year. Homecoming. Murphy Lake after the dance. A full harvest moon. Bare skin, fogged car windows, and exasperating bra hooks.

He smiled. For the first time in his life, he had stayed

out all night. When he'd parked his old Barracuda in the driveway at dawn, he'd prepared himself to find Pop up and waiting, pacing the floor, ready to lower the boom.

J.T. bit the inside of his cheek as the humor died. He closed his eyes and could still see the dim light sifting up the basement stairwell on that long-ago morning when he slipped by on his way to bed, could still smell the scent of sulfur, hear the clink and clatter of who-knew-what coming from Pop's laboratory below.

At first he'd felt relieved and smug to have managed getting away with missing his midnight curfew by an entire five hours. He decided that he must be the luckiest guy alive when Pop didn't punish him, did not, in fact, even mention the offense when he saw him in the kitchen heating up a can of soup for supper later that evening.

But the next Monday at school, when J.T. heard several other kids bemoaning their various fates for committing at least one of the same teenaged sins he had committed, he pretended his father had grounded him.

He never asked himself why he lied or why he avoided the questions that flickered through his mind. Had Pop not noticed he hadn't come home? Or had he noticed, but just didn't give a rat's ass? Either option filled J.T. with an uncomfortable sense of shame and embarrassment he had not wanted to face at the age of seventeen, shame and embarrassment he didn't completely understand even to this day.

J.T. sat on the edge of the bed. It hadn't changed, either. The waterbed mattress swayed and gurgled beneath his weight. He nudged out of his shoes, pushed them to the center of the small braided rug under his feet, making a careful mental note of where he left them since they, too, were transparent. He'd have the devil to pay if he didn't memorize their location.

Reaching toward a shelf on the bedside table, he pulled out a worn paperback novel, Truman Capote's *In Cold*

Blood. Man, how he'd been awed by that book the first time he read it when he was around fourteen. Awed by its power to disturb, to make him think about the human mind in ways he'd never considered before. Like what motivated human behavior, good and bad; the dark side of every mind; the reasons certain people ran, scared of that darkness, while others embraced it.

J.T. replaced the book and stretched out on his back in bed. He'd never fully satisfied those curiosities. They still intrigued him as much as before. He explored them with every criminal he studied, with each book he wrote.

He amended that thought. One criminal existed whose motives he refrained from examining too closely.

Now, for the first time, he let his mind drift back to the week after homecoming, to a crisp autumn night when he'd lain awake in this very bed, listening to the noises from downstairs while a breeze fluttered the curtains at his window. The chilly air that swept through the room that night failed to cool the burning hatred inside him, his overwhelming jealousy of his father's obsession.

Obsessed himself with far-fetched plans to destroy his faceless rival, J.T. had stared at the ceiling, stewing, listening, waiting. When the noises downstairs finally quieted and he heard Pop's footsteps on the stairs, he held off another few minutes, then crept down to the basement. Just as he had tonight, he took the laboratory key from beneath the loose floorboard. Then he opened the door.

Sixteen years ago, the basement lab had been less organized than today and as confusing and bizarre to J.T. as his father's personality. Pop's project, at the time, had something to do with teleportation, though J. T. was never able to make much sense of his father's ramblings about quantum systems and entangled particles and the transference of properties one to the other. On that night, as the door to the workshop squeaked shut behind him, he stopped trying to make any sense of it . . . stopped trying to make any sense of Pop . . .

J.T. stopped the memory, cut it off before it went too far, before the old bitterness could rise up and strangle him. He thought, instead, of Pop's partner.

Doctor Roselyn Peabody.

The woman, no doubt, was responsible for streamlining Pop's operation, for helping to focus his erratic genius.

Roselyn Peabody.

Now there was a mind whose motives he'd like to explore. In some ways, she seemed as over-the-top and out of touch with the "normal" world as Pop, but she also seemed more centered than the old man, as if she had at least a pinch of common sense sprinkled in with her high aptitude. He wondered if Pop had been the same in his younger days, before J.T.'s mother died, before the drinking started.

Roselyn.

Like Pop, she was probably used to being ridiculed. J.T. had lived with an eccentric intellectual long enough to know that mockery went with the territory. But while Pop had always seemed oblivious to the taunts, his new partner suffered them silently. He'd caught a brief glimpse of pain and defensiveness in her eyes when he teased her. It surprised J.T. that it bothered him as much as it did to discover that he'd wounded her. Who could blame him for shooting an arrow or two her way? She bore a lot of responsibility for his current condition.

Rosy.

J.T. yawned. That name suited her better. "Roselyn" was too elegant a name for the walking, talking train wreck he'd left in the den. Despite all he'd been through tonight, nothing surprised him more than the fact that he found her attractive in a funky sort of way. She was a female version of Pop, for chrissake. The electrical shock had obviously messed with his mind.

He yawned again.

Maybe he'd made a mistake by getting on her bad side. Female version of Pop or not, she would probably be manning the controls of that wired-up outhouse tomorrow if his "unfortunate condition" didn't wear off during the night and they had to juice him again. He'd be at her mercy. It might be in his best interest to adjust his attitude toward her in the morning. Play nice. Pretend her part in this whole disaster didn't tick him off big time.

J.T. thought of the protective way she'd placed her pretty long fingers on his father's shoulder, the stubborn set of her jaw when she defended the old man's integrity, the affection he heard in her voice every time she spoke of her mentor and all he'd done for her.

He closed his eyes, realizing Pop displayed the same sentiments when it came to his intriguing young partner. Protectiveness. Stubborn defense. Affection.

As he fell asleep, J.T.'s thoughts wandered to the untouched room he now occupied. Suddenly, the same questions that had nudged him sixteen years ago, after staying out all night and getting away with it, nudged him again.

Had Pop not dealt with the room because he didn't care enough to do anything about it? Or had his father simply not looked up from his work long enough to notice that his son no longer lived there?

Chapter Four

Hershel dug an umbrella out of the cluttered entry-hall closet. "Are you sure I can't drive you home?"

"Around the corner?" Roselyn shook her head. "No need for that."

The girl had a point. Her house was only two streets and one block over from his. Still, it was late, dark, and still sprinkling rain. "If it's my . . ." he cleared his throat, embarrassment smothering him. "If my driving worries you . . . because of the drink I had earlier, you could take my van, bring it back in the morning. Or Jerome's rental vehicle. He won't be needing it."

Roselyn accepted the umbrella he held out to her. "Thank you, but I could use the fresh air." She touched his forearm, her eyes soft with understanding. "That's the only reason I want to ride my bike. It's been quite a night."

It amazed him she could smile after all he and Jerome had put her through. But then, Roselyn Peabody was quite an amazing young lady. Hershel had known that after the first day he met her in his classroom ten years ago when she was only a college freshman. Her off-color eyes were the first thing to capture his attention, followed by the fact that the notes he'd scribbled beside each student's name told him she hailed from Las Vegas. Surprised to discover that this shy girl was the student he'd taken special effort to lure to the university, Hershel watched her with eager fascination. But after he spent the next hour lecturing, answering her questions, listening to her answers to his, he no longer cared quite so much about her Vegas roots or about the slim chance of what she might be able to accomplish for him. Nor did he notice the peculiarity of her eyes. He only saw the desire of discovery burning within them.

Roselyn was the only student that first morning of the new semester with enough courage and academic self-confidence to interact with him in a discussion of the lesson. He soon discovered that her scholarly abilities were the single area of the girl's life in which she felt confident.

Hershel patted her hand, wishing for at least the hundredth time he had never involved her in this project, wishing he'd been able to forget it himself. One truth he'd learned over the course of his life was that some things were better left alone; they simply weren't meant to be.

"Thank you for rushing over after I called."

Roselyn cocked her head to one side and scowled. "Well, of course I rushed over. What else would I do? We're in this together, you and I." She opened the door, looked out at the drizzle then back at him. "I still think I should stay the night to help you keep an eye on your son."

"No . . . no." Hershel shook his head. "You were right. We should start anew in the morning when our minds are clear and our nerves are more settled. You'll sleep better in your own bed."

With a nod, she poked the umbrella out the doorway, opened it, and then lifted it over her head as she stepped onto the leaky covered porch. Raindrops pattered as they hit the fabric.

"I'm not comfortable misleading Jerome," Hershel said.

"I know. I'm sorry. But I was afraid he wouldn't rest tonight if he knew the truth."

Though he found no humor in the situation, Hershel chuckled. "God, if he exists, has a twisted funny bone, don't you agree? What happened to Jerome . . . it's what we've worked night and day to achieve for the past two years. If only it had been a houseplant or a spider or even a mouse instead of my son, we'd be celebrating right now instead of worrying."

"Let's not second guess ourselves, Professor. God, either, for that matter. In the morning, we may find out we do have cause for celebration. Until then, Jerome doesn't seem to be suffering any serious side effects from his run-in with the refractor."

With one finger, Hershel pushed his glasses to the tip of his nose and peered at her over the top edge of the frames. "Other than the fact that he's transparent, you mean."

"Of course." She smiled. "But that's not a side effect, it's the desired effect as far as the refractor is concerned. What I meant to say was Jerome seems completely healthy. In perfect physical shape." Her voice trailed off. She drew her lower lip between her teeth and looked down at her boots.

When Wanda Moody came nosing over, Hershel had turned on the porch light. He could see Roselyn's face clearly. She was blushing, and he suddenly wondered what his son had said to her during the time they'd been alone. He knew the boy's mind better than Jerome thought he did. It didn't surprise Hershel that his son had found success as a writer. Jerome had a clever way with words. He knew just how to ply them to extract the desired emotion.

He cleared his throat. "I apologize for Jerome's—"

She silenced him with an upraised hand. "No need, Professor. He's under a lot of stress."

Turning, she started down the steps, but paused to look back at him. "What time shall I come over in the morning?"

"Is eight o'clock too early?" He glanced at his watch. "That's only six and a half hours from now."

"I'm sure I'll be wide awake and impatient to start long before then."

"Well, then. Make it seven-thirty." He stared at the dark, empty, rain-glossed street behind her. "Be careful. It's late for you to be out alone."

Roselyn dipped her chin, the corner of her lip twitching. "You forget I grew up in the concrete jungle of Las Vegas. I learned years ago how to take care of myself."

She called out one last "goodnight" as she ran toward the bicycle parked in the driveway.

Hershel stood on the porch and watched her ride away. She used her right hand to steer the handlebars, her left to hold the umbrella upright. Her back was straight as a ruler, her chin lifted.

When she turned the corner, Hershel went into the house and closed the door. Retrieving the suitcase and tote bag Roselyn had brought back from Jerome's hotel, he started for the bedroom where his son now slept.

Jerome's soft snores assured him a person truly did occupy the seemingly empty bed—that and the long deep indentation where the waterbed mattress supported Jerome's weight.

Hershel placed the bags by the door, walked to the

desk in the corner at the head of the bed, eased out the chair and sat. He stared at the impression in the pillow where Jerome's head rested.

His throat turned to stone as his thoughts traveled back to the happy family they'd once been, he and Evie and their little boy . . . long ago, before the unthinkable happened.

"Where are you going, Pop?"

Hershel turned around quickly, startled by the sound of the small, sleepy voice behind him.

Jerome stood at the bottom of the staircase rubbing his eyes, his pajama pants twisted at the waist, his dark hair mussed.

"I'm off to work," Hershel said in a hushed tone, lifting the boy into his arms for a hug and a smack on the cheek. "Why are you up so early?"

"I heard a noise," Jerome whispered. He touched the tip of his father's nose, blinked and yawned as he looked toward the window. "You go to work in the dark?"

Hershel stared into his son's eyes and nodded. Before now, he had never told the child he left the house long before sunup each morning to work with his team, that he had for the past three years. But since Jerome asked, he saw no reason to pretend otherwise. The boy was little more than a baby, after all, and Hershel was tired of secrets, of clandestine meetings and whispered codes. He missed talking about his work with family and friends, missed sharing the excitement it brought him. Ironic that his current project required "top secret" classification.

"The earlier I leave," he said, "the sooner I'll finish my work and the faster I'll be back home to spend time with you, little man. We can play hide-and-seek like we did last night. Would you like that?"

Nodding, Jerome rubbed chubby fingers across Hershel's chin. "Did you shave your whiskers?"

"I do every morning."

"Can I shave, too?"

"Soon enough, I promise."

The boy tapped on the lens of Hershel's eyeglasses, leaving a finger smudge, then tugged a lock of Hershel's hair. *"Can I grow my hair long, too?"*

"If you want to be a scraggly hippie like your dad, I guess you can." Hershel laughed. *"Right now, though, you should go climb in bed with Mommy. Snuggle up with her and try to catch some more sleep. Don't wake her. She's very sleepy."*

Hershel had the sudden urge to follow his own advice; forget the project for just one day, return to bed, hold Evie in his arms until she awoke. He worried about her. Though he couldn't divulge the details of the success they'd be celebrating, he had invited her to come to the breakfast party this morning at the research compound, as were many of the other spouses. He'd been disappointed when she'd begged off, saying she was simply too tired.

Evie hadn't been herself for days . . . weeks, really. Whenever he mentioned her lack of spark, she brushed aside his concern and told him to get accustomed to a sluggish wife. Chasing a three-and-a-half year old day in, day out, depleted her energy. And then she'd laugh and her eyes would dance in that way he loved. Because chasing Jerome was what Evie loved best and, exhausting or not, she had no intention of stopping for the next fifteen or so years.

"Can I go with you to your work, Pop? I'm not sleepy."

Hershel tickled the boy's ribs. *"May I go with you,"* he teased, mimicking Evie's habitual correction of their son's grammar.

Jerome giggled. *"Can I? Can I? Can I?"*

Why not? His son was no threat to the project's secrecy. No three year old, not even one as precocious as Jerome, would understand the workings of the refractor. Even if the boy tried to describe to anyone what he saw, his vocabulary was not extensive enough to communicate information that might expose the venture.

Jerome would enjoy the breakfast celebration, and Hershel could have him home by lunchtime. Evie might appreciate the hours alone to read and rest.

He thought of Reneau, thinking it a shame that he wouldn't be joining the rest of the team this morning. Hershel hoped the "family emergency" that had required Reneau to leave town this morning was not too serious.

Jerome squirmed in his arms. "May I, Pop? Please?"

Hershel wondered how he'd keep his son occupied once the party ended and work resumed. Though Jerome had a healthy curious streak, he might quickly tire of the lab. Then Hershel remembered the old typewriter his co-workers had shoved aside in a corner, the one nobody had taken the time to move to storage when the machine became obsolete. Evie was teaching Jerome the alphabet. He could entertain himself with the typewriter and a stack of paper, and Hershel would take along some of the books the boy loved, too, just in case the typewriter's appeal wore off too soon.

"I like that idea, Son. Let's go upstairs and find your clothes. Then we'll write a note to Mommy and pin it on my pillow. What do you say?" He offered his hand to the boy. "Shake on it?"

Jerome's tiny fingers wrapped around Hershel's palm as he recited the words that completed their familiar routine. "It's a deal."

Hershel's head jerked up when his chin hit his chest. He pushed his hair back from his face, removed his glasses and rubbed his eyes. The memory had seemed so real.

"Jerome," he whispered, reaching an unsteady hand

42

toward the dent in the pillow, closing his eyes as his fingers met the warmth of his son's stubbled cheek. "I miss you."

So many wasted years. Why hadn't he turned to the person he loved most instead of away from him? They had needed each other, he and Jerome, but Hershel had been blinded by obsession and anger and the quest for revenge, too guilt-ridden and self-pitying to reach out to anyone, even his son. So instead he pushed Jerome away slowly but completely, inch by inch, day by endless day.

The rain shower had stopped completely by the time Roselyn parked her bicycle in the detached garage beside her house. Closing the professor's umbrella, she let herself into the kitchen through the side door and immediately noticed the flashing red light on her telephone answering machine.

"My word," Roselyn muttered. Wondering who on earth would've called in the wee hours of the morning, she crossed the room and punched the button. A robotic, monotone voice informed her the call came in at 5:30 P.M. She had still been at her office at the university then. On arriving home an hour later after stopping by the Professor's, Roselyn hadn't even spared a glance in the direction of the machine. Janice and Melanie, two colleagues from the English Department, expected her to meet them for dinner by six-thirty. She'd been running late, so she'd rushed in, taken a quick shower, and then rushed out again.

A jazzed-up version of "Happy Birthday" filled the room, her mother's and Barb's well-trained voices belting out the tune.

"Hi, Baby," Darla Peabody said, after they finished their serenade. Her Texas upbringing was still evident in her accent. Even after all the years in Nevada she hadn't managed to lose it. "We hoped we'd catch you before you went out."

"You are going out, aren't you?" Barb's voice broke in. "Someplace you'll have to dress up for would be good. With a member of the opposite sex. And I don't mean that sweet old science teacher you're so crazy about."

"There's not a single thing wrong with Roselyn spending time with Professor Drake," her mother said. "At least he's safe."

"Damn, Darla. Listen to yourself. What girl wants to be with a safe old man on her twenty-eighth birthday?"

When her mother and Barb continued to argue as if the machine wasn't recording, Roselyn burst out laughing.

"Okay, okay maybe I am being too overprotective," her mother finally conceded. She sighed. "Hell's bells, honey, surely Pecan Grove has one or two *young* safe science types you find interesting."

"Nope," Roselyn muttered as her mother took a breath. "They're all even more boring than I am."

"Anyhow," her mom went on, "I wondered if the package Barb and I sent got there. The guy at the post office promised Barb it would be to you by today. I wish I was with you, Baby. If you did go out, I hope you remembered to carry a you-know-what in your purse just—"

"—in case," Roselyn finished her mother's sentence as the recorder cut off the final words. Shaking her head and smiling, she headed for the front door. Her mom meant well, but the fact remained that the "you-know-what" in Roselyn's billfold was the same one her mom put there ten years ago when Roselyn left Vegas to go away to college. The condom package was so wrinkled and worn smooth now that she could no longer read the writing on it.

Roselyn turned on the porch light and unlocked the door. Her mother simply couldn't comprehend that, unlike her, men only used Darla Peabody's daughter for her mind, not her body.

She peeked behind the huge pot of struggling geraniums beside the door beneath the porch overhang. She'd asked the mailman to stash any packages too large for the mailbox behind the plant if she wasn't home. Sure enough, a large box sat beneath the withering pink blooms.

Brushing dead leaves off the brown paper bearing her name and address, Roselyn lifted the package with one hand and turned on the water hose with the other. She wished she'd thought to pull the plant off the porch this morning so it could've had rainwater instead of tap water. After giving the thirsty geranium a long drink, she went back inside the house, scolding herself once again for neglecting the plant and everything else domestic in her life.

With the help of a sturdy pair of scissors, Roselyn tore into the box. When the lid came off, a rainbow of lingerie spilled out. A pale pink, sheer lace bra and matching thong panties, a purple satin teddy cut high at the thighs, a red bustier body suit. Roselyn laughed. These were Barb's contributions, no doubt. She wondered how Barb had slipped them in without her mother knowing.

Beneath all the sexy satin and lace lay a plain, conservative white blouse, a pair of baggy tailored navy blue slacks and a videocassette. These, she knew, her mother had purchased. Very sensible. Very safe.

Roselyn scooped everything into her arms and headed into her bedroom. She turned on the television and popped the cassette into the VCR. The picture on the screen flickered, and then her mother's face appeared. With her honey-colored hair swept up in a ponytail on top of her head, she looked impossibly young and as pretty as ever. The camera didn't pick up the lines fanning the sides of Darla Peabody's eyes, lines etched by years of laughter and heartache and more hard times than any forty-four-year-old woman deserved.

Her mother stepped back away from the camera and waved. "Happy birthday, Baby." She turned for a moment, covered her mouth, whispered something to someone out of sight.

"Ready?" asked the abrasive, deep voice behind the camera. It was a man's voice . . . Sully Tucker's. Roselyn had often teased him that he must gargle gravel before every meal. For years he had been her mother's boss and the only steady male influence Roselyn had ever known during her childhood.

Her mom nodded, the camera panned back, and there stood Barb, too, her mother's best friend and Sully's main squeeze, as Barb called herself. Darla Peabody had met Barb more than twenty years ago while working as a showgirl in the Las Vegas club Sully had managed. When he retired to do freelance security work part time, around the time Roselyn left for college, Barb stayed on at the club while Darla went to work at another establishment. Then, two years ago, the three of them joined forces and opened a dance studio.

On the video, her mom and Barb whistled, grinned, and waved, then shouted birthday greetings and blew kisses at the camera. The cake on the table they stood behind was covered with pink icing and burning candles.

"Twenty-eight . . ." Barb winced. "Damn, Darla. Roselyn was twelve years old when we were her age."

Roselyn covered her mouth with one hand and laughed as they started to sing. Though she couldn't see Sully, she could hear him. His off-key voice almost drowned out the others. When the song ended, he turned the lens on his ugly, lovable, bulldog of a face and winked at her.

The camera swung around again. Her mom blew out

the candles. Laughing, she slapped Barb's hand when the redhead dipped a finger into the icing.

Barb winced and licked off the evidence. "It's strawberry. Your favorite, Rosebud." She smacked her lips. "I'll be more than happy to eat your piece."

"We thought we'd give you a private showing of the new routine we've been practicing," her mother said.

"Let us know what you think," Barb added. "Hit the music, Sully."

The image on the screen blurred and scrambled. Roselyn saw the floor, the ceiling, a close-up of Barb's kneecap.

"Leave the cake alone, Sully," she heard Barb say. "Remember your cholesterol."

"Yeah, yeah, yeah," he mumbled. "How could I forget with you harping on it morning, noon and night?"

Roselyn giggled.

Barb groaned. "Would you please hit the music? We don't have all day."

The camera jerked up toward the ceiling again, down to the floor. "Sorry," Sully muttered when the dance floor finally came into view.

Keeping her gaze on the television, Roselyn unzipped her skirt. Memories flashed through her mind as the music began and the women moved to the beat. She had spent countless hours of her childhood backstage. Barb and Sully had watched out for her when her mom couldn't . . . and even when she could. Barb had taught her dance steps, dressed her up in costumes, and painted her face. And Roselyn could always count on Sully to help her with homework; he'd even given it his best shot after she advanced to high school honors classes and the lessons were over his head. Together, her mother and Barb had dried Roselyn's tears, defended and encouraged her. And when puberty rolled around, Barb had offered no-holds-barred advice on the opposite sex, whether Roselyn's mother liked it or not.

Wearing only her panties, Roselyn climbed into bed. She was far too tired to look for her nightshirt and too hot to wear it even if she found it. From the comfort of her pillow, she watched the graceful movements of her mother and Barb on the screen and remembered the soundtrack of her childhood. The beat of music, the clink and clatter of dishes, the scatter of voices and laughter.

Sully's club was one of the few places in the world where she had never felt like an outcast, where she'd been accepted for who she was, encouraged to be true to herself. No one at the club, Roselyn's childhood home away from home, ever ridiculed her.

Ridicule made her think of the professor's son . . . J.T., as he liked to be called, which was one of the reasons she persisted in calling him Jerome. She wondered what he'd think if he discovered her mom was an ex–Vegas showgirl.

Roselyn sniffed. She didn't really care what he, or anyone else, thought about it. Her mother had provided her with the best life she could in the best way she knew how. Roselyn had only kept quiet about her mother's occupation over the years because she'd quickly learned that while she could disregard taunts aimed at herself, she couldn't ignore any insults or innuendos directed toward her mother.

The last semester of her senior year of high school flashed to mind and, with it, Kyle Graham. He was one of the best looking, most popular guys in her class, a boy who, up until then, had never given her the time of day. And when he did, Roselyn found out later it had been on a dare and for his own personal gain. She would bet her last dollar that, at the age of seventeen, Jerome Drake had been a Kyle Graham clone.

Once, when she'd dropped by to check on the professor and found he'd had too much to drink, Roselyn had helped him to his bedroom. They'd passed by Jerome's old room on the way and she'd glimpsed the sports trophies and medals, the pictures of pretty girls pinned to his bulletin board, the countless other mementos of a teenager who'd been accepted and admired by his peers. Jerome Drake's old bedroom was a carbon copy of Kyle Graham's.

But Roselyn thought the two of them probably had more than that in common. Like Kyle, Jerome Drake undoubtedly considered her to be a joke. An attention starved, prudish geek, naïve about the opposite sex and the ways of the world. And while Kyle hadn't been far off, Jerome couldn't be more wrong. She wasn't the same gullible girl Kyle Graham asked to the prom eleven years ago. After that bad experience, she'd been educated about men by Barb, who'd chalked up enough experience with the opposite sex to qualify for a Ph.D. in the subject.

Propping up on the pillow, she tapped her fingers on the mattress to the beat of the song.

Jerome Terrence Drake.

Her own preconceived notions about the man undoubtedly contributed to her wariness of him. That and the fact he was invisible. She had so many unanswered questions about him, questions she'd never found the nerve to ask the professor. For instance, what had happened to put them at odds? To drive the son away from the father? To cause Professor Drake, on that night two years ago when she'd found him drunk, to tell her he'd lost his child?

Jerome.

He was intriguing . . . irritating . . . an enigma. She assured herself her curiosity about him stemmed, too, from the reactions of Pecan Grove's long-time residents whenever his name came up. Old or young, male or female, it didn't matter, the response was the same. Brows lifted, eyes twinkled and averted, voices became wistful and amused.

J.T.

Yes, the initials were a much better fit for the man who'd trapped her on his lap while Wanda Moody gasped and cowered on the sofa. The man whose voice scattered goose bumps across her skin, whose sturdy, well-built body she'd felt beneath her fingertips. He was quick—Roselyn couldn't deny that. Not only with his hands, but also with his sardonic wit.

Recalling Mrs. Moody's expression as the old woman stared at Roselyn's floating body and flailing arms and legs, she burst out laughing. Roselyn realized she'd been the target of all of Jerome Drake's jokes tonight, but at least his sense of humor, however sadistic, still functioned in a crisis.

The music on the television set wound down. Barb and Roselyn's mother did, too. They ended the dance with their butts in the air, aimed at the camera, mooning her. Not the true finale, Roselyn was certain, but one orchestrated to make her laugh, which it did.

It also made her homesick.

Sully set the camera down and went to stand in front of it with her mother and Barb. When the threesome waved, Roselyn grabbed the remote and froze their image. As seconds ticked into minutes, she focused on the faces of her family. Her eyelids grew heavy. Her heart lightened. Finally, comforted by their laughing eyes, she dropped off to sleep.

Chapter Five

J.T. picked up speed as he rounded the corner onto West Willingham and headed up the sidewalk. His heart pumped hard as he reached that euphoric place he was lucky enough to visit only after running five miles or having really great sex. Endorphins, he'd heard them called, the chemicals, or whatever they were, that surged through his brain now, making him feel like he could fly, like his feet weren't quite touching the ground.

It was early, not yet eight o'clock in the morning. He'd climbed out of bed an hour ago and found that nothing had changed. He still couldn't see his flesh or the clothes he'd slept in. But he could definitely smell them. He must've sweated buckets during the night; the fragrance drifting up from his clothing wasn't one any company would care to bottle. So he'd stripped off the foul-smelling T-shirt, shorts, and underwear, then found his shoes and socks and put them on.

Running in the nude wasn't half bad; J.T. had forgotten how much he liked it. No shorts or shirt clinging to his skin, no underwear to bind, no restrictions whatsoever. He hadn't experienced such a forbidden thrill since his junior year of high school when he'd streaked through the town library during the Pecan Grove Poets' Society's monthly meeting wearing only red high-top sneakers and a full-face stocking cap. The Poets' Society was a group made up of ten little old ladies and two old men. At least they'd seemed old to J.T., considering he'd only been sixteen at the time. As fate would have it, one of the more daring members grabbed the cap off his head as he passed by and the librarian recognized him. The group took a blind vote as to whether or not to file a complaint with the police. The tally came in at two for turning him in and ten against it. After that, whenever he met up with one of those little old ladies, J.T. always had a grin and a compliment for each of them.

Remembering those days, J.T. smiled. There'd been other capers that earned him local fame. Hiding out in the girls' gymnasium locker room. Climbing the town's water tower blindfolded. Flying Coach Temple's valentine boxers from the school flagpole.

J.T. jumped the curb onto his father's block. He'd always been a sucker for a risk. But thrilling or not, he knew running naked was pushing his luck. If the invisibility should wear off before he made it back to the house, he might get arrested; at the very least, he'd suffer some major embarrassment. After all, he wasn't sixteen anymore. And the *Pecan Grove Chronicle* would have a field day . . .

J.T. Drake, Pecan Grove's long-lost bad boy, was arrested for indecent exposure Saturday morning in the front yard of his father's house at 6623 West Willingham. Drake, a columnist for a Los Angeles–based magazine and a writer of true crime novels,

*was in town visiting his father, long-time resident
Hershel Drake, a retired Texas State University science professor best known for his numerous eccentric endeavors, including wandering the streets of
Pecan Grove three sheets to the wind in only his
underwear while singing '60s protest songs. In a
possible attempt to take family tradition to the next
level, the younger Drake started off for a jog yesterday wearing nothing but his Nikes . . .*

J.T. kept up his pace. Despite all the possible humiliating
outcomes, he wasn't about to wear his dirty invisible
clothing another minute, and he wouldn't let a little
problem like nudity keep him from his morning run, either. He was stressed to the max, and running was the
best addiction he'd found to relieve that malady. A legal,
healthy addiction—what could beat that?

He'd considered taking a clean pair of clothes from his
bag, which he'd found on the floor beside his bed when
he awoke. But he'd quickly nixed the idea. They might
smell good but they were visible. Explaining why a pair
of his jogging shorts were seen gliding through the air
above the sidewalk of their own volition seemed a lot
more complicated than explaining why he was running
around the neighborhood in his birthday suit.

As he neared Mrs. Moody's place, J.T. slowed his step.
She was sitting on the ground, working fertilizer into her
flowerbed. A dark-brown bulldog sat on her right side,
a tiny white poodle on her left. Both dogs' heads lifted
and turned toward J.T. The bulldog's snout quivered.
The poodle bared its teeth.

J.T.'s muscles tensed as a deep low growl serenaded
his start into the street. Swallowing hard, he headed for
his father's house.

"Toots! Curly!" Wanda Moody yelled. "Get your
prissy butts back here."

Glancing over his shoulder, he saw that Wanda was on her feet now. A cigarette dangled from the corner of her mouth. J.T. followed the direction of her irritated gaze toward two streaks of growling fur, one dark, the other white. Trailing leashes, they rushed into the street toward him.

"Toots! Curly!" she yelled again. "Stay out of the street, you—"

J.T. stepped onto the sidewalk in front of Pop's house then stopped and turned just as the larger dog lunged. Covering his crotch with both hands, he cried out. The bulldog rammed into his legs, and the growling stopped abruptly. It yelped and stumbled backward, eyeing with cautious curiosity the space where J.T. stood.

The poodle seemed less fearful. Prancing on its back legs and pawing the air, the miniature animal emitted the oddest bark J.T. had ever heard. The wheezy, strained sound was barely audible, as if the dog's voice box had been removed. That didn't stop it from hacking out the painful sound with relentless vigor.

Mrs. Moody was beside them in seconds. J.T. knew that, unless she'd gone deaf in the past few years, she could not have missed the sound of his yell when her bulldog hit him.

Reaching down, Wanda snatched the bigger dog's leash with one hand then bent and scooped up the poodle with the other. She stepped back, staring toward him with narrowed eyes.

J.T. froze and held his breath.

"Stay back!" she hissed. Transferring the poodle to the arm that held the bulldog's leash, she used her other hand to swipe the burning tip of her cigarette back and forth in front of him like a laser sword. "Or I swan, I'll . . ." Beneath the fair, parchment-thin skin at her temple, a blue vein throbbed. "It's you, isn't it?"

J.T. barely heard her words over the bulldog's growl, which had started up again.

Mrs. Moody backed up another step. "I saw you pull up on that bicycle a few minutes ago." The cigarette fell to the street as she pointed toward the driveway.

An old blue Schwinn with a basket between the handlebars sat alongside the garage door. It hadn't been there when J.T. left for his morning run.

"You don't fool me a'tall. You're the devil's spawn, that's what you are." Tugging on the leash, Wanda took another backward step, then another as she made her way slowly toward her yard. "You've cast a spell on poor Hershel, but now that I'm on to you, you won't get away with it, mark my words."

When she finally reached the curb, Wanda turned and high-tailed it toward her house with the barking bulldog scampering behind her on the leash. At the porch, the poodle jumped from her arms and took off into the bushes. "Curly!" she yelled.

Since Mrs. Moody was occupied searching the shrubs, J.T. released the breath he'd been holding. He crossed over to where the cigarette butt lay smoldering and ground it out with the toe of his shoe.

Seconds later, after one last glance back at Wanda, who was still poking around in the bushes surrounding her porch, he let himself into the house through the kitchen's side door, catching the screen before it slammed. At the sink, he turned on the tap, washed his hands, then splashed his face with cold water. He started down the hallway toward his old bedroom. Halfway there he heard voices coming from inside and slowed his step, pausing just outside the door.

Pop and Roselyn Peabody stood in the center of the room, staring down at his unmade bed. "He's not in here," Pop said, sounding exasperated.

Rosy sniffed. "Don't be so sure." She sniffed again. "Jerome, we're not amused by this little game you're playing. I know you're here; I smell you."

Smiling, J.T. leaned against the doorframe. She still didn't have even a trace of makeup on her face. But today, instead of a skirt and damp T-shirt, she wore baggy navy blue slacks and a plain, dry white blouse with the sleeves rolled up to her elbows. She hadn't missed a button, either. All that smooth, pale skin he'd seen last night was demurely concealed all the way up to her neck. Thinking he liked the damp T-shirt better, J.T. watched her as she began to move about the room.

Pop's head started to bob. "Surely Jerome wouldn't . . . you wouldn't, would you, Jerome? If you're here . . ."

Rosy paused at the foot of the bed. She stooped then pinched her forefinger and thumb together at the toe of her faded red sneaker. Slowly, she stood again. "No wonder I smell him," she said, wrinkling her nose, her arm held straight out in front of her. "I believe I've just found Jerome's shirt."

Pop stepped toward her then paused. "You mean—"

She nodded. "It's still invisible, so I'd say we can safely assume he is, too. Where do you think he might've gone, Professor?"

"I don't know. When he lived here with me, he ran every morning. Even in the summer when the cross-country track team was no longer in session."

Surprise shot through J.T. He would've bet money that Pop had not known about his membership on the track team, much less his habit of a daily morning run.

Rosy stooped again. She patted the floor around her feet. "Here are his shorts and . . ." Her hand stilled. She glanced up at Pop, her mouth forming a perfect circle. Without saying anything more, she quickly looked back at the floor.

"Is something wrong?"

"Um . . ." She lifted her hand into the air. "I think these are your son's . . . um . . . underwear," she said, though it appeared she held nothing between her clasped fingers but air.

Pop cleared his throat. "Here." He extended a hand. "I'll put all of Jerome's clothing in the laundry."

J.T. figured he'd stayed quiet long enough. He opened his mouth, intending to say something to make them aware of his presence, but Rosy spoke first, and her words gave him second thoughts about revealing himself.

"We should talk before Jerome returns," she said. "I'm sure it's important to you that we make him as comfortable as possible when we proceed this morning. It is to me, too, of course. I was wondering about the first—"

In the middle of her sentence, Pop turned away and started for the doorway where J.T. stood.

Blinking at the back of Pop's head, Roselyn followed behind him, her eyebrows puckered.

J.T. stepped aside to let them pass through then crept after them into the kitchen.

Rosy sat at the table and folded her hands atop the dull, scarred wood.

In the adjoining utility room, Pop started the washing machine, then dropped the transparent load of clothing inside of it.

"It's time, Professor," she finally called out. "There's no putting this off. Everything's going to be fine. We'll take every precaution."

Pop closed the lid on the machine. Turning, he paused, scratched his head, then slowly stepped into the kitchen again. "I don't mean to be rude, Roselyn. It's just that . . ." He took the chair opposite her. "There's a very good chance this isn't going to work. You do know that, don't you? We've never been in this position before."

J.T.'s pulse kicked up. He leaned against the stove, positioning himself to clearly see both their faces.

"*You* have, Professor. You made it work once, you—"

"That was years ago, Roselyn." He sighed. "Another lifetime."

She braced her forearms on the table. "The correct calculations are where they've always been, Professor. Safely stored away in your brain. You proved it yesterday. The refractor worked! *Completely.*"

"Only the initial phase. As for the final phase . . . I'm afraid there's more I haven't recalled. Until I do . . . *if* I do . . ."

"You can't be certain of that until we try. And then, if there's more, you'll remember, Professor. I know you will. I'll prod your memory with questions. I'll help you."

Pop's head moved up and down in quick jerky movements. "I have tried, Roselyn. Time and again, don't you see? I'm afraid it's lost to me. All of it. Yesterday's results were your doing, not mine." He glanced down at the table. "Jerome . . . what will we do if—"

She took his hand, silencing him, then leaned forward, her expression earnest and sure. "We won't stop until you remember everything. Look at yesterday . . . at how much we accomplished. *We,* Professor, the two of us together. With my assistance, it's coming back to you. This thing with Jerome is unfortunate, but it's also a huge achievement. Yesterday's adjustments to the refractor made possible the miracle that happened to your son. You remembered missing fragments of the equation, Professor, and if there're more, soon you'll remember them, too."

J.T. felt dizzy. *Soon?* His father would remember *soon?* What equation did Pop need to remember? He sure as hell hoped he misunderstood their conversation. Surely they'd done this before . . . made something disappear, then reappear. Surely they knew how to do it. *Surely* . . .

To brace himself, he reached back. His hand hit a pan on the stove. The skillet clattered against a burner.

Pop and Roselyn both jumped, their gazes darting in his direction at the exact same time.

After a moment, Roselyn scooted her chair away from the table and pushed to her feet. "Mr. Drake?"

"No more bullshit," J.T. said, as a cold, clammy sweat broke out on his skin. "Do the two of you know how to correct my problem, or not?

"No," the professor answered at the same time Roselyn said, "Yes."

"Which is it?" Jerome asked, his voice coming to Roselyn out of thin air.

She'd thought the odor of his clothing had lingered in the room, never imagining the sweaty scent she smelled was *him,* standing not six feet away, listening in on their private conversation.

"Maybe," Roselyn answered, scanning the space just in front of the stove. "Until you step into the refractor and turn it on, the answer to your question is 'maybe.' After that, if it turns out the answer should've been 'no,' then your father and I will simply go back to work. With your patience and cooperation, we'll come through for you, I promise."

A floor plank creaked. The chair next to Roselyn slid out from beneath the table. "So I'm the first, the guinea pig."

She detected a dangerous vibration beneath the smooth delivery of his words. Suspecting Jerome Drake's composure was shaky at best, Roselyn gripped the top edge of her chair and inched back. "You're not the first. If you'd been a more careful eavesdropper, you would've heard that your father achieved success with the refractor once before."

"That's a relief. When?"

"Thirty years ago," the professor said. "That was the first time . . . and the last."

A *smack* sounded on the tabletop. "Tell me you're kidding." Jerome's voice bellowed as loud as the thunder during last night's storm. "You haven't done this since 1972?"

Professor Drake cleared his throat. "You see . . . I'm afraid I lost my research. I've spent the years since trying to piece it back together. I'd give up for a while and move on to something else, but I always returned to the refractor. Until Roselyn came on board, I never gained any ground."

His eyes took on that faraway look that warned Roselyn his mind was wandering. "Perhaps I should not have . . . there are simply too many unpredictable elements that might affect the outcome," he continued, ". . . and the inherent dangers . . . I have a responsibility to mankind to consider . . . I refuse to approach it as I did in the past, with a lack of humility . . . a—"

"You were the key, Professor," Roselyn said, interrupting his sudden rambling, hoping to set his thoughts back on track. "The refractor was your brainstorm. Without your brilliant—"

"Please," Jerome said. "Would it be too much to ask of the two of you to adjourn this meeting of the mutual admiration society?" He sighed noisily. "Well at least now I can quit worrying about finding mutilated body parts buried underneath the house. I finally know what my father was doing down in the basement all the time I was growing up."

The room fell silent. Roselyn glanced at the professor. He looked as if he might choke, as if the neckband of his T-shirt was two sizes too small. "Well," she said, feeling almost as uncomfortable as he looked. "Let's all go downstairs. I'm anxious to get started."

"Oh, me, too," Jerome said, his words thick with sarcasm. "I've been looking forward all night to frying my brain again."

She waited for Professor Drake to make a move. When he did, she walked with him into the hallway and down the basement steps. She was spared the need to worry or wonder if his son followed. She heard the muttered curses, the disgusted tone of his voice, the clap of Jerome's shoes against the stairs.

Once inside the laboratory, the professor switched on the light, crossed to the refractor and opened its door. "You should dry off first, Jerome. Just to make sure there's no excess moisture on your skin. The drier you are, the less of a jolt you'll feel."

"Would have been nice to know that the first time I did this. I was dripping with rain."

"Yes, well . . ." Professor Drake coughed. "Perhaps if you'd told me—" He stopped talking and glanced at the ceiling when the phone upstairs rang. "I'll run up and get that. Never know who it might be. Quite possibly I've won that clearinghouse sweepstakes. I just received a notice last week that I was in the running, which is quite surprising since I never entered in the first place." He chuckled. "You'll find towels in the storage closet, Roselyn. Would you mind fetching one? Other than that, I'm afraid there's really no way to prepare for this or make it any easier on you, Jerome."

As the professor left the room, Roselyn walked to the storage closet and opened the door. Inside, on the lower shelf, she found a stack of faded, threadbare towels.

"I could use one of those," Jerome said. "And not just for drying off, either. It just so happens I'm in the buff except for my running shoes. If this works, I'd hate to offend you, Doctor Peabody."

Jennifer Archer

Roselyn's pulse stuttered as, towel in hand, she crossed to the refractor. *My word.* He'd been sitting right beside her in the kitchen wearing nothing but the shoes on his feet. That is, if she didn't count the smug sneer she knew, *just knew,* he had on his face. With all the talk about the refractor, she'd forgotten the invisible dirty laundry she found on his bedroom floor. Roselyn held out the towel. "Here you are."

The towel left her hand, floated through the air toward the refractor pod, then on inside the machine. Amazed, Roselyn watched the folded terrycloth fall open. She blinked. A *hand* towel. It was only a *tiny* hand towel . . . with a *rather large hole dead set in the center.* As an intriguing image of a visible Jerome Drake wearing only that towel flashed to mind, Roselyn bit down on her lip. The picture in her imagination was the same one that graced the back of his novel; the same raw-boned, broad-shouldered, narrow-hipped Jerome Drake, only minus his clothing. She swallowed.

"Interesting choice," he said. "I'm not sure if I should feel shocked or slighted. I know you've never seen me, Doctor Peabody, but I promise you'll have to do better than this." He tossed the towel. It landed on the floor in one corner of the refractor. "It won't even cover my—" He cleared his throat then laughed. "Let's just say I need something larger. Much larger."

What ego. Barb's lectures on the behavior of the male species had not gone unheeded. Roselyn had listened and learned. Clearly, this particular male was trying to get revenge for her offenses toward him, both real and imagined, by using the shock effect. He hoped to offend her, to make her squirm.

She smiled. Jerome Drake was in for a big disappointment. She might look like a prim and proper preacher's daughter, but despite her mother's best efforts to shelter her from the shadier side of the club scene, she'd heard more foul language, suggestive innuendos, and dirty jokes than a cockroach on a barroom floor. Not much fazed her anymore.

Roselyn wondered what Barb would say to him in this situation. And suddenly, she knew how to play Jerome Drake's game. "Hmm, something larger," she said, deciding to give him a dose of his own medicine. "I'm so sorry, Mr. Drake. I had no idea your ass was so huge."

He choked out a laugh. "Such language, Doctor, I expected more propriety from a modest woman like you."

"Whatever gave you the idea I'm modest?"

"Well, for one thing, darlin', you've gone to a helluva lot of effort to make sure no one catches a glimpse of your throat."

Instinctively, Roselyn's hand lifted to the stiff collar of the new shirt her mother had sent. She swallowed again. She would not get all defensive and end up looking like a fool. That's exactly what he wanted. "I'll get you a bigger towel." She started toward the storage closet.

"When I said I needed something larger," he said, his voice low and smooth, "I was referring to the *hole* in the towel, Rosy, not the towel itself."

Rosy. That was a new one. She wasn't quite clear what to make of it. Pausing, Roselyn looked over her shoulder and eyed the towel on the refractor floor. Once again drawing on Barb's backstage wisdom, she tilted her head to one side and raised her brows. "In that case, I'll look for one with a hole the size of a nickel instead of a dime."

Touché, she thought when he didn't snap back with a raunchy innuendo of his own. But she turned away quickly so he wouldn't see that she was blushing. She wasn't accustomed to taking part in such suggestive banter.

He made another choked sound as she pulled a second towel from the storage closet shelving. "You're enjoying this, aren't you?" she asked.

"Preparing to be shocked? Think again."

"Not that. Tormenting your father. Taunting me. You're getting some kind of morbid satisfaction out of it. You think you're entitled."

He didn't answer. She didn't really care. She had more to say. A lot more. "I couldn't care less if you badger me; knock yourself out, Mr. Drake. I'm used to being the brunt of the joke. But your father deserves your respect."

"You're not in a position to know what my father deserves from me."

"Oh, poor you. Let me guess . . . was he too strict on you growing up? Did he miss a track meet or two? Or is it simply that he made you eat your spinach?"

"I have a feeling I had you pegged all wrong, Doctor Peabody."

She'd expected him to bristle at her accusations, to defend himself. Instead he sounded amused, maybe even pleased. Not the expected male reaction; not typical at all. She didn't like that. It made dealing with him all the more difficult. "I don't give a damn what you think of me." Roselyn cast the dirtiest look she could muster at the space inside the refractor pod. "Once, when I was a child, I saw a man kicking a cat for spilling a saucer of milk. He kicked that poor animal again and again, laughing the entire time. The more distraught the cat became, the better he liked it." She drew a breath, surprised and annoyed that he could so easily bring her anger to the boiling point. "Right now, you remind me of that man, Mr. Drake. The only difference being that you're using words to kick your father instead of your foot."

"The analogy came through loud and clear."

"Sorry for the interruption," Professor Drake said as he entered the laboratory. "I turned off the phone so we won't be disturbed again."

Tamping down her temper, Roselyn crossed to the refractor pod and held out the beach towel she'd chosen.

"Thanks," Jerome said quietly as the towel left her hands. "I, uh, appreciate it. Really."

Surprised by his tame response, Roselyn turned away from him in time to see a tiny white dog dash into the room.

"For pity's sake," the professor said. "How did Wanda's pet get into the house?"

"I saw that poodle get away from her a few minutes ago when I was outside," Jerome said. "When I came in, Wanda was searching her yard for it."

Professor Drake crouched and reached a hand toward the trembling poodle that had taken refuge beneath the control panel.

"The animal's hardly larger than one of our mice," Roselyn said. "Poor thing. She's scared to death. Look at her."

"Come here, Curly," Professor Drake cooed. "You don't want to be on your master's bad side, now do you?"

Turning, the dog made a beeline for the storage closet. Roselyn had left the door open. The poodle ran inside.

Sighing, the professor stood. "We'll worry about her later. Remind me to fetch her from the closet after we're finished, and I'll return her to Wanda."

Roselyn rubbed her palms together. "Yes, let's not waste any more time. Make sure you're nice and dry, Jerome. We wouldn't want this to hurt any more than necessary. I, for one, can't bear the thought of all those volts of electricity connecting with your wet skin then coursing like a flash fire through your body from the top of your head to the tip of your—"

"*O* . . . kay, Doctor. Enough said. I can tell by your eager tone of voice that the prospect of my pain just cuts you to the bone."

Something twisted inside Roselyn. Sarcasm was one thing; Jerome deserved it. Callousness was another.

Though his attitude seemed to bring out the worst in her, in truth, she cringed at the thought of what he faced. Being shocked was no picnic. She wouldn't trade places with him for anything.

The towel fell open, hovered, moved briskly up and down. Finally it shifted lower and formed a hollow-centered circle around what she assumed was his lower body.

Roselyn tried her best not to cast more than a glance at the interesting contour the fabric took on, or the even more interesting bumps and bulges beneath the terry cloth. But, like always, curiosity got the best of her. She lowered her gaze. And stared.

Chapter Six

Doctor Roselyn Peabody was proof positive that the old saying "You can't judge a book by its cover" held true. It took a lot more effort to rattle her than J.T. had thought it would. Who would've guessed a woman like her would be the least bit interested in what hid behind his towel? Surprising. Her mouth surprised him, too. Sassy . . . with nice full lips. Why hadn't he noticed before?

He wondered if she'd be staring so openly at him if she could see his face and know he was staring right back at her. He wondered, too, why his common sense and intelligence flew right out the door whenever the woman was in his vicinity.

He'd intended to switch tactics with her this morning, to be cordial and cooperative and try to win her over. Instead, he'd done just the opposite. The woman hated him—most of him, anyway. The part she ogled at the moment didn't seem to displease her one bit.

"Let's get this over with." Trying not to think about the staticlike sensation that skimmed the surface of his skin and how it would soon be even more intense, he drew a deep breath. The faint odor of burnt rubber assaulted him, and he knew it was no use; no diversion could take his mind off of what was to come.

Rosy blinked like she was coming out of a trance. Still, her gaze remained on the towel. J.T. guessed that made sense. It was her only point of reference, after all. Still, her open curiosity caught him off guard. He'd figured her to be the queen of all prudes. He secured the towel tightly at his waist, deciding maybe he'd discovered an effective diversion, after all. If she didn't settle her attention elsewhere soon, they were all going to suffer some major embarrassment. Some things he couldn't control.

"Which switch do I hit?" he asked, studying the panel in front of him. "It was an accident last time. I wasn't paying attention."

"Don't worry about it," she answered. "We have controls out here, as well."

She and Pop started toward the panel beside a desk topped with a computer and various other pieces of electrical equipment, the same panel the poodle had escaped beneath earlier. A cord ran from the computer to the control panel to a machine on the floor beside it. A tangle of twisted coils connected that machine to the refractor pod in which he now stood.

"Just take a deep breath and relax," Rosy said. "Your father and I will handle everything."

While Pop and Rosy studied the computer screen and discussed in hushed tones matters J.T. didn't want to hear anyway, he closed his eyes. Anticipation sent a shudder through him and J.T. opened his eyes again, unable to look away from the two people who held his fate in their hands.

The slacks Roselyn Peabody wore cost fifty bucks. He

knew because a price tag hung from beneath the tail of her untucked shirt. Panic crept in. *Her shoes.* Holy crap, she wore two different sneakers; a red one and a dirty white one without laces. If the woman didn't even have the presence of mind to dress herself . . .

The saliva in J.T.'s mouth dried up. He glanced from Rosy to Pop, hoping . . . praying to see something in his father he'd never seen before—a hint of competence, rationality, stability. But Pop's eyes looked as wild and shifty as ever. They seemed unnaturally large and terrified behind the thick lenses of the little round wire-framed glasses he'd worn so long they were finally back in style again.

For the first time in years, J.T. forced himself to look at his father, to *really look at him.* From the long scraggly gray-streaked ponytail, to the faded Grateful Dead T-shirt, to the flip-flops peeking out from beneath a pair of old brown corduroy slacks. He scanned the room, noting the scattered evidence of the work that had been Pop's passion and obsession for as long as J.T. could remember.

Thirty years, Pop had said. Thirty years ago Hershel Drake lost his research on the refractor. But that wasn't all, J.T. realized with the force of a slap. Thirty years ago Pop had also lost his wife—J.T.'s mother. And now, as he studied the man across from him, J.T. thought he finally had the answer to the question that had always haunted him, the reason why he'd never really known his father. Thirty years ago, Pop had lost himself, too. While J.T. had grown up and moved forward, Pop had stayed behind, wandering around baffled in a world that no longer existed, searching for those missing pieces of his life that had once defined him.

"Ready?" Roselyn asked.

"Ready," J.T. answered, though he felt far from it. He closed the refractor pod door. Out of the corner of his eye, he thought he saw movement. He'd swear that the hand towel he'd tossed onto the floor earlier had moved an inch. This whole business was messing with his mind. No surprise there. His fate depended on the mental capabilities of two people so out of touch with reality they couldn't even take care of the minor, day-to-day details of their own lives. How did they expect to solve an enormous problem like this one?

Because she looked more confident than Pop, J.T. focused on Rosy's face, hoping some of her positive vibes might somehow channel on over to him.

As if some silent, magnetic force drew her attention to just the right spot, her gaze lifted. She stared directly into his eyes while Pop punched numbers into the panel . . . then pushed a button.

That old familiar vibration entered his toes. The humming started, making his ears ring. The white light brightened.

J.T. kept his eyes on Rosy's as the surge ripped through him, as his body went rigid and the green smoke swirled around him. And suddenly he saw more to her than a bad haircut and sloppy dressing habits, more than peculiarity and uptight propriety. In her eyes he recognized deep intelligence and limitless compassion. J.T. focused on those comforting truths as his vision blurred and everything faded to black.

Roselyn leaned forward and squinted. Through the haze of green smoke inside the refractor, she saw the silhouette of a man outlined by a sizzling blue and white aura. The refractor was going to work! She knew it. *She knew it!*

It was the most thrilling, yet oddest, experience she'd ever known. A moment ago, she had sensed Jerome watching her, felt the pull of his gaze, his desperate apprehension and need. After all the barbed words they'd tossed at one another, he had silently reached out to her for support.

Despite her opinion of the man, she couldn't dismiss his fear any more than she could walk away from an injured animal. How must he feel right now? Naked and alone and uncertain of his future? Afraid to trust? Afraid not to? She understood those inner turmoils all too well. Maybe she'd been unfair to judge him based on preconceived assumptions and his current behavior. In his situation she probably wouldn't be the most amicable person either.

Her heart pounded and dread filled her as the electrical aura faded from view. She no longer felt Jerome's presence or the magnetic tug of his gaze; except for the swirling green smoke, the refractor seemed empty.

"Turn it off!" Professor Drake shouted. "Turn it off; that's long enough! Something's in there with him."

"What?" Her pulse jumped. "What did you say, Professor?"

His rubber sandals squeaked against the floor as he ran across the room and lunged for the refractor pod's door. "Something was in there. On the floor in the corner."

"It was only a towel."

"It moved. I saw the towel move. And then . . . dear heaven, it looked like an animal."

Roselyn could scarcely breathe as she watched the smoke rush out of the machine and smelled the sickening odor filling the room. She forced her feet to move, to round the control panel, to walk to the place in front of the refractor where the professor knelt with his head thrust inside the conversion pod.

He'll be slumped on the floor inside, she assured herself, *exhausted, of course, and probably unconscious but fully materialized.*

She paused alongside Professor Drake. He turned and looked up at her, his stricken expression shattering all her hopes. Glancing over his shoulder, she stared down. Not only was Jerome not visible, neither of the towels were, either. "That's odd," she whispered. She should have watched the professor more closely. What if, instead of programming in the new calculations, he'd inadvertently repeated the initial phase? What if the current was too much for Jerome? *What if* . . . She swallowed. "Is he . . . ?"

"The same as before. His heartbeat is erratic but strong." Professor Drake closed his eyes. "I failed. I failed my son again." His head began its jerky tremor. "Think, man, think," he muttered under his breath. "The voltage . . ." He scratched his head and blinked. "It's possible . . ."

Roselyn laid a hand on his shoulder. "We're not giving up, Professor." She crouched down beside him. "Let's help him out of there." She heard a raspy, hacking sound and paused. "What's that?"

The professor's chin lifted. The sound came again. "Dear heaven."

"What is it?"

"It sounds like Curly . . . Wanda's poodle. The previous owner had him debarked." He sat back on his heels. "It caused quite a stir with Wanda and ended her friendship with the woman. Marion Tetly was her name . . . a member of Wanda's poker club. They met every month to play. At least, they did until the debarking incident. You see, Wanda was also the president of the Pecan Grove humane society at the time. She—"

"Professor?"

He blinked. "Yes, dear girl?"

"I thought the poodle was in the storage closet. That sound is coming from inside the refractor. You don't think . . ."

She felt something soft and fluffy brush against her ankle.

72

The professor met her gaze, his own gaze startled. "Wanda won't take this well. Not well at all."

Roselyn returned her attention to the floor of the refractor. "Mrs. Moody is the least of our worries right now."

"Yes, well . . ." The professor's voice sounded worried again. "Let's help Jerome out of there."

Dragging a grown man from the refractor was not an easy feat. Neither was rousing Jerome enough to pull him to a standing position. He was incoherent and only half awake as Roselyn draped his right arm around her shoulder while the professor draped Jerome's left arm around himself. Moving slowly, they helped him upstairs to his room, then into bed.

The professor sat at the edge of the undulating waterbed. Every few seconds he checked his son's pulse. He muttered under his breath, shook his head, and blinked as the minutes ticked by and Jerome continued to sleep.

Roselyn paced the floor alongside them, her mind already at work on the challenge ahead. One final glance at the professor told her that, for today at least, she was on her own. He was mumbling mathematical equations and rocking to and fro. But with or without him, she would proceed. She would not give in to defeat.

Slipping out of the room, Roselyn returned to the basement alone. She booted up the computer and went to work.

J.T. awoke with the mother of all hangovers. *Must've been one helluva party*. He tried to recall the event but only drew a blank. Then he moved and the bed beneath him swayed.

Home. Pecan Grove. Pop's house.

Everything came back to him at once. The invisibility, the refractor, the pain. And Rosy's eyes . . . giving him strength.

73

Afraid to open his own eyes, J.T. lay completely still. "Pop?" he said quietly. No one answered. Surely that was a good sign. The old man wouldn't leave him alone if he weren't in decent physical shape. Even last night, Pop had slept in the chair at his bedside.

J.T. blinked up at the ceiling. He drew long, even breaths and counted the blades on the fan as they circled. When his heartbeat slowed to a more normal rate, he lifted his arm from the bed and looked.

His heart took another leap and cold sweat beaded on his skin like rain on a freshly waxed car.

The machine hadn't worked.

He turned his head to check the clock and found he'd slept all day. Still he felt exhausted.

Pushing up onto his elbows, J.T. swung his feet around and onto the floor. He tried to stand but the muscles in his legs felt like jelly. They quivered and jerked convulsively. Lowering his head, he drew more deep breaths and rode out the wave of helplessness.

Five minutes later, he started off in search of Pop, doubting he'd get any answers about where to go from here but holding out hope for them, anyway. The old man wasn't difficult to find. J.T. just followed the snores, knowing from the familiar irregular sound of them exactly what he'd find.

Pop lay stretched out on the couch, one arm extended toward the bottle on the floor beside him like he was reaching for the next drink.

J.T. didn't pause. He continued on into the kitchen, then to the utility room. He recalled watching Pop put his shorts and shirt and underwear into the wash earlier. J.T. opened the machine lid and looked inside. The tub appeared empty. He stuck a hand in and felt the wet clothing. He transferred it into the dryer and twisted the knob to start a permanent press cycle.

He turned his head away from the couch when he

passed back through the den. The sight of his father lying there brought back too many bad memories, ones he couldn't stomach right now.

Midway through the room, J.T. paused. The snoring had stopped. He glanced toward the sofa. Pop's mouth was open but no sound came out of it, and he was so still. Too still.

Panic pricked at J.T.'s spine. He hurried over to the sofa, moved the bottle aside, then stooped down and placed his face close to Pop's, listening for signs of life. When he felt the soft brush of a breath against his cheek, he lifted his head and, feeling a mixture of relief and aching sadness, studied his father's features. Then he slipped Pop's glasses off of his nose and placed them on the lamp table.

Minutes later, J.T. stood beneath a warm spray of water in the bathroom shower. He told himself the water would wash away the refractor's effects, but he didn't believe his own lie. If it hadn't worked on his clothing, why would it work on him? He shampooed his hair, then frothed up a lather with a bar of soap and covered his body with it. The thick layer of suds took on the shape of his calves, his forearm, his hands, and he shuddered with relief at the affirmation of his body's existence, its physical substance.

If nothing else, the shower made him feel better. He returned to the utility room, took the clothes from the dryer and put them on, though they were still damp. Then he went in search of the cigars he sometimes smoked when he wrote. Not that they'd help the situation, but he doubted they would make matters worse, either. Right now, lung cancer and emphysema were the least of his worries. Could you pollute invisible lungs?

He headed out into the front yard, but paused when he saw Rosy's bicycle still parked in the driveway. He couldn't imagine she'd still be downstairs in the lab. Turning, J.T. went to find out.

She was there, all right. And she appeared to be so caught up in her work that he couldn't bring himself to interrupt. J.T. stood in the doorway and watched her. He didn't think he'd ever seen anyone so focused and intense, not even Pop. Were her efforts for him, he wondered, or for herself and the attention the refractor's success might bring to her career?

J.T. felt a twinge of regret. He hadn't been fair to her; he wasn't being fair now. The woman might appear to be a flake on the outside, but by all other accounts she was a serious scientist, a professional worthy of his respect. She was also funny and smart, indignant and compassionate.

He recalled her expression just before Pop pushed the button that had sent the surge through him. They had connected. The idea was ridiculous, but one he couldn't deny. Though she couldn't see him, Rosy had stared straight into his eyes. And the hope and assurance and intelligence he'd seen in her face had given him the strength to withstand what happened next.

Rosy. He didn't quite know what to make of her. Smiling, he thought of the way she'd focused on the towel around his waist, her quick clever comebacks, the way she defended herself and his father. He had tried his best to dislike her, to blame her for everything that was suddenly wrong in his life. But the truth was that Rosy could pretty much claim innocence. If he hadn't let himself into his father's laboratory uninvited . . .

A floorboard squeaked beneath J.T.'s feet when he shifted his weight.

Rosy stirred and glanced toward the doorway. "Hello?" She stared a moment, then returned her focus to the computer screen.

J.T. considered slipping out without speaking. Her lecture this morning had given him a lot to think about, and he wasn't sure he was ready to apologize for his behavior just yet. When he did, he wanted to do it right. He needed time to think about what to say.

Another step back from the door caused the floorboard to squeak again. J.T. froze.

Roselyn looked up, hoping to find the professor standing at the door. She sighed her disappointment when she found the doorway empty. The old house had its share of creaks; that's all she'd heard.

Yawning, she shoved her fingers through her hair, then looked at her watch. *Nine o'clock.* In the evening? She told herself it couldn't be so late. But her rumbling stomach confirmed that breakfast, lunchtime, and even dinner had long since passed. Unless her watch was on the fritz, she'd worked all day and then some.

After saving her file, Roselyn turned off the computer, then stood and stretched. Her muscles were stiff; her eyes felt gritty and strained.

"Hello."

She jumped and gasped at the sound of the voice in the doorway. "My word. Would you please stop doing that? You scared me to death."

"I'm sorry. How should I announce myself?"

She thought about that a second then answered, "Good question. I suppose you're in a no-win situation as far as that's concerned."

"Do you always work so late?"

Funny how one innocent question from him could make her feel self-conscious and defensive. "Not always. It depends."

"On what?"

His voice had moved closer. Roselyn smoothed the wrinkles from the front of her shirt. "On the work itself and whatever else my life demands at the time."

"I hope a little occasional fun is included in those demands. You know what they say all work and no play will do to a person."

"Are you implying I'm dull, Mr. Drake?"

"No, not at all." A paperweight on the desk lifted into the air, hovered a moment, came back down again. "I'm just saying everybody needs to relax now and then."

"I'll keep that in mind." Roselyn stepped to the side, away from where she thought he might be standing, and began shuffling papers. She heard his footsteps on the floor and, from the corner of her eye, saw the refractor conversion pod door open.

"This is really an amazing invention," he said.

"I'm sorry it didn't work."

"It will."

"How do you know that?"

"I've been paying attention to you." The pod's door closed again. "You're a very determined woman when it comes to your work. And Pop believes in your capabilities."

She looked up. "I was of the impression you didn't trust his judgment."

"I think he recognizes excellence when he sees it in one of his students." He cleared his throat. "I owe you an apology. I've been a real jerk." He paused. "I could tell you I'm out of sorts because of all that's happened to me but that wouldn't excuse anything."

Roselyn stared for a moment, then looked down at the desk and resumed her straightening of papers and books and files that were already in order. She would respect him more if he'd stayed true to form by continuing to badger her rather than resorting to brownnosing, as her mother called it. "An apology isn't necessary. I plan to resolve this problem regardless of how you treat me."

"I know that, I—"

"Now, if you don't mind, I have a few details to finish

up here before I can go home. Goodnight, Mr. Drake.
I'd appreciate it if you would close the door behind you."

She heard a baffled-sounding sigh of breath and then
his footsteps, followed by the closing of the laboratory
door.

Roselyn stopped fidgeting with the items on the desk.
Crossing her arms, she began to pace the floor while asking herself why she had allowed him to annoy her so.
Were his comments really all that irritating, or was she
being unreasonable, reading into them insinuations he
hadn't inferred at all?

She fed the mice, turned off all the lights, then left the
laboratory. After climbing the stairs, she passed by Jerome's bedroom and saw a piece of paper taped to the
closed door. She peeled it off and read.

*Rosy—you can rest easy and quit sniffing, I'm not
in the house. Went out for some fresh air. I forgot
to tell you that Pop drank himself into a stupor.
Maybe you should, too. Like I said before, you work
too hard. What I didn't say is that it's making you
grouchy. Go home and get some rest. I know you
didn't ask, but in case you're wondering, I feel fine.
(Though I'm still not much to look at.)
J.T.*

Roselyn smiled despite herself. He was right; she was
grouchy. She'd interpreted his apology as a maneuver, a
way to ensure she continued to help him. And maybe it
had been just that, but he at least deserved the benefit of
the doubt. She couldn't spend the rest of her life punish-
ing every man she met for an ex-boyfriend's abominable
behavior.

Roselyn read the note through again. The teasing tone
of it came through distinctly. When he dropped his usual
contempt, he could be quite charming and funny.

She rummaged in her purse for a pen, pressed the note to the door and, underneath Jerome's handwriting wrote: *If you need me for anything, just call this number, no matter how late.* After jotting down her phone number, she retaped the paper to the door.

As she approached the living room, she saw the professor passed out on the sofa, an almost empty bottle of scotch whiskey on the lamp table beside him. She came to a halt when the old threadbare throw draped over the chair next to him lifted into the air and fell open.

Roselyn took a quiet step back into the shadows of the hallway then peeked around the corner. She smiled when the comforter spread across the professor's body. So, beneath his calloused exterior, Jerome had a soft heart after all.

Seconds later, the front door opened, then closed. Roselyn waited another minute, then entered the room. Beneath the professor's dangling hand, a dark puddle soiled the rug. Sighing, she picked up the bottle, carried it into the kitchen and poured the remaining whiskey down the drain. She threw the bottle into the trashcan, returned to the living room with a damp washcloth and then went to work on the stain.

After returning to the kitchen and rinsing the cloth, she checked on the professor one last time. On the end table beside the sofa sat a framed photograph of a pretty young woman with dark hair. Roselyn lifted it and studied the image behind the glass. Professor Drake's wife, she guessed. Jerome's mother.

When the professor moaned and muttered something unintelligible, Roselyn replaced the picture and started for the door.

Thinking of the problem she faced with the refractor, Roselyn nibbled her lower lip and glanced back at him. She'd never felt more alone.

*   *   *

Night fell late during Texas summers. J.T. had forgotten the time-suspended expectancy of a warm and muggy small-town summer twilight. The hazy gray cast of the sky somehow made the colors around him more vivid; the green grass and the leaves overhead seemed more vibrant, Pop's Volkswagen minivan, parked in the driveway, seemed an even rustier shade of red, and Wanda Moody's hair, which he spied at the front window of her house, seemed more the color of a grape soft drink than the powdery, pale violet he remembered from last night.

J.T. sat in the rope swing that still hung from the tree at the side of his father's front yard. Any other kid's rope would've rotted by now. But no other kid had Hershel Drake for a father. Years ago, Pop had spent his days and nights concocting a chemical that would preserve the fibers through snow or heat or nuclear fallout. That's why Pop hung the swing, not so much for the enjoyment of his young son as to test his invention.

It was one of the few ideas Pop had come up with that actually worked. But instead of taking the time to patent and market it, Hershel Drake moved on to the next project. J.T. could never figure out why. Until now.

Pop's admission this morning that the refractor had always called him back answered a lot of questions for J.T. All of the old man's little experiments had only been distractions, a means of keeping his mind off his true obsession.

He took a puff of his cigar, then blew out a stream of smoke as he watched Mrs. Moody stare across at the swing where he sat. No doubt she'd spotted the orange glowing tip of his burning cigar. He chuckled. Too bad this hadn't happened to him when he was sixteen or seventeen. He would've had one hell of a good time being invisible back then.

When Mrs. Moody left the window and came out onto her front porch carrying a dog food bowl, he took another lengthy drag of tobacco, enjoying the look of suspicious, terrified fascination on her face. The thought occurred to him that he might not have changed all that much in some respects since he was a teenager.

"Curly!" Wanda yelled, then stuck her fingers into her mouth and let loose a shrill whistle. "Curly It's time for your supper."

Just for the heck of it, J.T. braced his feet against the ground and gave himself a push. Might as well give Wanda an eyeful, he decided, thinking that maybe Rosy had been right about him. Maybe he did get some kind of morbid kick out of tormenting people. Or maybe he just felt like poor old Mrs. Moody deserved a little excitement in her life. She might be snoopy, but she was a good-hearted woman. He admired her spunk.

As for Pop . . . J.T. felt a pang of guilt he didn't want to feel. A few minutes ago, when he'd covered his father with the blanket, he'd thought about all the reasons why Pop deserved his scorn, trying his best to justify his usual coldness toward the man who, for years, had put a roof over his head and fed him, if little else.

He blew a smoke ring into the air. Why should he feel any guilt? Losing a wife and a project in the same year didn't excuse Pop for throwing away the years that followed, for spending them in a hazed blur of alcohol and busy work. Right or wrong, J.T. *did* want to hurt his father. He wanted Pop to regret the lost years of his son's childhood, years J.T. had lived feeling confused and alone and unimportant.

A breeze drifted over him, rustling the leaves above, carrying the scent of Mrs. Moody's dreaded flowerbeds to J.T.'s sensitive nose.

He stifled a sneeze. When he'd decided to make this trip to Pecan Grove, he'd hoped he and his father might somehow finally find some common ground. While researching his last book and talking to the family members the murder victims left behind, he'd realized how important it was to mend fences with the people you cared about before it was too late. Life didn't last forever. So he'd come here with every intention of making an effort to reach out to Pop. The problem was that no matter how good his intentions, whenever he and Pop got together, whenever J.T. saw that slightly mad look in the old man's eyes or found him drunk like he had tonight, the memories returned and, in an instant, being reasonable and forgetting became something that was easier said than done.

Watching Wanda, J.T. pushed off for another swing. Behind him, a door squeaked. He looked over his shoulder.

Rosy stepped out of the house, then paused to look across at Wanda.

J.T. dragged his feet in the grass to stop the swing's movement. Dropping the cigar to the ground, he smothered it with his shoe. He leaned over and picked up the smoldering butt then shoved it into the pocket of his shorts.

"Curly!" Wanda yelled again.

"My word," Rosy muttered under her breath when she passed by J.T. on her way to her bicycle. "I forgot about the poor old woman's dog."

He started to call out her name but stopped himself. Mrs. Moody was honed in, ready to pounce on Rosy. He had a feeling a disembodied male voice coming from Pop's front yard would be just the push the woman needed.

As Rosy climbed onto her bicycle, J.T. stood. He watched her pedal away and, when the bike reached the corner, he jogged after her.

83

Chapter Seven

Roselyn pulled her bicycle to the side of the house. She climbed off, then nudged the rusted kickstand with the toe of her sneaker. When it refused to budge, she gave the metal bar a couple of hard kicks with her heel until it finally cooperated.

Once inside the kitchen, she turned to lock the door. The knob fell off in her hand. "My word," she muttered. No putting it off any longer. The place needed attention. Like it or not, she'd either have to make time for maintenance or watch the house fall down around her.

She placed the knob on the kitchen table, then dragged a chair across the floor and propped it against the door. Not much of a deterrent, she knew, should anyone care to break in, but Roselyn wasn't too worried. Locks or no locks, she felt safe in Pecan Grove. The town's crime rate was practically nonexistent. She didn't own anything worth stealing anyway.

As the earlier conversation with J.T. replayed in her

mind, Roselyn opened the refrigerator door and stared inside. Two bottles of water, a jar of peanut butter, a pitcher of tomato juice and *an empty glass.* "How did that get in here?" When she lifted the glass, it slipped through her fingers and shattered on the floor at her feet.

Roselyn ran a hand through her hair. She closed the refrigerator door, then picked up the biggest pieces of broken glass. The trashcan was full so she laid the shards beside the doorknob and then grabbed an apple from the basket in the center of the table. She was too tired and tense to mess with sweeping up the smaller slivers just now. She'd do it after a bath. Maybe soaking for a half hour would wash away the stress her encounter with J.T. had generated. Making a mental note not to walk into the kitchen barefooted, she started into the den on her way to her bedroom.

If the professor had been coherent, she would've spent this evening brainstorming with him. She thought she'd made headway today, but of course she couldn't be sure until they put the new calculations to the test. And Jerome would need some time to recuperate before he could handle another shock. Two episodes with the refractor in less than twenty-four hours was a tad much for one body to take. Perhaps they could put Mrs. Moody's poodle to the test first . . . if they could find him, poor thing.

As Roselyn passed the bookshelf in her den, she paused and bit into the apple, searching for her copy of Jerome Drake's last book. She had run across it at the bookstore a while back and purchased it out of simple curiosity. What she read later in the Foreword of that book had stunned her. It wasn't a typical Foreword, and especially not of the tone or content she'd expect to find in a true crime novel. In it, he spoke of forgiveness and the fragility of life. Roselyn shook her head and sighed. Perhaps he should read his own words more closely and relate them to his own relationships. Particularly the one with his father.

She had already made up her mind about the professor's son before buying his book, and his compassionate and sensitive words regarding the surviving victims of the crime he'd chronicled did not fit the portrait she'd painted in her mind. How could a man so irresponsible and heartless toward his own flesh and blood write something so sensitive and insightful?

And his photograph on the back . . . she didn't like to think about the amount of time she'd wasted staring at it, trying to tie the man in the picture to the gossip she'd heard around town. Gossip about J.T. Drake the scoundrel.

Faint evening light filtered in through the front window as Roselyn located the hardback book and pulled it off the shelf. She took another bite of apple and continued toward her bedroom. Chewing, she turned the book over and stared at Jerome Drake's image, studying the cocky half-smile, the sharp, inconsistent angles of his face. The harshness added a rough sort of edge that made his appearance more interesting, somehow more attractive than perfection.

Roselyn swallowed the bite of apple and took another. No one would ever guess this man was Professor Drake's son. Jerome's short hair was dark; the professor's, long and a faded shade of red streaked with strands of white. And while Professor Drake's uncertain eyes were the moody pale gray of a reluctant dawn, his son's narrow gaze was as black and intense as a moonless night, and just as disconcerting. Looking into his eyes now in the photograph made Roselyn shiver.

Such intensity; such attitude; such raw sex appeal.

They seemed exactly right for the man she'd met last night. Dangerous eyes. The kind she had learned to avoid. Getting caught in the pull of eyes such as his could easily make her yearn for things that weren't meant for the Roselyn Peabodys of the world.

In her bedroom, she switched on the lamp beside the bed, then propped the book against the dresser mirror with the photograph facing out. Though she'd called her mother earlier to convey thanks for the gift and had asked that the message be relayed to Barb, Roselyn was tempted to call Barb now. She could use a dose of the woman's backstage wisdom.

She hated to admit it even to herself, but Jerome Drake baffled her. Just when she thought she'd mastered his rhythm, he shifted stride. The way he'd covered up the professor with a blanket, for instance. And then there was the note he'd left for her on his bedroom door. She would never have pegged him as the sort of man who would realize it might worry her if she struck out to find him in the house and couldn't. Or the sort of man who would even *care* if she worried. Certainly not the sort to take the time to let her know of his whereabouts.

Roselyn laid the apple on the dresser beside Jerome's picture, then stepped back. Forbidden fruit. Both of them. She wasn't as daring as Eve had been in the Garden of Eden. Jerome Drake was tempting, but she wouldn't bite. If she did, he'd undoubtedly either reject her because she wasn't his type or he'd pretend to have a romantic interest in her because of what she could do for him with regards to the refractor, then turn away when he was once again visible. The man wasn't stupid. She suspected that, now that the initial impact of his condition had worn off, he'd realized his folly in getting on her bad side. He needed her knowledge and ability. She really couldn't blame him for changing his tune and pretending to want to be friends.

She sighed. *Friends.* As long as he left the pretense at that level, she would be okay. If they remained at arm's length, she wouldn't end up with a bruised heart when he no longer needed her.

Roselyn took another step back to distance herself from Jerome's photograph and the odd emptiness she felt whenever she looked at it, the uncomfortable awareness of all that was missing in her life. Kicking off her shoes, she walked to the television set and popped her mother's cassette into the VCR. She needed to lose herself in familiar sounds, in the pulse of the music, like she always had whenever depressing feelings weighed her down. After fast-forwarding to the start of the dance routine, she glanced again at Jerome's picture.

Those eyes.

The hypnotic beat of the song coursed through her blood; her body picked up the rhythm; her hips began to move.

Reaching for the top button on her blouse, Roselyn closed her eyes and let the music take over.

J.T. could barely breathe. That last blast of electricity had really zapped all his energy, even after sleeping most of the day. Running a couple of blocks normally wouldn't cause him to break a sweat, but he'd had to stop twice just to keep from keeling over.

He'd hoped to catch up to Rosy along the way, but the woman pedaled a bike like Lance Armstrong. Even though J.T. couldn't keep up, he'd stayed close enough not to let her out of his sight. He didn't know what he intended to say when he did catch her. He'd already told her he was sorry. If she expected him to grovel, she was out of luck. Wordy apologies made him squirm. The only thing worse than giving one was receiving one. Still, he felt compelled to take one more shot at a brief apology. This wasn't the first time in his life he'd acted like a jerk, but for some reason this time bothered him a hell of a lot more than the other times had.

J.T. stopped across the street from the house that Rosy had pulled up to only a minute before. He lifted the tail of his shirt to wipe his brow, trying to figure out what it was about Roselyn Peabody that had rubbed him wrong the instant he met her. He guessed it was the simple fact that she was Pop's partner. That and the fact that Pop treated her like a long-lost daughter. And she was so like the old man in all the ways he'd always resented and never understood. So he'd deemed her guilty of sharing his father's sins by simple association, which was crazy and unfair. If anyone should know that, he should. He'd spent a lifetime making certain he was known for his own antics, not nutty Hershel Drake's.

He'd been out of line—tossing off-color innuendos at her, teasing her about her proper clothing, pulling her onto his lap last night. Rosy wasn't anything like the other women in his life. She would find such antics offensive and shocking. Women like Rosy wore flannel pajamas to bed and made love under the covers with the lights out—that is, if she ever made love at all.

Besides all that, considering the fact that she was his best, possibly his *only* chance of getting out of this mess, he should be doing everything in his power to cooperate with the woman, to make her work easier instead of more difficult.

J.T. spent a few more minutes silently rehearsing his speech. Then he started across the street toward the little house with yellow siding, noting a pot of half-dead geraniums on the tiny front porch. Since Rosy had entered through the side door instead of the front, he followed her lead. He walked alongside the rickety white picket fence that edged the driveway, enclosing an overgrown yard.

The door squeaked and inched open when he knocked. He put his eye to the crack and looked inside. "Rosy?"

Music drifted from another room. Loud, pulsing music

with a slow, seductive beat. Not the type of thing he would imagine someone like Rosy enjoying.

J.T. pushed against the door. Whatever blocked it scraped the floor but offered little resistance. He poked his head inside and saw a chair blocking his path. Squinting, he scanned the room—a shadowy, cluttered kitchen. Uneasiness itched at the base of his spine when he spotted the doorknob on the table across the way and two large pieces of broken glass beside it. Pale light streamed from the window over the sink, glinting off slivers of glass on the floor, as well.

Something wasn't right here. "Rosy?" he called out again, louder this time. "Rosy, are you okay? It's J.T."

After several seconds passed and she didn't answer or show up, J.T. reached through the doorway and scooted aside the chair. He let himself in, then walked quietly through the kitchen, following the sound of the music. It led him through a small living room, down a short hallway, toward an open door. He glimpsed the headboard of a bed inside, a flash of movement. Preparing for a possible fight with an intruder, J.T. stepped into the room . . . and froze.

She was dancing. Not just any kind of dance . . . a strip tease . . . slow and seductive . . . eyes closed . . . smiling . . . unbuttoning her blouse inch by inch. When the last button fell free, she opened her eyes and looked across at the mirror-backed dresser.

J.T. followed her gaze. And felt his heart skip a beat. *His photograph.* She was dancing in front of his picture . . . the one on the jacket of his book. The book sat on the dresser, propped against the mirror.

He braced a hand against the doorframe. In the mirror, J.T. saw the reflection of her face. She kept her eyes fixed on his photo as she shrugged out of her blouse.

Too stunned to move or even utter a sound, J.T. watched the plain white cotton slide from her shoulders in what seemed like slow motion . . . drifting . . . billowing . . . swirling . . . pooling on the floor at her feet.

He looked up. *Sweet heaven, her bra.*

Roselyn Peabody, proper female scientist, wore a bra any fancy French whore would sell her soul to own. Pale pink see-through lace. Cups that accentuated rather than covered. J.T. blinked. A tiny white tag hung from the back of the left strap. He couldn't make out the price, but whatever the number, it was a small amount to pay for any strip of lace with the power to lift and swell like that one did.

She swayed; then, turning her back to him, grabbed the post at the foot of the bed with both hands. Arching backward, her head thrown back, she reached down with one hand to the button at the loose waistband of her baggy slacks.

J.T. opened his mouth to speak. As much as he was enjoying this, he had to let her know he was in the room before she went too far and embarrassed herself.

Hell.

He tried to swallow but his mouth was too dry. She would already be embarrassed if she knew. And pissed. She'd be furious. Something like this could push her over the edge; she might even go so far as to curse without blushing. He smiled at that thought, despite the situation. Now she wouldn't only think he was an asshole, she'd think he was a voyeuristic asshole.

He should leave the room. That's it. No need for Rosy to ever know he'd been here.

J.T. started to slip through the doorway but paused when her slacks hit the floor and she stepped away from the bedpost. Bending forward, she swept her fingers down toward her toes, providing him with a bird's eye view of her bottom.

"Damn," J.T. whispered. *Thong panties*. He blinked, looked closer. No mistake. Doctor Peabody wore thong panties and they looked unbelievably good on her. Fantastic. Who would've guessed?

Rosy's head jerked up; she stared over her shoulder, her mouth slightly open. Then she narrowed her eyes . . . and sniffed.

Tobacco. Roselyn smelled the rich, smooth sweetness of it . . . and recognized the scent. She shivered as, reaching down slowly, she grabbed her slacks off the floor, then held them against her chest. "You're here, aren't you?"

Backing toward her nightstand, she reached for the remote, then turned off the VCR. The room fell silent; her own staggered breathing was all she heard. "I know you're here. Say something."

"I'm sorry."

The sound of Jerome's voice made her jump, and in that instant, her wariness shifted to humiliation and then to anger. "Yes, you are sorry. You're a sorry excuse for a human being. Breaking into my house. Spying on me."

"I didn't break in. The door was open."

Her mind flashed back to the broken knob, the chair she'd shoved against the door knowing full well it provided only an illusion of safety.

"When I saw the knob on the table and all the broken glass," he continued, "I thought you might be in trouble. I called out to you but I guess, because of the music, you couldn't hear me."

Her emotions shifted again. Roselyn couldn't recall a time when she'd felt more embarrassed. Still holding her pants up to cover herself, she sidestepped to the place where her shirt lay on the floor. "How long have you been in here?"

"When I saw you . . ." He cleared his throat as she dropped the slacks on the floor.

Stooping, Roselyn scooped up the blouse, then stood and slipped it on.

"I was going to leave," he said. "I—"

"What stopped you?"

"Your panties."

"My panties stopped you from leaving the room?"

"Well . . . yeah . . . when I saw them I couldn't tear my eyes away, much less move."

"You—" Her heart felt like it might explode. The nerve of the man. *The nerve.* Her fingers moved from button to button, fastening each one as quickly as she could. "Why did you come here in the first place?"

"Because I wanted to take another shot at apologizing to you."

She lifted her chin. "You've already said you're sorry."

"Not really. You wouldn't let me. I've been rude to you since the minute we met. But tonight . . . well, this may sound stupid, but tonight it occurred to me that you're okay, and I've been blaming you for something that isn't your fault."

His voice drifted to her from the doorway. He hadn't moved into the room yet. Roselyn crossed her arms. If he was the least bit smart, he wouldn't. "When exactly did you decide I'm okay, Mr. Drake? Before you saw me in my underwear or after?"

He started to laugh, but cut it short. "Before," he said, the amusement still in his voice though she thought he was at least *trying* to sound serious. "But I'll be honest with you, Rosy. Now that I've seen you like this, well, the truth is, I like you even more."

Had his voice moved closer or was it just her imagination? Roselyn drew a deep breath, determined to keep her cool. "Do you expect me to find that comment funny? Or take it as a compliment? If so, you are seriously mistaken. You—"

"I'm human, Rosy. And I'm a man. I'd be a liar if I pretended I don't think you have great taste in lingerie and a knockout body to go inside of it. But I don't expect anything from you."

"Oh, really?" She swallowed, reached down and picked up her pants, backed up another step. He was near. Too near. Static electricity skimmed across her skin. "Hmm. What made you finally decide you liked me? Before the underwear, I mean."

"I think it was that wisecrack you made about my ass. That and the way you speak your mind. When I toss a load your way, you sling it right back in my face. I respect that in a woman. Then, when I was in the refractor and you looked into my eyes . . . I knew."

Her breath caught. He'd felt it, too. Blinking, she forced herself to breathe and pulled on one pant leg, refusing to let go of her anger so soon. "Or maybe you suddenly realized you needed something from me."

"Of course I need something from you. We both know that. Without you, I don't stand a chance in hell of getting out of this mess unless it takes care of itself. Pop's in no shape to deal with the problem. But, Rosy . . ."

The air crackled. She stopped breathing again.

"Even if I didn't need you, I'd still like you."

She wasn't sure what made her more nervous, the fact that she couldn't pinpoint his position or the fact that her anger was dissolving, that she was becoming hot and bothered over having the notorious J.T. Drake, Pecan Grove's legendary bad boy, in her bedroom . . . somewhere.

"So," he continued. "I guess it's time I got down to business."

She pulled on the other pant leg, tugged the slacks over her hips, then zipped her zipper.

"I'm sorry I've been rude to you, Rosy. I'd like to start over. Be friends."

The cigar scent grew stronger, making her think he'd stepped closer. The hair on her arms stood on end. Goose bumps scattered across her skin. "Why do you call me Rosy?" she whispered.

"It suits you. I like it."

"It's too—" *Familiar,* she started to say. *Intimate.* But then her tongue went numb because she felt a tiny shock, then his hand covering hers. His fingers were warm against her palm.

"Don't," she said quietly. "Don't touch me."

"I'm sorry." His hand left hers. "Do you want me to leave?"

"Yes . . . no . . . I—" Roselyn turned her head and closed her eyes. She was losing her mind, losing control. It had been too long since she'd felt a man's touch. And that man had been more of a boy. This man, however, was definitely full grown. She didn't need to see him to know it. And he was someone she'd been obsessively curious about for quite some time. Since becoming partners with his father, she had cursed and hated J.T. Drake, admired his prose and drooled over his photograph.

Her eyes shot open, her gaze darting toward the dresser and the mirror behind it. *His book.* She practically dove for it.

"Rosy," he said, as the book fell flat, title up.

His hands skimmed her shoulders from behind. She turned, blurted out the first thought that came to mind. "Are you still naked?"

"Are you hoping I say 'yes' or 'no'?"

"I'm hoping you at least had the decency to put your clothes on before you came over."

"Are you sure?" His voice lowered. "You looked at my picture while you danced."

She wanted to crawl underneath the bed and never come out again. Why didn't he just laugh out loud at her and get it over with? Tell her how foolish she was, how silly she'd looked in her skimpy underwear?

"No," she said. "You're mistaken. The book just happened to be there. I . . . I got it out last night after I left your father's house. I was curious about you . . . it's only natural considering the circumstances of our meeting. I . . . the professor gave me a copy when it came out," she lied, not wanting him to know she'd been so curious about him that she'd bought it herself. "I haven't had a chance to read it. I never even looked at it until—"

She felt his breath on her face a moment before his mouth brushed hers. Because her eyes were wide open, she saw the tiny spark flash between them, felt the quick strike of it against her lips. Roselyn pulled back. "Oh!"

He would kiss her again. She knew it. She wanted him to. Roselyn closed her eyes so it wouldn't seem so strange when he did, so she could imagine his face, the face from the book cover with the high defined cheekbones above hollowed cheeks, the narrow brooding eyes with just a hint of humor, the full but crooked mouth . . .

She thought she was prepared for the second electrical spark, but when their lips touched again, her body melted like candle wax, as did every promise she'd ever made to herself never to indulge in these feelings with anyone ever again. Especially not a man like Jerome. One in a position to use her until she'd served her purpose, then walk away.

Roselyn lifted her hand to his face, scraped her fingertips across his unshaven cheek. He felt so good, so male.

She savored the tang of tobacco on his tongue and went back for more. He tasted delicious, good enough to devour.

She took a deep breath of sandalwood-scented soap and shampoo. He smelled like pure—

It ended abruptly. One second he was against her, warm and hard and alive, and the next second he was gone. She leaned against the dresser, stunned and breathless as she glanced around the room.

"Rosy, I . . ." He cleared his throat. "Goodnight,

Rosy. Get some sleep. Tomorrow's Sunday, right?"

Blinking at the doorway where his words had come from, Roselyn nodded.

"I want to give the refractor another shot," he said. "You'll be over, won't you?"

She nodded again.

"Good." The door squeaked as it opened another few inches. "If you have a screwdriver handy, I'll fix that doorknob for you before I leave."

As much as she wanted to say something coherent, Roselyn couldn't speak. Nodding a third time, she pushed away from the dresser and started for the door.

Chapter Eight

Hershel sat beside Roselyn at the workshop computer as she explained the reasoning behind her latest computations. In spite of his pounding headache and the fact that it felt as if the entire Mojave Desert had relocated inside of his mouth, Hershel tried his best to listen.

Across the room, Jerome paced. Hershel knew because his son had not only been cooperative enough to wear clothing this morning, he'd worn visible clothing. Hershel did a double take each time he looked up and saw the T-shirt and shorts and Lakers cap gliding along through midair. The sight was beyond fascinating. It was somewhat hair-raising, too. But at least he and Roselyn knew where Jerome was and what he was doing.

It seemed that today they had decided there'd be no more secrets, no sneaking around, no more games. Both Roselyn and Jerome were acting unusually civil toward one another. Overly so. Politeness oozed in the room like pudding from the overfilled cream puffs Wanda Moody sometimes made for him. And, like the cream puffs, their forced congeniality was almost too sweet for Hershel's queasy stomach to take. Still, it was preferable to listening to them snap at one another.

Even more surprising than Roselyn's and Jerome's behavior, however, was the fact that Jerome wasn't snapping at *him,* either. He doubted last night's bottle of scotch had gone unnoticed. In the past, that had been more than enough to set his son off for at least a week. Hershel knew the drinking embarrassed Jerome, as did so many other things about him. The boy was ashamed of his father, and for very good reason; Hershel was ashamed of himself—for the drinking, at least. He couldn't change the fact that he was an oddball with an off-the-charts I.Q. For most of his life, he'd tolerated ridicule for his formal manner of speaking, his informal appearance, and the unusual conglomerate of interests that occupied his time. He'd learned to accept and brush off the typical reactions to his peculiarities and had hoped that, one day, Jerome would as well. But his son should not be expected to accept the drinking, ever.

Pathetic as he'd been in his drunken state, yesterday's bender had not been a total waste of time. While sipping himself into oblivion, Hershel had come up with a plan that just might solve this dilemma with Jerome.

When Roselyn finished explaining her calculations, Hershel looked into her eyes. With a nod, he shifted his gaze back to the computer screen. How could he tell her that after all her hard work, they were only slightly closer today, if at all, than they'd been yesterday to calculating the correct equation? How could he tell Jerome?

If they waited until he remembered what they needed to know, his son might spend his life in a state of transparency. More than three decades ago, when Hershel and his team of scientific wizards had worked on the project, it had taken them three long years to realize success, and he'd been at top form then. And while Roselyn was bright and dedicated, bringing the refractor to full working order went far beyond anything she could achieve on her own.

"Well, Pop," Jerome said. "What do you think?"

Hershel looked up. Jerome's clothing had ceased to float left to right. It hung in place on the other side of the computer, the bill of the ball cap pointed forward.

"Sit down," Hershel said.

"I'm too wound up to sit."

"Please, Jerome, humor me just this once. Pull up a chair. I have something to tell you." He glanced at Roselyn. "Both of you."

When Jerome sat next to Roselyn, Hershel cleared his throat. No more secrets. If they were willing, so was he. Terrified as he was, it might be liberating to finally tell the tale. And his mind was surprisingly clear this morning. The time seemed right.

"Well," Hershel said. "This is fine work, Roselyn."

She leaned toward him. "Is it?"

He nodded. "You've brought us a step closer."

"I hear a 'but' coming," Jerome said.

"I'm afraid you're right, Son. We're a step closer, but there are too many steps remaining to even count. And the problem is, I don't know the way, the direction to head from here. Not anymore."

Roselyn's brow crinkled and her eyes brightened in the way that so endeared her to him, the way that assured him she believed completely in their work, in herself, in him.

She shook her head. "But Professor—"

He held up a hand. "There was a time when I thought that by working together the two of us could pull this off. But, you see, I wasn't facing the truth. We're not working together; you're working alone. I'm simply here beside you." He glanced from one to the other. "I'm sure the two of you saw me yesterday. You both know I've pickled my brain; I know it, too. This isn't an easy admission for me to make, but I need help. Until I get it, I'm no good to either of you."

Roselyn's eyes filled, and though it almost killed Hershel to look into them, he forced himself. For too many years, he had put on a blindfold whenever his failures and weaknesses snuck up and tried to confront him. The girl clearly saw what he'd always refused to see. Her tears were for what he'd become, and he would stare that ugly reality straight in the face now so he could begin the long process of trying to change it. He only wished it hadn't taken another disaster such as this one with the refractor to force him to muster up some courage.

Hershel smiled at her. "Every success achieved in this basement for the past two years has been your doing, Roselyn. I merely started you off on the right foot, so to speak."

"But—"

He touched her arm. "But even you'll admit that, alone, it could take years for you to complete the necessary work."

She pulled a tissue from the pocket of her baggy jeans and blew her nose. "Or it could happen tomorrow."

"Yes, but do we want to risk Jerome's future on that possibility?"

"No," Jerome said. "We definitely don't want to do that. So what are the options, Pop?"

"We could bring someone else in on the project. Someone to work with Roselyn. That might shorten the time factor." He gestured toward the refractor. "But there are risks in sharing this with an outsider before it's complete."

The bill of Jerome's cap slid back. "Risks?"

"More than thirty years ago I assembled a team of men and women with whom I'd worked closely for years.

Then, when I couldn't convince the government to back my research, I approached a private investor. That was my first mistake. His name was Anthony Domani, and he agreed to finance my project. What I didn't know at the time was that Mr. Domani had more in mind than a mere investment. You see, he was sizing me up for something bigger, and when he decided I didn't seem the sort to go along with his scheme, he approached one of my scientists, Bartholomew Reneau." He shook his head. "I trusted Bart blindly, as I did all of the members of my team."

The old wound of betrayal reopened. Hershel found the sting to be every bit as painful and startling as it had been on that winter morning in 1972.

As she so often did, Roselyn seemed to pick up on his distress. She took his hand in hers and held on tight. "Is Reneau the one, Professor?" she asked, a tremor of excitement in her voice. "The man who stole your research files?"

"Yes. And he's our other option. Reneau stole my work. But only part of it, much to his dismay, I'm sure."

"I don't understand, Pop. How can he help us now?"

"He's still alive. I've kept tabs on him over the years. If we can steal the files back, we'll have the rest of the research, the missing pieces we need. But there are risks involved in that, too. Enormous ones. And before I'll involve you both in such an endeavor, I insist you understand completely what's at stake."

He leveled his gaze on the hovering Lakers cap, held it there, and took a deep breath. "It's time you learned about everything that happened outside of Bozeman, Montana, in 1972. We lived there, Jerome, you and your mother and I. Shortly after you were born, we left our home in Connecticut. Domani secured a place for my work in a remote location in the mountains where, as far as the outside world was concerned, we conducted ecological research for a private foundation.

"One morning when you were barely more than three years old, you asked to go to work with me." He shook his head and smiled as the memory took him back. "Three years old. And such a happy handful. Headstrong like your mother. It was your first time to visit the complex where my laboratory was located . . ." Hershel stopped smiling. His stomach knotted. "The first time and the last. . . ."

Carrying Jerome on his shoulders, Hershel entered the commissary on the front side of the duplex. The backside housed his laboratory, where the electromagnetic refractor sat safely locked away. For the sake of security, no hallway connected the two sections of the building. There was only one entrance into the lab and only one exit—through the same front door.

This morning, the commissary vibrated with noise and good cheer. Success was sweet, and Hershel's team had worked long and hard to achieve it. The men and women of Project ER deserved an hour or two of back-patting and bragging.

"Hello boys and girls," he called out. "I've brought a visitor this morning."

They gathered around him as he swung Jerome down from his shoulders and began to remove the boy's coat.

"Can we play hide-and-seek, Pop?"

"Not now. We're here to have breakfast and visit with our friends. But we might indulge in a game of it afterward. What do you say?" He draped the coat over his arm and offered the boy his hand. "Shake on it?"

"It's a deal," Jerome recited automatically, though he sounded none too thrilled about having to wait.

Lydia Haines took Jerome's coat from Hershel and waited while he removed his own. "The boy's grown at

Jennifer Archer

least three inches since I last saw him," she said as she carried the coats to a nearby wall rack.

Ned Witman rustled Jerome's hair. "You, boy, are the image of your mama." He nodded toward a food-covered table sitting close to the back wall. "Hope you inherited your papa's appetite, though. Lots of good stuff there, and the rule is we can't leave the room until we've sampled it all."

Hershel laughed. "Would you look at that, Jerome?" He crouched down and pointed. "There . . . in the center of the table. If I'm not mistaken, it's cinnamon coffee cake. It's a shame you don't care for it. I'll have to eat your piece."

Knotting his fists and placing them on his hips, Jerome frowned at Hershel. "I LOVE cim-a-non."

While waiting for the laughter to die down, Hershel stood and scanned the faces around him. "Now that we're all here," he called out, his voice causing the room to gradually fall silent. "I'd like to say a few words to all of you before we dig in."

"Doctor," came a voice from the back. "We're one body short. Reneau hasn't shown up yet."

"Oh, yes, I forgot. He called last night. It seems he had a family emergency. He assured me it wasn't serious but didn't offer any details."

He made his way to the front of the room, stepped up onto a chair, and turned to face his team. "We've traveled a long and bumpy road together these past three years," Hershel said. "I've always believed that if we pressed on, we'd reach this end and find it worth the walk." Emotion crept up and tightened his throat, surprising him. "Each and every one of you believed it too, or we wouldn't all be here today to celebrate this remarkable accomplishment."

While he spoke, Hershel kept one eye on Jerome,

104

watching as his small son wandered over to the food table to eye the goodies there.

"Words cannot convey how much I appreciate the commitment you made when you signed on with me three years ago. Your efforts and dedication, the countless hours each and every one of you devoted to this project . . ."

After circling the table, Jerome stopped in front of the coffee cake and lifted his index finger. A half-inch from touching the confection, he paused and his eyes shifted up.

From across the room, Hershel caught his gaze and held it. He arched an eyebrow and kept on talking, amused by the smug expression on Jerome's face as the boy lowered his hand and moved down to the next plate of food.

"But, while yesterday's breakthrough brought us to the end of one road, we're now at the beginning of an entirely new one."

Leaning forward, Jerome sniffed the donuts, then licked his lips and looked up at his father again.

"Excuse me a moment," Hershel said to the group. He winked and nodded at his son. "Go ahead, Jerome," he said, as every head turned to look at the boy. "Before temptation gets the best of you."

Laughter erupted again as, grinning, Jerome slipped a donut off the plate. Someone had spread a long white cloth over the table. It fell just short of the floor on either side. After one last glance at his father, Jerome disappeared beneath it with his prize.

A moment later, Hershel resumed his speech and when he finally wrapped up his thoughts, the small crowd applauded and cheered. He shook hands as he made his way toward the table of food.

A rush of cold air swept into the room. Hershel heard Evie's laugh and turned.

She stood in the doorway, bundled up in her long red coat, the one that so complemented her dark hair and eyes. She held a sack in one arm, a tray of fruit in the other.

"Champagne," she said, lifting the sack and heading his way. "I know it's a little early in the day but considering the occasion, I didn't think anyone would protest." When she reached him, she kissed his cheek. "I'd hoped to surprise you, honey, and if the expression on your face is any indication, I didn't fail. You didn't really think I was too tired, did you? Nothing on earth would keep me away today."

Hershel guessed he'd failed to hide his disappointment when Evie told him she wouldn't attend. She wasn't fooling him by pretending exhaustion had merely been an excuse to throw him off. The dark circles beneath her eyes were real. "Thank you," he said quietly. "I love you. You know that, don't you?"

She smiled. "Where's Jerome?"

Hershel nodded toward the food table. "Sneaking treats beneath the table cloth. He has his mind set on a game of hide-and-seek."

"Such a sweet tooth, like someone else I know. He's just as messy, too." Evie handed him the plate of fruit. "Maybe you could coax him to eat something healthy for a change. Heaven knows I haven't had any luck." She glanced around the room. "As I recall, this place has a kitchen."

Hershel pointed the way.

Glancing down at the sack, Evie said, "I'll slip out of this coat then pour up a toast."

After making room on the food table for the fruit, Hershel crouched down. "Jerome?" He lifted the edge of the tablecloth, expecting to see a sticky face staring back at him. But the space beneath the table was empty. Hershel *dropped the cloth and stood. Turning, he looked around the room. "Has anyone seen Jerome?"*

"He was over there just a minute ago," Lydia said, pointing toward the door with a laugh. "He had a doughnut in one hand and a muffin in the other."

Evie poked her head out the kitchen door. "Is something wrong?"

"I believe our son might've wandered outside," Hershel said, starting for the door. When he saw alarm flash in Evie's eyes he added, "Don't worry, sweetheart. To leave the complex, he'd have to get past Harry at the gate. Harry would call if Jerome showed up there. Go back to your champagne. I'll find him."

Hershel grabbed his coat off the rack and put it on.

Outside, the air was crisp and frigid. More snow was expected by nightfall; Hershel already smelled it in the breeze. The previous night's accumulation crunched beneath his boots as he started off around the building, thinking Jerome might be exploring out back.

"Jerome!" he shouted, shoving his hands into his coat pockets. "This is no time for hide-and-seek." He doubted the boy had seen his mother arrive. If he had, he would've run over to greet her. "Come inside. I have a surprise for you."

He scanned the grounds and kept walking, whistling a tune as he made his way.

When he reached the back of the duplex, the door to the laboratory opened. A man backed out, closed the door, then locked it with a key.

"Bart?" Hershel increased his pace, then paused at the foot of the steps. "What are you doing here? I thought—"

Reneau's startled expression froze the words on Hershel's lips. He glanced down. Bartholomew Reneau held a briefcase in one hand, a gun in the other.

107

Jennifer Archer

"What . . . ?" Hershel swallowed as he met Reneau's gaze again.

"It's a shame to have to destroy all our hard work." Reneau shrugged and lifted the briefcase. "But thanks to your penchant for detailed files I can easily rebuild the refractor." He shook his head, smiled. "You look baffled, Doctor. Let me clear things up for you. I'm afraid there is a side to your benefactor of which you're unaware. Anthony Domani knows a gold mine when he sees it. In addition to the many legitimate projects he funds, he also has a couple of lucrative sidelines only a chosen few insiders know about."

Reneau's eyes gleamed. "If we can make a mouse disappear and control when it reappears, then why not a man? Think of it, Hershel. An invisible man! Just imagine the access he'd have to all sorts of confidential information. Imagine the heists he could pull off. There'd be no evidence to leave behind. No visible hairs or fibers from his clothing."

Hershel felt dizzy. Where was Jerome? What if he walked up on this? What if—

"Now that everyone's accounted for at the commissary, it's time I left." Reneau pointed the gun at him. "Sorry, Hershel. I'd hoped I wouldn't have to do this face-to-face."

"My boy . . . what have you done with him? I swear to God, Reneau, if you've hurt him, I'll—"

"Your son?" Reneau stared at him. Then, with a nod of his head, he gestured behind him at the laboratory before slowly starting down the steps toward Hershel. "He's inside. Don't bother trying to find him." He glanced at his watch. "It seems the duplex has a gas leak. I wouldn't be surprised if this place blows sky high at any second."

Fury and fear took over. Hershel lunged at Reneau. A muffled "thud" sounded. Scalding pain ripped like a

knife through Hershel's shoulder. Reneau didn't try to
stop him as Hershel stumbled past, climbing the laboratory steps on hands and knees. The man was too busy
running in the opposite direction.

"Jerome!"

Gasping for breath, Hershel pulled a ring of keys from
his pocket, fumbled with the lock, then ran into the room
after finally unlocking the door. He paused, listened. All
he heard was the squeak of the metal wheel in one of the
cages across the way as a mouse ran around on it. There
were so many tempting places for a small boy to hide
here. Inside closets and cabinets or the refractor pod itself. Behind machinery, underneath desks.

"Jerome, it's Pop!" He tried his best to sound stern
instead of frightened but it was no use. The fear clawing
at him was too strong to push aside. "Come out this
minute. I don't want to play."

Clutching his shoulder, Hershel ran through the room,
screaming his son's name, throwing open doors, knocking over anything in his way.

Seconds passed. Twenty. Thirty. And suddenly he
knew . . . knew to the marrow of his bones that Jerome
was not in the lab. Reneau had set him up again, had
made certain Hershel stayed busy looking for his son so
that he wouldn't have time to clear the building. The lab
was not the only part of the duplex about to explode.
Reneau had left him knowing that if the bullet didn't kill
Hershel the explosion would.

He ran for the door. Domani's scheme . . . it was suddenly so clear. As crystal clear as if he had planned it
himself.

Evie . . . Dear Heaven . . . His team.

Reneau had known they would all be together this
morning, celebrating, having breakfast in the commissary. He intended to get rid of them all at once, every
last person who knew the truth about Project ER.

Would Reneau hide and watch? Wait for Harry, the guard at the gate, to come running, then slip away unseen?

If Harry had seen Reneau arrive, he would report that Reneau was with the others when the explosion occurred. There would be no one left to say otherwise. Reneau would be declared dead, too, and the disaster would be written off as a tragic accident caused by a gas leak that had gone undetected. If, on the other hand, Reneau had somehow slipped past the guard unseen, he would stick with his story about being away on a family emergency. Reneau and Domani had left no loose ends. They had thought of everything.

Hershel ran out the door and down the steps, his lungs aching from the cold air he drew into them. After making his way to the side of the building, he kept his focus on reaching the front, desperate to do so in time.

As he rounded the corner, the door opened and Evie stepped out. "Harry called," she yelled. "Jerome's—"

The force of the blast lifted Hershel into the air, the noise so loud he didn't hear his own scream . . .

J.T. felt numb, dazed.

"Evie was smiling," Pop said, wiping his eyes with the back of his hand. "Your mother's last word was your name. She had come outside to tell me you were with the guard at the gate. If you hadn't misbehaved that morning . . ."

Pop didn't finish the sentence, but J.T. knew what his father was thinking. He would've died, too.

"She was pregnant," Pop said. "Two months."

Rosy hugged him. "Oh, Professor, no."

"She hadn't even told me she suspected it or that she'd seen the doctor and was waiting to hear. After my physical wounds healed, he told me the test results were positive."

Stunned, J.T. took off his hat and set it aside. Pressure filled his chest, the weight of it almost unbearable. Grief, he realized. Grief not only for his mother, but also for Pop. When, as a small boy, he'd asked about his mother, Pop had led him to believe she died in a car wreck. His father had given him just enough information to temporarily satisfy his questions—sketchy information and a photo album containing pictures of the three of them before she'd died.

Growing up, J.T. had spent many hours studying his mother's image. Whenever he felt lonely and Pop was consumed with his work, or whenever Pop passed out or did something to embarrass him, J.T. would open the album and find comfort in her happy expression. If only she had lived, he'd told himself more times than he could count, everything would've been so different. Hershel Drake would've remained the sharp-eyed man standing alongside his mother in all those photographs. Pop would've valued his only child more than he did his experiments.

As the years passed and J.T. matured, that nagging belief created more complex questions in his mind. Did Pop somehow blame him for his mother's death? If so, why? Could he have been in the car with his mother when it crashed? Had he distracted her concentration? That possibility was the only thing he could come up with to explain Pop's remoteness toward him.

When J.T. found the courage to ask those questions, Pop was quick to assure him that he hadn't been in the car with her, that he'd had nothing whatsoever to do with his mother's death. Finally, frustrated over Pop's reluctance to talk about the details of the accident, J.T. had given up. The topic seemed off-limits. Now he knew why.

J.T. stood, stepped past Rosy then paused behind his father's chair. Taking a deep breath he placed his hands on the older man's shoulders. "I'm sorry, Pop. I'm so sorry."

Pop's head began to bob up and down.

"What about Reneau?" J.T. asked.

"He didn't count on me surviving, that's for certain. You see, he'd set it up to look as if he'd died in the blast, too, but I ruined that. The state had strong evidence against him. Then, at the last minute, Domani must've pulled some strings because the case was dropped on a technicality."

Rosy sighed and ran a hand through her hair, sending the layers in several different directions. "You said Reneau only stole part of your research. Why?"

"He thought he'd taken all of it but he had just one of two files. The one containing the second half of the research, the critical information about reversing the refractor's effects. I'd taken the other file home with me the night before to try to work out a minor glitch. I brought it back to the compound the next morning. It was locked inside my briefcase in the commissary when the building blew up."

"Could Reneau have recreated that initial part of the research since then?" she asked.

"It's possible, of course, but doubtful. I haven't seen any evidence to indicate he's had any success. I should have known I couldn't do it, either, without my files. After the explosion, my mind . . ." He lowered his head. "I wasn't the same. It's only because I'd taken the first file home that night that I've had any luck at all recreating it. It was more fresh on my mind than the rest and, after the tragedy, I scribbled down as much of it as my muddled brain would allow."

J.T. took his hands from Pop's shoulders and moved around to face him. "Why didn't he come after you? He and Domani were willing to kill to get what they wanted. And they got away with it. Why would they just give up and let you go on your way after all that? You were the key."

Pop kept staring down at his hands for a moment. When he finally looked up at the place where J.T. stood, his eyes looked worried and tired and miserable. "We took on a new identity when we moved to Pecan Grove. We changed our surname."

"What are you saying?"

"The name 'Drake' was given to us by the Witness Protection Program."

"Witness—" J.T. felt as if someone had kicked him in the ribs.

"It was risky to keep our first names, but I thought it would be too confusing for you if we didn't, so I insisted." He sighed. "I was born Hershel Carlisle, and up until the age of three you were Jerome Terrence Carlisle."

J.T. had thought nothing else could surprise him but he'd been wrong. He backed up a step, turned away, afraid of what he might say if he continued to look at his father. He could understand why Pop had shielded him from the truth of how his mother had died. But this lie was beyond comprehension. He wasn't sure he could ever forgive it. "You've let me live my entire life believing I'm someone I'm not?"

"Jerome." There was urgency in Pop's voice. J.T. heard it, as well as the squeak of his father's chair. A moment later, he felt someone touch his arm. "You aren't your name, Jerome, and that's the only thing about you that changed. You have the same mind, the same heart and soul."

More than anything, J.T. wished he could find it in him to turn to his father and break through the wall that they'd each taken part in building between them through the years. Today, Pop had ripped out the first brick. But this latest news had slipped it right back into place again.

"I'm sorry, Son," Pop said from behind him. "I

should've told you the truth long ago, but I just couldn't talk about it. Not until now. When you were a boy, I stayed silent for your protection. And later, well you see, the lie had gone on for too long." He sighed. "How can I make this up to you? Just tell me. I'll do whatever it takes."

"You can't do anything. I don't want you to do anything. I don't want anything from you at all." J.T. turned to face his father and saw that his words had hit their mark. Pop looked as if he'd just been slapped.

Instead of feeling vindicated, as he thought he should, sadness and shame swept through J.T. He couldn't change the past; he wasn't sure he could ever forgive Pop's deception. But if he wanted his old life back again, he needed to try to work with his father, cooperate with him. After that, he didn't know what relationship, if any, he wanted with the man. Not anymore. "I've heard of Anthony Domani," he said, unwilling to talk about this latest news another second. "He's been in more than a scrape or two with the law since you knew him."

Rosy's chin snapped up. She frowned. "Anthony. Anthony Domani. I know who he is. He owns businesses in Las Vegas. My mother worked for him for a short while right about the time I left for college."

"Yes, his headquarters and home are in Vegas," Pop said. "And Reneau still works for him, according to my information. As for his scrapes with the law, he always walks away free and clear, just as he did in 1972."

"Until you said his first name, his identity didn't click with me," Rosy said. "I never met him, and Mama never spoke of him much. I don't think she liked working for him, but she would never let on to me that she was unhappy." Her brows drew together. "This is quite a coincidence, isn't it?"

Pop shook his head. "Not really. I'm afraid I have another confession to make."

"This seems to be the day for them," J.T. said, unable to keep the sarcasm out of his voice.

"I hope you can forgive me, Roselyn," his father continued. "I'm ashamed to admit that your being from Vegas is the initial reason I sought you out when you were my student. In fact, I was on the scholarship board at the university when you applied, and I made it my mission to see to it you were awarded a substantial amount of money to attend school here. I wanted to make certain you chose Texas State over any other school you might have been considering."

"Really?" Roselyn scooted to the edge of her chair. "The scholarship *was* one factor in my choosing this school. I had other offers, but nothing as generous. Why did you want me to attend here, Professor?"

"Due to my identity change, I was always somewhat wary of running into someone who might know me, so I always took notice of where all new student applicants resided. When I saw your name listed, and that you were from Las Vegas, I did some research and learned that your mother was employed by Domani. I couldn't believe my good fortune! Please try to understand . . . I was consumed with the idea of recreating the refractor so that I could become invisible and seek revenge on Domani and Reneau. I thought if I got to know you and piqued your interest in the project, you might be of help to me in obtaining information about Domani. But after we became better acquainted, I couldn't bring myself to involve you in something so dangerous. If you hadn't found me drunk that night when you came back to town, I never would've told you anything about the refractor."

Looking stunned, Roselyn leaned back. "That's amazing, Professor. I never had the slightest clue . . ." She took his hand and patted it. "It's okay. I don't blame you for anything, and I don't want you to blame yourself. I wanted to be a part of this project. I don't regret it for a moment."

J.T. returned to his chair and sat. "So you're thinking I could go into Domani's headquarters, find the file and take it back?"

"Exactly," Pop said. "They have it. I know Reneau and Domani. They went to too much trouble to give up on this, even after thirty years."

"Pop . . ." J.T. shook his head and huffed a humorless laugh. "What you're suggesting is a long shot. Even if the file were there, how would I find it? I wouldn't have any idea what to look for."

"No, but I would." Rosy pushed away from the desk and stood. "I have an idea."

J.T. looked up at her. "What is it?"

"I need to call home."

Before J.T. could ask for a hint, she started for the door.

"I'll be back after lunch," she told them.

Chapter Nine

"I'll be in touch, Barb," Roselyn said, holding the phone to her ear with one hand while scrounging in the pantry for something to eat with the other. If not for the fact that she'd skipped breakfast and felt slightly light-headed she wouldn't go to the trouble of lunch. She was too keyed up to eat, too preoccupied by the idea taking shape in her mind.

The call home to Vegas had confirmed that her memory was on track. Years ago, her mother had worked for Anthony Domani. According to Barb, most women who'd been in the business as long as she and Darla had worked for the man in some form or fashion. Barb had even put in a short stint at one of his clubs, though she hadn't stayed on long enough to get to know him as well as Darla did.

"Don't talk to anyone about any of this," Roselyn warned, knowing even as she said the words the warning wasn't necessary. Barb could be trusted with any confidence. "I know I've left you in the dark about a lot of things, but I'll fill you in just as soon as I can."

"No problem. As long as I know there's a plan in the works that'll give Tony Domani what's coming to him and that I can take part in it, I'm willing to wait for the details." Barb made a sound of disgust. "That scumbag."

"The plan might involve Mama pretending to crawl back to him for a job. I hate that, and I don't think she'll like it any more than I do."

"Honey, I can't speak for Darla, but I'm betting if you put it to her in the right way, she'll go along."

"You're implying that it will take some fast talking on my part, am I correct?"

"Just tell her you don't mind if she bites him in the butt just before she stands up and walks out his door again. See if she doesn't jump at the chance. If not, I'll happily play the part of the pathetic, washed-up old broad and beg him for a job. I'd do it with a smile."

Laughing, Roselyn snatched a can of tuna off the pantry shelf. "I need to go now, Barb. Maybe you shouldn't tell Mama I called. She'll just worry herself sick. Let me figure out a way to break all of this to her."

"My lips are sealed. But whatever it is you're up to, you be careful. I've always suspected that man is dangerous."

Unease rippled through Roselyn as she thought of all the people Domani had killed. She hated involving anyone else in this, but Barb and her mother were street savvy. If anyone could take care of themselves, they could. "I'll be careful, I promise."

"Bye, Rosebud. Love you."

"Love you, too."

Roselyn punched off the telephone and placed it on the counter. Barb had had plenty to say about the man who'd once signed Darla Peabody's paychecks, and none of it was nice. It seemed that Anthony Domani consid-

ered his employees to be his private property—especially
the women. But he paid well and, since Roselyn's mother
had reached an age when work as a dancer was difficult
to come by, she'd controlled her tongue with her boss.
For a while, at least. Then she'd heeded Barb's and
Sully's advice and quit.

Roselyn opened the can of tuna, then put a couple of
slices of bread into the toaster. The odor of the fish made
her wonder if Wanda's poodle was being fed. She hoped
the professor's neighbor hadn't given up on the dog. Just
in case, she decided to stop by the grocery store later and
buy a bag of dog food. She would leave a dish on Professor Drake's porch next time she was there.

When the doorbell rang, she twisted the cap off a bottle of water and headed into the living room.

She opened the door and found the porch empty. With
a shrug, Roselyn stepped back to close the door again.

"It's me."

The sound of Jerome's voice made her jump. Water
sloshed out of the bottle and onto the carpet. "You almost gave me a heart attack. I don't think I'll ever get
used to talking to blank space."

"With any luck you won't have to, at least not when
I'm around."

Roselyn pushed open the screen and stepped aside. She
stared at the empty porch, wondering if he was naked or
if he wore the invisible clothing. The Lakers cap and
shorts and T-shirt were not in sight. She cleared her
throat. "Come in."

"I already did," he said from behind her.

"Oh!" She whirled around, adding more water to the
wet spot on the carpet. The screen door slammed.

"I'm sorry. When you opened the screen I took it as
an invitation."

"Don't worry about it." With her heart ticking like an
overwound clock, she started into the kitchen. She won-

dered what had brought him by so soon after she'd left his father's house. "I'm making a sandwich. Would you care for one?"

"Pop and I ate, thanks. If you have more water, I could stand a drink, though."

"Sure. How's the professor doing?"

"He's taking a nap."

"Bless his heart." Roselyn paused to open the refrigerator. "He must be emotionally drained."

"More like hungover."

She was uncomfortable with Jerome's frankness. To protect Professor Drake's dignity, she had gotten into the habit of making excuses for his behavior whenever he'd had too much to drink.

"Your father has had a difficult couple of days," Roselyn said as she took out another bottle of water and placed it on the table. At the counter she set her own bottle down, took the bread from the toaster, then opened the cabinet for a plate. The shelf was empty and she realized every plate she owned sat in the sink, dirty.

"He told me when this is over he plans to call a rehab center in Dallas to see if and when they can take him."

"That's wonderful." She smiled, relieved by the news. "I've been hoping the day would come when he'd be ready. He can triumph over his problem; I know he can." She turned on the tap and started scrubbing. "How are you? All of what your father revealed this morning couldn't have been easy to hear."

"You mean the fact that my mother was murdered and—" She heard a sound like fingers snapping. "Let's see," he continued. "What was that other little detail? Oh, yeah, the one about me living under a false identity for the past thirty years?"

Roselyn glanced over her shoulder. "I hope you had a chance after I left to talk to your father about all of that."

"What more is there to say?"

She shut off the water and reached for a dishtowel. "He needs to hear that you understand why he did what he did. He needs to know you love him."

"That was never a question."

Placing the dry plate on the counter, Roselyn pulled open the silverware drawer. No forks. She found a dirty one in the sink, then turned. "Where are you?"

"Here at the table."

"Sitting or standing?"

Wood scraped against linoleum as the chair slid back. "Sitting."

Roselyn glanced down. "If you're implying that it's your father's feelings for you that are questionable, I can assure you he loves you. Didn't you hear it in his voice when he talked about you as a child?"

"My mother was alive then." The chair creaked. He cleared his throat. "Maybe he thinks the only reason she really came to the lab that morning was because I was there."

Roselyn laid the fork back in the sink, then settled into the empty chair across the table from him. "It's obvious to me that he blames himself for your mother's death, not you. That's why he drinks, why he works from the time he wakes up in the morning until he goes to bed at night."

"Maybe."

The bottle of water she had set on the table in front of him rose into the air and hovered. The cap came off, then slowly lowered to the tabletop. The bottle tilted away from her and she half expected to see a stream of liquid fall from it as it poured down his throat. When the bottle lowered to the table again it was one quarter empty.

"I just wish I'd known a long time ago what was eating at Pop," he said. "I grew up hating that basement lab of his." His laugh was sharp and humorless. "I set it on fire once when I was a kid. Pop thought it was an accident and I never said otherwise. But it was no accident."

Roselyn didn't need to see him to know he was hurting and had been for a very long time. Giving up on trying to force an appetite, she leaned back in her chair. Now she knew why he'd come by; he needed to talk, to confess. And for whatever reasons, he had chosen to open up to her. According to Barb, soul baring wasn't easy for most men. She presumed a cocky, tough guy like J.T. Drake would find revealing conversations particularly uncomfortable.

"I guess you must feel as if you lost your father as well as your mother thirty years ago. That couldn't have been easy for you growing up," she said. "But at least your father was there, in body if not in spirit. Surely you have good memories as well as bad ones, times the two of you spent together when things were right."

"None spring to mind."

She stared in his direction, then blew out a long, slow breath. "I never met my father; I don't even know what he looks like. My mother met him on the Vegas strip in 1973 when she was barely sixteen. The only thing she knew about him was the little information he offered. That he was a student at a small college somewhere in Texas, that he was in Vegas for the weekend with a group of his fraternity buddies and that his name was Steven Bedford. How much of that information was true is anyone's guess. I think the fact that he was from Texas was part of the attraction. She'd run away to Vegas from a small town in Texas when she was fifteen, and I suspect she might have been homesick."

Roselyn shook her head as the story came back to her. "Anyway, when Mama found out she was pregnant, she tried to find him by contacting the different universities in Texas but she never tracked him down."

She recalled a statement she'd once overheard her

mother saying to Barb. "Except for a few stretch marks, I'm all Mama has to prove he wasn't simply a figment of her imagination."

The water bottle rose into the air again and remained suspended there. "Pop told me you earned your Ph.D. from Duke University."

"Yes."

"If I were betting, I'd put money on the assumption that a smart girl like you had scholarship offers from colleges all over the country when you graduated high school."

She nodded. "But as I told your father, none were as financially attractive as the one Texas State offered."

"Maybe not, but why would someone with your potential choose a small public university over some place more prestigious?"

She glanced down at her lap, then up to the spot where she guessed his face must be. "I think you've probably guessed."

"Because you thought your father might have gone here?"

"It was a slim chance, but he had told my mother he went to school at a small Texas college, and Texas State was offering me a scholarship. So . . ." She shrugged. "I didn't have any better leads for trying to trace his whereabouts."

"Did you check first to see if the university had record of a past student named Steven Bedford?"

Roselyn nodded. "A George Stephano Bedford went here for a semester about the time I was conceived. Supposedly he came from Amarillo, but I couldn't locate anyone there who knew him. That was as much information as I was able to find."

He took another drink, set the bottle down, twirled it left then right. "But you came here anyway and stayed until you graduated."

123

"Just by living here where he might have once lived, by walking the same university hallways, I somehow felt closer to him." She crossed her arms. "I came here looking for him; I stayed because I liked it. Pecan Grove was a nice change of pace for a Vegas girl. I felt comfortable around most of the students, and I liked the teachers. Professor Drake, in particular."

She heard a quiet thumping and realized his fingers drummed against the tabletop.

"You didn't find your own father, but you found mine."

The truth hit her like a cold blast of wind. So that was it. The reason he'd seemed to resent her since the moment they met. Roselyn braced her forearms on the table and leaned toward him. "I haven't replaced my father with yours," she said quietly. "I never planned on returning to Pecan Grove after I graduated. I only came back for a visit when I ran into an ex-classmate and she told me your father had retired because his health was declining—"

"You mean his drinking had gotten out of control."

"Call it what you like. The point is, he needed someone and rumor had it that you were unavailable to him."

"Did those rumors also inform you that I asked Pop numerous times to move to L.A. so he'd be closer to me but that he refused? Or about the times I checked him into rehab centers and he never showed up?"

"Long distance. You did all of that from afar . . . the coaxing . . . the making of arrangements. You never came yourself to talk to him face-to-face." She sighed. "I'm sorry. I have no right to blame you for anything."

"But you do."

"There was a time when I did, but now that we've met, I'm beginning to understand the problems you've faced with your father and how they affected you. Anyway, you're here now; that's what matters. And the point I was trying to make is that he has always been good to me. When I was his student, he took me under his wing, so to speak. He took my mind off my father's absence by nurturing my interest in science. So I came back to check on him and he ended up telling me about the refractor. I couldn't leave after that; I didn't want to. I guess you could say I became as obsessed with his project as he was. So I applied for his position at Texas State, left my prior job behind, and moved back to Pecan Grove. Don't you see, J.T.—"

The thumping stopped. "You called me J.T."

"So, I did. What about it?"

"Why?"

She tilted her head to one side, the corner of her lip twitching. "Because I've decided that, despite my prior suspicions, you're okay," she answered, repeating what he'd said to her last night.

He didn't respond, and the most irrational thoughts went through her mind. Was he sitting across the table, watching her, or had he left the room? Worse, had she only imagined him there all along? Months ago, on the night after she'd finally taken the time to read the Foreword in his book, after the revealing words on those first few pages had stunned and touched her, she dreamed about J.T. Drake. Maybe his presence right now, here in her kitchen, was simply a dream, too.

Roselyn shifted in her chair. "Say something."

His silence seemed strangely seductive; it made her feel exposed. Was it possible to feel another person's gaze like a touch? She'd swear his skimmed across her lips . . . her throat . . . her breasts, trailing heat and goose bumps, stimulating every nerve ending in her body. She crossed her arms. "Are you there?"

"Tell me, Doctor Peabody, did you decide I was okay before I kissed you or after?"

Roselyn heard the smile in his voice and caught her

breath. She wasn't good at the man-woman equation and normally avoided tackling it. But she found J.T.'s method of flirtation intriguing, an almost irresistible challenge.

Almost.

Roselyn knew from past experience how quickly the sweet taste of seduction could turn sour, how easily the blush of possibility could deepen to a red flush of humiliation.

"About last night," she said. "I want you to know that I recognize it for what it was."

"Which was?"

"A knee-jerk reaction to a situation."

"Most kisses are."

"Please, don't tease me. What I'm trying to say is that I understand that it didn't mean anything."

His chair slid back from the table. "It meant something to me. The only reason I left your bedroom so fast is that I was taken off guard by just how damn much I liked kissing you."

"For once, could you just be serious? I—"

"I am being serious." She felt static electricity in the air around her and, a second later, his presence beside her. "I seriously liked that kiss," he said, his voice low and only inches from her ear. "And I'd like to do it again if it's okay with you."

She thought she might shatter into a million pieces if she so much as breathed. His hand rested at the back of her chair, his fingers shooting tiny sparks off of her shoulder blade. She smelled the sandalwood soap she'd found in his hotel bathroom two nights before and placed into his bag. "You don't have to do this, you know. I intend to help you solve this predicament you're in no matter what. There's no need to—"

"What are you talking about?"

She flinched. His voice had changed; he sounded agitated. "You don't need to pretend to have a romantic

126

interest in me in order to obtain my help in reversing what happened to—"

"Is that what you think?"

"I think you realize I'm the person most qualified to help you and—"

"And so I'm screwing with your emotions in order to get what I need from you?"

His voice had moved away from her ear. She glanced up and frowned, baffled by his obvious offense to her statement. "Well, yes."

"I thought you said you decided I'm okay?"

"I did. You care for your father, that's clear. Before I wasn't sure, but I understand now why your relationship with him is on shaky ground."

"So that makes me okay? Even if I use you?"

"Well—" She swallowed. "Do you expect me to believe that your apology last night didn't stem from your realization that you'd been badgering the one person you need most?"

"At first maybe, but—"

"But what?"

"An apology is one thing. Faking an attraction to someone is another. The last thing I'd be is *okay* if I used you like that, Rosy. You deserve better."

She crossed her arms. "Then what's this all about?"

"This? You mean my wanting to touch you?"

Roselyn's pulse kicked up. She nodded.

"Who's the son of a bitch who gave you such a low opinion of yourself?"

"I . . ." She blinked. Was he defending her honor? Turning into the sensitive, caring J.T. Drake she'd found so appealing in the Foreword of his book? "I don't know what to say."

"Say whether or not you liked the kiss we shared last night and whether or not you'd like to do it again."

She swallowed. "Well, I don't know, I—"

"Did you like the kiss, Rosy? It's a simple yes or no question."

"I—"

"Yes or no?"

"Yes," she answered weakly.

"Good. That wasn't so hard, was it?" His breath tickled her ear again. "Now for the second part of the question. Would you like to do it again?"

"J.T., please, you're making this—"

"Yes or no, Rosy. It's that simple."

"Yes." She closed her eyes and blew out a noisy sigh. "I'd like it. Are you happy now?"

What was it about her that wouldn't let him back off? Ever since yesterday when he'd stood terrified inside the refractor and their gazes connected, J.T. had wanted to be with Rosy every second of the day and night. When they were together, he felt calmer, less freaked out about his current situation. That's why he'd walked over to her place after Pop took off to his room for a nap. He'd needed to see her again, to be with her. And for these past few minutes in her kitchen, he'd actually forgotten that he was in one hell of a fix, forgotten completely that he was invisible.

Stooped behind her chair, slightly off to one side, J.T. studied Rosy's profile. He'd never pursued a woman like her before, a woman so afraid to let go, to give in to her instincts. Her body was tight as a wire, her demeanor strictly hands-off. For the first time since he was about fifteen, J.T. felt as unsure of himself with a woman as Rosy looked to be with him. But he wasn't about to give up. Not unless she insisted.

He touched his mouth to the side of her neck, heard her quick intake of breath when a spark skipped between them. "See there? Sparks fly when we're together," he said, chuckling, moving his way up her smooth pale skin.

"That's only static electricity," she said. "Because of the refractor."

"I'm not so sure about that. I think it's a completely different kind of electricity. The kind generated between a man and a woman who like being together." He nibbled her earlobe. "Mmm. You taste good."

She pushed back her chair and stood. When she finally turned to face him, he saw the conflict in her eyes. It was disconcerting to stand only two feet from her and watch her scan the room, looking for him, to see her stare straight through his body as if it didn't exist.

"Whether I like this or not doesn't matter. It's a mistake," she said. "We shouldn't—"

"I've never been one to listen to shoulds and shouldn'ts. Seems to me they're usually just poor excuses for fear. That, or they hinge on the agendas of other people. I don't see how our kissing each other could hurt anybody."

"It could hurt you."

"Let's see." He stepped closer to her, brushed his lips across her mouth. "Nope. Didn't hurt a bit."

"That's not what I meant and you know it."

He smiled. She was so serious, so intense. And her strained expression told him what she wouldn't say. Rosy might be worried about him, for whatever reason, but she was afraid for herself, too. Afraid to be vulnerable, to give too much of herself. He wondered who'd instilled that fear in her, that insecurity.

Rosy nibbled at one corner of her lower lip. "I can't be distracted right now. I need to remain focused on solving this problem with the refractor so that you can have your life back and be whole again."

"I have faith in you, Rosy. And I'll only distract you a little bit. I promise."

He loved the way her eyes narrowed, the quick curve

of her smile. "You aren't accustomed to being rejected by a woman, are you?" she asked.

"No, as a matter of fact. But I think you're worth a possible bruised ego."

She reached out as if to touch him, her fingertips pausing just short of brushing his chest. "Last night after you left me," she said, her voice hardly more than a whisper, "It was almost as if you weren't really here and never had been. Like you were simply a figment of my imagination."

J.T. took her hand. "I'm real." Lifting her fingers to his mouth, he pressed them against his lips. "And I'm right here with you."

She slid her palm around to cup his cheek. "I'm terrible at this sort of thing. I lose all sense of competence. That's especially dangerous for you right now. I don't want to let you down, J.T., that's all. I need to concentrate."

"Okay. We'll back up a step or two. But I can promise you one thing . . . sooner or later we're going to end up right back in the same place again."

"We'll see." She smiled, her eyes no longer so serious. "If that happens it would be nice to be able to see the man who's kissing me. And in order to make that happen, I need a focused mind."

Moving around the chair, Roselyn walked to the counter and went back to work on the sandwich she had been making when he arrived.

J.T. crossed his arms and leaned against the sink, watching her. Whenever she smiled, he realized just how pretty she was. Pretty and unique, though no fashion magazine would ever put her face on a cover. She didn't fit society's mold for beauty. Rosy's face, with all its expressiveness, should be seen in person to be fully appreciated.

"Before you left the house earlier," he said, "you suggested you might have an idea."

"Yes." She carried her plate to the table and sat again, scooting the chair around to face him. "I have a friend in Vegas." She cocked her head. "Actually Barb's more like family. She and my mother and a man named Sully opened a dance studio together. Mama and Barb teach the classes and Sully takes care of maintenance and helps with administrative matters." She paused, lifted her sandwich. "Are you sure you don't want some lunch? I hate eating in front of you."

"I'm fine."

She took a bite. "When I was growing up," she said a few seconds later, "Sully managed a club on the strip and my mother and Barb performed in a long-running show there."

"Your mother is a Vegas showgirl?"

He didn't miss the quick lift of her chin. "She was. And she was good at it, too. One of the best. She and Barb are trained dancers. They worked hard."

Thinking of her solo performance in front of the mirror last night, J.T. smiled. "It must be in the blood. You most definitely inherited your mother's talent for dancing."

A flush of red crept up her neck. "I might have known you'd bring that up. I wish you'd just forget about it."

"Sorry, Rosy." He cleared his throat to keep from laughing. "That's not likely to happen."

Scowling, she took another bite of her sandwich and chewed for several seconds, then patted her mouth with a napkin. "Anyway, as I was telling your father earlier, Mama worked for a short time as a hostess in one of Anthony Domani's clubs before joining Barb and Sully in the studio venture."

J.T. pushed away from the counter. "Go on."

"I tried calling her this morning at work but she was out so I talked to Barb. I was vague about what's going on, but it didn't seem to matter to Barb. She can't stand

131

Domani and is more than willing to help us."

"How?"

"Any way we need her. It seems Domani wasn't too happy with my mother for quitting. He predicted she'd come crawling back to him for a job when she found out no one else in the business would be willing to hire a woman of her age."

"How old is she?"

"Forty-four."

He laughed. "Ancient."

"Unfortunately most showgirls reach the end of their careers long before then. It was difficult for Barb and my mom at the end . . . the physical demands of staying in top shape, competing with women half their age." Rosy placed her half-eaten sandwich on the plate and pushed it aside. "According to Barb, Domani had an interest in my mother. She said he acted as if his feelings were hurt when Mama left his club. He told Mama he'd take pity and find some sort of work for her when she came crawling back to him."

"What a guy. Would she do that? Pretend to crawl back to him for a job?"

"I don't know yet. Barb seems to think that if it will help give Domani his due, Mama will gladly swallow her pride. If so, it would be a way for us to look for information from inside his operation."

"You sound worried."

"I am. I can't bear the thought of asking my mother to try to get back into the good graces of a man like that. Even if she is only pretending."

"Then don't. Not for me."

"Even if you weren't involved, now that I know Anthony Domani has what your father and I need to complete our work, I'd be determined to try to get it back from him."

"You're sure?"

132

"Yes. I'll just have to talk to Mama and see how she reacts. Maybe the thing to do is to see if she can pull strings with Domani to convince him to hire me, instead of her trying to obtain a job with him."

"As a showgirl?"

Rosy laughed. "Hardly. Perhaps in his offices."

J.T. took another drink of water. "Let's say either you or your mother do hire on with one of Domani's enterprises. Then what?"

"To tell you the truth, I haven't completely figured that out yet. But at least we'll have someone on the inside. Maybe then we'll have better access to information that will lead us to your father's missing files."

"It's a start. So what's the next step?"

"I thought you and I should fly out to Vegas as soon as possible and talk to my mother in person. I'm afraid she'll think I've lost my mind if I try to tell her about you and your situation over the telephone. It might be a good idea if the two of you meet face-to-face."

"That's an interesting way of putting it considering my condition."

Rosy smiled. "I'm glad you can have a sense of humor about it." She stood. "As far as school is concerned, now is a good time for me to get away. The first summer session just ended, and I'm not teaching the second one. I have almost a month before my next classes begin. What about you?"

"I'll have to do some fast talking with my editor to convince him to extend my deadline. And I'll need to make a call to my boss at the magazine to ask for a leave of absence. It shouldn't be a problem, though. I'll tell them Pop's sick." J.T. knew his assistant could easily wrap up the last-minute details on his column for next month's issue.

As for Giselle . . . he winced. In all the chaos, he'd forgotten to call her and keep the peace. She'd be angry and pouty the next time he saw her. Coaxing another date out of the model wouldn't be easy but, to his surprise, he didn't much care.

"Well." Rosy shoved back the shaggy layer of hair that fell across her forehead. "That's that, then. Why don't you go home and make those calls? I'll contact the airlines and see if I can arrange a flight to Vegas for the two of us sometime tomorrow."

Chapter Ten

Hershel knocked on Jerome's bedroom door. "I just spoke with Roselyn on the phone. I told her we'd be by for her in ten minutes. By the time we drive into Houston, that will put you at the airport two hours in advance of your flight."

"I'm almost ready," Jerome called back. "I'll meet you out front."

"Why don't we take my vehicle? No need to add mileage to your rental car."

The bedroom door opened. "That hippie van of yours does good to go forty miles an hour floored. We'd miss the plane."

Hershel felt a nip of defensiveness for his and Evie's old VW. Jerome had never liked riding in it. When the doorbell rang, he sighed, then turned and started back into the den.

Wanda Moody stood on the front porch. "Hello, Hershel."

"Wanda . . . what a surprise."

She looked past him, her eyes narrowing behind the lenses of her glasses. "Is she here?"

"She?"

"That woman. I didn't see her bicycle out front but that doesn't mean anything. They're sneaky bastards. I don't trust them a'tall."

Hershel scratched his head as she shuffled past him into the room. "I'm afraid I'm confused, Wanda. Who are *they*?"

"Witches and warlocks and the like. I've been reading up on them." She sat on the couch and pulled a pack of cigarettes from the pocket of her long loose blouse. Hershel noticed the image of her bulldog, Toots, embroidered there. "They have a spell for every situation. Take you, for example. That girl needs something you've got and she's controlling your mind in order to get it."

"Wanda—"

"Now just you listen up for a minute. This particular witch or warlock is disguised as a young woman, a scientist, so's that you'll relate to it and trust it."

"I assure you, Roselyn Peabody is no more a witch than I am. She—"

"She's done something to my Curly." Wanda's lower lip quivered. "I hear that hacking bark of his from time to time but I can't find him."

Hershel felt a twist of compassion for the poor woman. "I'm sure he'll turn up soon, Wanda. He's run off before, hasn't he?"

She blinked back tears and nodded.

"Well then, you see? Don't worry yourself so."

"You don't understand. Curly's not gone. I poured food into his bowl and watched it disappear right before my eyes. Curly was eating it, I just couldn't see him."

"Now Wanda—"

The tears stopped as quickly as they'd started. "Don't

you *now Wanda* me, Hershel Drake. Curly was eating that food, all right. I reached down and petted him, felt his furry little body with my own two hands. That witch put a spell on him, that's what she did."

At a loss for what to say to sway her thinking, Hershel glanced at his watch. "I don't mean to be rude, but I'm running late for an appointment."

She tapped out a cigarette and stuck it between her painted-on lips. "With her?"

"When I return," Hershel said, ignoring her question, "I'll bring you a sack of cherries from the tree in my side yard. This evening, perhaps we could get together and discuss this problem with Curly over a slice of one of your delicious cherry pies."

Wanda lowered her lighter without striking a flame. She pulled the cigarette from her mouth, smearing her lipstick. "You never told me you liked my pies."

"They're the best I've ever tasted."

Tilting her head to one side, she smiled. *"Really?"*

"Absolutely." Forcing a smile of his own, he pushed the screen door and held it open.

"Okey-doke." She stood and started toward him. "But don't think for a minute I'm dropping this, Hershel. Curly's being cursed makes this my business. That girl is just a speck of dust in a sandstorm of evil. If we don't nip her plans in the bud before they go any further, mark my words, we'll both live to regret it."

Hershel closed the screen after she passed through onto the porch. "Have a good day, Wanda."

"I intend to."

As he closed the door he heard Jerome's laughter behind him.

"Well, well, Pop. I never knew you were such a smooth operator with the ladies. You played Mrs. Moody like a winning poker hand."

"Yes . . . well." He turned. "She's lonely, you know. Wanda has good intentions."

"She's been having good intentions for as long as I can remember. What happened to her dog?"

"Oh, yes, the dog. I guess Roselyn and I forgot to tell you. The poor creature must have slipped into the refractor with you the last time when we weren't paying attention."

"The dog's invisible?"

"So it seems."

Jerome swore under his breath. "Wanda won't back off now, that's for sure."

"Yes, well, I worry about the poor woman. The older she gets the more impulsive and outrageous her behavior. I wouldn't put anything past her."

Jerome huffed a short laugh. "That's funny. She said more or less the same thing about you when she called me in L.A. last week."

Hershel cleared his throat. "I don't take off for days at a time without telling a soul where I'm going. Bless the Hancocks next door to her. They sometimes find Wanda's dogs in their backyard with no explanation and assume she means for them to feed the poor animals."

As the full content of Jerome's comment finally registered, heat inched up Hershel's neck. "Wanda called you about me?"

"She was afraid you might blow yourself up when she saw all the green smoke pouring out of the house."

He looked down at the floor, reached into his pocket for his keys. "So that's why you came. To save me from myself."

"Considering your past history, I thought it might be a good idea."

The weight of disappointment hung heavy on Hershel's shoulders. He didn't know what he'd hoped. Perhaps that Jerome had come of his own accord, not because a neighbor had sent out warning signals that his father was becoming too dotty to live alone without supervision. He noted a subtle disturbance in the air around him, saw the front door open again.

"Let's go, Pop," Jerome said.

Fifteen minutes later Hershel drove down the highway with Roselyn beside him in the front seat and Jerome in back. He glanced into the rearview mirror. Only a few blocks away from Roselyn's house he had noticed a red car behind them. The car still followed.

"I want to surprise my mother so I didn't call her to say we were coming," Roselyn said. "She'd go to all kinds of trouble and, anyway, I'm hoping we can talk to Barb first and have at least a skeleton of a plan in place as far as Domani is concerned. When it comes to me, my mother's such a worrier. You'd think I was still five years old." She sighed. "I must admit I can't wait to see her. Barb and Sully, too. Barb said to give you her regards, Professor."

He glanced into the rearview mirror again as he took the next exit. The red car's blinker came on.

"Professor?"

"I'm sorry." Hershel met her gaze. "Did you ask me something?"

"Are you alright? You seem distracted."

"I believe we're being tailed."

Roselyn turned to look out the back window.

"Who would want to tail us?" Jerome asked.

"I can think of only one person. And it just so happens she drives a car exactly like the one behind us."

"Are you talking about that old red Chevy?"

"Yes, do you recognize it?"

Jerome chuckled. "Mrs. Moody?"

"I'm afraid so."

"Your neighbor?" Roselyn asked.

Hershel nodded.

"That's strange. Oh—" Roselyn reached down into the floorboard and lifted a small sack. "I bought a bag of dog food for her poodle. I thought you might want to put a bowl out for him now and then, in case Mrs. Moody's stopped feeding him."

"She's feeding him," Hershel said. "She told me she watched the food disappear. She believes you've cursed the animal, Roselyn."

Roselyn shook her head. "My word."

"Just what we need." Jerome said. "Wanda playing detective. That lady has too much time on her hands. But I have to hand it to her, she's persistent."

Hershel couldn't argue with that statement. He merged into the center lane traffic. Four car-lengths behind them, the red Chevrolet did the same.

Roselyn stood at the back of the car surrounded by luggage as the professor closed the trunk.

"I'll help you with the bags," he said.

"You'll get a ticket if you leave the car here," J.T. said. "I can help her."

Roselyn shook her head. "No, you can't." A passing elderly woman wearing a hat and dark glasses cast her an odd stare. Realizing she faced the empty space from which J.T. had spoken, Roselyn turned to the professor. "I'm not anxious to try and explain to security how my luggage moves of its own accord. I can manage."

"Guess you're right about that," J.T. whispered. "Sometimes I forget."

"That's one bad habit you'll want to break, Jerome. The last thing you want to do is slip up while in the presence of Anthony Domani." Professor Drake jingled his keys, stared down at them, his head bobbing slightly. "I wish I could go along. I started this more than thirty years ago; I should be there to finish it."

"That's not a good idea, Pop," J.T. whispered. "We

can't take the risk of Domani or Reneau running into you."

Roselyn reached for the professor's hand. She wanted to tell him how proud she was that he'd decided to seek help for his drinking problem but she knew such a comment would only embarrass him. "We'll be in constant touch with you. Jerome or I will call as soon as we've settled in."

"I'll be on pins and needles." He squeezed her hand. "Take care of each other."

"We will." She smiled then, releasing his hand, adjusted a tote bag's strap across her shoulder, her purse over the other.

"At least we seem to have lost Wanda in traffic. That's one less problem to deal with."

"For Rosy and me, anyway," J.T. said. "I have a feeling you haven't seen the last of her for a while, Pop."

Roselyn secured a satchel beneath one arm, then grabbed a briefcase. Both hers and J.T.'s suitcases were on wheels. She grasped a handle in each hand, then eyed the distance to the door, hoping she could juggle it all. "Ready, J.T.?"

"Ready," he whispered. "Are you? Only one of those bags belongs to me. You don't look like a clotheshorse. Why do you need so much luggage?"

She frowned. "I couldn't do without my research books. And I brought gifts for Mama and Barb and Sully."

"Women," he mumbled.

She lifted her chin. "Stay on my right side so I'll know where you are."

She only had to stop to readjust her load twice before reaching the ticket counter. The line there was short. After checking the two suitcases, Roselyn started off toward their gate, still juggling despite being two bags lighter.

Jennifer Archer

"You only bought a ticket for one seat?" J.T. whispered when they reached their destination.

She smiled at a passing couple, waited a moment until they were safely out of earshot, then whispered, "When I called yesterday to make reservations they said the plane wasn't full. Look for an empty seat."

The old woman in the hat who'd caught her talking to J.T. earlier outside at the car, passed by and eyed her suspiciously again. At least, Roselyn thought she was staring. Because of the dark glasses the woman wore, she couldn't be sure.

A short time later they boarded. Roselyn dropped her purse midway down the aisle and had to stop to gather the contents that spilled out onto the floor. Finally, she made it to her aisle seat at the back of the plane. After all the passengers were seated she was relieved to find the plane only about three-quarters full and the two seats beside her empty. The closest person to her was the little old lady who'd been eyeing her in the airport. She sat three rows up and across the aisle.

"You take the window," Roselyn whispered to J.T. He'd be out of the way there, with less chance of anyone brushing against him. Or smelling him. Roselyn drew a deep breath as she moved her knees aside to let him pass. She should have warned J.T. not to bathe with his usual soap. He smelled much too masculine. Any woman within a foot of him would pick up his scent and think Roselyn wore men's cologne.

She pulled a book from her tote bag, then put the bag with her others in the overhead compartment, affording J.T. a chance to settle in. After a moment, Roselyn sat in the aisle seat again, leaving an empty space between them. She slid her purse under the seat in front of her, then opened her book and started to read.

"You get a little groove between your brows when you concentrate, did you know that?"

Roselyn jumped. The book slid from her lap onto the floor. J.T. wasn't by the window at all, but in the middle seat beside her. His breath had tickled her ear.

Her heart pounded as, leaning down, she picked up her book and glanced around the cabin in front and behind. The passenger three rows up stared straight ahead. No flight attendant was in sight. "Jerome Drake," she whispered, "don't say another word the rest of the flight, do you understand?"

She opened the book again and returned to the paragraph where she'd left off. Thanks to J.T., her eyes skimmed across the words without registering their meaning. All she could do was wonder where he sat now. Beside her or the window? Was he watching her, or had he closed his eyes?

A couple of pages later, she heard a commotion and looked up. The elderly woman three rows ahead and across the aisle struggled to reach the overhead compartment. She dropped a bag, then stooped to pick it up, casting Roselyn a quick glance through her dark sunglasses when she stood again.

Roselyn stood, too, to offer assistance but the flight attendant beat her to it. Sitting again, she returned her gaze to the page, swiping a hand across the side of her head when something tickled her right ear.

"You have sexy ears," J.T. said, his voice a quiet murmur, so close she knew only she could hear him. "I never paid much attention to a woman's ears before."

She felt a gentle pinch of her lobe and, lifting her hand, swatted him away just as the flight attendant walked by.

The woman paused. "Is something wrong, Ma'am?"

"Oh, uh . . ." Roselyn blinked up at her and smiled. "It's nothing. Just a gnat, I think."

"I'm sorry. We'll be taking off in a minute." She glanced down at Roselyn's lap. "You might want to go ahead and buckle your seat belt."

As the flight attendant made her way to the back of the plane, Roselyn clicked her belt into place and pulled it comfortably tight. "You should buckle up, too," she whispered to J.T., then watched as the two straps in the seat next to her lifted and snapped together, leaving the buckled belt suspended around nothing. She blinked. "That won't do." The flight attendant was bound to notice.

"Then I'll have to unbuckle."

"No, don't. It isn't safe."

The belt separated. "I'll take my chances. If the plane goes down, I'll just hold on to you."

She released a jittery breath. It was going to be a long flight. "Move over by the window."

He kissed her neck. "I like it here better."

She leaned her head back against the seat, turned toward the window, and squinted. "Stop it."

She felt more than heard the vibration of his chuckle. Flustered, she resumed her reading as the intercom came on and the attendant went through her safety routine.

Moments later the plane took off.

Roselyn felt J.T's breath brush her ear again. "This is driving me crazy," he whispered. "Sitting here without anything to do but look at you. The first time we met, down in Pop's workshop, I didn't realize how pretty you are. It kind of crept up and surprised me."

"Quit," Roselyn said, too loud, she realized, when she glanced up from the page and saw the old woman in the dark sunglasses staring back at her.

Roselyn forced her attention back to the book. She felt J.T.'s fingertips stroke the inside of her elbow and her stomach muscles tightened in response. She drew in a quick breath that sounded more like a gasp.

The flight attendant paused beside her and grinned. "That must be some book you're reading. What's the title?"

"The title?" Roselyn wasn't quite sure. She'd been staring at the words, not really reading them. She closed the book and glanced down at the cover. *"Principles of Optics: Electromagnetic Theory of Propagation, Interference and Diffraction of Light."* She looked up again.

The attendant's brows lifted. "Hmm. Afraid that wouldn't do it for me." She studied Roselyn for a moment with a bemused smile on her face, then started off down the aisle again.

Roselyn reached under the seat in front of her for her purse, rummaged around inside of it until she found a pen and a scrap of paper. Quickly, she scribbled a note to J.T.

When I return from the restroom, I trust you'll be sitting in the empty seats behind us.

J.T. lifted the armrest, scooted to the aisle seat and turned to watch Rosy walk the short distance to the restroom at the back of the plane. It would be a hell of a lot more fun to stay put and tease her the rest of the trip. A lot more interesting, too. But he knew he was perilously close to crossing the line with her. Besides, he could use a nap.

He stood and slid into the three empty seats behind, the last row of seats in the plane. J.T. stretched out as best he could. Only a wall separated him from the restroom. When he heard the door rattle, he opened an eye and saw Rosy pass by. He closed his eye again and started to drift off.

"Can I sit here?"

J.T. jerked wide awake. A boy of about ten years of age stood in the aisle beside him staring off toward the back of the plane where the flight attendant was now preparing her cart to serve drinks to the passengers. The kid's bangs were spiked up with hair gel and he had a tattoo on his scrawny left bicep. J.T. blinked and squinted. Some sort of weird-looking troll or goblin or something. It was difficult to identify the image because the edges were smeared. One more bath and Joe Cool's tattoo would disappear altogether.

"Sure," the attendant answered. "Those seats are empty, help yourself."

J.T.'s heart jumped up to his throat. Lowering his feet to the floor, he pressed his body against the window.

"Good." A grin spread across the boy's tanned face. "My sister's up there hogging the window. I was about to kill her."

The woman laughed. "Good idea to put some distance between the two of you instead."

Holy crap, the kid wanted the window. No way could J.T. slip past him. Joe Cool had the aisle blocked. If he could move into the center seat maybe he could lift his feet onto the edge of it and scrunch up enough so that the boy would get past him without incident. He started to move but the kid stepped in.

Paralyzed, J.T. watched the kid pause in front of the aisle seat to juggle a CD player, headphones, and a paperback book. Willing his hand to move, J.T. reached over the seat in front of him and shook Rosy's shoulder.

She looked back just as the boy placed his paraphernalia in the empty seat by the aisle and turned toward the window.

"Wait!" Rosy squeaked.

The boy's chin lifted and, before J.T. could expel his held breath, she appeared in the aisle beside the young man. "Could you help me?" she asked.

The kid flattened a hand to his chest. "Me?"

"Yes. With my bag. It's in the overhead compartment." She smiled, her gaze lifting. "If you could get it down for me . . ."

"Sure. Whatever." Joe Cool wrinkled his nose and

shrugged. "But I'm even shorter than you are."

Wincing, Rosy grasped hold of her shoulder. "Arthritis. It's such a hindrance. Unfortunately, some day you'll probably understand." She gestured him to her with a nod of her head. "Come here. You can stand on the edge of my seat."

What a woman, J.T. thought. Not only good looking but quick thinking, too. He waited for Joe Cool to slip out into the aisle, but instead, the kid stepped onto the seat at the end of their row, leaned over and reached up.

"Oh, you'll fall," Rosy said. "You should use my seat so you won't have to reach."

"I can do it from here," the boy said. "It's easy." The door to the bin opened and a second later a blue tote bag dangled down. "This one?"

"Yes. That's it." Brows puckered, Rosy scanned the seats where J.T. sat then reached up and took the bag from the boy's lowered hand. "Thanks."

"No problem." Joe Cool closed the bin and jumped down.

"I could, um, use some company," Rosy said. "Would you like to sit up here with me? We can talk." She glanced down at the open CD player. "I see you like Lil' Bow Wow. She's one of my favorites, as well. Such a cute little singing dog."

The kid recoiled slightly as if Rosy were one of those strangers his parents had undoubtedly warned him to avoid. "Lil' Bow Wow's a guy. A human one." He stepped out of the aisle and toward J.T. "Thanks, but I'll sit here."

Rosy gave a nervous laugh as the young man dove full speed ahead for the window seat.

Everything seemed to move in slow motion except J.T.'s mind. A memory raced through it, an old Steve Martin routine about thinking small, or being small, or feeling small. Muscles clenched and gritting his teeth, J.T.

braced himself for the boy's landing while focusing on Rosy's pale face and round, staring eyes.

"Whoa!" The kid grabbed the edge of the seat with his left hand and slapped the window with his right palm. He looked down at his lap. "Whoa," he whispered. Slowly, he removed his hand from the window and reached down to probe the space between his thigh and the chair.

J.T. felt a finger poke his leg.

The kid shot to his feet and stepped off to one side. He stared, wide-eyed, at the chair where J.T. sat. "Did you see that?"

Rosy opened her mouth, then clamped it shut and shook her head.

Joe Cool took another side step toward the aisle, his gaze returning to the window seat. "Ma'am!" he called out to the flight attendant, his voice an octave higher than before. "Ma'am!"

"Please," J.T. whispered, the single word leaving his mouth before he could consider the consequences. If the boy insisted that the flight attendant or anyone else on the plane feel what he'd felt in the chair, J.T. couldn't imagine what might happen. "I won't hurt you. Please don't give me away."

The boy froze. His mouth dropped open. J.T. followed the shift of his gaze to the book that lay in the seat beside him. *True Accounts of the Supernatural.*

"Is something wrong?"

J.T. looked up at the flight attendant who now stood beside Rosy.

"He's . . . a . . . thirsty," Rosy stammered. "And hungry." She blinked repeatedly.

The young woman touched the boy's shoulder and frowned.

Grinning, Joe Cool glanced back at her. "I'm thirsty and hungry."

"I'm about to start serving. If you'll just have a seat and buckle up, it won't be a minute." She turned to Rosy. "You, too, please."

Nodding, Rosy did as she was told.

The boy picked up his book, sat in the center seat beside J.T., and buckled the belt. He waited until the flight attendant left, then opened the book, held it up to his face, and turned toward J.T. His tongue darted out across his upper lip. "Are you a . . ." He swallowed. "Are you a ghost?" he whispered.

J.T. spotted Rosy peeking back at them through the crack between two of the seats ahead. "No, I'm not a ghost," he whispered. "I'm invisible."

"Awesome." A slow grin lifted one corner of the boy's mouth. "I knew it. I *knew* stuff like this could happen. Just wait until I tell my sister. We'll see who's the dope now."

"What's your name?"

"Artie." He lowered the book, leaned over and glanced up the aisle, first in front of them, then behind. When he saw that the coast was clear, he lifted the book to his face again. "After my grandfather. My parents doomed me for life just to get on his good side. And he's not even my real granddad. My step dad married my mom even though she was having some other guy's kid. That's me. Grandfather's got a shitload of money. That's what my dad says. He's not very nice, though. I don't like him. My granddad, I mean, not my dad. He's nice." He drew a quick breath. "How'd you get invisible?"

J.T. couldn't even begin to digest all the kid had just told him. "It's a long story. But you can't tell anyone about me, Artie. Not even your sister. You have to promise, okay? It has to be our secret."

Artie chewed on his lower lip and frowned. "How come?"

J.T. tried to think what might have swayed him at age

ten. "I'm on a mission, Artie. And now you're a part of it. A lot of people's lives are at stake. Your silence is crucial to my success."

Artie quit chewing his lip. His eyes widened. "Awesome," he whispered. "I won't tell." He looked over the top of his book to the place where Rosy peeked. "Does the lady know?"

"Yes, she knows."

"Can I . . ." J.T. could hear the boy's rapid breathing, could see his chest rising and falling with it. "Can I touch you?"

"Sure. Lift your hand and I'll take it in mine."

Artie's hand shook as he raised it a foot off his lap. J.T. clasped his fingers and gave it a shake. "Whoa." An amazed smile spread across the boy's face.

"I'm J.T., Artie. We have to be careful, okay? Don't do anything to give me away. Adults are weird about this sort of thing."

"Are you—"

"Shhh." J.T. dropped his hand. "The flight attendant."

"What would you like to drink, young man?" She handed Artie a package of peanuts.

Placing his book on the empty aisle seat beside him, he cocked one brow and gave her a crooked grin. "I'll have a beer."

"Nice try, Slick. How about a root beer?"

He scowled. "Whatever."

She reached for a can, popped the top, and started to pour.

"Could I have two cans? And another bag of peanuts?"

"You are hungry and thirsty."

Artie lowered his tray table and the attendant put everything onto it, then moved on down the aisle. The boy lowered J.T.'s tray table, too. He put the extra peanuts and can of root beer on it. "I got these for you," he

150

whispered. "I'll keep a look out so you can eat 'em."

"Thanks. Where you headed, Artie?"

"To Las Vegas. For a big party my mom and dad go to every year." He popped a handful of peanuts into his mouth. "My dad's boss's birthday. My grandfather will be there, too. They work for the same guy only my dad works in the Houston division. He's sort of my great-uncle. Their boss, I mean. I don't like him, either." The kid leaned over and glanced down the aisle. "You can eat if you want. Nobody's coming."

Watching the delighted look of awe on the boy's face, J.T. lifted the root beer can and popped the top.

"Awesome," Artie whispered as J.T. drank. "I thought I'd be able to see the root beer going down inside you, but I can't." He stared another minute then asked, "Are you a spy like James Bond? Is your mission international espionage?"

"Not international exactly, but I guess it is a sort of espionage."

"How will I know if you pull it off?"

"Well, I don't know, Artie. Let's see. What if I find a way to get in touch with you?" That seemed fair in exchange for Artie keeping his mouth shut. "Give me your address before we land and I'll send you something to let you know I succeeded. Something you'll know is from me."

Artie tossed more peanuts into his mouth, his eyes lighting up. "How about a bag of peanuts?"

"A bag of peanuts it is."

Rosy looked back at them over the top of her seat. "Someone's coming."

J.T. set down the can then patted Artie's arm. "Shhh."

A brittle little old woman in dark glasses and an old-fashioned hat that covered her hair shuffled down the aisle toward the restroom. Pausing alongside Artie, she glanced back at Rosy's row of seats and muttered something under her breath.

J.T.'s nose started itching. Her perfume smelled familiar. Turning toward the window, he reached up and pinched his nostrils together. He needed to sneeze. Honeysuckle. The old lady smelled just like the honeysuckle in—

Holy—J.T. whipped around, stretched, looked over the back of the seat. The bathroom door closed.

"That old lady . . ." Artie wrinkled his nose. "She smells like the candles my sister always burns."

"I was thinking she smelled like flowers," J.T. whispered, turning back around in his seat and tapping his foot against the floor of the plane. Surely his mind was playing tricks on him. But just to be sure, he'd take another look when the woman came out.

A few minutes later, the old woman shuffled down the aisle again, trailing the mixed scents of honeysuckle and tobacco behind her. From beneath the edge of her awful hat, he spied a stray strand of hair. *Purple.*

J.T. sneezed.

"Bless you," she said, glancing back at Artie.

The boy sniffed. "Thanks," he said, sounding congested. When the old woman looked away, he winked and grinned in J.T.'s direction.

"Good job," J.T. whispered, leaning toward the seats in front of them to tap Rosy on the shoulder. When she peered back he whispered, "Go to the restroom. I'll be right behind you."

Rosy didn't complicate matters by bombarding him with questions like a lot of women might. That was one more thing he liked about her.

"Psst, Artie."

"Yeah."

"Let me by. I'm going to the restroom."

"You're not ditching me, are you?"

"Are you kidding? We're partners."

When Rosy passed them, J.T. scooted past Artie and followed. She stepped into the restroom and he stepped in behind her, then closed the door.

She frowned at his shoulder. "What's the matter?"

"You know that old woman sitting a few rows up from you?"

"Yes, why?" She wrinkled her nose. "It smells like cigarettes in here."

"Mrs. Moody probably snuck a smoke."

"Mrs. Moody?"

"I won't swear to it, but I think she might be the old woman who was in here right before us."

"You're kidding me. That's Wanda?"

"Maybe. It seems far-fetched that she'd go to such great lengths as to follow us to Vegas, but Pop did tell me her behavior bordered on outrageous these days. Seems she disappears for days at a time. And I saw a piece of her hair sticking out from under the hat she's wearing."

"Purple?"

"Yeah."

Rosy's eyes widened. She blew out a noisy breath.

"If it is her, you can safely bet she'll cause problems if we don't lose her at the Vegas airport."

The plane dipped and Rosy stumbled against him. J.T. took advantage of the opportunity to wrap his arms around her.

"Sorry about that." She looked up then tried to step away but he linked his fingers together at the base of her spine and drew her closer.

Her body stiffened. "You and your young friend have been whispering for the past ten minutes. You could've told me about Wanda without the two of us coming in here."

"You're right, I could have."

"Then why didn't you?"

The plane surged to one side. J.T. fell back against the door, bringing her with him. Her breasts pressed into his chest. Smiling, J.T. looked down into her startled upturned face. "Maybe I was hoping for turbulence."

He kissed her slowly, sliding one hand up her back and into her hair, coaxing the tension from her body little by little with his mouth until she finally relaxed, closed her eyes, and kissed him back. She tasted like wintergreen breath mints. She smelled like baby powder. She felt like—

A knock sounded on the door. Rosy jumped.

"Damn," J.T. muttered. "Hold that thought." Turning, he slid the lock and opened the door.

Artie stood just outside. He scanned the small restroom, his gaze finally settling on Rosy. "Is he in here?"

Rosy's face looked flushed, her hair even messier than usual, her lips puffy. Nodding, she answered, "Yes, he's here. But he's going back to sit with you now." Smoothing her shirt with one hand, her hair with the other, she stepped toward the door. "And he'll remain with you for the rest of the flight . . . or else."

Chapter Eleven

After Roselyn gave the cab driver the address to the dance studio, he pulled away from the curb in front of the Vegas airport. She looked out the back window. Just moments before, she'd watched the old woman from the plane climb into another cab behind them. It seemed paranoid to think Wanda might've followed them, but now that J.T. had placed the idea in her mind, Roselyn couldn't get it out.

She turned back to the driver. "I'll pay you an extra twenty dollars if you can lose the cab that's following us."

A pair of dark eyes peered back at her through the rearview mirror. "Sure, Ma'am. That's Pete Sullivan. I can outdrive him blindfolded." He chuckled. "Leaving ol' Pete in the dust'll be gravy."

He wove his way deftly around cars and jaywalkers, then hit the accelerator when they reached the main road. Roselyn caught her breath, dug her fingertips into the plastic seat cover to keep from sliding across it.

"You could've saved yourself the twenty bucks," J.T. whispered, then cursed under his breath. "The guy would've done this for free. He's getting a rush out of it."

They passed a Mazda, then cut in front of an SUV just in time to take the next exit.

The driver laughed. "That ought to do it."

"I think I'd rather deal with Wanda than die in the back of this cab," J.T. whispered.

"What's that?" The driver glanced over his shoulder. "I didn't hear what you said."

"Oh, nothing." Roselyn gave a jittery laugh. "Just talking to myself. An embarrassing habit of mine, I'm afraid."

Without slowing down, the cab made a sharp right at the next intersection, then another quick left down an alleyway. "Woo-hoo! See ya later, sucker." The driver looked over his shoulder, out the back window, then back at the road. "I hope you don't mind the scenic route, ma'am. Might be a little bumpy but it'll get us where we're going."

Roselyn braced a hand against the door for support. "Apparently your friend Pete is aware of that fact, as well. He just turned in behind us."

"That sorry so and so." The cab shot forward even faster than before.

J.T. slid into Roselyn as they whipped around another corner and onto a main street. "You're going to freaking kill somebody."

"Who said that?"

Roselyn met the driver's gaze in the mirror. "I did, of course."

"What's wrong with your voice? You sounded like a man."

She pressed a hand to her throat. "Laryngitis. It comes and goes."

Ten minutes later, they screeched to a stop in front of All That Jazz, the dance studio Roselyn's mother owned with Barb and Sully. Located just five minutes from the Strip, the street was alive with traffic and noise and people.

"Here you go," the driver said. "Safe and sound and all alone."

Roselyn fumbled inside her purse. Her adrenaline still soared from the ride and her hand shook as she handed the fare plus another twenty across to the driver. "Well . . . thank you. You certainly gave me my money's worth."

One corner of his mouth curved up. "I aim to please."

He met her outside, took the bags from the trunk, then climbed back behind the wheel and drove away.

"It's a good thing I didn't eat much breakfast this morning," J.T. said.

Roselyn's knees felt like rubber. "At least now we don't have to worry about Wanda." She shifted her gaze to the big window that stretched across the front of the studio, a rush of excitement flooding through her at the sight of the dancers rehearsing inside.

"Your mother's place?"

"Yes." Smiling, she reached for the bags. "I'm home."

Roselyn didn't miss the disturbed glances of the people passing by on the sidewalk who obviously thought she was talking to herself. She was pleased to discover she no longer cared if they dubbed her crazy. If any of them recognized her, which she doubted, they would simply assume that Darla Peabody's oddball daughter was back for a visit. Poor girl. So lonely. Always was a strange one. Shouldn't surprise anyone that she talked to herself now.

"Who's the gorgeous redhead leading the class?"

"That's Barb. And in case you have any ideas, she was wearing silk stockings when you were still in diapers."

He gave a long, low whistle. "No offense. I just didn't picture her as being such a knockout, that's all."

"None taken." Roselyn laughed. "But you haven't seen anything yet. Wait until you meet my mother."

"If she looks anything like her daughter, I'm in trouble. I'm not sure I can behave myself surrounded by so many good-looking women."

Smirking, Roselyn started for the door. "No need to flatter me, J.T. I grew up the ugly duckling in a lake of swans. I'm quite used to it."

"I wasn't flattering you, just speaking the truth." She felt his fingers encircle her wrist. "Wait a minute. I didn't know dance studios had bouncers. Who's the bruiser?"

Again, Roselyn shifted her attention to the scene behind the window. "Oh my word, look at Sully! He's lost so much weight!"

"You're kidding? That man must weigh at least two-fifty."

Impatient to see Barb and Sully, Roselyn started for the door again, but the grip around her wrist tightened. J.T. lead her around to the side of the building. "What's the matter?" she asked. "Sully won't be able to see you. Even if he could, he doesn't bite. He's gentle as a kitten."

"Looks more like a close relative of Mrs. Moody's bulldog to me. But it's not his teeth I'm worried about, it's his vocal cords. Barb's, too. Are you planning to let them in on our little secret?"

"I have to tell Barb. I already discussed it vaguely with her on the telephone." She frowned. "And I don't know how we'd hide you from Sully even if I wanted to. Not that I'd planned for you to stay with him. It's just that he's always around."

"Where am I staying? At Barb's?"

"Why would you stay with Barb?" Baffled, Roselyn

looked up and blinked. "She only has one bedroom."

"That's fine by me."

She heard the teasing note in his voice and hoped the twinge of jealousy she felt didn't show on her face. "I'm sure of that. In case you didn't know it, you have quite the reputation as a rascal around Pecan Grove. But I'm afraid it wouldn't be fine with Sully if you stayed with Barb. Even puppy dogs have sharp teeth."

"I don't want to get on Sully's bad side, that's for sure." He chuckled. "A rascal, huh? I haven't heard that word lately."

"That's how Miss Mullins described you."

"Miss Mullins?"

"The lady who owns the dry cleaners at Tenth and Vine."

"Oh, Betty." He chuckled. "Is she still around? She must be at least eighty by now."

"Eighty-two. But she blushed and giggled like a fourteen-year-old girl when she mentioned your name."

"She hasn't been able to look me in the eye without blushing since she saw me streak naked through the library during her poetry group meeting back in my wild and crazy days."

"You streaked through the library?"

"Sure did. Right in the middle of her recitation of Oscar Wilde's 'We are Made One with What We Touch and See.' "

"Interesting. No wonder Miss Mullins turns beet red when your name comes up."

"Betty," he corrected. "She lets me call her Betty."

"Oh, excuse me," Roselyn said sarcastically, rolling her eyes.

"Anyway," J.T. continued, "I was kidding you about staying with Barb." His hands skimmed up her arms. "Where you stay, I stay. We're partners in this. Besides, I get nervous when you aren't around."

His admission both surprised and pleased her and, despite the hundred-degree heat, goose bumps scattered across her skin. "We can trust Barb and Sully, if that's what you're worried about," she said, anxious to return the subject to safer territory. "They're my family."

"I'm sure they wouldn't intentionally do anything to give us away, but what about unintentionally? Can they remember to keep their mouths shut?"

She squared her shoulders and scowled. "Of course they can. Sully may look like a Neanderthal but he does have a brain and so does Barb. My mother, too, for that matter."

"I didn't mean to imply that they didn't."

"Good. Because, unlike you, I treat my family with respect, and I expect you to do the same."

She reached for the bags again and, juggling and tugging, started for the front of the building. After only two steps, she paused and looked back to where they'd been standing. "I'm sorry. That comment was uncalled for." She had taken his words and twisted them into something nasty because she wanted to be angry with him. Anger, she could deal with. Desire was another matter altogether. She feared the needs he stirred in her. Her ego would only remain safe if she kept those feelings buried.

When J.T. didn't respond, she started off again.

"Wait."

Roselyn felt his hands on her shoulders and turned.

"Apology accepted," he said.

As if to compensate for not being able to see him, her other senses intensified. She was hyper aware of his scent, the solid warmth of his body beneath her fingertips, the sigh of his breath on her ear.

J.T. took the bags from her, set them down, then backed her up against the wall of the building, out of sight of anyone who might pass by. "In case you're wondering, this isn't a knee-jerk reaction." His voice was a smooth low rumble, soft and seductive as velvet. "I planned this kiss. I've been imagining it and anticipating it ever since our encounter in the airplane restroom."

Just this once, she told herself as his mouth covered hers, just this once she would allow herself to give in to her needs, to enjoy the moment without worrying about the aftermath. Melting into him, she closed her eyes, slowly ran her hands up his chest, over his shoulders to encircle his neck. Before she knew what was happening, he'd coaxed her lips apart with his. His tongue swept across hers . . . once . . . twice . . . and in that instant she forgot she was in an alley with a man she'd never seen except in pictures, forgot that people walked by not five feet away, forgot the promise she'd made to herself to never lose control like this again. The honks and squeals of traffic on the street, the talk and laughter of pedestrians on the nearby sidewalk, faded to the background, drowned out by the rush of blood in her ears, the pounding of her pulse.

J.T.'s hands moved down to sculpt her bottom. She lifted her knee, skimmed it up his leg, trying to get closer to him, feeling as if she would never get close enough.

A strange sound filtered through the fog in her brain, one that didn't fit with the others. A hiccup . . . a slurred exclamation. Roselyn tumbled back into reality with a start. Her eyes sprang open. She dragged her mouth away from J.T.'s.

A dirty, scraggly haired old man clasping a bottle in a paper sack stood in the center of the alley staring at her through bleary eyes. He lifted the bottle to his mouth, started to take a drink, then lowered it. It slipped from his fingers and fell to the ground at his feet.

Roselyn turned toward J.T. and came face-to-face with a brick wall. Her arms seemed to encircle nothing, her lifted leg seemed only supported by air. Lowering her arms and foot, she pushed away from J.T. abruptly. She faced the street person again in time to see him rub his watery eyes with dingy, cracked knuckles, back up a step, then grin.

Grabbing the suitcases and bags, Roselyn started for the front of the building.

J.T. slipped through the door before it closed. He followed Rosy down a narrow hallway, his attention on the scantily dressed female dancers in the glassed-off room on their left. He decided the room must be soundproofed because he couldn't hear any music, though he felt it pulsing and vibrating the floor beneath his feet. And while Barb's mouth moved as if she were shouting instructions to her students, he couldn't hear her, either.

At the end of the hall Rosy stopped and tapped on a door that read Office.

"It's open," called a raspy, deep voice from the other side.

She turned the knob, pulled the door open, stepped in.

The man she'd called Sully stood in front of a cluttered desk, his back to the door. He glanced over his shoulder. "Well, son of a bitch! If it ain't my lucky day!"

J.T. stepped in behind Roselyn and made his way to a chair in the corner where he hoped he'd be out of the way. He sat and watched as Roselyn all but dropped the bags and dove into the giant man's arms. J.T. stared straight at Sully's delighted face. The man's eyelids consisted of a droopy flap of skin that hung from beneath his bushy brows to the tips of his lashes. Deep grooves lined his cheeks. He wore a poorly fitted beige suit, a silky maroon shirt open just enough to expose an abundance of chest hair and at least three gold chains around his thick neck.

"Sully Tucker." Rosy stepped back. "Oh how I've missed you."

"You, too, little girl, you, too."

She took his hands and looked him up and down. "What have you done to yourself? You look wonderful."

"Must be that miserable diet Barb put me on. It's cruel and unusual punishment, I'm telling you. Can't even have a nightcap without the woman bitching at me, pardon my French." He dropped one of her hands and tapped his chest. "Had a little scare with my ticker a couple months back. She's been the food Gestapo ever since."

"What? You had a heart attack and no one told me?"

"Not a heart attack, just a little blip on the radar screen. Didn't see any sense in working you up. Doc just said I gotta start living right or risk an early funeral. I'm not sure doin' without scotch and pasta is any better than being dead but—"

"But I want you around for a long time to come so you're gonna quit complaining and do as I say," Barb said as she strode into the room, her toned, freckled body glistening with perspiration. She stopped and shrieked when she caught sight of Rosy. "You're here!" Barb grabbed her. "Your mother will give me the silent treatment for a week when she finds out I knew and didn't tell her."

"She's not here, is she?" Rosy asked, stepping out of the older woman's embrace.

"No, but she's on her way. I tried to stall her but you know how Darla is when she's focused on something. She has an appointment with the banker in the morning to try to refinance our loan on this building and she's getting some figures together."

"We'll have to hurry then. I want to discuss my problem and how I might best present it to her."

"You mean whatever it is that's going on with Tony Domani?" Barb asked.

"Yes."

"What's that asshole up to now?" Sully growled.

"I'll explain everything soon enough," Rosy said.

"And I want to introduce you to a friend of mine. Professor Drake's son. He flew out with me."

Barb grabbed the end of the towel draped over her shoulder and dabbed her forehead. "Oh, really? When will he be here?"

Rosy looked left, then right. She sniffed. "He's already here."

Sully frowned. "What's he doing? Talking to one of the dancers?"

"I don't believe so, Sully." Rosy smiled. "I assure you that after I give you a little more background on the matter at hand, he'll make himself known."

Barb's brows lifted. "The tall, dark, and mysterious type, is he?"

"Tall and dark, yes. Or so I've been told. But not so mysterious." One corner of her mouth quirked up as she scanned the room. "He's really quite transparent."

J.T. smiled. Rosy seemed more relaxed here with the people she loved. He recalled how she'd dropped all her barriers and kissed him in the alley. He wanted to see more of this side of her, this less restrained, more earthy Rosy he'd first caught a glimpse of when she'd danced in front of her bedroom mirror.

"I can't wait to meet him," Barb said. Her chin lifted and she glanced toward the door. "I think your mother's already here. I heard someone come in."

"Barb!" a woman's voice called out. "Sully! I'm about to lose my mind. Do you know where—"

"Hi Mama."

"Oh, my lord!"

Darla Peabody was an older, more voluptuous, more polished version of Rosy. More polished, literally. Her lips were polished a pale pink, her fingernails and toenails a slightly more vibrant shade. Her tanned shoulders looked as if she'd buffed them with baby oil. She dropped her purse on the floor and pulled her daughter into her arms. "Why didn't you tell me you were coming?"

"I wanted to surprise you."

"Well, you did that, all right." Darla stepped back and glared first at Barb, then at Sully. "Did you two know about this?"

Sully lifted both hands. "Don't look at me."

Barb winced. "I swore to keep my trap shut, Darla."

"Since when did you start keeping promises?" She hugged Rosy again, then released her, a worried look passing over her face. "Okay, what's up? What are you doing here? Are you in trouble?"

"Does something have to be wrong for me to come visit my family?"

"Yes," they all replied in unison.

"It would take something pretty drastic to drag you away from whatever that secret project is you've been working on for the past two years," Darla said.

"As a matter of fact," Rosy wrapped an arm around her mother's shoulders and started toward the chair where J.T. sat, "the reason I'm here happens to have everything to do with the project." She nodded toward the chair. "You might want to sit down. What I'm about to tell you is pretty dizzying. You, too, Barb. Find a chair or lean on Sully."

When it appeared Darla Peabody was going to follow her daughter's advice, J.T. cleared his throat. "I wouldn't do that if I were you."

Darla gasped and stepped in front of Rosy. "What—"

"Who was that?" Sully asked, his droopy eyes suddenly alert.

Barb took Sully's hand. "Rosebud . . . ? What's going on?"

Rosy moved around in front of her mother and stared at the chair. "So there you are."

"There who is?" Darla whispered, her eyes wide.

"Mom . . . Barb . . . Sully," Rosy looked at each one of them in turn. "The project I've been working on with the professor for the past two years has been a continuation of one he started more than thirty years ago. It's a machine called an electromagnetic refractor. When an object is placed inside of it, the refractor generates an intense magnetic field. The—"

"Rosy," J.T. interrupted, causing the three pairs of eyes staring in his direction to grow to the size of saucers. "Why don't we just put it in layman's language?" He stood. "Simply put, the refractor makes things invisible. People, too, unfortunately."

"Mom . . . Barb . . . Sully," Rosy repeated, "I'd like you to meet J.T. Drake, Professor Drake's son."

J.T. reached for Darla Peabody's hand, pausing when a loud crash reverberated behind her. As everyone in the room turned toward the sound, he glanced over their shoulders.

All two hundred and fifty pounds of Sully Tucker lay sprawled on the floor at Barb's feet.

"Mama, put Gomez out, would you?" Roselyn said, when the cat clawed at the place where J.T. sat and hissed for at least the tenth time. "Considering the state he's in, I'm afraid to pick him up."

"That makes two of us," J.T. said.

They all sat around the coffee table in her mother's apartment living room eating take-out Chinese food.

Barb looked up from her plate as Darla crossed the room to grab the cat. "That's it, then," she said. "Tomorrow morning you and Rosebud will pay Tony Domani a little visit. You, too, of course, J.T, but they'll skip your introduction."

Roselyn watched her mother closely for a reaction as she carried the cat to the door. Darla had said little throughout the conversation. "Do you think Mr. Domani would really consider hiring me to work in his office, Mama? I'm not the least bit organized when it comes to administrative matters. My checkbook never balances and my filing system is practically nonexistent, everything goes into the same manila folder."

"He doesn't need to know that," Barb said. "It won't matter anyway. Tony'll jump at the chance to hire you if he thinks it'll earn him points with your mother. If not as an office assistant then maybe as a bartender or a hostess."

"Not as a hostess," Darla said firmly, closing the door and returning to the sofa. "She's not wearing any skimpy little hostess outfit. I did my time in a thong so my daughter wouldn't have to. Anyway, I'm not so sure he'll take her on, Barb. And I'm not so sure it's a good idea that he does. I can handle Tony, but Roselyn doesn't know the first thing about a man like—"

"Mama, please. I know more than you think. Do you really believe I was blind and deaf during all that time I spent backstage as a child?"

Her mother's brow puckered. "I regret that, baby, but it couldn't be helped. I tried to shield you the best I could."

"You did a good job of it, but I couldn't help but pick up a thing or two." Roselyn smiled. "Don't worry. I'm not completely warped by the experience."

"Darla, Tony's been chomping at the bit for another chance at you ever since you walked out his door," Barb said. "What is it he used to call you?"

Roselyn saw her mother cringe. "Sweet Pea," Darla said, sounding disgusted.

"That's right. You were probably the only woman in Vegas who ever turned down a chance to sleep in his bed and that hurt his overinflated ego. Just make it clear that you and Roselyn are a package deal. He hires you, he gets her, too."

"I don't like it any more than Darla does," Sully grumbled.

Barb took his hand and gave it a pat. "Don't worry, honey bunch. Darla's just gonna lead him on a little."

"Surely there's another way." Using her chopsticks, Roselyn's mother picked at the Moo Goo Gai Pan on her paper plate. "Tony's temper is unpredictable, and Reneau is just as bad. I don't want you any where near them, Roselyn. He could get angry over the least little thing and hit you or rape you or worse. As a matter of fact, I don't like the idea of you working anywhere on the strip or even close to it. I—"

"Oh, lock your doors, everybody," Barb interrupted, lifting her gaze to the ceiling. "Darla's about to remind us all that it's a big mean ugly world out there and everyone in it is out to get us."

Darla's jaw clenched. "Well it's true."

"Don't worry about me, Mama." Roselyn took her mother's hand. "It's not as if I'm going to be alone with the man."

"I'll be right there with both of you, Miss Peabody," J.T. said. "Domani just won't know it. Neither will Reneau."

At the sound of J.T.'s voice, Sully jumped and dropped his chopsticks. "Son of a—" He scrubbed a hand across his face. "I forget you're here sometimes."

"Sorry I scared you, Sully," J.T. said. His chopsticks rose into the air, lifting a chunk of chicken along with them.

"Well, I think we're jumping the gun," Darla said. "Tomorrow's too soon to meet with Tony. We're not prepared. I'll need one heck of a sob story to get him to give in and hire Roselyn to work in his office. And in case that doesn't work, it wouldn't hurt to have a backup plan."

Barb nibbled her lower lip. "Doesn't Domani have a

big bash every year about this time, or is that someone else I'm thinking of?"

Darla nodded. "It's Tony. He celebrates his birthday every year in his penthouse apartment. It's quite a shindig. I worked it once. That's how I first met him, before I hired on with him full time."

"So he doesn't pull staff from his clubs to work the party?" J.T. asked.

"He didn't like to leave the clubs shorthanded so he hired outside help for the party," Darla told them.

Sully leaned forward. "How many people are we talking about?"

"Three or four hostesses," Darla said. "A couple of bartenders and a bouncer or two."

Barb brushed a crumb from the front of Sully's silky shirt. "What are you thinking, honey bunch?"

He wiped his mouth with a napkin. "I could ask around. Find out who the s.o.b.'s hired and how much he's paying them. We have some money put aside at the studio for a rainy day. I think it'd be more than enough to convince three hostesses and a bouncer to get sick or have a family emergency or something else that'd make them have to bow out on Domani at the last minute."

It was a wonderful idea. Still, it only added another layer to the guilt already piled high and heavy on Roselyn's shoulders. Involving her family was bad enough; taking their money would be unbearable. "But it's your rainy day fund."

"Little girl," Sully said, "I'd say you and J.T. and his daddy are caught smack in the middle of a monsoon. We're family. If you drown, so do the rest of us."

Tears of gratitude sprang to Roselyn's eyes when her mother and Barb not only agreed with Sully's statement, but also confirmed his offer.

"I can't thank the three of you enough," J.T. said. "I'll see to it you're repaid."

Barb waved away any more talk about loans. "So, you can wait another day while Sully does his thing before approaching Domani?" she asked.

"I don't know why not." J.T. lifted another bite to his mouth. "At this point, all I have is time."

"Well . . ." Barb said, shaking her head at the sight of J.T.'s floating chopsticks, "Tomorrow's a busy day for all of us. I'll teach your class for you and visit the banker, Darla. That way you'll have extra time to catch up and visit with Roselyn." Standing, she turned to Sully and reached out a hand. "Ready?"

"Yeah." With his gaze also fixed on J.T.'s chopsticks, Sully took her hand and stood, too.

"J.T.," Barb said, "meeting you has definitely been the most interesting thing that's ever happened to me."

"I'll take that as a compliment, Barb. And Sully, I hope that knot on your head's feeling better. You hit the floor hard."

Sully blushed and cleared his throat. "First time that's ever happened."

Chapter Twelve

A pounding at the front door roused Hershel from a fitful sleep. Snatching his robe from the bedpost, he slipped it on and hurried into the living room. He'd forgotten to close the curtains before retiring last night. Outside the window, he saw that the sun was just now rising.

The banging increased.

"Just a moment!" Hershel called out. "I'm on my way." When he reached the door, he started to turn the deadbolt, then paused. "Who's there?"

"It's me . . . Wanda."

Expecting anything, Hershel unlocked the door and pulled it open. "Wanda . . . what in heaven's name? Come in, come in. Is something wrong?"

She held her arms in front of her body as though cradling a baby. One penciled brow arched above the crooked frame of her glasses. Hershel found himself wondering if the woman ever removed her makeup.

After staring him down for a good thirty seconds,

Wanda's bunny slippers finally passed over the threshold. She turned to face him. "We'll see who's the old fool now, Hershel Drake." She raised her cradled arms. "Look what I caught."

Hershel looked, but didn't see anything. He rubbed his eyes. "I'm sorry . . . I don't see—"

"Of course you don't see," Wanda snapped. "It's Curly. He's invisible, just like I told you. Here." She stepped closer. "See for yourself."

Before he could protest, Wanda reached out to transfer what she held in her arms into his. He heard a hacking wheeze just before a soft bundle of fluff brushed his wrist and a light but undeniable weight pressed against his forearms. "Dear heaven."

"What happened to Curly has nothing a'tall to do with Heaven, I'll promise you that. I followed that witch friend of yours all the way to Las Vegas yesterday."

Hershel came fully awake. "You did what?"

"I bird-dogged the two of you to the airport, found out where she was headed, then bought myself a ticket and followed her there. I don't know what she's concocted to convince you otherwise, but whatever that woman's got you wrapped up in is no good, I tell you, no good a'tall. I caught her talking to herself more times than I can count. Would of found out more, but she lost me at the Vegas airport. Took off like a bat outta hell. If she's so innocent, why would she run like that, Hershel? Answer me that if you can."

Weary with the whole ordeal, Hershel sighed. "I'm sure I don't know."

"Doesn't surprise me. You can't explain her weird behavior anymore than you can explain what she did to Curly. Well, I can explain it. The woman's a witch, I tell you. And I, for one, don't plan to let her get away with tarnishing our town. Curly and me, we're going to the university later today. I'm going to meet with Doctor

Peabody's superior. Then we'll take ourselves a little trip to the police station."

Hershel's heart dropped. He imagined nationwide news reports, imagined Anthony Domani or Bartholomew Reneau hearing them. "No, Wanda, you're not going to do that."

Her eyes widened. "Says who?"

"Says me."

For the first time he could remember, his neighbor seemed speechless. Hershel sincerely regretted the condition was only temporary.

Wanda grabbed Curly from his arms. "And just how do you plan to stop me?"

"I haven't been completely honest with you. You see, I do know why it appeared to you as if Doctor Peabody was talking to herself and why she ran from you at the airport."

She blinked. "You do?"

"Yes. And I also know what happened to Curly."

She blinked again. "Tell me then."

"Better yet, I'll show you. Let's go down to the basement." He turned and took a step then glanced over his shoulder.

Wanda started to follow him, then hesitated. "Oh, no you don't, Hershel Drake. That woman really did brainwash you, didn't she? You're planning to get me down there and lock me away so I can't expose her." She backed toward the door.

Hershel went after her. "Now Wanda—"

"Stay away from me, Hershel, I'll scream."

Panic streaked through him. The situation was getting entirely out of hand. "Wanda . . . for pity's sake," he said as he reached out to calm her.

She flinched. "Don't touch me!" Stumbling backward, she lunged for the door. "Help!" she screamed. "Someone help me!"

Alarmed by her hysterics, Hershel followed his instincts. He encircled her wrist with one hand, and then covered her mouth with the other to silence her cries. The invisible poodle hacked and wheezed.

"Wanda, you know me. I would never hurt a fly, much less you. Please let me explain."

After a moment or two, she quit struggling. Hershel lowered the hand he had clasped to her mouth.

She drew a deep breath, then let loose a blood-curdling screech.

Hershel covered her mouth again, appalled by his own actions but at a loss as to what else he might do to stop Wanda from kicking up a fuss. Though the dog nipped at his fingers he didn't pull back. He couldn't let her take that poodle to the authorities and tie this entire incident to him and Roselyn Peabody. He couldn't risk the possibility of Domani catching wind of the situation, no matter how remote that risk might be. Not now when J.T. and Roselyn were right under the man's nose. Hershel *refused* to risk it. He wouldn't. Even if he really did have to lock Wanda Moody in the basement.

The day proved worth the wait. Sully knew just who to talk to in order to get the information they needed about the people who'd been hired to work Anthony Domani's party. Sully also knew what strings to pull to tug those people over to his side. Tomorrow, Rosy and Darla would pay Pop's former benefactor a visit, and J.T. would sit back and listen, unobserved.

That night it was too hot to sleep. J.T. paced the floor of the tiny pink bedroom that had once been Rosy's. No baby dolls here. And, with the exception of one three-foot-wide hairy spider perched in a corner, no collection of stuffed animals, either.

On the shelves lining her walls he touched an old microscope, a bug collection under glass, books about particle physics and quantum mechanics and other scientific topics that only sounded vaguely familiar to him. Centered over the desk beside the bed was a framed certificate proclaiming Roselyn Grace Peabody the winner of her school region's science fair her senior year. To the left of it hung the certificate for first place in the same contest her junior year. To the right, hung the first place certificate for her sophomore year.

On the adjoining wall, stuck to a bulletin board with thumbtacks in no particular order were snapshots. A gangly prepubescent Rosy with a long crooked pony tail, her mouth too big for the rest of her face, standing between her mother and Barb, all three of them in glittery costumes, with feathered plumes in their hair. An even younger Rosy sitting atop Sully's shoulders when the man still had a full head of hair. A teenaged Rosy with serious, almost defensive eyes, sitting in a classroom alongside an older woman who might've been her teacher. No pictures of friends or boyfriends, though. No yellowed homecoming mums. No torn concert ticket stubs.

J.T. paused at the dresser to pick up a bottle of perfume. Apparently Pop wasn't the only parent reluctant to let go of the past. From the looks of Rosy's old room, Darla Peabody suffered the same dread. He twisted off the lid on the bottle and sniffed the contents. The fragrance smelled exotic and spicy, more like something Barb or Darla might dab behind their ears, not Rosy. No wonder the bottle was full. J.T. felt a tickle in his nose as he recapped the bottle and sat it back on the dresser. The tickle intensified. He should've known better than to sniff that perfume. He never could tell what might set off his allergies.

When he sneezed, he thought he caught a glimpse of someone in the mirror. J.T. glanced behind him, but the bedroom door was closed, the room empty.

He slipped out into the hallway, telling himself he'd lost his mind to even consider that a woman like Rosy might want to be with a man like him, telling himself it would never work anyway. They were too different. Rosy had the same intellect and interests as Pop. J.T. had never understood any of it and had, long ago, given up trying to do so. Besides that, Pop had never found J.T., or J.T.'s interests, to be worth his time, so why would Rosy?

He walked quietly past Darla Peabody's bedroom, which tonight she shared with her daughter, then moved into the shadowed living room toward the lamp table, thinking he'd turn on the light so he could make his way into the kitchen for a glass of water. A draft of cool air swirled through the room and flowed over him like a breath of heaven. Wondering where it came from, J.T. reached for the lamp switch, but before he could twist it, a movement on the terrace caught his attention.

Rosy stood out there, her elbows propped on the railing, her head turned slightly to one side so that he could see the profile of her face in the moonlight. She wore a long white sleeveless nightgown that brushed the tops of her bare feet.

J.T. walked toward the sliding glass doors, saw that Rosy had left one open far enough to step through. That explained the draft. For a moment, he stood there and watched her. She looked troubled and so alone. Quietly, he stepped out onto the terrace, forgetting about their differences and the aspects of her intelligence he'd never understand.

The sound of traffic on the street below was as steady as a heartbeat. The city twinkled like a carnival with red, green, and blue lights, and stretches of glowing gold.

After a moment, she turned to face him. "You're here, aren't you?"

"Yes."

She reached out her hand. "Where?"

He took hold of her fingers, felt the sting of a spark.

Rosy drew him up to the railing beside her, then turned back to stare at the sprawling city below. "When I was a child, I wished for a house with a yard and a white picket fence in a quiet neighborhood. I wanted a tree swing and a bicycle to ride up and down the block. I thought all of that would make me normal." She laughed. "Whatever normal is."

J.T. thought of the bike she rode in Pecan Grove rather than driving a car. "I had all of that," he said. "The house, the yard with the picket fence. The paint was peeling, but it was white. And the neighborhood was quiet, at least when I wasn't creating chaos. I even had the tree swing."

She smiled, turned toward him, but looked over his head instead of into his face. "How was it? Having all of that?"

"I wanted out just like you did. I grew up and high-tailed it to the city; you grew up and high-tailed it to the small town I'd escaped."

She was quiet for a moment then said, "I wanted my mom to stay home and bake cookies instead of dancing in the clubs."

"I wanted Pop to coach my Little League team instead of playing mad scientist in the basement."

"I wanted to know my dad," she whispered.

"I wanted to know my mom."

He touched her chin, shifted it so that her eyes were aimed more at his face instead of the top of his head. "It seems we have a lot more in common than I ever guessed, Rosy."

"Yes, I guess we do. Or perhaps all children want something other than what they have when it comes to parents and lifestyles and all of that."

"You're probably right."

She looked back out at the lights. "It sounds crazy, but now that I'm gone, I sometimes miss all of this. I guess it's more a part of me than I thought."

He smoothed the wrinkle between her brows with his fingertip. "You're worried. Why?"

"I'm afraid I won't be able to pull this off."

"The refractor . . . its success means a lot to you."

She sighed. "I've devoted the past two years of my life to it. But it's more than that now. Now that I know what Domani and Reneau did to your mother, what they did to your father." She lifted her hand, pressed her fingers to his cheek as if she could see it. "And you."

Her words tightened the knot in his chest. "I feel the same way. Maybe it's wrong to want revenge, but I do. I want it for her, for Pop. I want it for myself. I can't help but wonder how my life might've been if . . ." He stopped himself. Even if he got his revenge, it wouldn't bring his mother back or erase the loneliness of all the years he'd spent without his father's attention. And like Rosy had suggested, maybe all children wanted what they didn't have.

Rosy lifted her other hand, reached forward tentatively. As a blind person might, she read his features with her fingertips, tracing the ridge of his nose, his lips, his chin. "J.T., what if we don't find the files? What if I can't make the refractor work? If I fail, you'll—"

"You won't fail, Rosy. We won't." Turning his face into her palm, he kissed it. "Hey . . ." He laughed. "This situation I'm in is a crime writer's dream come true. When we pull this off I'll have the story of a lifetime."

"And then you'll be free to go back to your life in L.A. To the magazine and writing your books."

She pressed her lips together for a moment, and he wasn't sure if the expression he saw in her eyes was relief or sadness.

"I read the Foreword in your last book," she finally

said. "I haven't had a chance to read more of it."

"We writers are sensitive sorts. You're killing my creative ego."

"No, no, what you wrote touched me. I wasn't expecting it."

The embarrassment that swept over him surprised J.T. He laughed.

"Really. You seemed to have come away from your research with so much more than just a story. When you talked about the victims of the murders, I felt your compassion. It was almost as if they were personal friends of yours."

"I did begin to feel like I knew them after all the research I did, all the time I spent with their families." He stopped her when she started to step closer to him. "It's only fair to warn you . . . I'm naked."

Her grin spread slowly. "It's only fair to warn you that I'm not as prim and proper as you think I am."

When he drew her into his arms she didn't tense or try to draw back. She laid her head on his bare chest, kept it there while he stroked her hair.

"I want so much to see you, J.T." She lifted her head, looked up. "I want to look into your eyes and see you looking back at me."

"It'll happen, Rosy. I know it will."

J.T. thought he should feel nervous about what they would begin tomorrow. His very life hung in the balance. But right now, with Rosy in his arms and the sultry night breeze washing over them, he felt more calm and content and needed than he'd ever felt in his life.

Hershel couldn't recall ever feeling more ashamed of himself. He had disconnected the power source to the refractor so that Wanda would not get into trouble should she become curious after he left. Now, he stood in the doorway and looked toward the sofa where she sat beside the blanket and pillows and food he'd brought down for her.

"It doesn't have to be this way, Wanda. Please ... won't you let me show you what happened to Curly? We'll use a book or something like that. All you have to do is watch me."

"I don't want anything to do with that machine. If you turn it on I'll close my eyes and scream bloody murder; I don't care if nobody hears me but you. It's the work of that woman; I know it is. I don't want any part of it, no part a'tall, do you hear me?"

He nodded. She was already close to hysterics; he didn't want to cause her any more distress. "Everything's going to be fine, Wanda. I'm sorry about having to detain you. I assure you, it's only temporary. As soon as Doctor Peabody and my son arrive, they can help me explain everything to you."

She glared at him. Somewhere in the room, the poodle hacked.

"If you need anything, anything at all, use that broom in the corner to tap on the ceiling. My bedroom's right above you. I'll come running."

He waited a moment. When she didn't respond, he closed the door and locked it. Leaning against it, Hershel shut his eyes. He was holding an old woman prisoner in his basement. Dear heaven, he needed a drink.

Chapter Thirteen

"Well, well . . . look who's here." Anthony Domani walked around to the front of his desk, then leaned on the edge of it, eyeing Roselyn with interest before turning a self-satisfied smirk Darla's way. "I thought you'd rather eat out of the dumpster than look at my face again, Sweet Pea?"

"Yeah, well, hunger pains can change a woman's mind, you know? Not to mention those nasty ol' maggots." Darla lifted her chin, her expression tinged with just the right mix of pride and humility. "I made a mistake, Tony. You were right and I was wrong. There, I said it. Now can we just forget the past?"

He crossed his arms. "You shouted some pretty nasty insults at me the last time I saw you, Darla. They aren't so easy to forget."

Before Roselyn's eyes, her mother had changed into someone she didn't recognize. A coy seductress. Tough and manipulative, but vulnerable, too.

Jennifer Archer

Darla dipped her chin and looked at him through her lashes. "I didn't mean any of it. I've got a temper, Sugar, you know that."

Laughing, he reached out and nudged her cheek. "Do I ever. You took your sweet time coming back, but I knew you'd be here sooner or later."

Roselyn had expected a larger man. Someone more menacing. Anthony Domani was short, solid, and undeniably handsome. Especially for a man close to seventy, if he hadn't reached that birthday already. He had a full head of wavy silver hair, a strong curved nose, wide lips, and olive-toned skin.

He also had a way of making Roselyn feel small, meek, and insignificant. Or maybe it was the combination of him and her mother in one room together. Darla's and Domani's personalities clashed and tangled even when they only stared at each other. But woven into all that knotted tension was an unmistakable smooth thread of sexual awareness. Roselyn almost felt as if she were spying on a private encounter she had no business seeing.

She caught the scent of a cigar and wondered if J.T. stood nearby. Surely he'd known better than to smoke this morning. The last thing they needed right now was for him to draw attention to himself. She almost groaned with relief when Domani lifted a cigar from a humidor on his desk.

"Let me guess," he said, sticking it into one corner of his mouth. "You need work."

"Are you hiring?" Darla moved to a chair, sat, and blinked up at him.

"Maybe," Domani answered. "Maybe not."

She'd dressed carefully, Roselyn noted. Her mother's short skirt was casual, but it accentuated two of Darla Peabody's trademark features. Her mother might be forty-four years old, but her legs remained twenty. Slowly, she crossed them, obviously aware that the dirty

182

old coot was salivating at the sight of them.

When Domani finally met her mother's gaze, Darla looked him square in the eye. "This isn't easy for me, Tony," she said. "You know how I hate to eat crow. You promised if I came back you'd take me on again."

His laugh was a low rumble. "Sweet Pea, you always did know how to get to me. But as much as I'd like to hire you, I'm afraid that old offer expired. You waited too long."

Darla's chagrin appeared genuine. Rosy was amazed. Her mother deserved an Academy Award.

"You want me to beg?" Tears glistened in her eyes. "Is that it, Tony? Is that my punishment?"

"Hell, no, I don't want you to beg. I can't stand a sniveling woman; you know that. Besides, the Darla Peabody I used to know had spunk."

With a sniff, Darla squared her shoulders. "She still does."

"Good." He chewed on the cigar tip, rolled it between his teeth as his attention shifted to Roselyn. "Maybe if you laid something on the table, Sweet Pea, offered an incentive in return for my generosity, a peace offering, so to speak."

From the corner of her eye, Roselyn saw her mother's body tense.

"My daughter's not up for negotiation," Darla said firmly.

"Your daughter?" Domani's gaze skipped from Roselyn to Darla then back again. His smile slowly widened. "I should've guessed. Add a little makeup, do something with her hair, and she'd look just like you did when I first set eyes on you, Darla." He pushed away from the desk. "What's your name, sweetheart?"

He looked amused when Roselyn offered her hand. "I'm—"

"Her name is Roselyn Grace," Darla answered, her

tone clearly indicating that her daughter was strictly off-limits.

Domani took Roselyn's hand. But instead of shaking it as she'd intended, he lowered his head and brushed his lips across her knuckles. "Your mother gave you a damn classy name. I like that. Now . . ." He winked. "A young thing like you I'd have no problem finding a place for in my operation. You ever danced before, Roselyn Grace?"

"Yes," Roselyn answered before her mother could protest. The situation was not proceeding as they'd imagined. But, like it or not, she couldn't chance losing an opportunity to get closer to Domani, whatever that opportunity might entail. "I have danced." She decided the performances in front of her bedroom mirror should count for something. "But I'm not particularly skilled at it. I prefer office work."

"Office work—" Domani barked out a laugh. "Sweetheart, hiding you away in an office would be a crime against nature. How about working as a hostess?"

"Roselyn has a college degree. Several, in fact. She isn't interested in—"

"Yes, I am, Mama." Roselyn's heartbeat accelerated. She couldn't believe what she was setting herself up to do. Though Sully had been successful in persuading several of Domani's party staff to quit, they'd planned to only use the party as a last resort, hoping that Domani might be talked into hiring her as an office worker. But she sensed they walked a risky line with Domani. She thought he might only be playing cruel games with her mother, trying to make her sweat, to irritate her before giving in. Then again he might have another tactic in mind altogether. Domani could be mad enough over her mother jilting him years ago that the only salve strong enough to sooth his wounded pride was the satisfaction of rejecting Darla's pleas. Roselyn couldn't let him turn her away. "I'd be very interested in working for you as a hostess."

"Good."

"Oh, no you don't." Darla shook her head. "My daughter's not squeezing into one of those indecent costumes you seem to prefer and parading around for a bunch of horny old men. Two years I busted my butt for you, Tony. I pretended not to know where you were whenever collectors showed up wanting to break your kneecaps, which was often. I ran the club when you were too hungover to function. Not to mention putting up with long hours, late paychecks, and your filthy mouth. You owe me. Roselyn's smart as a whip. Put her to work in your office as an accountant. I'll take the hostess gig." She gave him a meaningful stare. "And whatever else you might have in mind for me."

He studied her mother through hooded eyes, his expression amused. "That's a very interesting proposal." His cigar bobbed. "But the fact is, I don't owe you the time of day, Sweet Pea. And I don't need an accountant."

"Okay, then, she can answer telephones, type, anything of that nature."

"All those positions are filled."

"Then let her do errands and make coffee. She can keep things running smoothly whenever you have a conference or a meeting."

"What I have available," Domani said, clearly enjoying her mother's distress, "is a hostess position." His gaze shifted to Roselyn. "You look to be the right size for the costume."

An image of herself in spiked heels and pasties flashed through Roselyn's mind. "I do brew a delicious cup of coffee," she said, more meekly than she liked.

"I'm sure you've got all kinds of hidden talents, honey. But I'm more interested in your physical attributes than your résumé. I'm throwing a shindig in a couple of nights for my birthday. I celebrate every year with about three hundred of my closest friends." He gestured overhead. "Upstairs in my penthouse. My sister and her husband are in charge of all the details. Last I heard one hostess and a bouncer quit yesterday. You got experience as a bouncer, Roz?"

"Roselyn," Darla snapped. "As in Rose."

"Whatever." He walked around his desk.

"No, sir," Roselyn answered. "I'm afraid I don't. But I don't have much hostess experience, either."

"It'll be easier to teach you to smile pretty and carry a tray than to kick butt and take names." He pushed the intercom button on his phone. "Shanna, I need you to take one of these gals upstairs to Sophie for a fitting."

"Better make that both of us," Darla said. "My daughter and I are a package deal. You want her, you get me, too."

"You surprise me, Pea. I never thought you to be the jealous type." *Tsk*-ing, he shook his head. "Sorry, Darla, but I just can't use you."

His focus moved to the door when a knock sounded. "Yeah?"

The door opened. An elderly horse-faced man stuck his head into the room. "Anthony, could I speak to you in private?"

"Can't it wait?"

The man's shoulders slumped. He looked as if he might back out the door, but seemed to gather courage at the last second and lifted his chin instead. "No, it can't."

"Then spit it out."

"Okay." His Adam's apple quivered. "Sophie just called. Two of the other young ladies we hired as hostesses and the other security person resigned this morning."

"That's not my problem. My sister's in charge of the party, Bart, and you're in charge of her."

The withered old man pursed his lips, his tired eyes bitter and defensive. "But it is your problem, Anthony."

"Oh, yeah? How's that, Reneau?"

Roselyn's breath caught. *Bartholomew Reneau.* The scientist who'd turned traitor against the professor. The hair at the back of her neck stood on end, telling her J.T. was nearby. Or was it his anger she felt crackling in the air around her? How must he feel, standing face-to-face with the two men who had murdered his mother?

Certain everyone present must sense the altered energy in the air as well, she glanced at each person in the room. But they didn't seem aware of the electric presence she couldn't ignore.

Reneau looked first at her and then her mother before returning his gaze to Domani. "Are you sure you want to discuss this in front of your guests?"

"If I wasn't sure, I wouldn't have asked you the question. I don't have all day."

Reneau cleared his throat. "In short, Anthony, the party is to take place day after tomorrow and we're without a full staff or security."

"Then I advise you to stop bothering me and get on the phone."

"It will be next to impossible to find reliable help on such short notice."

"The people you took your time hiring couldn't be counted on, either."

Reneau's gaze made a nervous scan of the room, though he didn't meet anyone's eyes. "There must be a virus going around. All but one of them were sick. The other had a family emergency."

Domani shrugged. He turned to Darla. "Looks like you've got yourself a job after all, Sweet Pea."

Darla looked smug. "I can get you one more hostess," she said. "And I know a man who can handle security for you, too."

Domani sat in his chair and leaned back, his hands clasped behind his neck. "They got experience?"

"They're pros," Darla said, tilting her head to one side, a coy smile on her face. "You can trust my judgment, Sugar."

"Okay, you win. But I'm still going to hold you to that peace offering. I've been waiting a long time for it, Sweet Pea. I won't wait much longer."

He glanced across the room at Reneau. "Problem solved," he said.

J.T. stayed behind in Domani's office after Reneau ducked out and Rosy and her mother left for their costume fitting. He didn't like the way Domani had sized Rosy up like a piece of merchandise, and felt like kicking himself for allowing the two women to get involved with such a scumbag. His only peace of mind was knowing Barb and Sully would probably be hired, too. If J.T. couldn't be around to keep an eye on things, he sensed that Sully was perfectly capable of handling matters.

When Domani slipped into the private restroom adjoining his office, J.T. ran his hand along the cherry wood file cabinet that sat beside the massive matching desk. He scanned the walls and floor, looking for signs of a hidden safe. Crossing to the far wall, he lifted the bottom edge of a framed painting and looked behind it. Though the wall appeared smooth, J.T. skimmed his fingers across it, feeling for any suspicious crack or hidden button. He stooped, lifted the edge of an oriental rug, tapped the planks of the polished wood floor.

He heard the toilet flush and dropped the rug, then returned to the corner by the window where he'd stood during Darla's and Rosy's visit.

Domani made a beeline for the telephone on his desk. He didn't sit; he seemed too agitated. Leaning down, he punched the button on his phone and all but shouted into the intercom. "Call Reneau and tell him to get back in here." When he finished giving the order he stretched, mumbling to himself, "I don't know why I've kept that slow-witted son of a bitch on the payroll all these years. I'm surprised he can get dressed in the morning without someone telling him how to pull on his pants."

Domani stepped back, shoved a hand through his silver hair. Sunlight drenched his desk. Turning, he started toward the stretch of windows where J.T. stood.

Quietly, J.T. eased off to the side, but no more than two feet separated him from Domani as the older man lowered one window shade. Domani shot a glance over his shoulder to his desk, which was now cast in shadow. "That's better," he mumbled, stepping toward it.

J.T. held his breath when Domani looked again at the place where he stood. The old man's brows pulled together and he sniffed and scratched his head. After a moment, he turned, walked to his desk and sat.

As J.T. studied the handsome crook, hatred clawed its way up to his throat. He wanted to yell, to lunge at Domani, to do his level best to give him a heart attack. Instead, he choked off the impulse, let the hatred burrow deep inside of him, let it feed on the blood that pumped through his veins. His mother's blood. Pop's. He'd never felt an emotion more frightening or overwhelming.

Backing up to the wall, J.T flattened his sweating palms against it and drew a breath to steady himself. Perspiration broke out on his forehead. His heart tripped in his chest.

Domani glanced up from the papers on his desk. He stared at the windows, his gaze piercing straight through J.T. One bushy eyebrow twitched. Finally he returned his attention to the papers again.

J.T. decided if he couldn't hurt the man, he could at least make him question his own sanity. He drew another deep breath then blew out a noisy sigh.

Domani's chin came up again. He pushed his chair away from the desk.

J.T. whistled quietly.

Domani pushed the intercom.

"Yes, Mr. Domani?" came his secretary's voice.

"Come in here."

"Yes, sir. Should I bring anything?"

"Just you. Hurry."

A few seconds later, Shanna slipped into the room. Domani didn't look at her; his focus remained on the window. "You needed me, sir? I called Mr. Reneau."

"Have you been burning a candle in here when I'm not around, Shanna?"

"No, sir, I—"

"What's that odor, then?"

"What odor, sir?"

"Don't tell me you don't smell it," he said, his voice rising. "It's like," he sniffed, "I don't know, hell, soap or something, men's cologne."

Shanna drew a deep breath. "Sandalwood. I do detect—"

"You know I don't like candles. And the only men's cologne I wanna smell is the stuff I'm wearing. You haven't been playing patty cake on my desk with some sugar daddy when I'm not here, have you?"

On impulse, J.T. huffed a laugh.

Shanna flinched. "I assure you, sir, I haven't been burning any candles, and I most certainly haven't—"

"Be quiet!"

The young woman's mouth snapped shut like it was spring-loaded.

"Do you hear something?" Domani glanced at her, then back toward J.T. "By the window. An air leak or something."

She leaned forward, tilted her head, squinted. "No,

sir," she finally said, her voice almost a whisper. "I don't hear anything."

A flush of red crept up Domani's neck. He scooted his chair closer to his desk and glanced down at the papers there. "Okay then, got out of here."

"Yes, sir." Shanna scampered like a scared mouse out of the office.

J.T. gave Domani a moment to relax and regroup, then reached for the window shade the older man had lowered a few minutes before. He tugged and let go. The shade shot up, snapping as it settled into place.

Domani popped out of his chair like a jack-in-the-box, his gaze darting toward the window. "Holy Mother—"

"Anthony? What's wrong?"

Gasping, Domani whirled around to face Reneau, who stood in the doorway. He stepped back, stumbled against his chair. His feet went out from under him and he fell backward into it, a lock of wavy hair straggling across his eyes. "Damn it, Bartholomew!" He swept his hair back with shaky fingers, then sat up straight and cleared his throat. "Don't you ever come in here unannounced, understand?"

"Miss Timmons said—"

"I don't care what Shanna said. *I* said . . ." He cleared his throat again. "Get in here and shut up."

Bartholomew Reneau was the last person J.T. would ever suspect to be a killer. He looked like a skittish whipped puppy, uncertain whether to pounce and bite or tuck tail and run.

J.T. watched him quietly close the door. Shoulders drooping, he faced his boss. "The Peabody women are upstairs. Did you want to meet Sully Tucker before I hire him?"

"Sully Tucker?"

"The man Miss Peabody recommended to handle security."

Domani waved a hand. "Just have him checked out. If he's legit sign him up; I don't need to meet him. I know Darla. She's a tease, but she doesn't have a dishonest bone in her luscious little body." He cursed. "Why are we talking about this anyway? That's not why I called you in here." Pointing a finger at Reneau, he continued, "Don't you ever interrupt me again about the party when I'm with people. Or ever, for that matter. Can't you make one simple freaking decision on your own? I swear on my mother's grave, if you weren't married to my baby sister you'd only be a bad memory to me now. You would've been finished when you screwed up the first time thirty years ago." His eyes narrowed. "That's the only smart thing you ever did, asking Sophie to marry you. Saved your hide, and you know it."

Reneau looked everywhere in the room except at his brother-in-law. "Is that all?"

"Pathetic. That's what you are. I can't figure what Sophie ever saw in you. She could've done better." He shook his head and cursed. "Can't even handle the nothing jobs I give you, you stupid, worthless piece of—"

Rubbing a stubby hand over his face, Domani puffed out his cheeks and exhaled noisily. "This year, all my stuff better be where I left it when the party's over. I don't want nobody on the second floor in my private quarters. Especially not that spooky kid. If I catch him snooping around, I'll whack him like an eight ball. Got it?"

"Don't worry about him, Anthony."

"Don't worry . . ." He slapped the heel of his hand on the desk.

Reneau seemed to shrink into himself. He leaned back against the doorframe as though to stay as far away from the other man as possible. "I've been overseeing this party of yours every year for more than a decade," he said, his voice indignant but faltering. "I know what I'm doing."

"If you know what you're doing, why did you let that slimy kid out of your sight last year?"

"That slimy kid just happens to be mine and your sister's grandson, Anthony." With renewed bravery, Reneau stepped further into the room.

"He's no blood of mine or yours, either," Domani said. "As I recall, someone else knocked up his mother six or so months before that sucker of a son of yours married her. Besides that, the kid gives me the creeps with those books he reads. All that supernatural crap ought to be banned from the planet. Just keep an eye on him while he's in my house, understand?"

"I'll do my best."

"That's what I'm afraid of."

"If it makes you feel any better, I'll insist that his older sister skips the party to watch him."

He huffed. "You can't trust that girl. She needs a babysitter, too."

Waving a hand, Domani dismissed Reneau. He shuffled the papers on his desk, then picked up his telephone receiver.

J.T. recognized the hatred in Reneau's narrowed eyes as he stared at his brother-in-law. "Will that be all?" Reneau asked again.

"Yeah." Domani punched in a number. "Get out of here."

J.T. hurried quietly across the room. He made it to the door just before Reneau pulled it open. J.T. slipped through as the old man paused to glare at Domani. J.T. waited then, moving cautiously, followed Bartholomew Reneau down the hallway. They paused at an elevator where Reneau pushed the down button, then waited some more. When the elevator arrived, they rode down to the fourth floor.

Jennifer Archer

Reneau's office was poorly lighted and not much larger than a walk-in closet. Stacks of files and books cluttered the floor. J.T. had to do some fancy footwork to dodge it all and find a place out of the way to stand. The dingy white walls needed paint and shelving, the desk was metal, even the telephone was outdated. There was no window, no extra chair.

Looking drained and defeated, Reneau sat at his desk and stared into space. After a minute, he picked up a paperweight and hurled it. It hit the opposite wall with a loud thud, chipping the flaking plaster.

The door opened and a pretty, plump middle-aged woman stepped into the room. She glanced at the paperweight on the floor, then lifted her troubled gaze to Reneau. "Your wife called," she said, her accent French.

He sighed. "Again?"

"She wants you to meet her for lunch to discuss the party."

"I don't have time to meet her, Marie. And I'm sick to death of the details of Anthony's self-absorbed extravaganza." He hung his head.

Marie eased the door shut. She walked across the room to stand behind Reneau. Lifting her hands to his shoulders, she began a slow massage.

"I might need a babysitter for my grandson and his sister," he said after a moment, sounding miserable. "Don't bother asking anyone who knows of his antics last year."

The woman smiled. "He's just a curious boy, he means no harm. I'll look through the personnel file." Her fingers stilled for a moment. "Why do you put up with all of this, Bartholomew?"

"Anthony and I . . . we share a history you're unaware of."

"I know, I know. You've told me this a hundred times. Why won't you trust me with the details?"

"You're safer not knowing." He sighed. "Put simply, I failed him once."

"But so did all the others who followed you. That much you've told me before."

"Yes." He looked up at her. "But what I didn't tell you is that each and every one of them died in a so-called accident. I was the only one spared."

Her fingers stilled on his shoulders. She bit her lip.

"As long as I stay married to Sophie, he'll let me live."

Marie sighed when he turned to stare down at his lap. "It doesn't have to be this way, Bartholomew. You know the combination to his safe, where he keeps the keys to his files. You know his secrets. You could ruin him."

"His secrets are mine, as well. If I implicate him, I implicate myself."

"Then forget the secrets. We don't need them."

When Reneau twisted his chair toward her, she eased to her knees on the floor beside him. "With what's inside his safe," she said, "we could disappear, you and I. We could live the rest of our lives together and never have to answer to anyone again." She took his hands. "You've let him steal your self-confidence, your dignity. Take it back, Bartholomew . . . with interest. He owes that to you. The party is the perfect time. He believes that you would never turn against him, that you're too fearful. And he'll be distracted; you know how he is when surrounded by his entourage. He won't be concerned with you."

"I would never know peace unless . . ." Reneau frowned, his mouth a tight, thin line. "This secret Anthony and I share, it's his obsession . . . his dream. The only way to truly destroy him is to end it once and for all."

"Then do it, Bartholomew." Marie kissed him. "For me if not for yourself."

A chill raced up J.T.'s spine. Retrieving Pop's files might turn out to be easier than he'd ever expected. And the man to help him do it might be the very person who'd stolen them to begin with.

Chapter Fourteen

Roselyn paced in front of the sofa where Barb and her mother sat. "What could be taking him so long? I knew we should've waited."

"I'm sure J.T.'s fine," Barb said.

Darla tucked her bare feet up under her. "Maybe he found something in Tony's office."

"Or maybe he's in some kind of trouble." Roselyn rubbed her palms up and down her arms. "Domani isn't someone to underestimate. I don't know how you ever worked for him, Mama."

"We needed the money. But if I'd had any idea the horrible things he was capable of, I would never have worked for him, money or not."

"Well, don't worry about J.T.," Barb said. "Domani's no match for him. Being invisible, he has the advantage over that bag of hot air and everyone else, for that matter. Short of getting chased down by a pack of dogs with sensitive noses, what kind of scrape could he get into?"

"The refractor's effects could wear off unexpectedly. What if that happened and Domani saw him?"

"You're borrowing trouble, Rosebud."

"Barb's right, Baby. Why don't you sit down and try to relax. Get your mind off him for awhile."

No chance of that, Roselyn thought, though she wouldn't admit it aloud. Even if he hadn't been gone for hours her mind would still be on J.T. She didn't want to feel anything more than friendship for him and had tried her best not to let her feelings stretch beyond that limit. But it was too late. She felt. And wanted. In the end, when he went back to California and his life, she would probably regret getting too close to him. But right now, that didn't matter much.

"Save your breath, Darla," Barb said. "She's not going to sit. She's crazy about him, can't you see that?"

Roselyn caught a glimpse of the worry in her mother's eyes. "I see it," Darla said. "It scares me."

"What scares you?" she asked, still pacing.

"The way you look at him."

"What?" Roselyn paused to scowl before resuming her trek, back and forth, across the carpet. "I can't see the man; how can I possibly look at him any certain way when I can't see him?"

Barb laughed. "Good point, Rosebud."

"Okay then." Darla blinked. The manipulative seductress had disappeared. The worried, overprotective mother had taken her place. "I see the way you listen to him, then. The way your face changes whenever he talks. The—"

"—way you squirm whenever you smell him," Barb finished, closing her eyes and shivering. "Damn, Darla, who can blame her? He smells so male. Like shaving cream and—"

"Sandalwood," Roselyn said, a sigh leaving her lips

before she could stop it. "Shaving cream and sandalwood soap."

Barb sighed, too. "Whatever it is, it makes me want to strip off all my clothes and howl at the moon."

"Barb!" Darla's feet hit the floor. "Watch your mouth."

Roselyn bit back a laugh. "My word, Mama, I'm a grown woman."

"A grown woman with a bad case of the hots for one sexy see-through man," Barb added.

Darla grabbed Roselyn's wrist when she passed by. "Is that true?"

"I don't know." She glanced down, felt a flicker of annoyance at the concern she saw in her mother's eyes. "What if it is? What could it hurt? Maybe I'll finally get a chance to use that condom you gave me just before I left home for college almost nine years ago."

"That con—" Her mother's eyes widened momentarily then narrowed to slits. "You're the one it could hurt, Roselyn."

"Why did you give it to me if you didn't expect me to use it?"

"I gave it to you just in case you found yourself in a . . . situation." Darla bit her lip. "And because the realistic side of me expected you'd get involved with someone, someday, and I wanted you to be safe, not make the same mistake I did."

Mistake. She tried to pull away but her mother grasped her wrist tighter. "Well, I'm here to tell you," Roselyn said, her throat closing, "that you shouldn't have wasted your time worrying about me. My reality is not the same as yours or Barb's or most any other woman's, for that matter. A *situation* never came up." She huffed a laugh. "No, that's not true, it did come up, but I recognized what was happening and put a stop to it. The guy was using me for the A I could help him make in calculus.

He figured if he showed weird, lonely, pathetic Roselyn Peabody a little attention, she'd help him with his homework. And if he went even further, she might even *do* his homework. Sound familiar, Mama? Just like my high school experience with Kyle Graham? Well I wasn't about to repeat that old song and dance."

"Roselyn—"

"I know you don't understand. That's why you gave me the condom." She tugged at the top button on her shirt. "Why you bought my clothes two sizes too big and taught me to button up to my chin. Guys don't use women for their minds, right? Well, I'm the exception. A freak of nature, I guess. A mistake."

"Stop it, Roselyn." Her mother let go of her wrist. "I didn't mean it like that. You know I didn't. I've never once thought of you as a mistake. I loved you and wanted you from the second I found out I was pregnant. And I'm proud of you. So, so proud. You're smart and beautiful and so much stronger than I've ever been. I just meant that, when it happens to you, I want it to be with the right man, a man who'll stick around, who'll be there for you."

"And how do you know J.T. Drake's not that man?"

"I like J.T., but I also recognize his type. He may be ready to settle down some day but it won't be anytime soon."

"Could it be," Roselyn asked, feeling defensive, "that he reminds you of my father?"

Darla's face paled. For a moment she didn't speak, just stared into Roselyn's eyes, her own eyes hurt and haunted. "J.T. does remind me of him. An older version, of course, but the sort of man I imagine Steven Bedford might have grown up to be."

Feeling drained, Roselyn sat on the sofa between the older two women. "I'm sorry. I didn't mean to hurt you

by saying that. And I don't mean to shock either of you
by saying what I'm about to say."

"It would take a lot to shock your mother and me,"
Barb said with a nervous laugh, cutting it short when
Darla shot her a look.

"Did it ever occur to you," Roselyn continued, "that
maybe I'm not ready to settle down anytime soon, either?
That maybe I might enjoy just having a good time with
a nice, sexy man?"

She wasn't sure whom she was trying hardest to convince, her mother or herself. And though the concept,
spoken aloud, sounded good, like something she wanted,
she didn't quite buy it. She wondered if her mother did.

Darla stared at Roselyn for a long minute. "Well, in
that case," she finally said, pausing to nibble her lower
lip. "Don't use that old condom I gave you, buy a new
one. That thing's so old it's probably defective."

For a moment, Roselyn could only stare back at her
mother. Then she laughed. Barb grabbed her around the
waist from behind and started laughing, too. They
rocked back and forth, tears streaming down their faces
while her mother gawked at them as if they'd gone crazy.

"I can see you think this is funny," Darla said, "but
you should think long and hard about it."

"Long and hard . . ." Barb shrieked. "That's always
good."

"Go ahead and laugh, you two." Darla crossed her
arms. "I've had a few blind dates. Sometimes a man can
sound good on the telephone, then you meet him in person and he looks like Sully."

"Hey," Barb said, wiping her eyes. "My Sully's an ac-
quired taste, that's all."

"Yeah, and it took you almost twenty years to acquire
it," Sully said as he came through the door.

Barb stood and met him in the center of the room. She
smacked a noisy kiss on his mouth then pinched his

cheeks together. "I happen to think this is an adorable mug."

"I do, too, Sully," Roselyn's mother said. "I was only kidding when I said that. I think you're cute as pigs' feet."

"Yeah, right." Sully blushed. "And you're so full of crap your eyes are turning brown." He draped an arm over Barb's shoulder. "Go ahead and talk mean about me. I'm used to being abused."

Darla threw a pillow at him. "Poor thing."

He grinned, then turned to Barb. "You ready to go?"

"Sure. We all have a long day ahead of us tomorrow. Your payoffs worked."

"They did?"

She nodded. "Which means we'll have to call off a class if we're all going to be working Domani's party in a couple of nights."

"Expect a call from Bartholomew Reneau later today," Darla said. "He's Tony's right-hand man. He'll want to check you out. You know, ask you a few questions about your experience, that sort of thing."

Roselyn stood. "I'll walk you two out."

Halfway down the stairs to the parking lot, Barb paused. "You go on to the car, Sully. I'll be right there. I have something to say to Rosebud in private." She winked at him. "Girl talk."

"Okay, but hurry. I want to get something to eat. I'm so hungry I'm fartin' fresh air." He started down, shaking his head. "Abused, that's what I am," he mumbled. "Neglected. Taken for granted."

"What is it?" Roselyn asked.

"I stopped at the bookstore on the way home last night. I found J.T.'s book." Barb grinned. "He doesn't look a thing like Sully."

Roselyn bit the inside of her cheek. "No, he doesn't."

"I don't know what it is you've got in mind for him."

Barb touched her arm. "Whether it's something permanent, or something temporary. But whatever it is, don't waste any time. Your Mom means well, but if you follow her advice and tiptoe through life 'cause you're afraid of getting hurt or making a mistake, you might avoid getting your toes crushed but you'll miss out on a lot of fun and joy, too. It's not a big mean world out there, Rosebud. It's a big beautiful world with a little bit of mean stuff mixed in with a whole lot of good." She glanced down at Sully in the parking lot below. "It took me twenty years to figure that one out. Don't you take so long."

"I'll try not to, Barb." She smiled. "And I'm happy Sully finally made you see the light. The two of you are perfect for each other."

"Yeah, well, don't change the subject on me. It's you and J.T. Drake I'm talking about now." She reached into her purse, pulled something out of it and pressed it into Roselyn's palm. "I figured that considering the condition he's in, these might make things a little more interesting for the two of you. If you want to, you can let me know if they're worth the money I spent. If you don't," she shrugged, "well, I'll be disappointed not to get at least a few juicy details, but I'll understand. Besides, my imagination is vivid." She kissed Roselyn's cheek. "Have fun, Rosebud."

As Barb made her way down the stairs, Roselyn opened her fingers and looked down at what rested against her palm. A folded strip of at least twelve condoms. Multicolored. Glow in the dark.

Roselyn's heartbeat sped up. Laughing out loud, she slipped them into the pocket of her jeans and turned to climb the stairs.

J.T. jogged all the way back to Darla's apartment. He had sat on the floor in a corner of Reneau's office waiting for at least half an hour for the man and his secretary to leave for lunch. When they did, he looked through Reneau's desk drawers. But the most interesting thing he found was hidden beneath one drawer, not in it. A computer disc labeled simply, *ER*.

Slipping the disc into the pocket of his invisible shorts, J.T. had let himself out of Bartholomew Reneau's office and left the building.

Now he took the stairs up to Darla's apartment two at a time, then knocked on the door. In seconds, it opened and Rosy stood in front of him wearing a tired and worried expression on her face.

"It's me," he said, panting from the exertion of running.

"Where have you been?"

When she stepped back away from the door, he walked in and closed it behind them. He saw her mother shift to the edge of the sofa, heard an old Beatles tune playing softly in the background. "I was stuck in Reneau's office for a while, but it was worth it."

Rosy's eyes brightened. "You found something?"

"Maybe." He pulled the disc from his pocket. "Take a look at this."

Darla shook her head and pressed a hand to her chest. "How did you do that? Make that disc appear out of nowhere?"

"It was in my pocket. I had on these clothes when the refractor zapped me, so they're invisible, too."

Rosy reached for the disc. "You can't see what's in his pockets because, like J.T., the clothes he's wearing have substance. They didn't dematerialize, they're simply not visible."

With another shake of her head, Darla said, "Sorry to be so dense but this blows my mind. I don't understand any of it."

"That makes two of us, Darla," J.T. said.

Rosy looked down at the disc, her breath catching when she read the label. "Didn't the professor refer to his work on the refractor as Project E.R.?"

"Yeah. That's why I thought I'd better bring that with me."

She started toward the computer that sat on a desk in one corner of the living room. "Can I borrow your PC, Mama?"

"Sure," Darla said. "Help yourself."

J.T. stood behind Rosy, watching over her shoulder as she booted up the machine, then brought up the information stored on the disc. She opened one file after another, scanning notes and studying calculations.

"What do you think?" he finally asked her.

"This all looks very familiar. Where did you say you found the disc?"

"Hidden beneath one of Reneau's desk drawers. There's nothing high-tech or fancy about his office. Compared to Domani's it looks like a broom closet." He studied the screen. "Is that it? I can't believe finding Pop's research could be this simple."

Roselyn reached for the telephone. "I'd rather not speculate until I talk to your father. I'll pay you back for the call, Mama."

Darla stood beside them now. She nibbled on her thumbnail, her expression as tense as her daughter's. "Don't worry about that. Just call him and see what he says."

Twenty minutes later, Rosy called J.T. to the phone. "Your father wants to speak to you. It seems he has a problem on his hands."

J.T. took the receiver from her. "Pop? What's up?"

"It's Wanda."

"Mrs. Moody?"

"Yes." He cleared his throat. "You see, she found her poodle."

J.T. puffed out his cheeks. "Great. Is he still invisible?"

"Quite so, I'm afraid. Wanda blamed it on Roselyn. It seems she still believes her to be a witch. She threatened to bring the animal's condition to the attention of the Dean of Science at the University as well as the police."

J.T. stared into Rosy's worried eyes. "What did you do?"

"Knowing Wanda's persistent nature, I thought my only option was to take her into our confidence by showing her the refractor and how it works. I intended to demonstrate with an inanimate object but she refused to cooperate, so I—" He cleared his throat again. "I locked her in the basement."

"You did what?"

"I didn't know what else to do. She's beyond reason. Whenever I mention showing her how the refractor works she becomes hysterical. I'm really quite worried about her."

"How long has she been down there?"

"Since yesterday morning. She—"

"Do you mean to tell me," J.T. interrupted, bracing a hand against the computer desk where Rosy sat, "that Wanda Moody spent all day yesterday and last night held against her will in your laboratory?"

"She's quite comfortable. I made her a place on the sofa. And this morning I cooked her a nice breakfast. Scrambled eggs, bacon, and biscuits with homemade plum jelly. Nelda Pettibone brought me the jelly last week from—"

"Pop . . ." J.T. shook his head. Rosy and Darla had their heads together and were staring wide-eyed at the receiver he held in his hand. "You can't keep Wanda locked up in the basement."

"I know that." Pop sighed. "I was hoping you might speak to her. Wanda has always been quite fond of you,

Jerome. She reads your books. Perhaps she'll listen to you."

"Put her on."

J.T. heard arguing in the background. He mulled over what to say to Mrs. Moody to soothe her injured pride over being held prisoner, while at the same time convincing her to keep quiet about their secret. Artie, the boy from the airplane, came to mind. Wanda liked being in the know. Maybe the same tactic he'd used on the kid would work with her, too.

"Jerome Drake, is that you?" she finally said into the phone.

"It's me, Mrs. Moody."

"How do I know it's not that witch disguising her voice?"

"Remember that time when I was a kid and I pulled all the vinca from your flowerbeds thinking it was a weed?"

"Sure do." She hesitated a moment. "You'll have to give me more than that to go on."

"Okay, let me think. There was the time you caught me setting off firecrackers on old man Miller's front porch but you kept your mouth shut about it because you were mad at him for cheating you in some card game."

"Old geezer deserved a good scare." She laughed. "J.T. Drake, what are you up to? Do you mean to tell me you know about whatever it is your daddy has going on with that cockeyed woman?"

"I do. I can explain everything, Wanda. But you have to promise me you won't tell anyone. A lot of lives hang in the balance, not the least of which is mine." He gave her a brief overview of what had happened to him and talked her into letting Pop give her a demonstration with the refractor. She only agreed to do so after he promised he'd mention her in the book if he ever wrote the story.

Finally, he hung up the phone.

"I couldn't help overhearing," Roselyn said. "Is everything okay?"

"I hope so. It's a long story. I'll fill you in later. First I want to hear what you and Pop decided about that disc."

"Well, just as I expected after quickly looking at the files, it seems what you've found is Reneau's attempt to recreate the calculations he's missing. The part of the formula your father and I have spent the last two years perfecting."

J.T. scratched his head. "Attempt?"

She smiled. "It's incorrect. But he's almost there. And that's what's frightening. With only a slight change in his calculations he'll have what he and Domani were after all along. The complete formula and the ability to make people invisible, then visible again. Then there'll be no limits to what they can achieve."

"That's assuming they still have the stolen research," J.T. said. "And after what I heard this morning, I suspect Domani has it locked away somewhere and he doesn't even let Reneau near it."

Darla and Rosy both waited for him to elaborate.

"Reneau and his secretary are pretty cozy. They had a private conversation in Bart's office. At least they thought it was private. I got an earful of information." J.T. walked to the sofa, sat down, and relayed what he'd overheard.

"I don't understand." Rosy frowned. "You don't think his secretary wants him to steal your father's research on the refractor, do you? If Reneau had no luck with it in the past, what would be any different if he took it now? How would he profit? He probably has it memorized anyway."

"My guess would be that Marie referred to jewelry or money when she encouraged him to steal whatever's in that safe. But I also think that, to get back at his brother-in-law, Reneau would like to take the research, too. Or maybe even destroy it. Reneau kept mentioning Domani's *obsession*. If I'm right, that obsession is the refractor. And it was pretty clear to me that if Reneau is going to risk double crossing Domani, he wants to go all out. He doesn't just want to steal from him, he wants to ruin his plans . . . his obsession."

"Do you think Reneau will really follow through, though? I mean, he hasn't ever managed to find the courage before. Why now?" Rosy asked.

"I think it will only take a few more humiliating putdowns from Domani to push Reneau to action. I can help in that department; make sure some things go wrong. Things Domani will blame on Reneau."

"And then?"

"Then, when Reneau's had enough of his boss's harassment, I'm betting he'll lead me right to what we're after."

Rosy stood and started to pace again, her hands clasped behind her back.

"I realize it's a long shot," J.T. said. "But we have to start somewhere. And after what I heard this morning, I believe Reneau could become our accomplice without even knowing it."

"I don't understand why Domani would be keeping the formula away from Reneau. Reneau was his secret weapon, the man with the knowledge he needed to pull it all together."

"But his secret weapon shot blanks. You saw how Domani treats him."

Darla turned off the CD player. The room fell silent. "Worse than a mangy dog."

"Exactly," J.T. agreed. "He only keeps the guy around because Reneau's married to his sister. That's what Reneau told his secretary. And he said Domani had hired others who failed, too, and that they each died in freak accidents afterward."

Darla shook her head and sat back down on the sofa beside J.T. "I knew he was capable of a lot of underhanded things, but I never dreamed he'd stoop to killing people on a whim."

"Which is why I don't want either you or Barb to let him get you off alone at that party. Especially if I'm occupied with Reneau and Sully's distracted by something else. Just to be cautious, let's get everyone together tomorrow night and come up with a concrete plan."

"This better be good." Wanda crumpled an empty cigarette pack. "I smoked my last fag more than two hours ago; I'm about to have a nicotine fit."

Hershel placed a textbook inside the refractor pod, then closed the door and turned to face her. "Are you ready?"

"As ready as I'll ever be." She backed to the wall, her arms wrapped protectively around her transparent poodle. "If you and that woman are pulling a fast one on me Hershel Drake, if that wasn't really your boy on the phone, mark my words I—"

"It's my understanding that you've been calling my son long distance to discuss my sanity."

One penciled-in eyebrow rose. "Not your sanity exactly, just—"

"Considering those conversations, I can only assume that you know what Jerome's voice sounds like on the telephone."

"Yes, but—"

"Did it sound like Jerome on the telephone?"

"That woman could've disguised her—"

"I confess I was eavesdropping on your end of the conversation. Didn't Jerome tell you things of which I have no knowledge? Things I would not have known to convey to Miss Peabody?"

She scowled. "You've made your point, Hershel."

"Good. You've known me for years, Wanda. I can be trusted." He smiled as he made his way to the control panel. "You, dear lady, are about to become one of the first witnesses of what might be the most amazing discovery of the new millennium."

"I'll believe it when I see it with my own two eyes. Let her rip."

Hershel hit the switch.

Wanda coughed and sputtered and complained as the swirling green smoke began to seep into the room. Minutes later, when he turned off the power and the smoke had cleared, Hershel had to coax her over to the pod to take a look.

"Well, I'll swan," she said, her voice uncharacteristically quiet and awed. "Where'd it go?"

"It's still there." He motioned her closer. "Come and feel for yourself."

She kneeled on the floor beside him and, still cradling Curly in one arm, reached down to touch the place on the pod floor where his hand rested against the now-transparent book. "Well, what do you know about that?" she said when her fingers brushed the book's binding.

An hour later, Hershel had a shelf filled with invisible books. He also had an invisible stool, an invisible paperclip holder and at least two dozen invisible paper clips. Wanda had transformed from a reluctantly skeptical observer into a wildly eager participant.

She walked around the room looking for other objects to zap. "With this little tidbit, I'd be the center of attention at my poker club for the next year. Marion Tetley would be green with jealousy that I was in on something this big and she wasn't."

"Now, Wanda, I thought you understood that you can't tell a soul about this until Miss Peabody and I say so. She and Jerome are in a very precarious position at the moment. If this was leaked to the press too soon by anyone, their lives could be jeopardized. Not only that, Curly's conversion might be delayed, as well."

Wanda winced as she glanced down at the invisible bundle she still held in the crook of one arm. "I'll keep quiet. It won't be easy, though." One corner of her mouth curled up. "Just to make sure I don't accidentally spill the beans, you might not want to let me out of your sight until it's safe." She walked to the sofa, sat, and plumped the pillow. "I was right comfortable here. I wouldn't mind staying another night or two." Her brows bobbed. "Just to be safe, mind you. 'Course I'd rather you didn't lock me in."

Hershel sighed. Since Jerome and Roselyn had left for Las Vegas, he'd felt helpless, as if he no longer had a role in or control over the situation. But now, like it or not, his purpose was clear. "Actually, that's not a bad idea, Wanda," he said. "Just to be safe, as you said." He cleared his throat. "Might I interest you in an early dinner tonight?"

"With you?"

He smiled. "Of course. There's a new Mexican food café in town I've heard good things about. Would you join me?"

Patting her hair, which was awry after a night spent in the basement, she smiled back at him. "Why Hershel, I'd be delighted."

Chapter Fifteen

Roselyn stood on the patio but didn't look at the city lights twinkling below against the dark of the night. She looked at the moon instead, a full golden circle that seemed to simmer with the same summer heat that threatened to suffocate her. She and J.T. and her mother had discussed a sketchy plan before retiring to their rooms tonight. Tomorrow they would work out the details with Barb and Sully.

Roselyn nibbled her lip. She couldn't remember the last time she'd been so nervous. Day after tomorrow, she would squeeze into that silly excuse for a costume Domani's sister had given her and pretend to do what the old man expected of her. Serve cocktails and hors d'oeuvres, smile and flirt and mingle when, all the while, she'd be watching for a sign from J.T. When she received his cue, she would have to find a way to slip out of the party and meet him somewhere—a place he'd designate later after scoping out Domani's penthouse apartment.

213

Below on the street, tires screeched and a horn blared long and loud. Roselyn sighed. She was awkward at social functions, and flirtation was her mother's forte, not hers. That particular skill was as foreign to her as solving a mathematical equation would be to her mother. But if for no other reason than to help J.T., she had to find a way to follow through. Domani liked her, that fact was obvious. She needed to play on that attraction, though finding a cure for cancer seemed a far less daunting task, in Roselyn's opinion, than using her so-called feminine wiles to manipulate a man she couldn't stand to be near. A caterpillar didn't transform into a butterfly overnight. But because so much was at stake, she would try.

J.T.

She closed her eyes and let the thought of him sift through her. When he had put his arms around her and held her right here on this patio, for one wonderful moment all her worries and insecurities, all her doubts and inhibitions had simply disappeared. She wanted that feeling of freedom again, the strength and security of his arms around her, the sound of his heartbeat steady and sure against her ear.

Roselyn slipped her fingers into the pocket of her jeans. The condoms Barb had given her were still there. She pulled them out, stroked her thumb across the packets. She was such a liar; she couldn't even be honest with herself. What she wanted from J.T. right this minute went beyond security and support, beyond having him chase away her fears.

She had tried dating the type of men her mother encouraged her to spend time with. Nice, safe men. Gentle and unassuming. The type who would provide her with intellectual stimulation and not ask much more from her in return. The kind of men whose kisses, if they kissed her at all, were sweet and undemanding and far too easy to walk away from.

214

J.T. could give her intellectual stimulation, too. But when the conversation ended, she felt certain that he could also provide a very different sort of stimulation, the kind of excitement she felt whenever she danced, only better. She suspected he would be a demanding lover, but one who would give as much as he took. Roselyn already knew for a fact his kisses weren't easy to walk away from. She found it difficult to walk at all after kissing J.T.

Sometimes, when he spoke her name or she sensed his presence in a room before she had proof he was there, she became too aware of things . . . her own heartbeat, the weight of her breasts, a tightening deep inside.

Needs.

She had ignored those needs for too long. Whenever they'd become too persistent, too overwhelming, she had tried to satisfy them through music and dancing, alone in her room, alone and lonely while her pulse ticked with excitement, her blood pumped faster, her mind let go.

She didn't have to be alone tonight. She didn't have to be lonely. She didn't need the music. J.T. was just down the hallway. So close.

Roselyn left the patio and made her way through the living room. She promised herself she would keep her relationship with J.T. uncomplicated. Just some fun with a nice, sexy man, like she'd told her mother. Nothing more.

As she walked down the hallway, she told herself that if worse came to worst and she couldn't keep it simple, it would be worth any humiliation that came afterward, worth a broken heart, to spend one night with him.

She paused at the door of her old bedroom, reached for the knob, and twisted it, swearing she would have no regrets.

The curtains were drawn. The room was dark, almost pitch black. She smelled the heady, sweet scent of J.T.'s cigar. The pleasant, masculine scent had become familiar, and she'd begun to like it, much to her surprise. It was an aroma she would forever associate with him.

Blinking, Roselyn scanned the room, jolting a bit when she spotted a round orange glow suspended in midair above the chair by the bed. Her eyes gradually adjusted to the darkness, and she detected the curl of white smoke swirling up from the burning tobacco. Turning, she closed the door and locked it.

When she looked toward the chair again, the glow of his cigar had extinguished. She heard a noise at the window, glanced up, watched the curtains open. Moonlight poured into the room. Roselyn could see everything . . . the twin bed she had slept in as a girl, the nightstand on one side of it, a chair on the other. Her old dresser. Her stuffed animals. Her first microscope. She could see everything . . . everything but him.

She walked to the center of the room, paused, turned slowly around in a circle. Her breath came too fast. She felt dizzy with anticipation. Hot. Her skin was so hot, so sensitive. The touch of his gaze was as real as any caress she'd ever felt.

Roselyn kicked off her sandals, first one, then the other, knowing he watched her, welcoming his gaze. Closing her eyes, she stopped thinking and tried, instead, just to concentrate on sensation. Cool air against her skin . . . hard, cool tile beneath her feet . . . her clothing brushing against all the most sensitive places on her body. She listened to the rush of distant traffic . . . the hum of the air conditioner . . . her own quiet breathing.

A moment later, the hair on her arms stood on end. The air around her sizzled with energy. She caught a stronger scent of the cigar again, remnants of smoke mingled with sandalwood.

Roselyn opened her eyes, glanced down at her chest. The top button of the sleeveless black blouse she wore came out of the buttonhole. She held her breath, watched the second button slip free. Glancing up, she searched the space in front of her, wanting to see his eyes, the expression on his face when he looked at her. *Where would his eyes be?* J.T. was tall; she'd had to stand on tiptoe to kiss him. She lifted her chin, stared up at the place she guessed his face would be, hoping he saw in her eyes that she wanted him to continue.

The message must've gotten through. One by one, the buttons parted. Neither she nor J.T. spoke and, as before, she found the silence seductive, filled with anticipation and promise.

When, finally, the last button came free, Roselyn drew a shaky breath. He'd accomplished it without touching her; not once had she felt his fingers against her skin. He managed to do the same as he opened her blouse. Slowly, it fell from her shoulders.

She wore a red satin bra Barb had given her for Christmas last year. Roselyn glanced down, saw that her nipples had beaded against the satin. The first trickle of self-consciousness found its way into her psyche, but before she could let it consume her, a new sensation drowned it. A quick snap against her right breast, then something warm and wet, dampening the cup of her bra, spiraling need down deep into her belly. His mouth, she realized, his mouth on her breast. And then his hands on her hips, her stomach, sliding down the zipper on her jeans, popping the snap at her waistband.

"Do they match?" he asked, his voice like coarse velvet.

"Wh-what?"

"Your panties. Do they match the bra?"

"Yes . . . I—" Oh, God, his breath felt so warm. It tickled her navel as he slid her jeans down . . . down . . . down. "I'm sorry. I—" She closed her eyes, her laugh nerve-tinged and self-conscious as she stepped out of her jeans, then nudged them aside with her foot. "I might as well just tell you now that I have a thing for . . . well . . . I guess some people might call it kinky underwear."

"You're apologizing for this?" She felt his fingers brush gently across the silk triangle that barely covered her bottom. "For *this*." His hand came around, traced the lacy elastic band in front that stretched from hipbone to hipbone. "I should be thanking you, not listening to you apologize. Don't ever feel embarrassed with me, Rosy. I like your taste in underwear. I'm crazy about it."

"It doesn't surprise you that someone like me would wear lingerie like this?"

His hand stilled and, for a moment, he didn't say anything. Roselyn realized his answer meant everything to her, though she wasn't sure what words she hoped to hear him say.

He swept a kiss across her lips, cupped her face in his palms. "Someone like you? I don't know what you mean. You're a beautiful, sexy woman and you like beautiful, sexy underwear. Why should that surprise me?"

Roselyn thought it was the perfect answer as he kissed her again, this time not so gently, but with the same urgency she felt, the same hunger. She reached up, found his shoulders, wrapped her arms around him.

She realized he was naked when he pulled her against him. Naked from head to toe. She ran her palms down his arms, traced her fingers over lean muscle, bulging veins. His chest . . . so warm . . . she skimmed her hands across it, felt a light dusting of hair. Her hands traveled down, down to his stomach . . . and oh, her breath caught, his stomach was hard and flat and . . . Roselyn went still as her hand moved lower still.

"J.T.—"

She heard his breath catch. "We were doing just fine without conversation, darlin'." He caught her lower lip between his teeth, scraped it gently before releasing it.

"I'm sorry. I forgot you don't like me calling you that."

"I do now."

"Good." He laughed quietly. "I was going to ask you to just keep doing what you were doing. I was liking it just fine."

"Me, too." Her voice sounded breathless, shaky. "But I really want to see you."

"Wish I could help you with that, but—"

"No." She stepped away from him, stooped, reached behind and grabbed her jeans off the floor where she'd kicked them. She slipped one hand inside the pocket, then pulled free the strip of condoms, holding them out for him to see.

"We have plenty of time before I'll need those," J.T. said with a low chuckle, his voice vibrating over her, teasing her nerve endings. "I've got a few things planned first."

"J.T. . . . Look closer." She held the packets up higher so that the strip fell open like slats on miniblinds. "They're multicolored. Glow-in-the-dark." Her grin spread slowly. "As I was saying, I really, really want to *see* you."

His quiet laugh wrapped around her like the music she loved so much.

"Where'd you get those?"

"Barb gave them to me."

"I suspected Barb was my kind of woman."

"I knew you'd like her."

"Well . . ." he said, his palms sliding down her shoulders, scattering goose bumps all over her skin. "Do you want to do the honors or shall I?"

Roselyn hadn't expected that question. She'd just assumed he'd do it. Her experience at such matters amounted to zilch. Still, she guessed now was as good a first time as any. She tore off one packet, then tossed the strip on the bed.

"I think I'd like to," she answered. "I might need some assistance, though, considering the circumstances."

She opened the package, removed the contents. Reaching out tentatively with her free hand, she came in contact with what felt like his stomach and heard the hitch in his breath.

"I don't know about that. Trial and error on your part might be fun."

She hesitated. "J.T. . . . I've never . . ."

"You don't mean . . . ?"

"No . . . no, not that. I've done *this* before. I've just never done *this* part of this."

"Take your time," he said, his voice amused.

Roselyn did take her time. A minute or so later, she stared down at him, stunned.

"Blue," J.T. said, sounding stunned himself, but still amused. "My favorite color."

"Um . . ." Her mouth had gone dry. She cleared her throat. "Mine, too. Blue, that is. It's my favorite color. It is now, anyway."

He laughed. "Well . . . this is interesting. I'm . . . uh . . . pretty sure I've never been in this situation before."

"Situation?" she asked, still staring.

"Yeah, a situation where a woman carries on a conversation with my—"

"Oh!" Roselyn pulled her hand away, averted her eyes, winced. "I'm sorry. Oh, my word. I didn't mean to look there while we . . . it's just that it's the only part of you I can see and—"

"I don't mind." He took her chin, turned her toward him. "Stare all you like."

"I don't know if I can now." Her eyes were closed. Opening them slightly, she peeked at the blue glow again. "It's weird."

"Weird? There you go again. Bruising my ego."

She covered her face with her hands. "*It's* not weird,

this entire *experience* is weird. It's as if I'm conversing with a talking—"

"It's—" His fingers left her chin. "What's . . . ? *Damn*."

Roselyn lowered her hand, heard a hiss, felt something soft and warm and furry pass across her ankle. She looked down and saw a dark movement at her feet. Blinking, she realized it was Gomez, her mother's cat, teeth bared, hissing and swiping out toward the blue glow, which slashed left then right like a frantic laser beam. She bent down. "Gomez, how did you get in here?" When she reached for the cat, he leaped away from her toward the moving blue glow, spitting wildly.

J.T. swore. "Never mind how he got in here, get him out before he attacks me."

The glow hovered over the bed now; Gomez jumped up there, too.

"I'm trying. He's tricky." Roselyn said. "Gomez, come here, boy."

"That animal's possessed. Watch out! Don't let him scratch you." He gasped. "Don't let him scratch me."

Roselyn tiptoed up to the bed. "He won't hurt me." She grabbed the cat from behind. "Gotcha!"

J.T. blew out a noisy breath of relief.

A giggle worked its way up Roselyn's throat as she let the cat out, closed the door again, and turned to find the blue glow still suspended above the bed. "You can come down now." She giggled again.

"Very funny," he said.

She watched the light move down, away from the bed, toward her. "Sorry about that. Maybe the glow in the dark thing wasn't such a good idea. It's sort of spoiled the mood, hasn't it?"

When he stopped in front of her, she couldn't stop her eyes from lowering. Perhaps it had only spoiled mood, Roselyn decided. From the looks of it, J.T. was still ready, willing, and able.

"Close your eyes, Rosy."

"What?"

"Close your eyes."

"Why?" Instead of closing them, she opened them wider as the stunning blue streak of light moved even closer and, beneath her stare, became even more impressive than before.

"We're going to work on getting that mood back," J.T. said.

Rosy's eyes closed. J.T. took her hands in his and led her to the bed. He couldn't remember ever wanting a woman more. She blew his mind with her constant surprises. Her Vegas family. Her fancy underwear. Showing up in his room tonight.

The women he normally romanced were easy to figure out because they always stayed close to the surface. Nothing complicated. He had always thought he preferred that type. Shallow, predictable women were nonthreatening; they kept life simple.

Then he met Rosy. She made him think and look deeper inside of himself. She made him feel. He was discovering those particular activities weren't so bad, after all. A little scary at times, maybe a little uncomfortable. But challenging and insightful. No denying that fact.

And more interesting by the moment, J.T. thought as he moved the strip of condoms off the bed and tossed them onto the nightstand. Talk about surprises. When she'd pulled those out of her pocket he'd felt like a kid again. For days now, he'd imagined going to bed with her. He'd been doing exactly that when she opened the door and walked into his fantasy for real. But in all those imaginings, the sex had been intense, serious, sultry. He'd never dreamed it would also have a light side, a fun side, with multicolored condoms and titillating conversation.

He sat on the bed, drew her down beside him, watched her. Rosy's short hair was tousled; her eyes remained closed. J.T. looked lower, skimmed his attention between the red bra and panties. He started to sweat. Amazing. Her body amazed him. The sight of it was enough to drive him crazy. Some might say she was too thin, too pale. But he thought she looked perfect. Perfect and unique. One of a kind. His kind.

He touched her cheek with the palm of his hand, slid it down her neck, across her shoulder. Bending forward, he eased her back against the pillows, then lowered his mouth to her lips.

Her hands came up, found his face, his shoulders, his back. She traced her fingers down the length of his spine, then opened her eyes.

"Rosy," he said quietly. "Can you feel me looking at you?"

"Yes," she whispered as he moved on top of her, settling his elbows at either side of the pillow where her head rested.

She touched his nose then his mouth, lingering there to stroke his lower lip.

J.T. kissed her fingers, then took one of her hands and slid it up to his eyes. He pressed her fingertips gently against each lid. "Look here."

Her gaze lifted to the place her fingers touched.

"You're looking into my eyes," he said. "I'm looking into yours."

She lowered her hand, but kept her gaze steady. "What do you see?"

He pushed a lock of hair off her forehead while his pulse went wild and his body ached. She looked at him as if she could see his face. More than that, as if she saw inside of him. Her eyes shone in the moonlight, so warm, so honest, so clear he thought he, too, could look right down to her soul. "I see your heart," he said. It was as fragile as it was beautiful, and she trusted him with it. The enormity of that responsibility awed and frightened him. "Rosy, are you sure you want this?"

She smiled. "Yes, I'm sure."

"Why?"

Her laugh was soft as a breeze. "Look who's chatty now." She found his mouth with her fingertips, then kissed him. "Don't ask questions. Just make love to me."

When she pulled his head toward her, J.T. covered her mouth with his, anticipation shivering through him. Her lips parted in welcome, and she tasted even better than he remembered. Sweeter. Wilder. He nipped at her lower lip the way he'd imagined doing as he sat in the dark earlier, thinking of her, of them together and how it might be. He wanted her in every way he'd fantasized. Slow and easy, hard and fast. Under him. On top of him.

Just as he'd imagined doing, he explored every dip and rise of her body, the texture of her skin, the jut of each bone. And as he did, Rosy's hands and mouth moved over him too, twisting the needs and wants tighter inside of him.

He fumbled for the hook between her breasts.

She reached up to help him.

Their fingers bumped. The bra fell away.

Soft laughter drifted across the room, became murmured words of pleasure as he learned the curve of her breast, dissolved into a soft, sweet silence punctuated by sighs when he tasted her.

Rolling to his back, J.T. took her with him so that she was on top of him now. The moonlight reached through the window and found her, bathing her in silver, letting him see her more clearly. He fought every instinct urging him to hurry, to feel her warm and wet and tight around him, to release the tension building inside. As much as he wanted that, he sensed she was keeping a part of herself remote and detached, separate from what was happening between them. He didn't want only part of her; he wanted everything. He wanted her so drunk with needs that she couldn't hold anything back if she tried, that she couldn't think of anything but him and the pleasure she felt.

He stroked his palms over the satin covering her bottom, around and up to her breasts, slowly back down, teasing and tormenting until her eyes were hazy and the sounds she made were almost desperate with longing. Finally he slid her panties down her legs, helped her out of them.

The sight of her naked above him, so small and pale and soft, made his breath catch, started a pounding in his head and chest that staggered him. "Rosy," he murmured, drawing her to him, absorbing the feel of her bare breasts against his chest, sliding his fingers through her hair as he guided her mouth to his. "Open your eyes. I'm here. Look at me. I want to see your eyes."

A moment before their mouths touched, she blinked and their gazes connected . . . just as they had once before. Their kiss was hot and needy, and when it ended Rosy sat up, her knees at either side of him.

Watching her face, J.T. moved his hands to her hips, shifted her body slightly. And then he slowly sank into her, into her warmth and her sigh, memorizing each subtle change in her expression, hearing her whisper his name. The sound of it echoed through him, and he went still, savoring the sensation of her body wrapping around him.

Slowly . . . slowly . . . her shadowed silhouette moved above him, starting the pace. It was a different sort of dance, her movements all the more erotic because he couldn't see his own body, only hers . . . arching in the filtered moonlight, swaying to a silent beat.

He wondered what thoughts drifted through her

mind . . . if she imagined his face and body beneath her own . . . if this felt as real to her as it did to him, or more like a seductive dream. And then she cried out, and he had no more questions, no thoughts at all.

He'd planned to crumble all her barriers, to empty her mind of doubts and questions until nothing remained but him and the way he made her feel. Not once had he expected to end up mindless, too, completely lost to all but her and a yearning so intense it obliterated everything except the tangle of heat as they melted together, the mingling of sounds . . . her breath and his, the salty taste of her skin as he finally let go.

Chapter Sixteen

Roselyn drifted back slowly, aware first of a comforting, pleasant, moving presence underneath her, supporting her. She didn't dare open her eyes for fear it had all been a dream and she'd find herself alone in the room, alone in bed.

She felt something nibble at her ear, something warm and wonderful, and knew she hadn't been dreaming. J.T. Drake had just made love to her and she'd loved him back and it had been the most incredible experience of her life.

Still, she wouldn't open her eyes because, if she did, she knew that, though he lay underneath her right this very second, she wouldn't be able to see him. It was easier without sight to imagine the silky dark hair between her fingers, his broad shoulders and muscled back, his firm buttocks and the long legs now entwined with hers. Just by touching him, she thought she knew exactly how his face and body looked, even the strong hands that had

Jennifer Archer

stroked life back into her soul and brought her indescribable pleasure. It would be too strange to look down and see herself sprawled naked above the bed, her legs apart, her arms encircling nothing.

"Mmmm, that feels good," he said, as her hands moved slowly over him.

After a moment, when he stirred as if he meant to get up, she wrapped her arms tighter around him. "Don't go."

He laughed. "I thought you might've worked up a thirst. I know I did. Wouldn't you like some water? I promise I'll be right back."

She nuzzled his neck. "Okay. Just don't take too long. I'll miss you."

"I'll be back so fast you won't even know I've been gone."

"Watch out for Gomez."

"Thanks for reminding me."

When she heard the door open then close, Roselyn blinked and sat up. Suddenly, the fact that she'd just experienced sex in her childhood bed, in her mother's home, cast awkwardness over the moment. She almost felt as if she'd done something sneaky and would get into trouble if her mother found out. Roselyn smiled. Not that her mother wouldn't have something to say about it. Keeping this a secret from Darla Peabody would be next to impossible, and Roselyn knew her mother well enough to know there would be plenty of warnings as well as words of advice, asked for or not.

She switched on the lamp, then stood to smooth the rumpled bed. J.T.'s suitcase lay open on the floor. She grabbed a T-shirt from it and slipped it over her head. The garment fell to mid-thigh and smelled like him.

Roselyn walked to the dresser, picked up an old bottle of perfume she'd been given as a gift years ago but never

228

used. At the time it had seemed too frivolous for her; she would've been embarrassed to wear it.

She pulled off the top and sprayed a little onto her wrist. The exotic and mysterious scent seemed appropriate for what she'd just experienced. Making love with a man she couldn't see had been arousing in a way she had not anticipated. There had been an edge of forbidden impropriety to it that she'd found irresistible.

Roselyn sprayed her other wrist and then her neck before recapping the bottle and placing it back on the dresser.

The door opened. Two glasses of water floated, side by side, into the room. "You're up."

"I was restless waiting for you."

"I almost ran into your mother in the kitchen. Seems she's having trouble sleeping."

"You spoke to her?"

He handed her a glass. "Not until she spoke first. When I saw her I decided to forget about the water and just slip back in here without her knowing any different but it seems she smelled me."

Roselyn winced. "You do have a very distinctive scent."

"Guess I should buy a stronger deodorant."

"No, it's a good scent. Believe me." She sat on the edge of the bed and motioned him to join her. "So, what did she say?"

"Your mother?"

J.T.'s glass glided toward her then made a smooth landing on the nightstand. Roselyn felt his weight settle on the mattress beside her.

"She said that you and I are both adults, and that she won't try to stop what we've started even though it's taking place under her roof."

Roselyn winced again.

"I know what you mean. I felt scolded. Worse, I felt

as if I deserved it. I told her I'd sleep on the sofa from now on so you could each have a room to yourself, but she said there was no sense in that. She suspects the deed's already been done and that, anyway, how would she know I was really on the sofa? It's hard to keep an eye on someone you can't see."

"Smart woman, my mother."

"Yeah. Scary, too. She told me she'd kick my voice up two octaves if I hurt you like that asshole Kyle some-body-or-other once did."

"Oh." Roselyn turned her head away from him so he couldn't see the embarrassed expression on her face. "I wish she hadn't said that."

"Who's Kyle?"

"Nobody important." She lifted her glass of water and took a long drink.

"What's that you're wearing?"

"Your T-shirt. I hope you don't mind."

"Not a bit. It never looked that good on me. But I wasn't talking about the shirt." He drew a long breath. "I meant the scent."

"Oh." She pointed to the bottle on the dresser. "It's some old perfume." She lifted her wrist toward him. "Do you like it?"

"Nice. But it makes my nose itch. I have allergies. Flowers and anything closely related tends to set me off."

"I wish I'd known that." Dipping her chin she looked up at the place where she thought his eyes would be. "Does that mean you won't kiss me until after I take a shower?"

She squealed when he grabbed her, then laughed when he pulled her down on the bed and nibbled at her neck. "Try keeping me away. Now . . ." He pinned her wrists over her head. "Tell me about Kyle what's-his-name."

"You sound congested," she said, trying to free her

hands and squirm out from under him. "Let me wash off this perfume."

"I'm fine. Quit trying to change the subject."

"I told you he's nobody."

"Then why do you tense up whenever I mention him?"

"Okay." She sighed. "He's a bad memory from my senior year of high school."

He released her wrists. "Must be a really bad one to still get such a reaction out of you after all this time."

When she sat up, she felt his arm go around her. She leaned into him, laid her head back against his shoulder, thankful for the support. "Every high school has at least one student nobody pays any attention to unless it's to poke fun at them. You know, the boy or girl who doesn't fit in, who blends in with the woodwork, blows the curve, and keeps quiet. I'm sure you had such a classmate."

He nodded. "Her name was Jayne Nelson. She was at least a hundred times smarter than the rest of us but she lived in her own strange little world. And talk about bad fashion sense." He laughed. "She didn't have any real friends that I can think of, which is sad. Kids can be brutal. I was never mean to her but, like you said, I never paid her much attention, either. If she just wouldn't have done such offbeat things, life might've been easier . . . better for her."

"What kind of offbeat things did she do?"

"For one, she would sit in her desk and rock slightly back and forth. And I remember that whenever she read aloud in English Lit, she used a different voice for each character in the story." He laughed again. "Jayne was a very odd girl."

"Well . . . I was the Jayne Nelson of my high school."

"I don't believe you. You're too damn pretty to blend into the woodwork. Besides, I seriously doubt that Jayne ever wore red satin and lace underwear. I'm positive it was white cotton all the way for her."

"Believe me or don't, that's up to you. But the truth is your Jayne and I had a lot in common from what you've told me about her, though she may have been a tad more eccentric. I didn't rock, and instead of reading in character, I took my science book to pep rallies and assemblies and studied or worked problems. I was a joke to my classmates, the school oddball. I knew it, but I didn't know how to change it."

When he didn't say anything for almost a full minute, Roselyn feared he felt sorry for her. Pity was the last thing she wanted from J.T. Which was why she wished her mother had never mentioned Kyle. "It's okay." She patted his leg. "I'm not sure I would've changed it if I could have. I played the egghead role for so long I guess I became almost comfortable in it. At least it was safe. I knew what to expect. I did until Kyle pulled his little stunt, anyway."

"Stunt?"

"He asked me to the prom. He was the captain of both the football and lacrosse teams and he asked me, nerdy, plain-jane little Roselyn Peabody to the senior prom. I couldn't believe it. As it turned out, I shouldn't have. But I was just so thrilled. I might've been an oddball but I was also a teenaged girl and I wasn't immune to Kyle's good looks and raw sex appeal. He had plenty of both and he knew just how to work them to his advantage with the girls." She paused then said, "Somewhat like you."

J.T. cleared his throat but didn't defend himself.

"Kyle planned it all carefully. First he became my friend, then he asked me to the prom, then he spent the next couple of weeks making me believe he was serious."

"Wasn't he?"

"We were in the same chemistry class together. He

asked me to tutor him. That's how it started. He would come over here after school or I'd go to his house and we'd study." She huffed. "Or rather, I thought we were studying. I studied, he seduced."

The heat of a blush crept up her neck. Telling the story brought back the old feelings . . . the exhilaration, the hope that things were finally changing for her and, fi-. nally, the humiliation.

"Rosy." J.T. drew her closer to him. "You don't have to tell me any more. I shouldn't have forced the issue."

"No. I want to tell you. I need to say it. It's ridiculous that I've let something that happened when I was just a girl affect me for all these years."

She swallowed the knot of shame that had lodged in her throat, angry with herself for feeling such an emotion over something that had not been her fault.

"Kyle was the first boy to ever kiss me. It started out innocent enough. At least I thought it did." She laughed. "I was pathetically idealistic. I wanted to teach him chemistry; he wanted to copy my work. I was adamantly opposed to it. All it took was a peck on the lips and I gave in a little. I did a little less teaching and he did a little more copying. I'd insist he work the problems, then I'd check them and help with corrections. That took quite a lot of extra time, though, because I wanted to make certain he understood the changes. He complained about the time it took and tried to convince me he'd learn just as much only a whole lot faster if he watched me work the problems for him. When I stood my ground, his kisses became less innocent and more passionate. I gave in a little more. He asked me to the prom. The more interest he showed in me, the more of his work I did, until finally we were sneaking quickies in his bedroom while his parents watched television in the den, and I was doing all of his work, no questions asked."

She shook her head, smiling. "I remember getting

ready for the prom. I think Mama and Barb were more excited than I was. Sully, too, bless his heart. After Mama and Barb helped me dress and fixed my hair and makeup, he oohed and aahed and took pictures. I felt like a princess." She lowered her head, looked down at her hands where they rested in her lap. "You can probably guess what happened."

"The bastard didn't show up."

The tears mortified and surprised her. When the room blurred, she blinked until everything came back into focus again. How could a high school heartbreak still do this to her? She had never loved Kyle; he had simply hurt her pride. "Come to find out," she said, swiping at her eyes, "he was flunking chemistry and was not going to get to play the last lacrosse game of the season if he didn't make a good grade for the six weeks. Kyle knew I was the perfect person to help him. Not only was I the smartest girl in our class, I was the loneliest. I suppose he thought that if he showed me enough attention and made just the right promises, I'd do anything he asked. He was right."

J.T. wrapped both of his arms around her and held on tight. "Almost all teenaged boys are insensitive jerks from time to time. I know I was. But what he did went beyond insensitivity. It was just mean. He was the loser, Rosy, not you."

"I know that now. I found out later it had all started out as a dare from his friends. They dared him to pretend to be interested in me and to ask me out. I guess it occurred to Kyle that I could be the answer to his chemistry problem, so he took things even further." She lifted her chin. "I'm angry with myself more than him. I let a seventeen-year-old boy's selfish prank affect every relationship I've had with the opposite sex ever since."

Turning in his arms, she reached up and touched his face. "Do you want to know how truly pitiful I am? You are the first person I've had sex with since Kyle. Because of that one incident, I've been celibate since I was seventeen years old."

"I don't know what to say."

"Oh, I had a few opportunities, though it's a miracle any guy ever looked twice at me I was so uptight. I was just so afraid of being used again. Any time anyone showed an interest in me I became suspicious of their motives."

He kissed her, a hard, possessive, protective kiss that made her heart lift and swell, that made her feel desirable and beautiful and important; for the first time in her life she felt cherished as a woman.

"I don't have an ulterior motive when it comes to you," he said against her lips. "I'm with you because I like being with you, is that understood?"

She caught her breath. "Yes."

"You're sure? I don't want any doubts on your part."

"I—" She pressed her lips together, looked away. "I admit I wondered at first. Other than your father, I'm the one person who might be able to make you normal again. You and I both know that the professor is slipping somewhat when it comes to his mental capabilities."

He took her chin in his hand, turned her head toward him and kissed her again. "After knowing you for only five minutes," he said, "it was clear to me you have a strong sense of honor and morality. I suspected you hated my guts and I knew you disapproved of me. But I also didn't doubt that none of that mattered. You would do whatever you could to help me."

Roselyn smiled. "I didn't hate your guts. I only strongly disliked them."

"That didn't stop you from staring at my picture while you danced in your underwear."

The teasing note in his voice did funny things to her stomach. "I disliked your guts, not the way you look. I happen to like the way you look very much. At least in your picture. I'm hoping you're not simply extremely photogenic. I'd hate to be disappointed when I see the real thing."

The hem of her T-shirt lifted. Roselyn raised her arms as he pulled it over her head. "You saw one part of the real thing tonight," he murmured. "What did you think?"

"I liked what I saw very much," she said, then let out a sigh as he cupped her breast. "I can only hope I like it just as much when it isn't blue."

"Oh, you will. I promise."

"Such ego," she said, then felt his mouth warm her skin.

Suddenly, he pulled back and sneezed.

A flash of dark wavy hair, broad shoulders, bare skin appeared.

Roselyn gasped.

"Excuse me," J.T. said, sounding more congested than ever. "It must be that perfume you have on. Maybe you should wash it off, after all."

"I saw you," Roselyn whispered, grabbing the shirt off the bed again and tugging it over her head.

"You what?"

"When you sneezed. I saw you for just an instant. You flashed into view, then disappeared."

"That can't be. Can it? You must've imagined it."

She covered her mouth with her hands, blinked at him, her pulse kicking up. "Your hair is dark. It's a little long in back, a little wavy."

"You know that from touching it."

"Your shoulders are wide. You have quite a nice body."

"Rosy . . . you would know that better than anyone. You've had your arms wrapped around me and my shoulders a good part of the night." He laughed. "Oh,

236

and thanks for the compliment, by the way."

She stood quickly and hurried over to the dresser. After uncapping the bottle of perfume, she splashed more on.

"What are you doing?"

"Take a deep breath," she said, rushing back to the place where he sat. "Let's see if we can't make you sneeze again."

"This is crazy."

"Just do it."

She heard the rush of air as he drew it into his lungs. "Rosy, I—aah . . . ahh . . . ahh . . ."

"That's it! That's it! Just let go!"

He groaned. "I lost it. I can't sneeze on demand. It doesn't work like that."

She sat on the bed. "Then kiss me. Kiss me and don't think about sneezing and maybe you'll sneeze."

"I'll be more than happy to kiss you but now that you've put the idea in my mind I'm not going to be able to forget about sneezing."

"Have you so little faith in the power of my kisses?" Glancing down, she stuck out her lower lip and frowned.

His sneeze vibrated the bed.

"My word, it *is* impressive!" Her chin lifted. "Even when it's not blue."

"You didn't—"

"Oh, yes I did! I saw you. Just for a second, mind you, but that was enough." Grinning, she fanned her face with one hand. "Verrrry nice."

"I think you're trying to pull a fast one on me."

"I'll prove it." She crossed her arms. "I'll prove I saw you. You have a scar . . . on your right hipbone, if I'm not mistaken."

"You did see me! How did you spot that so quickly?"

"I was staring at just the right spot, I suppose." Roselyn stood again and started to pace, her mind trying to outrace her pulse.

"What do you think this means?"

"I don't know for certain. I've never dealt with this before. As you already know, your father and I never made it this far with the refractor. But I'd say it's a very good sign. We should call the professor first thing in the morning and tell him about this latest development. That is, if you're not already completely visible by then."

"Do you think that's possible?"

"I don't know why not. On the other hand, it might take the effects a while to wear off completely. Or this could simply be something that's been happening all along but we just weren't aware of it. I can't recall ever hearing you sneeze before now."

"Well, whatever it is, make sure you don't wear that perfume to Domani's party tomorrow night. I'd hate to flash into view at the wrong moment."

"I didn't think of that." She drew her lower lip between her teeth. "Please be careful."

"We all need to be careful around Domani, not just me. In fact, as long as I stay invisible, I'm the safest one of all. I may flash into view from time to time, but I'm still transparent. And like your mom said, it's difficult to keep an eye on something you can't see."

Chapter Seventeen

Music throbbed like an anxious heartbeat throughout Anthony Domani's penthouse apartment. J.T. stood a few steps up the staircase. Since arriving at the party, he'd overheard Domani remind Sully at least twice that upstairs was off-limits to the guests, so J.T. felt confident he'd be out of the way there, without any chance of anyone bumping into him.

This morning when he awoke to find he was still invisible, he and Rosy had called home. Pop was as surprised as they'd been by the flashing incident. He'd had no advice to give them or predictions of what to expect. J.T. assumed that as long as he didn't sneeze, he'd be okay.

Below, at the foot of the stairs, Domani pulled Reneau aside. He glanced across the room where Sully stood watch over the crowd. "You're sure that clown's on the up and up?"

Though the party had only been in swing for a little

more than an hour, the old man's words already slurred, and his nose glowed like a shiny red apple.

"His references were impeccable," Reneau answered. "Tucker worked security for years on the strip then managed one of Lou Linville's clubs for more than a decade."

"Lou didn't fire him, did he?"

Reneau shook his head. "Tucker retired. With full benefits, I might add."

"Good. Lou's a regular Sunday school teacher. He wouldn't have anyone on his payroll who wasn't first class and squeaky clean." Domani's gaze strayed back to Reneau. "So I'm counting on nothin' going wrong tonight, understood?"

"As always."

"I'll hold you responsible for any foul-ups."

The ligaments in Reneau's neck pulled tight. "I have everything under control, Anthony. Just enjoy yourself."

Domani emptied his glass, then leered at Rosy as she passed by with flutes of sparkling wine on a tray. "You can bet on that." He took off after her.

Reneau swore under his breath, then smiled brightly at an approaching middle-aged man and his young female companion. "Ed Baruski!" Turning his back to J.T., Reneau shook the man's hand. "This must be your lovely wife. Olivia, isn't it?" He executed a half-bow. "I'm Bartholomew Reneau."

J.T. zeroed in on the lady's bustline. There was no ignoring it; some plastic surgeon had given the woman her money's worth. Her dress fit so tight that if she drew a deep enough breath, champagne corks wouldn't be the only things popping at the party tonight.

The woman fluttered her lashes and smiled. "I'm flattered you'd remember."

Ed Baruski paid little attention to the exchange between Reneau and his wife. He seemed more interested in Domani, who was drinking champagne out of Rosy's spike-heeled pump.

Rosy giggled like Marilyn Monroe when the old man slipped the shoe back onto her foot. She played her part well. Better than J.T. had expected considering how nervous she'd been about it. And she looked incredible in the revealing tuxedo-like costume all the hostesses wore. When they'd met with Barb and Sully and Darla last night over dinner, they'd decided that the women should see to it that Domani got good and blasted tonight. They didn't want him thinking about security or the valuables in his safe, wherever it might be. In fact, the hazier his thinking, the better. From the looks of things, he was fast approaching a heavy fog.

"I haven't had a chance to talk to Tony yet tonight," Baruski said. "He plans on making time for me, doesn't he?"

J.T.'s irritation reached the boiling point when Domani slapped Rosy on the butt. For just a second, before she recovered her composure, he saw her cringe and her face flush red.

"Oh, yes, of course," Reneau assured Baruski. "Anthony has been looking forward to talking over his business proposal with you. He mentioned it just before the first guests arrived, as a matter of fact."

So Ed Baruski was a potential business associate of Domani's. J.T. knew opportunity when he saw it. When Olivia Baruski lifted her flute of champagne for a sip, he nudged Reneau in the small of the back with his foot. Reneau stumbled into Olivia. Her glass tipped. Wine trickled down between her cleavage.

"Look what you've done!" Mrs. Baruski shrieked as Reneau righted himself. "Edwin! My dress . . . It's ruined! Do you have any idea how much I spent on this?"

At least half the heads in the room turned to stare. Domani's was among them. He didn't look happy.

241

Reneau's hand trembled as he pulled a handkerchief from his pocket and held it out to the woman. "I'm so sorry. I don't know how that happened."

She glanced down at her damp chest, then glared at the handkerchief, her nostrils flaring.

J.T. stepped down two steps and off to the side of Reneau. He grasped hold of the older man's outstretched wrist and pulled, guiding the hanky toward the stain on Olivia Baruski's overfilled bodice.

The next seconds seemed to pass in slow motion. Reneau made a strangled noise of surprise, his face wrinkling with confusion and horror as he stared at his own hand. He struggled to pull back his arm but J.T. was too strong for him.

Olivia gasped as the handkerchief made contact with her bosom and one breast broke free of her low-cut bodice.

J.T. bit back a laugh, released Reneau's wrist and backed quietly up the staircase.

"Forgive me," Reneau said, his voice choked, "I didn't—" He crashed backward into the curved banister as Ed Baruski's fist slammed into his face.

A hush fell over the room, the only sound audible the beat of the music. Domani rushed forward and jerked Reneau up by the collar. "You stupid moron. I don't wanna see your face another second tonight, understand? Get the hell out of here." He shoved Reneau back against the staircase again, then faced Mrs. Baruski, apologizing profusely.

Sophia Reneau looked as angry as her brother as she barreled her way through the crowd to her husband's side. Laughter scattered throughout the room when she grabbed Bartholomew Reneau's arm and, speaking in angry whispers, hauled him off toward the kitchen.

J.T. scanned the faces of the guests until he found Reneau's secretary, Marie. She watched her lover and his wife depart, her eyes bitter and determined.

Smiling, J.T. whistled quietly under his breath. Things were looking good.

Roselyn slipped into the powder room and sighed. Two wooden swinging doors led into an adjoining small room with a toilet. Roselyn peeked beneath them, relieved when she didn't see any feet.

Her own feet felt like she'd hiked Mount Everest on tiptoe. She kicked off one shiny black high heel then the other. Both of her big toes had poked through the little diamond-shaped holes in her fishnet stockings, turning them into big round holes the size of quarters. "Attractive," Roselyn muttered. Her right foot was still damp from the champagne Domani had poured into her shoe. As if that weren't uncomfortable enough, her skimpy faux-tuxedo strapless bra top was starting to bind. She pulled out the silicone inserts and plopped them on the vanity top, thinking they looked like two beached jellyfish, lying side by side.

Leaning closer to the mirror, she saw that she'd licked off the siren red lipstick Barb had insisted she wear. "I'm not cut out for this."

Something pinched her butt. Roselyn's hand flew back to the black stretchy panties beneath the tiny ruffle of her skirt. She glanced over her shoulder.

"How are you holding up?" J.T. murmured.

She turned. "You scared me to death."

"Sorry. I've always had a hard time resisting temptation." She felt the light sting of a spark at her bare shoulder, followed by the touch of his hand. "And you do look tempting in this getup."

"I look ridiculous."

From out of thin air, a kiss brushed her lips. "Ridiculously tempting," he said.

"When I felt that pinch I was afraid Domani might've

followed me in here. That dirty-minded old geezer has been putting his hands all over me the entire night."

"I know. I'm finding it tough to keep from poking the guy's eyes out. If he slaps your bottom one more time, I just might do it." He nuzzled the side of her neck. "Relax, darlin'. Instead of that dirty-minded old geezer you got this dirty-minded young one."

Roselyn felt his hands encircle her waist. He lifted her onto the vanity then stroked his palms down her bare back to her bottom.

"You wouldn't let him get this far, would you?"

"Who?" Roselyn asked, feeling light-headed. She'd always heard that falling in love could make a person dizzy, but she'd never really believed it.

"Domani."

Falling in love. Where had that thought come from? She pressed her hands against his chest, slid them up to encircle his neck. "Of course I wouldn't let Domani get this far. What kind of girl do you think I am?"

"My kind."

"Exactly. Which is why I'm not stopping you."

But she did think of protesting when he reached for her legs and coaxed her to wrap them around him. They could easily get caught; someone might walk in at any second. But, somehow, that only added to the excitement pulsing through her.

Leaning her head back against the mirror, Roselyn closed her eyes. She felt the warmth of his lips at the side of her neck again. "Who's watching Reneau?" she asked, surprised by the low, throaty sound of her own voice.

"Barb is. He's busy getting his ass chewed by his wife. From the look in her eye, I'm guessing she's planning to draw out the torture, so when I saw you headed this way I found Barb and told her I needed to talk to you. She'll let me know if Reneau leaves the kitchen." His kisses moved lower, across her collarbone, over the curve of her breasts.

"What happened out there with Reneau and that woman . . . I'm assuming that was your handiwork?"

He laughed. "Yeah, pretty effective, wasn't it? I expect that right about now Reneau would do anything to get back at Domani for humiliating him."

Roselyn was having a difficult time concentrating on his words. She'd never done anything so spontaneous, so reckless, so wild. It dawned on her that J.T.'s chest was bare. Moving her hands further down, she found that his shorts were gone, too; he only wore his underwear. She knew he'd dressed in his invisible clothing for the party, the T-shirt and shorts and shoes he'd worn the night he'd stumbled across the refractor. "Your clothes . . ."

"One of the guests was standing near me when she dropped her bloody mary. It splattered all over me . . . stained my shirt and shorts. It was the weirdest sight you ever saw—just those stains suspended in the air. The lady saw them too, for a second, anyway." He laughed. "She looked like she thought she might be hallucinating. I turned to face the wall as fast as I could. Then I hurried down the hallway, took off my clothes, and stuffed them in a closet."

"I'll be distracted the rest of the night, imagining you running around here in only your underwear."

"You think it's not driving me crazy watching you run around in yours?"

"This isn't my underwear."

He slid his fingers beneath the elastic band around one leg of her panties. "It might as well be. You don't have on anything under it but skin." With a groan, he found her center. "Nice, smooth skin."

Roselyn closed her eyes again as he stroked away the last of her inhibitions. She heard the rush of blood in her ears, the sound of his breathing, the sound of hers. The party on the other side of the wall seemed another world away, so far, in fact that at first the sound of the door opening didn't penetrate her hazy brain.

"Rosebud . . . ? What are you doing?"

Barb's voice snapped Rosy back to attention. Her eyes flew open and, when she felt J.T. jerk back his hand, she lowered her legs and scrambled off the vanity, grasping at her clothing to make certain nothing was amiss.

"Oh!" Barb's laugh sounded startled. "I came looking for J.T. I thought he . . . goodness he is, isn't he?" She bit her lower lip, and then started to laugh again. "I interrupted something, didn't I?"

Roselyn's tongue wouldn't work. She turned to face the mirror, grabbed the silicone inserts off the vanity and stuffed them back into her bra top.

"Hello, Barb," J.T. said.

Roselyn glanced up and saw Barb's delighted grin in the mirror. "Hello J.T., wherever you are. No wonder you needed a break."

"Is something up?" he asked.

Lifting a brow, Barb placed a hand on her hip. "You tell me, Sugar."

"Very funny, Barb," Roselyn said, finally finding her voice again. She couldn't recall the last time she'd been so embarrassed.

Barb stepped further into the powder room, then turned and twisted the latch beneath the doorknob. "This locks, you know," she said, grinning. "Might not be as much fun that way, though." She nodded toward the swinging wooden doors that led to the toilet. "I'm assuming no one's in there."

"I checked for feet when I came in. We're alone."

"Good." Squinting, Barb looked around the powder room. "J.T.?"

"Right here," he answered, his voice coming from Roselyn's right.

"Reneau finally escaped his wife and left the kitchen. He's been holed up in the hallway for the past few minutes with his secretary. They've had their heads together, and I don't think they were talking office politics. Just before I came in here, he started upstairs."

"Did Domani see him?" J.T. asked.

"No. Reneau watched from the hallway until Domani was out of sight before he went up there."

"Okay, this is it," J.T. said.

The excitement in his voice started Roselyn's heart racing. "What should we do?"

"I'll go upstairs and see what Reneau's up to. Give me ten or fifteen minutes, then follow me up. Wait in here so you don't have to deal with Domani. If we're lucky enough that Pop's research is hidden away up there somewhere, you're the only one who can identify it."

"How will I get up the stairs without Domani seeing me?"

"Barb, you tell Sully what's going on. He needs to see the way clear so Rosy can come upstairs while you and Darla keep the old man busy."

"That should be easy enough. We'll just pour more drinks down his throat."

"And keep 'em coming until Rosy's back downstairs. Stay surrounded by people. I don't want the two of you alone with him."

"You got it," Barb said, starting for the door. "I'm out of here. Good luck."

J.T. pulled Roselyn to him and gave her a quick kiss. "Be careful," he said.

She smiled. "You, too. I'll see you in ten minutes."

After he let go of her, Roselyn watched the door until it opened and closed before returning her attention to the mirror. Pulling a lipstick from her cleavage where Barb had showed her to hide it, she went to work on repairing the damage J.T.'s kisses had done.

A minute later, a noise behind her had her glancing up.

Anthony Domani came through the door, closed it behind him, locked it. His grin spread slowly. "Sneaky, sneaky." He wagged a finger at her. "Bet you thought you could hide from Tony, didn't you? You didn't know I saw you come in here a while ago and never come back out." He winked and moved closer. "I been trying to join you, but Baruski's had me backed into a corner talking business." He took another step. "Which is juss where I wanna get you." The grin widened. "Backed into a corner, that is. But I don't plan to talk business."

Roselyn lowered the lipstick to the vanity and turned to face him, her heart pounding. She forced a smile. "Now, Mr. Domani—"

"Call me Tony, sweetheart." He stepped closer still. "You and me, we're about to become very good friends."

Her stomach knotted, but Roselyn reminded herself to play the game. She thought he was too drunk to be of much threat to her. All it would take was one little shove to knock him off his feet. And if she could pinpoint what made him tick and tie that in with his interest in her, she could manipulate the situation to her advantage. Her mother, she'd discovered, was good at such maneuvering. Surely she'd inherited at least a fraction of the skill. She simply hadn't developed it.

In her mind, Roselyn replayed the encounter with Anthony Domani on the morning he'd hired them. Her mother had said things to make him feel superior, powerful, impressive. *Ego.* Roselyn's pulse jumped. That was the key to this man.

"Tony . . . it wouldn't be fair for me to keep you all to myself, as much as I'd like to. I don't mind sharing you with the guests at least until the party's over. Let's go out and dance." She gave him what she hoped was a coy look. "You haven't danced with me all night."

He trapped her against the vanity, bracing his hands at either side of her hips. "Have I tol' you that you look juss like your mother did back when she worked for me?" His tongue flicked out to moisten his upper lip. "Does Darla ever talk about me?"

Roselyn's knees felt weak. The stench of liquor on Domani's breath was suffocating. She'd never been in a tight spot such as this one before. For the first time in her life, she realized just how good a job her mother, Barb, and Sully had done in sheltering her from the more ugly side of their occupations. They must have dealt with drunken slobs on a frequent basis. For her, Roselyn thought. Her mother had put up with the likes of Anthony Domani and never once complained because she'd wanted to give her daughter a better life.

Though her heart raced and her stomach churned, Roselyn smiled into his bloodshot eyes, hoping the liquor had loosened his tongue. "Mama told me she regretted leaving you and playing hard to get. She said you were something special, that she wasn't sure what it was you had in the works, but she suspected it was something spectacular. Something most men wouldn't have the nerve to attempt."

"Darla said that, did she?" He puffed out his chest. "Well, she was right. I got things in the works the lightweights in this town never dreamed of. Big things."

She stroked her hand across the lapel of his jacket. "Oh, really? For instance?"

"You wouldn't be interested in the boring details, sweetheart."

"Oh, but I would. Big things excite me, Tony." She almost groaned at the tacky double entendre. "But you can't expect me to simply take your word for it. I have to see the proof with my own two eyes."

He chuckled. "Well, you're in luck. I'm not shy."

She giggled. "I'm talking about the big thing you've

got in the works. You know, your big project or whatever it is." She cocked her head to one side the way she'd seen Barb do a thousand times when flirting with men. "Will you show me?"

"Sure, sweetheart." He patted her fanny. "But first things first. Before I strike a bargain, I like a little sample of the merchandise being offered in exchange."

J.T. looked over Bartholomew Reneau's shoulder as he opened a door midway down the upstairs hallway. The bedroom the older man peeked into was tidy and empty. Reneau went inside, then poked his head into the adjoining bathroom. Seconds later, he came out again, closed the door and moved on down the hallway to the next room, where he paused and repeated his previous actions. When he came to the last door at the end of the hall he reached for the knob, then paused. J.T. noticed the tremor of Reneau's frail hand. The older man turned his head to stare toward the stairway at the hallway's opposite end, his gaze piercing straight through J.T. Reneau licked his lips, swallowed, his Adam's apple bobbing convulsively. Finally, he faced the door again, grasped the knob, then twisted it.

The curtains were open, and the city lights below illuminated the shadowed bedroom. It was different than all the others, larger and more masculine, with a more lived-in feel to it. *Domani's bedroom,* J.T. thought.

Reneau paused a moment before stepping inside and closing the door.

J.T. waited a few seconds, then opened it slightly himself. Reneau was entering the adjoining bathroom. J.T. quietly slipped into the room and followed the older man.

Once inside the bathroom, Reneau pulled a small flashlight from beneath his jacket and flicked it on.

J.T. looked around. The bathroom was massive, with

an ornate sunken tub, marble everywhere and mirrored walls from ceiling to floor. Bracing a hand on a vanity covered with men's toiletries, J.T. watched Reneau move into a walk-in closet across the way.

The closet looked big enough to hold a king-sized bed. Reneau sat the flashlight on a shelf, positioning it so that the beam shone on a row of business suits organized along the back wall. Then he shoved aside a number of the blazers to reveal the wall underneath. He ran his hand down the plaster, then paused to glance over his shoulder.

The flashlight beam glared on Reneau's long, gaunt face, exposing the uncertainty in his eyes. Holding his breath, J.T. stared at his mother's murderer and silently willed him to proceed.

After a moment, Reneau turned back to his task. He pushed against something J.T. couldn't see and a part of the wall slid aside, revealing a metal door with a numbered panel on the front. Reneau blew out a shaky breath, then reached back for the flashlight. He punched several numbers on the panel. A faint *click* sounded, then another shaky sigh as Reneau pulled the door open.

With the aid of the fragile light sifting in from a small window on the adjacent wall, J.T.'s vision had adjusted to the darkness. He shifted to try to see what was inside the safe and, when he did, his hand hit a bottle on the vanity. It clinked against the mirror. He froze.

Gasping, Reneau looked back. He shined the flashlight beam straight at J.T. and moved cautiously out of the closet.

J.T. watched the tension slide from the old man's shadowed silhouette when he found himself alone in the bathroom. Reneau closed his eyes for a moment and drew several deep breaths. Then he opened his eyes again, returned to the closet and started to close the door to the safe without removing anything from inside of it.

Before Reneau could close the safe, J.T. grabbed a cologne bottle off the vanity and stepped quickly inside the closet. He jabbed the bottle into the small of the old man's back. "Don't move."

Reneau's hands went up, shooting the flashlight beam to the ceiling.

Chapter Eighteen

J.T. took the flashlight out of Reneau's hand.

"This isn't how it looks. Please . . . don't tell Anthony. I can explain."

"Relax, I'm not security."

"Who . . . ?"

"It doesn't matter. What matters is the fact that we can help each other."

"Help?" Reneau's head turned slightly, as if he intended to look over his shoulder.

J.T. pressed the cologne bottle harder against his spine. "I said not to move. Keep your eyes on that safe."

"I don't understand. How can we help each other?"

"I want something; you want something. You give me what I want, and I'll keep quiet about you being a thief."

"I wasn't going to take anything."

"What were you doing then? Polishing the silver?"

"I—" Reneau drew a wheezy breath. "I changed my mind. I couldn't double-cross Anthony."

"Well you're about to change it again."

The wheezing intensified. "What do you want? The cash? The jewelry? You can take all of it. Just leave me out of this."

"I don't care about any of that. What I want is information."

Reneau remained quiet for several seconds, then blurted, "Some of it he keeps here. He launders the rest through banks outside of the country. Please . . . I'll tell you whatever you want to know, just promise you won't implicate me. I only did as I was told. The records are here in the safe. Take a look at them if you'd like. Compared to what he profits, my portion is insignificant."

J.T. smiled to himself as Reneau continued talking. He was getting even more than he'd bargained for; enough on Domani's dirty sideline occupations to put him and Reneau away for the rest of their lives. All it would take was an anonymous tip to the police when this was all over.

"That's all very interesting," J.T. finally said, "but that's not the information I'm after." Remembering the story Pop had told him, the ruthlessness with which this pathetic old man had killed more than a dozen people, J.T. shoved the cologne bottle harder into Reneau's back, eliciting a whimper from him.

"What information?" Reneau shook his head. "I don't understand."

"Thirty years ago you stole files from a scientific research laboratory in Montana."

Reneau's chin jerked up. "Research?"

"Does the name Project ER bring back any unpleasant memories, Reneau? I hope so. I hope it makes you sweat whenever you think about it. I hope you've lost sleep these past thirty years. I bet you told yourself time and again that it was all over, didn't you? That you didn't need to worry."

J.T. took a breath, warning himself not to let his emotions take over and jeopardize the plan. Getting Pop's files back would be his revenge; he would have to settle for that, at least for now. Later he would see about taking things further.

"What do you want?" Reneau whispered.

"I want the files."

"They aren't here."

"Then where are they?"

"They're worthless. I've tried . . . Anthony has hired other scientists. Everyone failed. What makes you think it will be different for you?"

"Because I have something the rest of you didn't. Someone." Rage clenched like a fist in the pit of J.T.'s stomach. "We've met before, Reneau, but you wouldn't recognize my voice since I was only three years old at the time."

Reneau turned quickly, catching J.T. off guard, bumping the hand that held the flashlight.

"My God," the aging scientist whispered, as the beam slanted up to where his captor's face should've been. "Where . . . ?"

J.T. watched realization slam into Reneau as his focus lowered to the hovering cologne bottle. His eyes widened, and before J.T. could react, Reneau swung at him, knocking the cologne bottle out of J.T.'s hand. It hit the wall and shattered.

A spicy fragrance filled the closet, almost choking J.T. and causing his nose to itch. When he lifted the flashlight and shone the beam on Reneau again, he saw that the old man had pulled a gun and was waving it in every direction, his eyes wild and terrified.

Afraid Reneau would start shooting, J.T. dropped the flashlight, ducked, and rammed into him. When his head connected with the frail man's chest, Reneau grunted and air rushed out of his lungs. The gun fell to the floor. J.T.

dropped to his knees and scrambled for it in the dark. He could hear the old man wheezing and felt like doing the same, thanks to the potent cologne fumes filling his lungs.

"Stay where you are," J.T. gasped. "I have the gun." He picked up the flashlight again and shined it on Reneau, who lay slumped on the floor clutching his middle.

J.T. pointed the gun at him, then stepped back to the closet's entrance, reached out and flipped on the light. He closed the closet door, then sat the flashlight on the floor.

"Hershel Carlisle . . ." Reneau wheezed, staring up at the hovering gun. "We heard he had died shortly after our trial. Anthony obtained proof."

It took a moment for Pop's real name to register with J.T. "His proof was wrong."

"The refractor . . . he finally succeeded, didn't he?"

"I want the files you stole from him thirty years ago," J.T. said, trying to control his urge to sneeze and his even stronger urge to pull the trigger. "The research you took right before you killed my mother."

Reneau flinched. "You're Hershel's son . . ." Wheezing overtook him for the next several moments. "He can't reverse it, can he? He can't make you visible without the remainder of the research."

J.T. wiggled his itching nose and sniffed. "Where is it?"

"You won't find it in the safe, if that's what you're thinking."

"Then—" The sneeze erupted before he could stop it.

"My God," Reneau said in an awed whisper. "I saw you."

"Where is my father's research?"

"Across the hall. There's a laboratory."

Reaching down, J.T. hooked a hand under Reneau's arm and tugged him up off the floor. "Show me."

"Don't hurt me, please. I'll tell you everything. There's an electronic keyboard by the door." He recited several numbers. "That code will allow you inside. The files are locked in a cabinet in the adjoining office. You'll see it once you're inside. The key to the cabinet is taped beneath the middle desk drawer."

Reneau whimpered when J.T. grabbed a necktie from a hanger and tied it around the old man's eyes. Rosy should be upstairs looking for them right this minute. He didn't want Reneau to see her and know she was involved in what was happening. He kept one hand beneath the old man's arm to guide him, kept the gun at his back as he shoved him toward the door. "Let's go."

"I—I'm not certain I know where he keeps the key to the office."

"You'll find it."

Reneau surprised J.T. by chuckling. "How perfect. This serves Anthony right. Losing his precious project after all these years."

Once outside of the bedroom, J.T. scanned the hallway for Rosy. He'd been upstairs at least fifteen minutes. She should've been up there by now. Worried about her, he started for the door across the way, taking a stumbling Reneau along with him.

A noise in the direction of the staircase made him pause halfway to the door. He expected to see Rosy at the top of the steps but instead Darla stared back at him. She came to a halt when she spotted Reneau, her expression cautious and uncertain.

"I'm here," J.T. said quietly. "If you have to talk, whisper." He didn't want Reneau to recognize her voice. "Where's . . . ?"

She rushed toward them. "I don't know," she whispered. "We can't find Domani, either. I'm afraid they're together."

"Is someone checking the restroom?"

Darla nodded.

When a man's off-key singing sounded on the stairway, Darla and J.T. both turned to look. Seconds later, Domani and Rosy appeared at the top of the stairs. The old man leaned heavily on Rosy as he guzzled champagne straight from the bottle.

Darla quickly stepped to Reneau's side and put her arm around him, hiding from Domani's view the gun J.T. had pressed into the old man's back.

Domani paused midway down the hall and stopped singing. He blinked then broke into a grin. "Well would you look at that," he slurred. "A blindfold. Seems my brother-in-law's got a kinky side I didn't know about."

"Anthony, I—"

J.T. nudged Reneau in the back with the gun, cutting off his words while Darla giggled and rubbed up against the old man.

"Don't worry," Domani said, dragging his hand up and down Rosy's arm as he took another drink of champagne. "I won't tell my sister, Bart. I'm just damn happy to find out you're not the stick in the mud I've always thought you were." Laughing, he winked at Rosy. "Hey, sweetheart, maybe we ought to join 'em. What d'ya think?"

Roselyn's heart felt as if it might jump from her chest. Just before her mother had stepped to Reneau's side, she had caught sight of the gun at his back. *Don't blow it now,* she warned herself. This was no time to let Domani get suspicious, not when J.T. was finally making progress. She faced the old man and stuck out her lower lip. "I'd rather be alone with you, Tony. You know . . . after you show me that great big impressive project of yours?" She spoke loud enough so that J.T. could hear her.

Domani chuckled. "I like the sound of that even better."

Behind him, Roselyn saw Sully coming up the stairs.

"Everything okay up here, Mr. Domani?"

"Yeah. Go back downstairs. Don't let anyone else come up here, understand? 'Specially my sister." He chuckled again. "My brother-in-law and me, we're having our own little private party. Wouldn't want her to crash it and ruin the fun." He turned and looked at Reneau. "Would we, Bart?"

"Come on, Sugar," Darla said, then gave a throaty laugh as she led Reneau toward the nearest bedroom door. "Let's go in here where it's nice and quiet. Just you and me." She looked pointedly at Sully. "Or maybe that big boy over there would like to join us."

Roselyn looked at Sully, too, and saw the question in his eyes. He wasn't sure where he was most needed . . . with her and Domani or with Darla and Reneau. "You should take her up on the offer," she said. "Mr. Domani promised to show me something. Then we're planning a little threesome of our own."

"Threesome?" Domani lowered the champagne bottle from his lips and leered at her.

She cuddled up against him. "You'll think you've had a threesome after I get through with you." *But not quite the sort you're anticipating. J.T. will see to that,* she silently added as she smiled into Domani's liquor-dulled eyes.

She felt confident Sully had understood her subtly delivered message. He nodded and smiled before returning his attention to Darla. "I'd sure like to join you, ma'am, but I have work to do. I'll check out that room for you, though, before you go in. I thought I saw someone come up here ahead of all of you. That okay with you, Mr. Domani?"

Domani was too busy staring at Roselyn's chest to pay much attention to anything else. He glanced up briefly when he heard his name. "Yeah, whatever."

Sully passed them by and went to join Darla and Reneau. Then Roselyn distracted Domani by nibbling his earlobe, while keeping one eye on the gun that floated behind a decorative vase on a plant stand at the hall's far end. When the gun was safely hidden and her mother and Reneau were inside the bedroom, Roselyn pulled back, knowing full well that J.T. stood beside the plant stand, waiting to follow them.

"Slow down," Roselyn said with a laugh as she wiggled free of Domani's grasp. "Remember our deal."

"Yeah . . . yeah . . . the project," he mumbled under his breath as he wove his way toward the room at the end of the hall. "You're as stubborn and unpredictable as your mother. Who'd a guessed she had a thing for Bart?"

Roselyn stood behind Domani while he punched in a number on the control panel by the door. She sensed J.T.'s presence behind her, so much so that she wasn't the least bit startled when she felt his hand on her shoulder. When the door opened and Domani walked in ahead of her, J.T. sniffed, then whispered in her ear, "I'll stay behind you. Lead me over to someplace I can hide the gun."

She nodded, then followed Domani into the dark room, stopping when she heard a muffled sneeze behind her. At least the light was off. If J.T. had flashed into view, with any luck Domani hadn't seen him.

"Cold?" Domani asked.

"It gets a little chilly running around with so few clothes on." She rubbed her hands up and down her arms.

"Close the door." He switched on a light, then faced her. "Then come here. Tony'll warm you up."

Roselyn shut the door, her attention fixed on the machine in the center of the room. Her heart skipped a beat. It was an electromagnetic refractor very similar to the one she and the professor had built. A wall of windows separated an adjoining office from the laboratory. Inside of it she saw a desk and a computer, shelves and a file cabinet.

Praying J.T. wouldn't sneeze, she made her way slowly to a worktable that held a control panel connected to the refractor pod by cords and coils. J.T. could stand beside it and the gun he held would be hidden amidst the equipment. When she stopped walking, from the corner of her eye she saw the gun lower to the tabletop and knew J.T. was there. Unless someone was looking for it, she thought the weapon would go unnoticed.

Roselyn started toward the glass pod. "What is this?"

"A machine that makes things go *poof*." Domani lifted one hand into the air and spread his fingers wide. His eyes were even blearier than before and fixed on her as he swigged from the champagne bottle he'd brought with him from downstairs.

She ran her fingers across the refractor's glass door. "It makes things disappear?"

"So I was told." Domani took another swig, then started toward her.

"And it works?" Realizing his intention to grab her, she maneuvered her way around the refractor, backing toward the office wall.

"Not yet, but it will."

She paused at the door to the office. "Why doesn't it work?"

"I promised to show it to you, not spend all freaking night talking about it." Swaying, Domani proceeded toward her, blinking then widening his eyes as if trying to clear his vision.

"The door to the office," J.T. whispered. "Get the key."

Domani went still and blinked again. "What's that? What did you say?"

"Nothing." Roselyn reached for the doorknob to the office, twisted it left then right. "Just talking to myself. An embarrassing habit, I'm afraid. What's in here?"

He started walking toward her again. "Nothin' for you to worry about."

Before she could slip out of his reach, he lunged, pressing his palms against the wall at either side of her shoulders, trapping her between his arms. "You got away from me downstairs, you're not getting away from me again." His mouth lowered to the curve of her neck.

Just before his lips connected with her skin, Roselyn ducked. She slipped beneath his arm and backed quickly away from the wall, not letting him out of her sight.

Domani turned. "So you wanna play games, do you?" Weaving and stumbling, he stalked her.

"I want to see inside the office, Tony." She wiggled her brows and kept backing away, moving left, then dodging right. "Unlock the door and I'll let you catch me."

Chuckling, he pulled a ring of keys from his pants pocket and dangled it in front of him. "You want in, you come get the key."

Roselyn drew a deep breath, paused, then switched her direction. When she stood close enough to reach out and take the key, she lifted her arm to do so.

Domani snatched the key back just before she touched it. He hid it behind his back and took another drink. The bottle lowered. His mouth curved up at one corner. "You can have the key, sweetheart, you just have to get it."

She stepped so close their bodies pressed together. Meeting his gaze, Roselyn grinned. "I believe you're the one who likes games, Tony." She wrapped one arm around him and groped blindly for the keys.

Behind his back, Domani shifted his arm, keeping the keys just out of her reach. "That's better, Sweet Pea," he said, his words thick, "but not good enough." He nipped at her shoulder. "I've waited a long time for this."

Sweet Pea. Roselyn realized Domani was so drunk that he thought she was her mother. She twisted and squirmed, trying to see over his shoulder.

"That's it," Domani said. "I like the way you move." The arm clutching the champagne bottle came around her waist then tightened. Her silicone inserts squashed against his chest. "Nice." He licked his lips. "Real nice."

Roselyn wished she could say the same about his breath. It wafted over her as his mouth lifted from her shoulder so that he could ogle her enhanced bustline. When she spotted J.T.'s hovering gun behind Domani, she stood on tiptoe and wiggled some more. The keys dangled at the small of Domani's back. Lowering her arm, Roselyn grabbed them, grazing his butt in the process. Ignoring Domani's inebriated laughter, she held the keys out behind him for J.T. to take.

The keys left her hand. Another sneeze sounded. *Blue boxer briefs.* She'd seen them clearly and the legs beneath them, too.

"Excuse me," Roselyn said.

"Not warm enough yet, Sweet Pea?" The hand Domani had held the keys in now covered her right buttock. "Let's go over here and I'll put this bottle down." He moved toward a table alongside the refractor's control panel, taking her with him.

Over Domani's shoulder, Roselyn saw the floating keys and gun, saw the office doorknob wiggle slightly. Then she felt the zipper at the back of her bustier bra top slide down. Her silicone inserts plopped onto the floor at her feet. The tube of lipstick followed. She drew a startled breath.

One second Domani was looking down with a puzzled expression at the two flesh-colored silicone blobs, the next he was being tugged away from her by a gun and a key ring. His bloodshot eyes widened as he shrieked his confusion. Roselyn heard a loud sneeze, saw J.T. flash into view just as he slammed Domani into the wall, saw the keys and the gun fly through the air and hit the floor. The gun slid one direction, the keys the other.

J.T. sneezed again. Once . . . twice . . . three times, flashing into view like photos on a slide projector with each explosion.

Domani slid down the wall and stared, his ruddy face paling. When his butt finally hit the floor, he muttered a curse.

J.T. sneezed and flashed again.

In his second of visibility, Roselyn saw his hand reaching out toward the gun.

Domani saw, too. The gun lay on the floor six feet away from him. Shifting to his hands and knees he scrambled toward it.

Rosy pressed one palm to her bra top to hold it on and headed the same direction, her ankles twisting on the spike-heeled shoes. J.T. was in a sneezing frenzy; he couldn't seem to stop. She saw him in fragmented still-frames, like a jerky old cartoon. *Head thrown back, mouth open as the sneeze built.* Then nothing. *Bent forward at the waist, hand over his mouth as the eruption sounded.* Nothing again. *Face twisted, head back . . .*

He was in no condition to grab the gun, much less fight Domani for it. She knew it was all up to her. She reached the weapon at the same time the old man did. He grabbed. She kicked. The pointed toe of her shoe connected.

Holding his breath in an attempt to curb the sneezing, J.T. watched the gun spin across the floor toward the office. It seemed to move in slow motion, and as it came to a stop, a sound in the opposite direction distracted his attention. He turned. The laboratory door opened. A boy ran through. When he spotted Rosy, the boy came to a halt. "I know you. You're the lady on the plane."

J.T. gave the kid a closer look. *Joe Cool.*

"Remember me?" Stooping, the boy scooped up the keys that had landed just short of the door. "My name's Artie."

"Give me those keys, kid," Domani said as he tried to stand. The massive quantities of liquor he'd consumed had affected his coordination. Every time he got his feet under him, he fell down again.

J.T. couldn't hold his breath any longer. He released it, drew another. A tickle threatened his throat. A second later, he sneezed.

"J.T.?" Artie said cautiously, "Is that you?"

"It's me, Artie." He sneezed again. "Don't give him the keys."

Rosy stood between Domani and Artie. She glanced from one to the other.

Domani still floundered as he tried to push to his feet. "Bartholomew, Junior," he growled, "give me the keys or I'll fire your grandfather."

Artie glanced at the keys in his hand. "J.T.?"

The sneezing subsided. J.T. hesitated. Bartholomew Reneau was the boy's grandfather. No telling what the two men might do to him after this. "Leave the keys on the floor and go on out of here, Artie," J.T. said. "I don't want to cause you any trouble with your grandpa."

Artie shrugged. "He's not my real grandfather. Anyway, I don't like him. He couldn't find a babysitter for me and my sister so when my parents left our room, he came and locked us in. He should know I'd find a way out. When I told my dad, he said that after all that's happened tonight, he's had it with this family. He's quitting his job and we're moving to Timbuktu. Wherever that is."

Domani grabbed hold of Rosy's ankle and tried to pull himself up. She kicked her foot but the old man held tight.

J.T. started over to help her, but was seized by another sneezing fit.

"Watch out!" Rosy yelled.

In the middle of a sneeze, J.T. looked up. Sometime during the confusion, Domani had found his feet and managed to get to the gun. He lifted it, and Rosy hit the floor.

Domani pointed the weapon and moved toward the place where J.T. stood. "Where are you, you son of a—"

"Get down, Artie," J.T. managed to whisper before he sneezed again.

When he flashed into view, Domani adjusted his aim.

J.T. recovered and saw Rosy inching toward the old man on hands and knees. Artie also took a step in that direction.

"No!" J.T. yelled, then ducked to his left as a bullet whizzed past him. "Get down Artie! Rosy stay put!"

Domani scanned the room with frantic eyes, waving the gun in every direction. "You can't hide forever. Sooner or later I'll—"

J.T. sneezed again. He saw his own hand fly up toward his face.

Domani whirled toward him, pointed the gun, fired.

Dropping to the floor, J.T. rolled and missed the bullet. When he looked up, Domani had grabbed Rosy and was jerking her up off the floor. "It's you or her, take your pick," the old man shouted.

Before J.T. could react, Artie lunged, ramming his head into Domani's stomach. Jarred away from Rosy, the old man stumbled forward, then fell to his knees, his forehead hitting the floor. He lifted his head and turned slightly, his eyes rolling back, just before landing nose down on one of Rosy's silicone inserts.

Sully, Barb, and Darla rushed into the room.

"Close the door!" Rosy yelled at them. "Lock it!"

Sully didn't waste any time with questions. He did as

Rosy said then wedged a chair beneath the doorknob.

J.T. ran over and snatched the keys from Artie's hand. "Thanks, kid." He held them high. "Rosy!"

Wobbling on her heels and holding her top in place, she hurried over, took the keys and darted for the office.

"Why didn't you tell me on the plane that your grandfather is Bartholomew Reneau?" J.T. asked the boy.

Artie shrugged. "You didn't ask. Besides, how was I to know you knew him?"

"Reneau said the key to the filing cabinet is taped beneath the center desk drawer," J.T. called out to Rosy.

Through the glass windows into the office, he saw Rosy open the file cabinet and start to rifle through it. He glanced to the refractor where Sully, Barb, and Darla tied up and gagged Domani. "What did you do with Reneau?" he called out to them.

"Tied and gagged that s.o.b., too," Sully answered. "Left him in the bedroom closet next door."

"I think I've found it!" Rosy yelled, running out of the office.

She skidded to a stop when voices sounded in the hallway. Everyone went silent and stared at the door. The doorknob rattled. J.T. recognized Reneau's voice. He shouted something, then started banging.

"I know a secret way out of here," Artie whispered, "I found it last year at the party."

He ran across the room and opened a closet, then pushed against something just inside. A panel covering the entire back wall slid up. It left an opening large enough to step through. "Come on," he said, turning back to them. "There's a hidden stairway out of the building in here."

"I don't want you getting into any more trouble for our sake," J.T. said, then frowned when the pounding at the door intensified.

Artie shrugged. "I'm always in trouble. But my grand-

267

father and Mr. Domani won't know I helped you. After you're out, I'll lock myself in the office and say the burglars put me in there."

"How about I stick around and make sure they treat you right? At least until your folks show up. I need to slip downstairs and grab my clothes out of the closet anyway."

"Sure," Artie said.

"Just forget I'm here, okay?"

Artie nodded, then waved the others over. "Come on," he said. "Hurry."

Chapter Nineteen

Hershel sat back on his heels, pulled a handkerchief from his pocket, and wiped his sweaty brow. He had come out to the garden to try to quiet his mind. At least that's what he had told Wanda, and it was half true. What he didn't tell her was that he also needed a reprieve from her constant company. At the moment, she was in his kitchen preparing a cherry pie for the oven. It was all a smidgen too cozy for his comfort. He didn't even want to speculate on the gossip they must be generating about town.

Gardening was a new diversion. Mainly because he'd never considered his options before. In the past, he'd simply turned to the tried-and-true method of overindulging in liquor to escape reality or to simply numb his thoughts. He found that most effective, if only temporary. Gardening, on the other hand, was not as certain, but due to his new no-alcohol resolution, he'd decided to give it a try.

Scooting along on his backside, he made his way to

the shade of the pecan tree and leaned against the trunk. He searched the branches for the bluebird that had made a home in the tree. Watching it each day brought him comfort. The secure reliability of a loyal, familiar friend, he supposed. Other than Roselyn, he hadn't taken the time to make many true friends over the past thirty years.

He eyed the cordless telephone lying within reach. Jerome or Roselyn should've called by now. He'd been in the shower last night when Jerome had left the message with Wanda. They would contact him again today. Everything was fine.

Fine.

What in heaven's name did that mean? That they'd succeeded? Or merely that matters were progressing in a positive way? When he'd tried to call back, there'd been no answer at Darla Peabody's number. And so he'd waited.

And he was waiting still.

Easy enough. Hershel was good at waiting. Over the years, he'd perfected the skill. As a young man, he'd waited for funding for his project so that he could see the electromagnetic refractor become a reality. As the work proceeded, he'd waited for the day he could share his invention with the world. And later, when that world fell apart, he'd waited for his wife's murderers to be brought to justice. When that never happened, he'd simply waited for the pain to subside, had sought to ease it by devoting himself to revenge. He would recreate the refractor, use it to ruin his enemies, to finally bring Evie the justice she deserved.

A breeze flickered the leaves overhead, bringing with it a moment of blissful relief from the heat.

Hershel returned his attention to the branches. Soon it would be autumn. He and Evie had brought Jerome home three days after his birth on a crisp New England morning in October. The trees lining either side of their street that day had reminded him of the skirts of gypsy dancers, rustling and swaying in the wind, flashing gold and red in the dappled sunlight, welcoming them as he drove his family home. Alive. The trees had seemed so alive, as alive as he'd felt back then. So happy and proud, so full of plans for himself and his son and his wife.

Hershel sighed. Evie would not recognize the man he'd become. A scientist who wasted his intelligence seeking senseless revenge that would not bring her back. A bitter widower who drowned his sorrow in a bottle. A father who had allowed their son to grow up alone and lonely.

Shifting to his knees, Hershel crawled back to his tools. The garden had gone neglected for too long. Weeds had taken over, and though he'd made a small amount of progress with them, plenty remained to pull. They were stubborn, but he would stick with it until he'd uprooted them one by one. Then he'd start over. Plant seeds. Nurture them. With any luck, something would sprout.

When the back door slammed, he paused and glanced over his shoulder. Roselyn stood on the porch, a thick bound expandable file clasped to her chest. Because it looked familiar, a shudder rippled through him. She smiled. Without looking away from her, he pushed to his feet and turned.

"We were lucky enough to book an early flight," Roselyn said. "We thought we'd surprise you."

She held out the file. After a moment, it drifted from her, seemed to move through the air toward him of its own accord, coming to a stop and hovering in place two feet away.

"Here," he heard Jerome say. "I believe this belongs to you, Pop."

With an unsteady hand, Hershel reached for the file, but when his fingers brushed Jerome's, he left them there. Warm. Alive. His reason to go on . . . to finally live again.

"It's finally almost over," Jerome said.

Yes, Hershel thought as he closed his hand around his son's. His old life was finally ending. But a new one was beginning.

He would plant seeds. Nurture them. With any luck, something would sprout.

J.T. entertained Mrs. Moody upstairs while Roselyn worked with the professor on the refractor all day and into the night. Shortly after midnight she yawned and stretched, then logged off of the computer. She walked to the laboratory door and paused. "Professor?"

Intent on his work, he didn't look up.

"Professor Drake," Roselyn said again, louder this time.

With the expression of someone who'd just been roused from a long, deep sleep, he blinked up at her. "Yes?" He blinked again. "Are you leaving already?"

Roselyn smiled. "It's almost twelve-thirty, Professor."

"You don't mean it!" He glanced at his watch. "Where did the time go?"

"I'm going home to sleep. You should, too. Exhausting yourself will only defeat our purpose. You won't do Jerome any favors by making yourself sick."

He placed his pencil on the desk. "I suppose you're right. But I'm much too keyed up to sleep."

She understood that feeling well enough since she, too, found it impossible to shift from work mode to relaxation mode without a soothing activity in between to help her wind down. "I suggest you go up to your room, kick off your shoes, and start a good book. It just so happens I can even recommend a couple. I have a feeling you haven't found the time to read them, though you know the author quite personally."

Thanks to the laboratory's bright lights, she detected a blush on his face despite the distance between them.

"Yes, well." He cleared his throat. "You're right. It's time I read Jerome's books. I'm ashamed I haven't long before now. I wanted to . . . I planned to. But at the end of the day I was always either too tired from my work or too drunk to do any reading."

"What's done is done. It's your actions now that matter."

"I'm counting on that."

She cocked a brow. "I read his first book while in Las Vegas and the second one on the flight home. If I were you, I'd start with the second book first." Leaning forward, she whispered in a confidential tone, "You'll find that the writing's much stronger in that one, though I'd never tell Jerome so." She leaned back again. "Don't skip the Foreword. I think you'll find it to be quite interesting. It seems researching the murders opened Jerome's eyes more clearly than ever to the fragility of life. Getting to know the victims' family members touched him deeply. He says that each and every one of them expressed remorse over words left unspoken."

The professor's head began to bob. "Do you think it's possible that's the true reason he finally came home after staying away so long? Not because of Wanda's call, but because he was making an effort?"

Roselyn smiled. "I'll let you decide that for yourself."

He pulled off his glasses. "Shall I drive you home?"

"Thank you, but no. I'll manage." She smiled. "Goodnight, Professor."

"Sleep tight, dear girl."

Roselyn closed the door, then climbed the stairs. When she and J.T. had flown in that morning, they'd taken a cab to the professor's house. Roselyn had not been home since, so she didn't have her bicycle. She stepped out onto the porch. The night was warm. She would walk home. Her muscles could use the stretch, and she could use the fresh air after being cooped up all day down in the lab.

Drawing a cleansing breath, she gazed up at the stars and let the hum of cicadas drown out the busy chatter in her mind. The trip to Vegas had been good for her. She'd always referred to the city as her home. But despite her mother and Barb and Sully being there, Pecan Grove was where she belonged now, where she felt comfortable, where she would stay. Even if her contribution to the refractor's success brought her professional recognition and offers of other work, as she'd always hoped it would, she knew now that Pecan Grove would remain her home base.

Roselyn twisted her stiff neck from side to side as she started down the steps. When she heard a creak and saw the tree swing move forward then back again, she paused. A round orange glow pierced the darkness between the two ropes, and Roselyn caught a familiar whiff of cigar smoke in the air.

The night breeze ruffled her hair as she walked to the tree. The swing came to a halt. The orange glow fell to the ground, then snuffed out. Without a word Roselyn grasped a rope with each hand and climbed onto J.T.'s lap, facing him, she knew, though she couldn't see his face. It was a tight fit, and not particularly comfortable. The ropes dug into her thighs on either side.

"This has interesting possibilities," J.T. said, "but it hurts my butt."

"Hello to you, too. And tough beans about your butt. From the feel of things, other parts of you don't seem to mind."

He laughed. "You've changed since we first met. Was that only last week?"

"Yes it was. And I haven't changed, really. I'm just letting you see the real me. That's not something I do with everyone."

"I'm aware of that. I like the real you. Your mother and Barb and Sully raised quite a woman."

"They're something else, aren't they?"

"We couldn't have accomplished what we did without them. Artie, too."

"So have you found out anything more about what's going on with Domani and Reneau?"

"I talked to your mother a little while ago. They've been arrested."

Roselyn felt a weight lift from her shoulders. "That's fantastic! Sully's visit to the police obviously paid off."

"It didn't hurt that he's old friends with the chief. The records of Domani's and Reneau's money-laundering accounts were right where Reneau told me they'd be. In the safe, along with several hefty stacks of cash."

"I'm relieved. I was afraid Domani and Reneau might tie Mama, Barb, and Sully to what happened at the party and track them down."

"Domani was so wasted on champagne I'm sure the whole party is one big blur to him. And as for Reneau, even when he wasn't blindfolded, he couldn't see me to describe me and he never saw any of you, either. Even if he wanted to speculate and talk, what's he going to say? That an invisible man held him up? They'll think he's crazy. The only way anyone could trace us would be based on Artie's description." He chuckled. "You should've heard what the kid told them. He made us out to look like bad guys from an old Dick Tracy comic strip. It was all I could do to keep from laughing out loud. I'm sending him a whole case of peanuts tomorrow."

J.T. must have pushed off because they started gliding slowly back and forth.

"Where's Wanda?" Roselyn asked.

"About a half hour ago I convinced her to go home and sleep in her own bed tonight. I figured it's too late for her to call anyone. I'll check in on her first thing in the morning before she has a chance to get the itch to gossip. Maybe I should ask her to breakfast."

"Better yet, ask her to cook it. She'll be flattered." She laughed. "Your poor father. She has a thing for him, you know."

"No kidding?" J.T. said sarcastically.

"I have to admit that now that she's finally accepted the fact that I'm not some sort of sorceress with wicked plans in the works for you and your father, she's really quite charming."

"Shoot," J.T. said. "You don't have something wicked in mind for me? I'm disappointed."

Roselyn wiggled her eyebrows. "Wanda doesn't have to know all my secrets, does she? Besides, the wicked things I have in store for you are nothing at all like she suspected."

"I like the sound of that. When can we start?"

"My supernatural powers won't kick in until I've had at least six hours of sleep," she teased.

"Six hours?" He groaned. "Wanda was right; you are wicked."

He pushed the swing harder. Except for the cicadas and the creak of the rope, the night was quiet. Roselyn thought if she listened closely enough, though, she could hear J.T. mulling over more serious things than her need for sleep.

"You know," J.T. said after several moments of silence, "there's a lot more to most people than what you see on the surface. Take Wanda's charm, for instance. And then there's you. When we first met, you reminded me of Pop in some ways. That scared me."

"Your father and I do have a lot in common. Some of the same interests and passions—"

"And quirks."

She smiled. "That, too, I suppose."

"But I've seen another side of you."

"Your father has another side, too. Perhaps if you'd look at him as closely and spend half as much time with

276

him as you do the criminals you write about, you'd uncover it. And you might be surprised to find that the two of you have more in common than you ever suspected."

He seemed to think that over for a minute then said, "I'll tell you one thing Pop and I have in common."

"What might that be?"

"We both love you."

She felt the warmth of his mouth as it covered hers. "I love you, too," she murmured.

"After only knowing me such a short time?"

"It doesn't take long to love you, J.T. Not if a person's willing to dig through all your bullshit. If they do, they find a quite loveable man underneath all the stink."

The swing came to a halt. "Bullshit, huh?"

"Yes, bullshit."

"That sounds like something Sully or Barb would say."

"They aren't stupid. You carry around quite a load of it at times."

"Your honesty is brutal, you know that?"

The swing started moving again.

"While you and Pop worked today and Wanda grabbed a nap," J.T. said after a moment, "I finished my book and put it in the mail to my editor. Then I gave him a call and pitched another idea. Pop's story."

"And?"

"And he went for it. With the advance he offered, I could take a leave of absence at the magazine and work on it full time."

"Would you do that?"

"Well . . . yeah, I think I might. If Pop doesn't mind me writing the story, that is. If I handle it right, I think it might reopen the investigation into Domani's and Reneau's involvement in the explosions at the compound that killed my mother and Pop's team. I'm not sure he's ready to face all of that again. I need to talk to him about it."

"I think you should." Roselyn chewed on her lower lip. "Are *you* ready?"

"What do you mean?"

"If you write the whole story, it won't only expose your father, it will expose you, as well. How your mother's murder affected not only the professor's life, but yours, too."

"And the fact that I've spent a lifetime feeling ashamed of him. Is that what you're saying?"

She didn't answer.

After several seconds, he blew out a noisy breath. "Now I'm ashamed of myself."

"You were a boy."

"Not last month. Not even last week."

"You were given an opportunity to see the truth. You didn't look away. It takes courage to change an ingrained attitude."

"Don't make me out as a saint. Part of me is still angry with him. Part of me still hurts."

"He's not a saint, either. He made mistakes that affected you deeply."

When he remained silent for a good long while she asked, "You'd really take a leave of absence?"

"I'd kind of like a break from the magazine." He cleared his throat. "From L.A., too. I can write a book just as easily in Pecan Grove as I can there."

Her pulse hiccupped. "Whoa. Stop the swing."

"What?"

"Stop the swing."

He did.

"Now . . . what exactly are you saying?"

"Just that I don't have to be in L.A. to write the book. I'd have to travel some to do research, but I do that anyway."

Did he mean what she thought he did? Or was she just hearing what she wanted to hear? The truth of the matter was that she'd been waiting for him to tell her he'd be leaving as soon as she and the professor made him whole again. She'd been preparing herself to tell him good-bye.

Roselyn took two long slow breaths. "You'd move back here?"

"I would if I could find a roommate."

"Do you mean the sort of roommate you share a bed with, or the sort with whom you just share the bills?"

He laughed. "That depends. Which sort are you?"

"Nice try, Mr. Drake, but I'm not sure I'm ready for that yet." She lifted her fingers to his face. Moved from his cheek to his nose to his mouth, found it curved up at the corners. "I wouldn't mind having you as a frequent overnight visitor, though."

"For how long?"

"Until I'm satisfied that you're content here," she answered, trying hard to keep the tremor from her voice, but failing. "Content with me."

He kissed her fingertips. "That won't take long."

Her throat tightened as she wrapped her arms around his neck. The kiss they shared was full of hope and promise, so tender it surfaced the tears that Roselyn had tried very hard to hold back. "You're sure that's what you want? Even though I haven't yet been successful in helping you?"

"I'm sure *you* are who I want to be with, no matter what happens."

"Even if you remain invisible?"

"Even then. That is, if you could handle carrying on a relationship with a man you can't see."

She smiled through her tears. "As long as I kept plenty of perfume on hand and Barb kept us supplied with a few other necessities, I'd do just fine." She laughed. "But you won't remain invisible, J.T. I'll see to that if it's the last thing I do."

Roselyn reached for the ropes again, then scooted off his lap.

"Where you going? I'm not through with you."

"I need to sleep. Though I'll put up with you being invisible, I much prefer to be able to see the man I share my bed with. Which means I have a lot of work ahead of me tomorrow. Your father and I almost have it. Almost."

"I'll walk you home."

"Oh, no you don't. I know you." Roselyn cocked her head to one side as she gazed at the swing. "I said I needed to sleep."

"And I know you. You'll need to wind down first. I have a better method of doing that than dancing."

She smiled. "What did you have in mind?"

"I thought I might try electric pink on for size tonight . . . see how you like it."

Roselyn reached out and took his hand. "I do love the way you think."

It was 3 A.M. when J.T. walked back to his father's house. He had intended to stay all night with Rosy but he couldn't sleep. He felt at peace as he made his way down the street he'd grown up on. Ironic, he thought, that he'd finally found happiness when his life was turned upside down and inside out.

As he neared the house he saw that Pop's bedroom light was on. He knew Pop was worried about the success of the refractor and all that lay in the balance, and hoped his father had not become so stressed out that he'd turned to a bottle.

J.T. let himself in, then made his way toward the hallway that led to the bedrooms. At Pop's door, he paused, weighed the pros and cons for a moment, then raised a fist and knocked.

"Come in," Pop's voice sounded from the other side.

J.T. opened the door. Pop was propped up in bed, his long hair unbound and flowing free over his shoulders. A book lay open in his lap. His little round glasses sat perched at the tip of his nose.

"It's me," J.T. said, relieved to see that his father's eyes were clear. "I noticed your light."

"What time is it?"

"Three A.M."

Pop yawned. "I lost all track of time." Holding his place in the book with a finger, he closed the cover.

J.T.'s heart lurched when he saw his own name printed in large letters across the front.

"I can't put this down," Pop said. "It's top notch, Jerome. You have a talent for grabbing the reader and not letting go."

"Thank you." J.T. didn't know what else to say. His father had never commented on his writing before. And the few times J.T. had mentioned it, Pop had little to say in response, leaving J.T. to wonder if he thought it unimportant, or maybe even embarrassing.

"Your mother had great respect for the power of the written word. She'd be quite proud of you."

"I hope so."

"I'm proud of you."

Stunned speechless for a moment by the comment, J.T. swallowed and nodded.

Pop placed the book beside him on the bed. "I've always been proud of you. I should've told you a long time ago."

"Pop, I—"

"No, let me finish. Please. I owe you an apology. Ever since your mother was killed, I've been so wrapped up in my own work, in my quest for revenge, that I haven't paid nearly enough attention to *your* work." He shook his head. "I haven't paid nearly enough attention to you, period. It's the biggest regret of my life, I—"

Jennifer Archer

"Pop . . . before you go on, I need to confess something. That time when I was a kid and I broke into your lab. The fire . . . it wasn't—"

"I know you started it. I've always known."

J.T. stepped further into the room. "Why? Why did you let me off the hook by pretending to believe it was an accident? I wanted to destroy your work. I did it out of anger because—"

"You were jealous of it. I understood that. And you deserved to be angry. I wish . . ." He shifted and put his feet on the floor so that he sat at the edge of the bed. "I wish I had found the courage then to put the past behind me and straighten out my life with you, but I didn't. I was just too bent on revenge. I'm sorry. For all we've missed. For everything."

"Pop—"

"If I could bring back all those years and make them right, I'd do it in a second, but of course I can't. Perhaps, though . . ." Pop cleared his throat. "Perhaps we could start anew."

The floor creaked beneath J.T.'s feet as he moved toward his father. When he reached him, he sat beside him at the edge of the bed. "I'm willing to give it a go if you are." He reached his hand out toward Pop, though he knew his father couldn't see his arm. "Shake on it?"

Pop's eyes softened with recognition of the old routine they'd shared during J.T.'s childhood. Then his own hand lifted, and he reached out, too. A spark flashed. They found each other. "It's a deal," he said.

Chapter Twenty

J.T. could think of at least one good thing about being invisible; Rosy, Pop, and Wanda could not see him trembling. He watched Pop reach for the door to the cage that sat on a back counter. The wheel inside spun continuously, though the mouse running on it could not be seen. Less than an hour ago, after almost a week of constant work by Pop and Rosy, they had placed the mouse inside of the refractor and made it disappear. Now they were waiting for the rodent's system to stabilize before they zapped it again.

Pop placed one hand in front of the tiny cage door before opening it. "Aha! I caught you my little friend! You're not quick enough to escape me this time." His fingers closed, forming a circle around what appeared to be nothing more than thin air.

Inside the refractor pod, Rosy replaced the sticky tape on the floor then stepped out. "That should hold him long enough for us to close him inside."

Wanda, perched on the sofa across the room, patted the space between her arms when a repeated hacking sounded. "Wait your turn, buster," she told the poodle.

"If we're successful with the mouse," Pop said, "I'll recalculate the voltage to Curly's body weight. After he goes through, I'll recalculate again for yours, Jerome." He chuckled. "Otherwise, we might make your big toe visible but not much more."

J.T. shoved back the bill of the cap he'd worn for everyone's benefit. "Couldn't you two have come up with a way to buffer the electrical surge? Curly there might not remember enough to be worried but my eyes are bugging out just thinking about it."

Roselyn came up behind his chair and placed her hands on his shoulders. "If we had more time we might be able to do just that. Are you willing to wait?"

He tilted his head back and looked up at her. True concern for his welfare clouded her eyes. "No way," he said.

"Good." She looked relieved. "But I don't want this to be too traumatic for you, either."

"I can stand the pain." He swallowed his apprehension. "Let's get on with it."

While Rosy moved to man the controls, Pop stepped inside the refractor pod, stooped, then lowered his hand to the place on the floor where Rosy had placed the sticky tape.

"If this is successful," J.T. said, "you do plan to proceed with it, don't you Pop? To get the credit you deserve?"

"I had decided not to. But then it occurred to me that far too many people I cared about gave up their lives because of this project. I can't keep it a secret. And it wouldn't be fair to Roselyn to keep it quiet, either. She deserves half the credit. But I'll want to take steps to make certain the research doesn't fall into the wrong hands this time. The potential for danger is far too great."

"Then you won't mind if I write the book? After you've taken those steps, of course. Because of the sensitive nature of the subject matter I've been toying with the prospect of marketing it as fiction rather than True Crime. You know, changing the names to protect the innocent and all that. I'd handle it in the right way. I—"

"Write it." Pop backed out of the pod, then stood, and closed the door. "I trust your judgment completely, Jerome. Just make certain that Roselyn's character is as crucial to the plotline as mine."

Roselyn shook her head. "Oh, but I shouldn't be portrayed as such, Professor. The glory is yours and yours alone. The refractor was your brainchild. I only helped you to remember what you'd already—"

"Dear girl—"

"Please," J.T. interrupted. "I'm sorry I brought it up. You can argue this later. Let's start those sparks to flying."

Pop turned to him, his eyes clearer than J.T. thought he'd ever seen them before. "Ready?"

J.T. nodded.

"Me, too," Wanda said from across the room. "But Curly and I are staying right where we're sitting until the smoke clears."

Rosy flipped a switch and the refractor pod hummed and shimmered with white light.

J.T. held his breath. Inside the glass walls, green smoke began to swirl and, after only a few moments, filled the pod like a dense morning fog.

When the humming ceased and the light inside the refractor dimmed, Pop dropped to his knees beside the machine. Smoke seeped out into the room. The scent of burnt rubber started J.T.'s stomach rolling. He fanned his face and coughed.

"See anything, Hershel?" Wanda asked, still keeping her distance.

"Not yet."

Rosy's chair legs scraped the floor as she pushed away from the controls and hurried to Pop's side, her eyes wide and anxious. She crouched beside him. "The smoke is clearing," she said. "Are you watching, J.T.?"

"I'm afraid to look. I'll let you tell me."

Except for an occasional cough, the room fell silent for at least the next thirty seconds. Even Curly stayed quiet. Then J.T. heard a tiny squeak. He breathed a sigh of relief. At least the mouse had survived. Whether or not it was visible remained to be seen. He stared at the backs of Pop's and Rosy's heads.

"Oh, my," Roselyn finally said, her voice breathless.

"Incredible," Pop added.

"I'll swan," Wanda whispered.

Swallowing, J.T. glanced at the old woman who now stood beside his father, then shifted his attention back to Pop and Rosy. "Well?"

With a squeal, Rosy threw her arms around Pop's neck. "We did it, Professor! We did it!"

Tilting his head back, Pop laughed like J.T. had never in his life heard his father laugh before. While they hugged and laughed and squealed, he moved toward them, his eyes on the refractor. He walked around his father and Rosy and Wanda, then crouched at the door of the machine. Inside on the floor, the tiny mouse squirmed and twisted, fighting the sticky tape that held him in place.

Laughing too, J.T. opened the door and freed the rodent. He held it in the palm of his hand, thrilled to see that during the process of transformation, no body parts seemed to have been rearranged. "We're in the clear,

Curly old boy," J.T. yelled. "The head bone's still connected to the neck bone."

Rosy looked puzzled. "You mean the skull is connected to the—"

"Whatever," J.T. interrupted. "The point is, the mouse still looks like a mouse and not some horrible disfigured monster. I halfway expected to see a foot sticking out of an ear or a tail where the nose should be."

"Why didn't you tell me you were worried about that? I could have explained that the refractor doesn't rearrange molecules. It—"

"Stop. I don't want a headache going into this. I'll feel bad enough afterward as it is." He crossed the room and returned the mouse to the cage. "This is what I had to see to ease my mind."

Wanda stretched her arms out toward J.T. "Would you like to do the honors?"

He tipped his hat, then reached for the poodle that he knew she held. "I'd be happy to, ma'am."

"You could go in together," Pop told him.

J.T. carried a squirming Curly to the refractor pod, sat him inside, then closed the door. "No, thanks. I understand what Rosy said about rearranging molecules and all that, but I'm still not taking any chances of ending up with a tail."

Minutes later, Curly's pom-pom tail wagged, though weakly, for the entire world to see. Mrs. Moody scooped him into her arms and let him lick her face. "If that machine don't beat everything, I don't know what does. Hershel Drake, you're a bona fide genius, that's what you are."

"I didn't do this alone," the professor said, his gaze shifting pointedly from Mrs. Moody to Roselyn.

Roselyn watched Mrs. Moody's lip curl slightly; then, slowly, the woman smiled. "You're bona fide, too, Doc-

Jennifer Archer

tor Peabody. I guess I've been kind of hard on you. Truth is, you're alright. You got the job done." She chuckled. "And you didn't even use a wand."

"Why, thank you, Mrs. Moody. I appreciate that," Roselyn said. She turned to J.T. "Your turn."

His hat floated toward the refractor pod. The door opened and, after the hat drifted in, closed again.

Roselyn felt the pull of J.T.'s gaze again, just as she had the last time they'd attempted to make him visible. She focused on the place just beneath the bill of his cap, calling on every fiber of her being to channel her strength and love his way. This time would be different. This time, when the smoke cleared, she would not only feel his presence, she would see him.

She stood beside the professor as he punched in the new calculations for J.T.'s body weight, then reached for the switch.

"Are you ready, Jerome?" the professor asked.

"Yeah, Pop."

Roselyn couldn't speak. Her heart drummed, her head started to spin, a cold sweat broke out on her skin. From the corner of her eye she saw Mrs. Moody step up beside her. The older woman took Roselyn's hand and gave it a squeeze.

Widening her smile until her cheeks hurt, Roselyn gave J.T. a shaky thumbs up. She kept her gaze steady on him as the light intensified and the humming started. Her smile didn't waver when she saw his sizzling blue silhouette or even when the smoke swirled and clouded the inside of the box, obstructing her view of J.T.'s ball cap.

When it ended, her composure crumbled. Releasing Mrs. Moody's hand, then stumbling around the control panel, she made her way to the front of the refractor, jerked open the door and, coughing, waved away the wretched-smelling smoke.

Her heart dropped. Except for the ball cap crushed in

a corner of the refractor pod, the machine appeared empty.

"It can't be," Professor Drake whispered from behind her.

"Where is he?" Mrs. Moody whispered back.

Roselyn fell to her knees and reached inside. Relief swept over her when her hand connected with warm skin. "He's here and he's alive."

"Thank Heaven."

J.T. moaned.

"Why didn't it work?" Mrs. Moody asked.

"We did everything right," Roselyn murmured, fighting back tears. "Everything." Panicked, she stood and faced the professor. "Let's go over the calculations one more time. We can't fail at this. We can't, do you understand? I won't let him stay this way."

Professor Drake stared at something behind her, his face pale and startled.

Mrs. Moody gasped. "What in the blue blazes . . . ?"

"Roselyn . . ." The professor pointed. "Roselyn . . . look."

She turned. The first thing she saw was a mass of tousled dark hair suspended slightly above the floor in the right hand corner of the refractor. As she watched, the dim image of a face shimmered beneath it. Slowly, the image clarified. And then, before her eyes, a body appeared beneath the face and hair.

J.T. lay slumped in the corner, his knees up in front of him, his head between them, his arms hanging limply at either side of his body.

"Remarkable," she heard the professor whisper. "Astounding."

"Spookiest dad-burned thing I ever saw," Mrs. Moody added.

Professor Drake stepped up beside Roselyn. "Let's get him out of there."

Without uttering a syllable, Roselyn grabbed one of J.T.'s feet while the professor grabbed hold of the other. Mrs. Moody lowered the now-sleeping poodle to the floor and came to help them. Together the three of them maneuvered him out of the refractor pod until he lay flat on his back, spread-eagle on the workshop floor.

Roselyn sat down and cradled J.T.'s head in her lap. She felt for a pulse, found it; then scanned him quickly, checking for fingers and toes, making certain she counted ten of each like a mother with a newborn baby. When she found everything intact—even his boxer shorts—her interest instantly shifted, becoming anything but motherly. He looked even more handsome than his picture on the book cover, more rough around the edges, darker, bigger, *real*.

"I don't know where he inherited his size," the professor said, as if he'd read her thoughts. "I'm only of medium build, and Evie was such a tiny thing."

Roselyn couldn't quit staring at J.T.'s face. She ran her fingers through his hair, massaged his temples. His lips . . . she wanted to kiss them but thought it might be inappropriate to do so in front of Mrs. Moody and the professor.

"He has your nose, Professor," she whispered, tracing the bridge of it with one fingertip.

"I guess he does at that," Professor Drake agreed, his voice filled with pride. "But everything else about him is Evie through and through."

Mrs. Moody sighed. "She musta been a looker, your wife."

He nodded. "Evie was beautiful and strong and good."

Roselyn glanced up at him. "He's the best of both of you, Professor. You've raised a fine man. His mother would be so proud." She looked back down at J.T.'s face. "I love him, Professor. I love your son."

Mrs. Moody huffed a laugh. "Tell him something he don't know."

"Rosy . . ." J.T. moaned. "Rosy, I love you."

The professor smiled. "Nothing could please me more than seeing the two of you find happiness together."

J.T. stirred, then moaned long and loud.

"I think he's coming around," Roselyn said.

He moaned again, then cursed.

Professor Drake chuckled. "Perhaps I should warn you that Jerome's not always the easiest person to live with."

"Then he's met his match. I'm not easy to live with, either. Just ask my mother."

"I guess this means you'll be going away," Mrs. Moody said. "Joining J.T. in L.A."

Roselyn met the professor's gaze. He smiled. "I'll miss you both," he said.

She shook her head. "I'm not going anywhere. He's coming home."

"Home?" Professor Drake looked baffled. "You mean here? To Pecan Grove?"

"Didn't he tell you? He wants to write the book here."

"He does?" The professor blinked back tears. "Thank you for bringing my son back to me, Roselyn."

"You did that yourself, Professor. You did it yourself."

That evening, J.T. swung a leg over Rosy's bicycle. "Get on," he said.

She scowled. "You're joking. You must be exhausted."

"I'm not joking. I feel great. Sit your cute little butt on top of these handlebars. I'm driving you home."

"But the basket . . ."

He unhooked the two straps that secured it to the bars, then lifted it off and handed it to her. "Pop won't mind if you leave it on the porch."

J.T. noticed that the little dent between her eyebrows

had deepened when she returned from putting the basket away.

"I've never taken a ride on bicycle handlebars before," she said.

"Then it's high time you did."

"Have you?"

"Have I what?"

"Taken a ride on the handlebars of a bicycle?"

"More times than I can count."

Her eyes narrowed. "Name one."

"Okay. Remember when you asked me if I had any good memories of Pop and me together?"

Rosy nodded.

"Well, today when we were celebrating over dinner and I saw him so happy and relaxed, a memory surfaced."

She stepped closer. "Tell me."

"I couldn't have been more than five or six years old at the time. I recall being surprised when Pop stopped working and came upstairs early. I was reading a book and the house was very quiet so I heard him immediately when he came into the room. I looked up and found him staring at me. His eyes . . . they looked so sad, as if he were seeing me for the very first time. But then he smiled."

Just thinking about that smile brought one to J.T.'s lips. He could see his father's face so clearly in his mind, the way it had looked on that long ago day. "I remember him saying, 'It's a beautiful day, my boy. We should be outside, soaking up the sunshine.' "

Laughing, J.T. shook his head. He remembered the joy that had swelled inside of him, the sweet thrill of having his father's attention.

"I followed him outside, and he took me for a ride on the handlebars of an old bicycle that had belonged to my mother. He whooped and hollered and swerved all over the road, on purpose, I think, but I didn't know that at the time. I screamed and laughed and held on for my life. And I remember seeing neighbors as we passed by, standing in doorways and yards, looking up from their gardens, whispering and shaking their heads. Pop told me we'd have to work as a team to avoid a wreck. I was the navigator. My job was to watch for bumps in the road . . . to tell him which way to go."

He swallowed, surprised to find that his throat felt as hard as cement. "That day is one of the few times, maybe the only time, I felt connected to my father. Like he needed me as much as I needed him. Like we were two wings of a bird, him one and me the other, flying down that street, capable of anything because we were together."

J.T. looked down at the ground, embarrassed that he'd become so emotional, that his voice had wavered and his eyes had blurred on that scene from the past.

"That's a fine memory, J.T.," Rosy said. After a moment, she walked in front of the bike then backed up and straddled the wheel. "How am I supposed to do this?"

"Here." Obliged to her not only for giving in, but also for not dwelling on his emotional state, he reached under her arms and lifted her up. "You're on."

Across the street a screen door slammed, diverting J.T.'s attention.

"Howdy do, Rosy, J.T." Waving, Wanda Moody started toward them with Toots and Curly on leashes.

This evening, her hair had a red cast instead of purple and, as she drew closer, J.T. noticed that she wore different glasses. The new frames were cat-eyed and sprinkled with tiny rhinestones. Her polyester pantsuit looked new, too, as did the hot pink high-heeled sandals that slapped the soles of her feet.

J.T. whistled his appreciation.

Jennifer Archer

Stopping alongside the bike, Wanda struck a pose. "So, you like the new me, do ya?"

"Wanda Moody, you're a knockout," J.T. said, sizing her up.

"Very unique," Rosy added. "Not just any woman could pull off that look, Mrs. Moody, but you do it with flair."

"You think so, do you?" She lifted a rhinestone-studded cigarette holder that matched her glasses, stuck it into her mouth, took a drag, then blew a smoke ring into the air. "You don't think it's too showy?"

"Not at all." J.T. was careful not to meet Rosy's eyes for fear of losing his composure. "What's the occasion, Wanda?"

"None to speak of. Just went shopping today. Bought your daddy a little gift too. A token of my appreciation for the I-talian dinner the other night."

J.T. coughed. "Dinner, huh?" Rosy gave him a subtle nudge with her elbow. "Pop didn't mention that."

Wanda reached into the tote bag she had slung over her shoulder and pulled out a silky tiger print short sleeve men's shirt that buttoned up the front. "You think he'll like it?"

J.T. cleared his throat. "Well, now." He cleared it again. "I can see Pop wearing that, can't you, Rosy?"

Rosy's mouth opened but nothing came out.

"Rosy?"

"Oh, yes! I'm certain the professor will love it."

Wanda stuffed the shirt back in the bag, then took another puff of her cigarette. "What are y'all up to now?"

"I'm trying to convince Rosy that she's safe on my handlebars."

Wanda cackled a laugh. "I don't know about that a'tall. I seem to recall talk of you giving all the girls in town a ride when you was younger, but never on a bike.

294

And I have my doubts about any of 'em being safe."

"That's what I was afraid of," Rosy said dryly.

"You're giving Rosy the impression I was disreputable, Wanda."

"Shoot. You don't need help in that department. Seems to me you worked hard enough on your own to earn that reputation."

Rosy pursed her lips and gave him a bemused stare. "I'm not sure I want to hear any more of this."

"Good," he said. "I'm not sure I want you to."

She shifted to the center of the bars and held tight. "Let's proceed, before I lose my nerve."

Grinning ear to ear, J.T. started off. "Bye, Wanda."

"Bye, now," she said, then started toward Pop's house.

"Bless your poor father's heart," Rosy said, glancing back at him with a smile.

"Don't let him fool you. He can hold his own with her just fine."

She smirked. "Don't be so sure. A woman on a mission is tough to stop. And that woman has definite plans for the professor."

The bicycle wobbled. Rosy gasped and shrieked.

"Hang on. I've got her under control."

"I'm closing my eyes," she said, her voice shaky.

"Fine with me, but it's a shame you'll miss that gorgeous sunset."

J.T. swerved on purpose, eliciting another shriek from Rosy, just as he'd intended. "Woo-hoo!" he yelled. "Don't fall off now, darlin'."

Ahead, he saw a man scoop a newspaper off his porch, then pause to turn and stare.

On the other side of the street, a blonde-haired woman walked down the sidewalk toward them holding the hand of a little boy. She shielded her eyes with one hand then waved. "J.T. Drake, is that you?"

"Hey there, Libby." *Libby Bakersfield.* His senior year

homecoming date. "You're looking good. That your kid?"

"Sure is. What are you doing in town?"

"Came to check on Pop. Stayed to find myself, you might say."

He saw her baffled frown as they passed, and he imagined her thinking he'd become as kooky and unpredictable as his old man. For the first time in his life, that possibility pleased him.

"Old flame?" Rosy asked, glancing over her shoulder.

"Guess you could call her that."

"First love?"

He shook his head. "No, just first time to make it around all the bases."

"Oh." Her brows drew together just before she turned to stare ahead. "*Oh!*" When she looked back at him again, her face was bright red.

"Jealous?" J.T. asked.

"Immensely."

"Don't be. Libby might've been my first time to round all the bases, but you're my first love. My first and only."

Her eyes softened. "Stop the bicycle."

"What?"

"Put on the brakes."

When he did and his feet were braced on the ground, Rosy wrapped her arms around his neck and leaned into him. "You do know just what to say, Mr. Drake. Before we even met, I loved your way with words."

Their lips connected, and J.T. soared . . . faster than he had on the bike, taking Rosy along with him . . . two wings of a bird, flying high into the sunset.

Epilogue

Two Years Later

Roselyn signed for the package, then thanked the mailman and watched him walk away. Too excited to take it inside and prolong her curiosity, she went to her knees on the porch, using her gardening shears to tear into the box. J.T. was out of town chasing down a lead on Steven Bedford. He had insisted that she'd helped him find his father, and now that he wasn't on deadline, he was going to help her find hers. He had also given her permission to open this particular parcel if it arrived while he was away.

When the cardboard flaps came open, she caught her breath at the sight of the title printed on the spines of his first foray into fiction "based on a true story."

The Invisible Truth . . . J.T. Drake

"It's beautiful!" Roselyn whispered as she lifted out one novel. "Perfect." The perfect gift for J.T. to give his father in celebration of Professor Drake's two years of sobriety. The perfect gift for her in celebration of the award for scientific achievement she'd accepted at a private ceremony recently in Washington D.C. In the past two years, she had logged more miles between home and the Capital than she'd traveled in her entire life. She and Professor Drake had gone to great lengths to make certain their calculations would not fall into the wrong hands again. The details of their research were to remain highly classified, and the scientists chosen to assist Roselyn with the continued study of electromagnetic refraction were to be screened and monitored by the government agency now in charge of the project.

Roselyn opened the cover of J.T.'s book, then flipped to the dedication page.

> I dedicate this book to the memory of my mother,
> Eve Carlisle;
> And to my father, Dr. Hershel Drake,
> Who gave me the gift of his memories;
> And to my inlaws, Darla, Barb and Sully,
> Who took on my mission and accepted me sight unseen;
> But most of all, this book belongs to my wife,
> Dr. Roselyn Grace Peabody-Drake
> Visible or not, without her heart, I wouldn't be whole.

Smiling, she closed the cover. *Visible or not.* That should have more than a few readers scratching their heads, speculating as to whether or not the book was more fact than fiction. Roselyn placed her palm on her stomach. "You have quite an amazing father, my love," she whispered. "An amazing family, too. I can't wait for you to meet them."

Jennifer Archer
Once Upon A Dream

The gambler who comes to Robin in her dreams satisfies all her desires. Too bad he is nothing like the men she meets in reality, nothing like the nerdy scientist who lives next door. And yet, behind the professor's glasses doesn't she detect the same sexy blue eyes of her fantasy man?

Alex Simon wants nothing more to do with women. Then a bold lady saunters into his dream world. Unfortunately she is nothing like the women he encounters in everyday life, nothing like the peculiar artist who lives next door. And yet, looking past Robin's purple nail polish, doesn't he see the same promise in her shining eyes?

By day they have nothing more in common than a property line. By night they fulfill each other's wildest fantasies. But as their attraction spills over into the light of day, Robin and Alex know they share more than a property line, more than a dream world—they share a love to heal their souls, a love that began . . . once upon a dream.

Dorchester Publishing Co., Inc.
P.O. Box 6640
Wayne, PA 19087-8640

___52418-X
$5.50 US/$6.50 CAN

Please add $2.50 for shipping and handling for the first book and $.75 for each additional book. NY and PA residents, add appropriate sales tax. No cash, stamps, or CODs. Canadian orders require $5.00 for shipping and handling and must be paid in U.S. dollars. Prices and availability subject to change. **Payment must accompany all orders.**

Name: _____

Address: _____

City: _____ State: _____ Zip: _____

E-mail: _____

I have enclosed $_____ in payment for the checked book(s).

For more information on these books, check out our website at www.dorchesterpub.com.
____ *Please send me a free catalog.*

TRISH JENSEN

Stuck
with
You

Paige Hart and Ross Bennett can't stand each other. There has been nothing but bad blood between these two lawyers . . . until a courthouse bombing throws them together. Exposed to the same rare and little-understood Tibetan Concupiscence Virus, the two archenemies are quarantined for seven days in one hospital room. As if that isn't bad enough, the virus's main side effect is to wreak havoc on human hormones. Paige and Ross find themselves irresistibly drawn to one another. Succumbing to their wildest desires, they swear it must be a temporary and bug-induced attraction, but even after they part ways, they can't seem to forget each other. Which begs the question: Did the lustful litigators contract the disease after all? Or have they been acting under the influence of another fever altogether—the love bug?

___52442-8 $5.99 US/$6.99 CAN

Dorchester Publishing Co., Inc.
P.O. Box 6640
Wayne, PA 19087-8640

Please add $2.50 for shipping and handling for the first book and $.75 for each book thereafter. NY, NYC, and PA residents, please add appropriate sales tax. No cash, stamps, or C.O.D.s. All orders shipped within 6 weeks via postal service book rate. Canadian orders require $2.50 extra postage and must be paid in U.S. dollars through a U.S. banking facility.

Name_____
Address_____
City_____State_____Zip _____
I have enclosed $ _____ in payment for the checked book(s).
Payment <u>must</u> accompany all orders. ☐ Please send a free catalog.
CHECK OUT OUR WEBSITE! www.dorchesterpub.com

SUSAN SQUIRES

BODY ELECTRIC

Victoria Barnhardt sets out to create something brilliant; she succeeds beyond her wildest dreams. With one keystroke her program spirals out of control . . . and something is born that defies possibility: a being who calls to her.

He speaks from within a prison—seeking escape, seeking *her*. He is a miracle that Vic never intended. More than a scientific discovery, or a brilliant coup by an infamous hacker, he is life. He is beauty. And he needs to be released. Just as Victoria does. Though the shadows of the past might rise against them, on one starry Los Angeles night, in each other's arms, the pair will find a way to have each other and freedom both.

Dorchester Publishing Co., Inc.
P.O. Box 6640
Wayne, PA 19087-8640

___5036-6
$6.99 US/$8.99 CAN

Please add $2.50 for shipping and handling for the first book and $.75 for each additional book. NY and PA residents, add appropriate sales tax. No cash, stamps, or CODs. Canadian orders require $5.00 for shipping and handling and must be paid in U.S. dollars. Prices and availability subject to change. **Payment must accompany all orders.**

Name: _____

Address: _____

City: _____ State:_____ Zip: _____

E-mail: _____

I have enclosed $_____ in payment for the checked book(s).

For more information on these books, check out our website at www.dorchesterpub.com.
_____ *Please send me a free catalog.*

ROBIN WELLS
OOH, LA LA!

Kate Matthews is the pre-eminent expert on New Orleans's red-light district. It makes sense that she'd be the historical consultant for the new picture being shot on location there. So why is its director being so difficult? His last flick flopped, and he is counting on this one to resurrect his career. Maybe it is because he is so handsome. He's probably used to getting women to do as he wishes. And now he wants her to loosen up. But Kate knows that accuracy is crucial to the story Zack Jackson is filming—and finding love in the Big Easy is anything but. No, there will be no lights, no cameras and certainly no action until he proves her wrong. Then it'll be a blockbuster of a show.

Dorchester Publishing Co., Inc.
P.O. Box 6640
Wayne, PA 19087-8640

_____52503-8
$5.99 US/$7.99 CAN

Please add $2.50 for shipping and handling for the first book and $.75 for each additional book. NY and PA residents, add appropriate sales tax. No cash, stamps, or CODs. Canadian orders require $5.00 for shipping and handling and must be paid in U.S. dollars. Prices and availability subject to change. **Payment must accompany all orders.**

Name: _____

Address: _____

City: _____ State:_____ Zip: _____

E-mail: _____

I have enclosed $_____ in payment for the checked book(s).

For more information on these books, check out our website at www.dorchesterpub.com.
_____ _Please send me a free catalog._

Those
Baby Blues

SHERIDON SMYTHE

Hadleigh Charmaine feels as though she has been cast in a made-for-TV movie. The infant she took home from the hospital is not her biological child, and the man who has been raising her real daughter is Treet Miller, a film star. But when his sizzling baby blues settle on her, the single mother refuses to be hoodwinked—even if he makes her shiver with desire.

Treet knows he's found the role of a lifetime: father to two beautiful daughters and husband to one gorgeous wife. Now he just has to convince Hadleigh that in each other's arms they have the best shot at happiness. He plans to woo her with old-fashioned charm and a lot of pillow talk, until she understands that their story can have a Hollywood ending.

Dorchester Publishing Co., Inc.
P.O. Box 6640
Wayne, PA 19087–8640

52483-X
$5.99 US/$7.99 CAN

Please add $2.50 for shipping and handling for the first book and $.75 for each additional book. NY and PA residents, add appropriate sales tax. No cash, stamps, or CODs. Canadian orders require $5.00 for shipping and handling and must be paid in U.S. dollars. Prices and availability subject to change. **Payment must accompany all orders.**

Name: _____

Address: _____

City: _____ State: _____ Zip: _____

E-mail: _____

I have enclosed $_____ in payment for the checked book(s).

For more information on these books, check out our website at www.dorchesterpub.com.
_____ *Please send me a free catalog.*

UNDER THE COVERS
RITA HERRON

Marriage counselor Abigail Jensen faked it, and she is going to have to keep on faking it. She wrote *the* book on how to keep a relationship alive, and now the public is clamoring for more than her advice—they want her to demonstrate her techniques! But Abby has just discovered that her own wedding was a sham. Adding insult to injury, her publicist produces a gorgeous actor to play her husband, and with him Abby experiences the orgasmic kisses and titillating touches she previously knew only as chapter titles. Longing to be caught up in a tangle of sheets with her hunk of a "hubby," Abby wonders if she has finally found true love. She knows she will have to discover the truth . . . under the covers.

Dorchester Publishing Co., Inc.
P.O. Box 6640
Wayne, PA 19087-8640

___52488-0
$5.99 US/ $7.99 CAN

Please add $2.50 for shipping and handling for the first book and $.75 for each additional book. NY and PA residents, add appropriate sales tax. No cash, stamps, or CODs. Canadian orders require $5.00 for shipping and handling and must be paid in U.S. dollars. Prices and availability subject to change. **Payment must accompany all orders.**

Name: _____

Address: _____

City: _____ State: _____ Zip: _____

E-mail: _____

I have enclosed $_____ in payment for the checked book(s).

For more information on these books, check out our website at www.dorchesterpub.com.
_____ *Please send me a free catalog.*

Bait & Switch

DARLENE GARDNER

To catch a criminal and save his sibling's skin, Mitch agrees to switch places with his identical twin. But nothing could prepare him for the gorgeous knockout on his doorstep. The blond bombshell is spitting mad, and Mitch's course of action is clear: He will have to win back his brother's girlfriend. Wooing the funny, smart, and caring Peyton is no hardship. It's keeping his hands to himself and ignoring all the steamy fantasies she evokes that is pure torture. And it doesn't take a crack detective to realize Mitch has set a baited trap, but it's *his* heart that has been ensnared. Which leaves only one question: Has Peyton fallen for him or his mirror image?

Dorchester Publishing Co., Inc.
P.O. Box 6640
Wayne, PA 19087-8640

52521-6
$5.99 US/$7.99 CAN

Please add $2.50 for shipping and handling for the first book and $.75 for each additional book. NY and PA residents, add appropriate sales tax. No cash, stamps, or CODs. Canadian orders require $5.00 for shipping and handling and must be paid in U.S. dollars. Prices and availability subject to change. **Payment must accompany all orders.**

Name: _____

Address: _____

City: _____ State: _____ Zip: _____

E-mail: _____

I have enclosed $_____ in payment for the checked book(s).

For more information on these books, check out our website at www.dorchesterpub.com.
_____ *Please send me a free catalog.*

THE LAST MALE VIRGIN
Katherine Deauxville

Leslie expects a great deal of publicity for Dr. Peter Havistock—heck, the hunk has survived a plane crash, spent nearly fourteen years living with a Stone Age tribe in the wilds of Papua New Guinea, and returned to write a best-selling book about it. But his tour of colleges is too wild. Frankly, Leslie has never seen a doctor of anthropology act the way Havistock does. And while his ceremonial g-string is . . . authentic . . . she doesn't see the need for him to go flaunting his perfect body across the nation. And then he announces on *Harry King Live* that he is a virgin! And that he is looking for a wife! And that he'd like to marry her! Well, she decides, there is a first time for everything. . . .

Dorchester Publishing Co., Inc.
P.O. Box 6640
Wayne, PA 19087-8640

52497-X
$5.99 US/$7.99 CAN

Please add $2.50 for shipping and handling for the first book and $.75 for each additional book. NY and PA residents, add appropriate sales tax. No cash, stamps, or CODs. Canadian orders require $5.00 for shipping and handling and must be paid in U.S. dollars. Prices and availability subject to change. **Payment must accompany all orders.**

Name: _____

Address: _____

City: _____ State:_____ Zip: _____

E-mail: _____

I have enclosed $_____ in payment for the checked book(s).

For more information on these books, check out our website at www.dorchesterpub.com.
_____ *Please send me a free catalog.*

CONTACT
SUSAN GRANT

A BEAUTIFUL CO-PILOT WITH A TERRIBLE CHOICE.

"After only three novels, Susan Grant has proven herself to be the best hope for the survival of the futuristic/fantasy romance genre." —*The Romance Reader*

A DARK STRANGER WHO HAS KNOWN NOTHING BUT DUTY.

"I am in awe of Susan Grant. She's one of the few authors who get it." —*Everything Romantic*

A LATE-NIGHT FLIGHT, HIJACKED OVER THE PACIFIC.

COMING IN OCTOBER 2002

ATTENTION
— BOOK LOVERS! —

Can't get enough of your favorite **ROMANCE**?

Call **1-800-481-9191** to:

✴ order books,

✴ receive a **FREE** catalog,

✴ join our book clubs to **SAVE 20%**!

Open Mon.-Fri. 10 AM-9 PM EST

Visit **<u>www.dorchesterpub.com</u>**
for special offers and inside
information on the authors you love.

We accept Visa, MasterCard or Discover®.
LEISURE BOOKS ♥ LOVE SPELL